KU-032-706

A Summer Breeze

COLETTE CADDLE

**SIMON &
SCHUSTER**

London · New York · Sydney · Toronto · New Delhi

A CBS COMPANY

First published in Ireland by Simon & Schuster UK Ltd, 2015
A CBS COMPANY
Copyright © Colette Caddle 2015
This paperback edition 2015

1 3 5 7 9 10 8 6 4 2

Simon & Schuster UK Ltd
1st Floor
222 Gray's Inn Road
London WC1X 8HB

www.simonandschuster.co.uk

Simon & Schuster Australia, Sydney
Simon & Schuster India, New Delhi

A CIP catalogue record for this book
is available from the British Library

PB ISBN: 978-1-47113-822-5
EBOOK ISBN: 978-1-47113-823-2

Typeset by M Rules
Printed and bound by CPI Group (UK) Ltd, Croydon, CR0 4YY

For my mother, with love.

Chapter One

Three lines in the first act, five in the last and some soulful looks and sighing in between. How on earth would she be able to memorise all that? Zoe tossed the script out of bed in disgust. The play was truly dreadful. Rumour was, it was only being staged because the playwright was the daughter of a wealthy and indulgent director. Why had Zoe taken the part? Because you couldn't afford not to, she reminded herself, and wriggled down under the duvet. How would her career ever get off the ground? If it wasn't for the few quid she made from helping out with her friend's catering business, she would be flat broke. At twenty-eight, she wondered was it time to admit defeat and do something different. But what? She wasn't trained for anything else, she wasn't interested in anything else. She'd always loved movies and loved to perform in school productions, but her real passion for acting had only been ignited when she saw her first live play at the Gate Theatre in Dublin. After that, she knew she just had to act. Her euphoria on her first day at drama school would forever be etched in her memory. She was on her way! Anything and everything seemed possible back then. And she had got off to a promising start. She had played small parts in a few plays and then won a slightly more challenging role in a large production. She was over the moon when one reviewer singled her out for a special mention – she still had the tattered news-cutting. Not that she needed to read it. She knew every word by heart. *Zoe Hall's performance was understated and flawless: she's definitely one of our rising stars.* Tears filled Zoe's eyes. That had been written nearly nine years ago, and what did she have to show for it? Nothing, not even a place of her own, and she was as poor as the proverbial church mouse.

She grimaced as she heard the unmistakable sound of a headboard thumping the wall. She'd diplomatically come to bed early to allow her brother privacy with his latest squeeze, but she should have known they'd have graduated to the bedroom before the first glass of Chardonnay had been downed.

She pulled the pillow tight around her ears. The only thing worse than not having a sex life was having a ringside seat to someone else's.

Shane's love life never ceased to entertain. He was, in essence, an introvert, yet he seemed to attract women like moths to a flame. Like Zoe, he'd inherited their mother's dark hair and black-brown eyes but, whereas she was an optimist and a bit of a giggler, there was an air of melancholy, mystery and moodiness about Shane. He reminded her, on his more sullen days, of Rupert Everett. Though Zoe was tall at five eight, he dwarfed her at six three and had a slight stoop, as if he were apologising for towering over others. Though he occasionally wrote poetry and once a rather sweet little children's book, he was, in the main, a playwright and a damn good one.

He'd managed to get her a part in a couple of his plays but he wouldn't help her more than that. No one would ever take her seriously if she became successful because of him, he'd point out, and she knew it was true. But it was a chicken-and-egg situation. If no one got to see her on stage for more than five minutes, how could she prove herself? Of course, things would have been different had she stayed in Ireland. As Shane pointed out on a regular basis.

'You're dropping a promising career to go trailing around England after that loser?'

Zoe had never seen him as furious. She adored her big brother, almost a parent to her since Mam and Dad died, and she couldn't bear him being angry with her. But though she cried every day until she left, she still left.

She'd never met anyone like Ed McGlynn before. Three years older than her at twenty-five, he was a far cry from the boys she'd dated. Taller than many men, Zoe was used to being ignored when there were petite, curvaceous girls around, so she never gave him a second look – she wouldn't be one of his sad drove of admirers. Although it was damn hard to pretend to be unaffected by Ed. He was gorgeous with those piercing green eyes, thick auburn hair and the body of an athlete and he was a good actor too. But he could have any woman he wanted and she very much doubted that she was his type. Their paths didn't cross often, until she secured her first meaty role since leaving drama school, and he was playing one of the lead roles. Her nerves were in danger of getting the better of her, but Ed surprised her by joking around and helping her to relax. And though she tried to resist his charms, sure she was on a hiding to nothing, when he talked to her, he made her feel as if no other woman existed. It was only when she started getting dirty looks from other female cast members that she realised he made a point of singling her out. It gave her a warm fuzzy feeling and she needed all of her acting skills to play it cool.

They'd had one brief, but pivotal, scene alone together, and he suggested they should work on it to get it just right. Zoe didn't argue. Truth was, she was glad of any excuse to spend time with him. If it was raining they huddled over coffee in the grotty fast-food café across the road from the theatre. If it was fine they sat on a bench in the small park nearby. Zoe found it hard to concentrate when he was that close. She had never been so conscious of a man's scent and presence and, when his arm brushed hers, it sent a shiver through her that reached her toes – among other parts.

One day, as they sat on the bench, she fluffed her line, and they'd cracked up laughing. And then he'd told her she had a beautiful smile, touched her cheek, gazed into her eyes, and then they were kissing and she was lost.

She had no illusions. This was just a fling, short but sweet, and when it was over she wouldn't weep or beg him to stay. But weeks turned to months and they still couldn't keep their hands off each other. Even if he was walking by, she'd feel the pressure of his hand on her back and, if she whispered in his ear, she couldn't resist pressing her lips to his pale skin. Everything about him was intoxicating. He became the centre of her world. Everything and everyone seeming colourless and blurred by comparison. She was obsessed with the man and, it seemed, miraculously, he felt the same way about her.

When Ed got the lead in a play in London and asked her to go with him, she didn't hesitate. There was no role for her and it would mean starting her career from scratch but the idea of being separated was intolerable. He romanticised their future. They were going places together. They would be Ireland's answer to Burton and Taylor. She was carried along on the wave of his dreams. Everything would have been perfect if only her brother had given her his blessing but he wouldn't even listen to her. Leaving Shane on bad terms broke her heart but there was simply no way that she could let Ed go without her.

But her happiness was short-lived. As the weeks in London turned to months it was as if she'd become invisible. Ed was the bright shining star with the sexy Dublin accent and she was his shadow, barely acknowledged, grudgingly tolerated. Though the cast were polite, she was very much the outsider. Ed pressurised his new UK agent to take her on and soon she was getting bit parts here and there. When they were both working it meant they saw very little of each other. She would come home to the cold, empty flat in Slough and Ed would arrive back hours later, stinking of smoke and booze. Zoe would give him the silent treatment and turn her back on him in bed although she longed to be in his arms and was punishing herself as much as him. After a few days he'd arrive home with flowers, a bottle of cheap wine and a sheepish grin, and they would spend a couple of days in bed, vowing never to let anything come between them again ... until the next time.

When they found themselves in a small, damp theatre near

Stratford-upon-Avon, Ed proposed. Zoe had never given much thought to marriage and none at all to children, but carried along by his enthusiasm and the romance of marrying in Shakespeare country, she'd said yes. She had called Shane and asked him to give her away, but he'd told her she was a fool and hung up. Zoe was gutted. Why couldn't he just accept that she loved Ed? He didn't have to like him, they didn't have to be best buddies, just civil, that's all she had asked. Of course, she'd invited Uncle Gerry and Aunt Hannah, too, but they never left the farm unattended and Zoe wasn't surprised when they sent their regrets along with their good wishes, and a cheque for €100. In the end, only her friend Tara and her husband were there from her side on her big day.

They were back in London and had moved to a slightly larger, more comfortable flat in Putney when Zoe got her first real break since leaving Ireland, a key role in a big production with an eminent director. She was over the moon. Ed wasn't. He was playing the lead in a play that was about to go on tour, and was flabbergasted that she was even considering not accompanying him. And she'd caved. Looking back, she couldn't believe she had given in to him. What spell had he cast over her? As for her brother, Shane nearly had a fit when she told him she'd turned down the role.

'You're throwing your career down the toilet for a man with half your talent, who couldn't possibly love you or he wouldn't ask you to do this.'

But despite silently agreeing that Ed was being unreasonable, she proceeded to traipse around the country in her husband's wake. As she watched rehearsals or wandered down yet another high street, staring in store windows at things she couldn't afford, bitterness began to set in. She felt worthless. What had she become? Ed McGlynn's wife, an appendage to him rather than an actor or even a person in her own right. She'd put Ed's ambition and dreams before her own, but, isn't that what you did when you loved someone? But what did that say about Ed? Shane was right. It had been a ridiculous sacrifice. She could have easily taken the part she'd been offered and, if it hadn't worked out, joined Ed then.

They were only married a year and already Zoe was a smouldering cauldron of resentment. When it would get too much for her to bear, she went home to Dublin for a couple of days, staying at Shane's. If she timed it well, he was out of the country and she could laze around the house without being nagged. If he was there, she had to listen to his rants or, almost worse, tolerate his sad, reproachful looks.

And then one night before a performance, Zoe was seeking Ed out to wish him luck and found him with his tongue down the throat of his leading lady. It was like a knife through the heart – she'd actually felt faint. Sure, he was an outrageous flirt but they were as close as ever. He always wanted her, reaching for her like she was his anchor. How could he be like that with her and then screw other women? Because when she confronted him it was clear that it wasn't the first time he'd done it, and that he didn't stop at kissing. He didn't see anything wrong with it. He loved her. The other women meant nothing. It was just sex. Feeling as if she'd been punched in the stomach, Zoe packed her bags and left for Dublin.

Shane had been right. He'd seen what she was too besotted to notice. Ed was self-centred. When things were going his way he was the best company in the world, but when they weren't he was sullen, bitter and manipulative. It was only in hindsight she realised that his darkest moods coincided with the few occasions when she was doing better than he was. Whilst she'd always been proud and happy for him when he triumphed, he was envious and petulant when her talent was recognised. That realisation had made their break-up that bit easier. It wouldn't have mattered if he'd been faithful, she'd realised. They were doomed from the start.

It had gone quiet in the next room and she was just settling back to enjoy her paperback when her phone rang. She groped around the bed for it. 'Hello?'

'Zoe? I need you.'

'If I was that way inclined, darling, those would be the sweetest words in the world,' she said *à la* Mae West. She squinted at the clock radio. It was only nine o'clock. 'What's up, Tara?'

'I'm serving supper for thirty and Andrea's let me down. Can you help me out? I'll pay you double.'

'You can't afford to,' Zoe reminded her.

'I can tonight,' Tara said, a smile in her voice. 'This is a big-league gig. Their kitchen probably cost more than my house.'

'On my way.' Zoe said, sitting up and throwing back the duvet.

'You're a sweetheart! Grab a pen and I'll give you the address. Take a taxi, I'll pay.'

Zoe crept out to the outdated bathroom, the tiles icy under

her bare feet, and splashed water on her face. Back in her room, she tied her long dark hair into a neat ponytail and dressed in the uniform that Tara preferred, black pencil skirt, white blouse, black tights and flat black pumps. A dash of lipstick and eye-liner and she was ready and waiting when the taxi pulled up outside.

Zoe had just finished school and moved to Dublin when she first met Tara Devlin. Someone had given Shane a voucher for a sailing course, but as he had no interest in watersports other than skinny-dipping, he'd passed it on to his sister, who adored the water and swam like a fish. Tara had been in her group and they'd taken an instant liking to each other and been firm friends since. Getting to spend more time with Tara had been one of the few good things about moving back to Dublin after her marriage broke up. She'd taken to helping her friend out when she needed an extra pair of hands. She needed the cash and it kept her mind off the fact that, despite registering with an agency and going to several auditions, the phone remained stubbornly silent.

Her brother just shrugged at her situation. 'It will take time.'

Things had improved since then but she still spent more time catering than acting, and there wasn't much difference in the salary. Luckily, she didn't have to pay rent as, despite all his rants about her wasted opportunities, Shane had taken her in. Zoe was grateful but, at the same time, longed for a place of her own. It got a bit much, though, bumping into strange women on the way to the bathroom or at breakfast – toast and coffee if they were lucky.

Tara had bemoaned the fact that such an enormous kitchen in their house in Terenure was rarely put to good use, and she was always appalled at the contents of the fridge and bin. The first held little, the second was always brimming with take-away and microwave cartons.

'It's better now I live here,' Zoe had protested. 'We can't all be cordon-bleu chefs!'

Her friend had laughed. 'Shane must be thrilled to have you back to look after him.'

'I'm like his little serf. I clean and tidy and buy the loo rolls – of course he's happy! Still, it's the least I can do for free lodgings. Not that anyone in their right mind would pay to stay here.'

'It's seen better days,' Tara had admitted, wandering around the huge kitchen with its ancient cupboards with wonky doors and a cooker that seemed to be held together by grease. Incongruously, in the midst of the drab fifties room, stood a hi-tech white washing machine, a microwave, an espresso machine and a kettle. 'It would be an amazing restoration project.'

'For someone who was creative and had a lot of cash,' Zoe agreed. 'The window frames are rotten, there's no central heating, the house needs to be rewired and the plumbing is completely unreliable. Shane had great plans when he bought it but you know what he's like. All enthusiastic over a project and then something else comes along to distract him and he's off.'

'I remember,' Tara had said with a wry grin. She and Shane had dated for a while but she'd ended up marrying someone much more dependable, although the downturn in the market had seen the successful builder become one of the many unemployed. Once confident and hard-working, Greg

Coleman was now a depressed and difficult man. Tara was being amazingly patient with him but Zoe wondered how long her friend could put up with his moods.

Tara threw open the back door of the impressive three-storey house in Donnybrook, looking hot and flustered. 'Oh, I could kiss you, Zo.'

Chuckling, Zoe hurried after her, down a narrow hallway and into the state-of-the-art kitchen. 'Nice place. Now, what do you want me to do?'

'If you can take round the hors d'oeuvres, I'll get started on the mains.'

'Do I need to sort the drinks too?' Zoe balanced one platter in the curve of her arm and then picked up the other two.

Tara peeked out the door before answering: 'No, the lady of the house, Cynthia Mahon, doesn't trust staff with drink.'

Zoe raised her eyebrows. 'Charming.'

'Oh, she's a total witch,' Tara whispered, 'but she pays well and on the night. Whatever you do, steer well clear of William, the husband. He's a lecherous old goat, but if she catches him feeling you up, she'll blame you.'

'Of course she will. What does he look like?'

Tara put her head on one side as she considered the question. 'Like a lecherous old goat?'

'Gotcha.' Zoe laughed. 'Where am I going?'

Tara waved a spatula towards the hall. 'Follow the noise. They're in the drawing room, last door on the right. The dining room is opposite. Will you double check the table settings for me? I'm pretty sure it's okay but I've been rushing around so much, I don't trust myself.'

'Consider it done.' Zoe knew from experience that the dining room would be perfect – Tara never forgot anything. She'd once caught her rearranging the cutlery so that it was all an inch in from the edge of the table! She carried the food down the impressive hallway and into the drawing room, where she was immediately set upon by the hungry guests. Keeping a smile pinned to her face, she struggled to hold the platters steady as the glamorous and well-heeled, already three sheets to the wind, fell on the food like savages. Zoe thought about the care and attention poor Tara was currently putting into the confit of duck main course, knowing this lot would be as happy with a kebab. The food was almost gone when she saw a woman signalling her, eyebrows knitted in a frown – obviously the hostess. Zoe immediately made her way over and smiled.

'Is everything okay, madam?'

'No, it isn't. Where's Tara?'

'Preparing dinner.'

'I thought she'd have all that done and be able to help out here.' She tutted. 'Go and get more starters.'

'Er, I don't think there are any. The main course is quite large and there are three desserts and a cheeseboard to follow—'

'You don't have more? Well, really!' Face like thunder, Cynthia stood up, turned on her heel and headed for the kitchen. Zoe was about to follow when she felt a hand on the small of her back.

'Don't worry, dear. My wife gets rather stressed when she's

entertaining, but Tara will calm her down. Lovely girl, quite the cutesy.'

Zoe turned to face the man, who stared openly at her breasts and licked his lips. God, he really was a lech. She moved closer and stuck out her chest, making his eyes pop. 'Tara is gorgeous, isn't she? Great in bed too,' she said, and, with a wink, left him with his mouth hanging open, and went back to the kitchen.

'You did not say that!' Tara laughed, when Zoe related the conversation as they finished cleaning up three hours later.

'Did too,' Zoe assured her, and sighed. 'He'll be fantasising tonight about a threesome.'

'Ugh.' Tara shuddered and collapsed into a chair. 'Lord, I'm exhausted.'

Zoe packed the last of the pans into a box and washed her hands. 'I'm not surprised. You gave them a great night and the food was amazing.'

'Half of them will probably throw up within the hour, and the rest won't remember if it was good or not,' Tara grumbled.

'Stop with the pessimism, missus. I'm sure you'll get more bookings out of this. I recognised a lot of famous faces here tonight.'

'I hope so or we're going to end up living in a tent.' Tara gave a wide yawn.

'I'm sure you'll be able to run to a campervan,' Zoe joked, wishing she could do something to take the anxiety from her friend's eyes. 'Go get that big cheque and let's go home. You need sleep.'

Chapter Two

Tara crept into the house and eased the door closed, hoping it wouldn't squeak. She really had to get some oil and sort it. No point in asking Greg, even though he was the one who complained when she woke him. She eased off her shoes and padded into the kitchen. It was almost two in the morning and she was dog-tired, but she knew that she wouldn't be able to sleep, not immediately. She reached into the cupboard over the freezer for the bottle of gin and poured a small measure into a glass. She hesitated, the bottle in hand, and then splashed in some more. She looked around and fumed at the mess. A dirty plate sat congealing on the table along with an open carton of curry sauce and a bag of prawn crackers, some of which had spilled onto the floor and been trodden in. Tara banged down her glass, dumped the food and scrubbed the plate, before wiping the table and sweeping the floor. After she was satisfied that the kitchen was clean, she carried her drink through to the sitting room and stretched out on the sofa. Balancing the glass on her stomach, she let out a weary sigh. More and more she was feeling like a hamster in a wheel and she couldn't even talk to Greg about it. Not that she wanted to talk to him when she came home to a mess like the one he'd left tonight. Couldn't he see how tired and stressed she was? If only she could persuade him to get some sort of work – his inertia was driving her crazy. She had taken time out of her own busy schedule and put together colourful, eye-catching flyers to attract custom. Add a conservatory to your house, convert your attic or garage into a room and transform your home into a modern, open-plan family space, that sort of thing. People couldn't afford to move these days and were instead improving and extending their homes, jobs Greg could do with his eyes closed. She had been so pleased with the flyers, but when she'd presented them to him with a flourish, he'd been completely dismissive.

'You go into people's homes and feed them and suddenly you think you're an authority on running a business?' he'd jeered.

The disparaging tone and disdain in his eyes wounded her more than the words. She tried time after time to reach him, but he had built a barrier round himself that she just couldn't seem to penetrate. Sex was infrequent but, even when he did take her in his arms, he wasn't gentle or loving. It was angry sex, almost a punishment. And she embraced it, God help her, because at least he was holding her and she didn't feel quite so lonely. But afterwards he'd turn away without a word and sleep. Tara had never felt so helpless or miserable. She was losing him and she didn't know how to make it right. He hated her for working. He hated that it was her money putting food on the table. He seemed to hate being around her and yet complained when she was out so late. She couldn't win. She tried to make herself invisible so as not to irritate him, but as she prepared food for a function she felt his eyes boring into her, accusing her. Of what? Of making a living? Of supporting him? Was that her sin? If he didn't want her help, why didn't he get off his arse and do something? She wanted to scream at him, to shake him, to make him come to his senses, but she was very afraid that it would send him over the edge. So she did nothing.

Tara drained her glass and went upstairs. Though the bedroom was in darkness, she knew instantly he was awake. When she slipped in beside him, he was lying on his back. Leaning over, she pressed her lips to his chest. 'I love you,' she whispered as she did every night. Sometimes he was silent, sometimes he turned away and sometimes . . . She moaned as he flipped her on her back and started to kiss her, his mouth hard against hers. She wound her arms around his neck and pulled him closer. Any contact was better than none.

When Shane's phone went straight to voicemail, Adam O'Brien flung his mobile across the room. He didn't like it, not at all. He had that pain in his stomach again, the one brought on by stress, aka Shane Hall. Why had he ever agreed to go into the theatre? What did he know about actors or plays? But Shane was like a brother, they had a lot in common and he'd always found it hard to say no to him.

Adam had grown up in a small community in County Meath. When Shane and his sister had arrived from Dublin to live with their aunt and uncle, it had caused quite a stir. Their parents had been killed outright in a horrific car crash, which made them a huge subject of morbid curiosity in the town. Shane had ended up in Adam's class at the local boys' Catholic school. He still remembered awed silence when the principal led Shane into the class and introduced him. The boy had stared at them, his dark eyes defiant, as if warning them not to dare ask any questions, and it had worked. Everyone gave him a wide berth and he'd kept himself to himself.

It had been a while before they became friends but, when they did, the bond was strong. Shane moved back to Dublin as soon as they left school. They'd kept in touch but Adam was working on the production line at the local plastics factory and didn't have time or money to visit, and Shane rarely came home. But the older he got, the more stifled Adam felt in the small terraced house he shared with his mother, and Shane made city life sound so exciting. Finally, he bit the bullet and followed his friend to the bright lights. He got a job working in Clerys department store, which might have been interesting enough if he'd been on the shop floor but he was stuck in the back, stock-taking, and was almost as bored as he'd been at home. When he complained about it, Shane suggested they work together. Adam could take care of all the administrative details, allowing Shane to concentrate on writing and directing his plays. Adam had laughed at the idea. His job might be monotonous, but at least he had a steady wage. Whereas, despite Shane's success – he'd written, directed and produced three plays already – he had zero security and usually seemed to be broke. But once Adam attended his first play, he had been gobsmacked that his friend had written a story that completely absorbed him for two hours, and suddenly the thought of being a part of that world seemed a hell of a lot more exciting than stock-taking. The job title producer sounded very grand and off-putting but, at the end of the day, it just meant taking care of the legwork involved in staging a play and Adam was a natural-born organiser. And so he agreed and was so very glad that he had, taking to it like a duck to water. His success with Shane led to other directors seeking him out and within a couple of years he had a relatively healthy income and his stock-taking days were behind him.

But as Shane had warned, it wasn't all glamorous. Artistic types were an unpredictable and unreliable lot and Adam almost had to babysit them through each production. He would boost egos, nudge procrastinators, bully a little and beg a lot. Shane was one of the worst, always doubting the quality of his own work. He rarely met deadlines as he struggled for perfection, ignoring reassurances that he'd already achieved it. It frustrated the hell out of Adam but he'd learned that the only way to handle Shane was to back off and let him come out of his self-inflicted torture in his own time. He always got there in the end but there had been many hairy moments over the years and the uncertainty played havoc with Adam's gut.

The director of Shane's current work-in-progress, John Whelan, was one of the best but wasn't a patient man and he and Shane tended to clash a lot. Adam would find himself in the middle, trying to keep the peace. Luckily, John was working on a production in Belfast at the moment and seemed too preoccupied to notice that he hadn't received Shane's script yet. But it was only a matter of time before Adam got that call. Still, he could handle John and buy Shane more time, that wasn't a problem. It was Shane not returning his calls that made Adam nervous. He had provisionally booked a theatre for an initial two-week run and if he reneged on that it could be costly. Fuck it, he deserved better than this. He was going to pay Shane a visit. In a way he hoped there was just a new woman in his life and he was too busy screwing to bother with work. That was infinitely preferable to the possibility Shane had torn up the script in disgust and was in a bar somewhere, drinking himself into oblivion. If Shane wasn't home, though, there was a good chance Zoe would be, and that would be worth the trip in itself.

Adam still remembered the first time he'd laid eyes on Shane's sister as an adult, a far cry from the skinny little kid who used to trail Shane round. Tall and willowy with a mane of dark hair that was almost down to her waist, at eighteen, by then, Zoe was a beautiful young woman but still had the same friendly, sunny nature. Shane had noticed the way Adam had looked at her and warned him off with an icy glare. Which was fair enough, after all he was nearly six years older. But nowadays she was very much a woman and a divorced one at that and fair game. But despite his attempts to flirt with her, she'd shown no interest in him. She was always nice and would welcome him with a wide smile – she had such a lovely smile, it lit up her entire face – and she'd chat away about anything and everything, but it was clear that she only saw him as a friend. He'd learned to accept that but he still couldn't resist seeing her any chance he got, happy just to be in her company and admire her from afar. She carried herself like a queen, shoulders back and head held high, and she had the most amazingly expressive brown eyes. Adam couldn't understand why she hadn't had more success in her career or why Shane didn't try to use his influence to help her when he obviously idolised his little sister.

Adam was disappointed to see Tara Devlin's little van outside the house when he drove up. That girl didn't like him and made no effort to hide it. He thought about driving off, but he was here now and he really did need to talk to Shane.

He heard laughter as he walked up the path and rang the bell. Zoe opened the door, dressed in a loose shirt, ripped jeans, her hair piled in an untidy knot on the top of her head, and looking bloody gorgeous.

'Hi, Adam.' There was that smile. 'Come in.'

He heard Tara's groan come from the kitchen.

Zoe laughed. 'Don't mind her, she's grumpy today.'

'Is she ever any other way? How are rehearsals going?'

She rolled her eyes. 'Put it this way, I'm getting through a lot of novels.'

'Hanging around between scenes?'

'That's putting it mildly. How come you're here?' Her eyes twinkled. 'Oh, I know, you've come to tell me that some director spotted me in the street and wants me to star in his new play?'

'Afraid not but I'll keep my ears open,' he promised. 'I wanted to talk to your brother and as he never answers his phone I decided it was time for the mountain to come to Muhammad.'

'But he's in Spain.' Zoe said as she led Adam down to the kitchen, where Tara sat at the kitchen table. She gave him a limp wave.

'Spain?' He stopped in the doorway, searching his memory.

Had he missed something? Had Shane mentioned he was going away? He didn't think so.

'Yes, he flew out yesterday.'

Fuck. The pain in his stomach had been right again. 'What the hell is he doing in Spain?'

Zoe's eyes widened. 'You didn't know? Sorry, obviously not. He's having some issues with the script, apparently, and decided he needed a change of scene.'

'He might have mentioned it. And if it's no big deal, why isn't he taking my calls?' Adam thought for a moment, remembering a late-night session recently when Shane had disappeared early with a girl. He looked at Zoe. 'I don't suppose there's a new woman on the scene?'

Zoe pulled a face. 'Now you mention it . . .'

'Great.' Adam sank into a chair.

'What does it matter where he is once he's writing?' Tara piped up.

'If there's a woman with him, I doubt he's doing a lot of that,' he retorted.

'I don't know that for sure, Adam. He should have let you know he was going. But I only found out myself yesterday.' Zoe shook her head at her brother's unpredictable nature.

The kettle boiled and Zoe looked at him, her lovely eyes full of sympathy. 'Tea, coffee or do you need a real drink?'

'A lager would be great, thanks.'

'Tara?'

Thankfully, Adam noted, the girl stood up. 'Not for me, I need to go to the wholesaler's. Talk to you tomorrow.' She hugged Zoe. 'Great to see you again, Adam. Don't keep Zoe too long – she's got a hot date later. Byeee!'

The door slammed and Adam looked back at Zoe. 'If you're in a rush—'

'Don't mind Tara, she has a warped sense of humour.' She set a bottle in front of him and made a coffee for herself. 'You seem pretty rattled, Adam. What's up?'

'Shane promised he'd deliver the script soon and John gets difficult when people let him down.'

Zoe's eyes widened in disbelief. 'But what writer meets a deadline?'

He laughed. 'Okay, he gets difficult when they don't meet their deadlines and don't make contact to explain why, or to give an estimate as to when it will be ready. When is he due home?'

'He didn't say. I wasn't here when he left. He just sent me a text from the airport. It all seemed a bit last-minute.'

'Your brother is going to be the death of me. We're supposed to be putting on a show in six weeks.' Adam couldn't hide his irritation. 'It's not fair of him to mess me around like this, or John either for that matter.'

'Of course it isn't,' she said, looking helpless.

'I don't suppose you know where he's staying?' Perhaps if it was with someone in the theatre, he could track down a number.

'No, sorry. Let me try calling him.' Zoe reached for her phone and rang her brother but shook her head. 'It's gone straight to voicemail but I have an idea.' She waited for a moment and then in a breathless, panicked tone she spoke. 'Shane, it's me, I need your help. I've locked myself out and I can't remember where you said you'd hidden the spare key. Call me ASAP, for God's sake. I've left the pan on the stove. Shit, maybe I should just call the fire brigade. Oh, call me, Shane, please, for fuck's sake, call me!' And she hung up.

Adam stared at her in astonishment and then burst out laughing. 'And the Oscar for best actress goes to . . .'

'Why, thank you.' She bowed and sat down again. 'Let's see if it works.' The phone started to ring almost immediately and she grinned at Adam. 'Gotcha!'

'Get a number off him, tell him you have to be able to reach him. Oh, shit, I don't know, but just see what you can find out, please.' Calm down, Adam told himself. It wasn't the first time that Shane had gone AWOL and arrived back in the nick of time. But he'd never done it quite like this before. Leaving so suddenly and sending his sister a text from the airport? It was very odd. Damn it, why had he ever got into this game? Directors, actors, writers were such a paranoid, emotional and unreliable lot. He tuned back into what Zoe was saying and had to suppress a laugh. Though she hadn't moved from the counter, she was breathlessly pretending to be digging in the flower pot outside the front window, searching for the key. He could hear Shane's voice raised in panic as he urged her to hurry, terrified that his house was going to burn down.

'Got it!' Zoe yelped and, reaching over, took Adam's car keys and pressed them against the wood of the table before hurrying to the back door and opening it. 'I'm in. Just hang on while I turn off the cooker.' She winked at Adam, sat down and took a sip of tea. 'Okay, it's fine – my chops aren't even burned.' Shane said something and she laughed. 'Listen, before you hang up, Adam's been looking for you. Where the hell are you? Why the sudden departure?'

Adam watched her face as Shane answered her. When she

23

bowed her head and turned slightly away, his uneasiness grew.

'Okay, then,' she said finally. 'Talk to you then.'

'Well?' Adam searched her face and wasn't convinced by the reassuring smile.

'He couldn't talk but he said he was very sorry.'

Adam held her gaze.

'I need to know where I stand, Zoe.'

'I understand that. When I talk to him later I'll find out exactly what's going on.'

Adam stood up, not entirely happy with her response but at a loss as to what else he could do. He could see sympathy in Zoe's eyes. 'Will you phone me after you talk to him?'

'Of course.'

'Great, thanks, Zoe. I appreciate that.'

As soon as she was alone, Zoe picked up her phone. She held her breath as she waited for Shane to answer. As soon as she'd heard his voice she'd known that there was something wrong and it frightened her. He was prone to bouts of depression but it had been a long time since the last one. He finally answered, the same tremor in his voice. 'Hey, it's me, Shane. Sorry about that but Adam was here.'

'What? Shit. What did you tell him?'

She could hear sheer panic now. 'Nothing. What's wrong, Shane? Where are you? Are you okay?'

'Not really.'

She waited for him to volunteer more but there was silence.

'Shane, talk to me. I'll need to tell Adam something. He seems really on edge.'

'He should be,' Shane mumbled. 'I can't do this play.'

'I thought it was going really well.' Zoe had watched Shane prowling around, lost in thought, and come down some mornings to coffee mugs, empty crisp bags and beer bottles strewn round the place, clear evidence that he had pulled an all-nighter. He had seemed completely consumed and so excited by what he was working on. She had been hoping there might be a part in it for her and, when he was out, she had ransacked his room, longing to get a glimpse of the script, but without success. The fact that he was keeping it under wraps fuelled her curiosity. So much for giving up on acting and moving on. 'Shane?' she said, worried by his silence.

He sighed heavily at the other end of the phone. 'There's just something not quite right about it and I can't figure out what it is. I thought some time in a different location might help but it's not coming.'

'You only went yesterday,' she pointed out, exasperated.

'True.'

'You know the more pressure you put yourself under the less chance the ideas will come.'

'I suppose.'

Zoe sensed there was more to it than he was letting on. 'You'd tell me if there was anything wrong, wouldn't you, Shane?' She gripped the phone tight to her ear and paced the kitchen. 'Apart from the play.'

'Sure.'

She wished she was convinced but he sounded miserable.

'Forget about writing for a few days,' she said gently. 'I've watched you go through this many times before and you always panic when you come close to the end.'

'Do I?'

She smiled at the surprise in his voice. 'You do. And everyone knows that but you still need to let Adam know what's happening. It's not fair to leave him in limbo like this.'

'What do I say? That I can't write, that I don't know what to write? That I've literally lost the plot?'

Zoe heard the unmistakable sound of wine being poured. 'Please don't drink, Shane. Where *are* you? Who are you with?'

'I'm in Nerja in Diana's villa.'

'Diana?' Zoe paused in her pacing. The only Diana she knew was the one Shane had had an affair with on and off for the last few years. 'Diana Nelson?'

'Yeah.'

'Shane, this is madness. Will you please stop messing about with married women?'

'Keep your hair on, I'm alone,' he said, sounding weary. 'She just said I could crash here for a while.'

'And does her husband know that?'

Again a sigh. 'I don't know and I don't really care. Look, Zoe, I have to go.'

Zoe wracked her brains for a way to get through to him. 'Is there a copy of the manuscript here?'

'Why?' he asked, sounding wary.

'Let me give it to Adam. It will buy you some time.' There was silence. 'Shane?'

'But I'm telling you, it's not ready!'

'It doesn't matter. It's proof that you're working.'

He gave another weary sigh. 'Okay. Tell Adam I'll email it to him.'

'Isn't there a hard copy?' She'd thought she was finally going to get her hands on the script. Jeez, you would think it was a treasure map. Writers!

'No. Tell Adam not to show it to John unless he has to. It's not ready,' he warned.

'Fine. I'll just say how hard you've been working and that you want to get the ending just right. How does that sound?'

He gave a humourless laugh. 'There's no way in hell of getting the ending right.'

She heard him take a drink. 'Lighten up, Shane. Take some time out, chill. The ideas will come and the words will flow – they always do. This play is important to you, Shane. I can feel that and I know it will be brilliant.'

'No, Zoe, I think you're going to hate it,' he said, his voice cracking slightly.

'I doubt that.' She smiled. She loved her brother's writing and almost burst with pride at every premiere. 'If it's stressing you this much, I'm sure that, not only will you finish it, but I will love it. But you need to get some rest first and lay off the booze. You know it will just bring you down.'

Again silence and then another sigh. 'You're right.'

She let out a breath she hadn't realised she'd been holding.

'Don't go asking Adam for a copy. I don't want you to read it, Zo,' he said, sounding alarmed.

'I won't, I promise – but why, Shane?'

Another sigh. 'Please, just humour a crazy writer.'

She smiled. 'Okay, but you must promise me that you will keep your phone on and that you will answer my calls.'

'I will, and, Zo?'

'Yeah?'

'I love you, you know that, right?'

'Love you too. Bye, Shane.' She hung up on him and called Adam.

Chapter Three

'There goes one very angry young man.' Terence Ross eyed his daughter over the top of his newspaper. He'd taken to dropping in more often lately. His excuse? That he was at a loose end or just passing, but she knew that it was really his way of trying to put pressure on Greg. He meant well but his visits didn't help the tension in the house. It was ironic, really. All her life she'd wanted more of her parents' time and now, when she least needed it, Terence had finally decided to behave like a dad.

'Please don't wind him up, Dad,' Tara said through gritted teeth, though she knew she was wasting her breath. A door slammed in the distance, making her jump.

Terence gazed at her, all innocence. 'All I asked was how the job-hunting was going.' His expression darkened as his eyes travelled over the platters of food covering every surface. 'I think that's a fair question from a father whose daughter's working round the clock. You can't continue at this pace, darling – you'll make yourself ill.'

'I enjoy it,' Tara insisted, and she did, although it would

have been nice to have the occasional morning in bed and sleep through the night instead of lying awake worrying about money.

'The very least he could do is roll up his sleeves and give you a hand. I assume he does your accounts.'

He didn't. But she wasn't going to fuel her father's anger. He had always been civil enough to Greg but the two men had little in common and not much to say to each other. And since Greg's business had gone belly-up and she was the sole earner, her dad was always taking pot-shots at his son-in-law. 'He does help with some of the deliveries.'

Terence snorted. 'How very noble of him.'

'I thought you had a play coming up. Shouldn't you be home, learning your lines?' she said pointedly.

He waved a hand in the air. 'You know I don't work like that, darling. I need to get a feel for the character, *be* that person, before I can even think about the words.'

Tara bent her head over the chicken she was hacking into portions to hide a smirk. 'Right.'

But he had tossed aside the newspaper and was glaring again. 'Seriously, Tara, are you really planning to do all this and then go and serve it too?'

'No, Dad, Zoe is going to help me. Stop worrying, it's all under control. When do rehearsals start?'

'Probably next month.' Her father put down the paper. 'Actually, speaking of Zoe, is she working?'

'Only for me. Well, she has some tiny part in a play in some tiny theatre.'

'When?'

'Next week, I think. Why?'

'Hmm, I might be able to put some work her way. It's only a short run but it *is* in the Abbey and I think that she would be perfect for the part.'

'Oh, Dad, that's fantastic. She'd be absolutely thrilled.' Zoe usually joked about 'resting', but Tara had noticed that she hadn't been her usual bubbly self lately.

'She'd have to audition, of course,' her father was saying, 'but I think she'd be well able for the part. Ridiculous the girl isn't doing better. She has that certain something, I can sense it, and I'm never wrong.' His blue gaze narrowed. 'Yet another woman's ambition thwarted by an egotistical, selfish man.'

Tara chuckled as she put the chicken, vegetables, herbs and garlic into a large pot and set it on the gas. 'I'd love to hear what Mam would have to say on that subject.'

'Excuse me, Vivienne is the success she is today because I let her go.'

'Er, the way she tells it, she let *you* go,' Tara said, but she was smiling. It was a conversation they had on a regular basis but without malice. Her parents were still on good terms though they had never married and, in fact, split up shortly after she was born. Which was probably just as well. Terence seemed incapable of fidelity and her mother was a fiercely independent woman whose career in musical theatre was more important than any relationship. 'Will I call Zoe and tell her?'

'No, that's okay.' He glanced at his watch. 'I'll drop by and say hello. Is your mother still seeing Boring Bob?'

She shook her head, smiling. 'Don't call him that, he's nice.'

Terence groaned. 'Nice? The most insulting description known to man but, in this case, accurate.'

'No, harmless is the worst description.'

'He's that too.'

'Speaking of partners, how is Rosemary?' Tara had learned long ago not to get too attached to any of the women in her father's life as they rarely lasted long. Some she liked, most she didn't.

'Who?' Terence stood up.

'You're impossible,' she said, laughing.

'But you love me.' He put his arms around her and dropped a kiss on her brow. 'Should I go and find your husband and say goodbye?'

'No, leave him be! Things are difficult enough for him at the moment.'

He scowled. 'They're difficult for you too.'

'We'll be fine,' she said with a reassuring smile, wishing she believed it.

Not long after Terence had left, Greg strolled back into the kitchen, put on the coffee machine and opened the biscuit tin. He turned and Tara could see he was still smarting from her dad's comments.

'Aren't there any custard creams?'

She gritted her teeth. She was in the middle of making pastry. Did he seriously expect her to drop everything to help him search for biscuits? 'You're looking in the tin – you tell me.'

He banged it down. 'You know what I meant. You need to do a shop.'

'No, Greg, *you* need to do a shop. In case you hadn't noticed, I'm working, and you're not.'

He stiffened and glared at her. 'Why the dramatics? It's just a bit of shopping.'

'Exactly.' Tara gave him a sweet smile. 'Even you should be able to manage it.'

He gave a world-weary sigh. 'Okay, fine. If you're going to make an issue of it, give me a list and I'll do it if it will stop you nagging.'

'I'm busy. You make a list,' Tara said, keeping her eyes on her pastry. 'You live here too, you'll figure out what's needed.'

'Why are you being so bloody difficult?'

'I'm just busy, Greg, and tired.' She looked up at him, feeling suddenly tearful. 'Really tired.'

A flash of guilt crossed his face. 'Fine. I'll do the shopping,' he said and stormed out of the room.

The front door slammed a few minutes later. It was a wonder any of the doors in this house were still on their hinges. Tears of frustration spilled out onto Tara's cheeks and she wiped them away on her sleeve. The idiot would probably come back laden down with all sorts of rubbish and forget the basics. Tara looked round at the array of wonderful food she had prepared. From the leftovers she would make soups and stews or stir-fry. Even though they were technically on the breadline, Greg was eating like a king and he was moaning about bloody biscuits. The tension in the house was building every day and it was only a matter of time before it came to a head. Nothing she did was right. He got annoyed when she tried to discuss their situation yet, when she was silent, he accused her of being moody or sulking. These days it was a relief to get out of the house and, when she was stuck at home with no job to prepare for, she threw herself into the house-work. It was infinitely preferable to sitting in the same room as him, tension and anger crackling between them.

She had never thought anything could come between them. Any problems that life threw their way, they would deal with together, as a team. But when he'd gone out of business, he had just shut her out, retreated into himself and, it seemed, given up. Two years on and there was still no sign of him pulling himself out of this depression. Zoe maintained that, because he'd been such a successful man, their current situation had emasculated him.

'This isn't the Stone Age,' Tara had protested. 'We're equals.' But the more she thought about it, and the more sarcastic and scathing and distant Greg became, the more she realised that Zoe was right. If she didn't have the catering business and they'd had no other income, would it have given him the incentive to get out there and find work? There was no point in wondering about that now and there was no point in her worrying about Greg. He had chosen to go through this alone and, if that's the way he wanted it, so be it.

The food preparations complete, Tara got stuck into cleaning up. With luck she'd have time to tidy the cutlery drawer too.

Zoe wasn't sure what woke her. She peered at the clock and was stunned to see it was almost lunchtime. It had been a bad night and the noise of the wind and rain rattling the windows had kept her awake for hours. When morning finally came, she had stayed put, dozing and reading, glad there were no rehearsals. The doorbell rang and there was a rap on the knocker too. So, that's what had woken her. She ran to the window and peered out and was stunned to see Terence Ross on the doorstep. She quickly grabbed her robe and tied it over her flimsy nightshirt and then groaned as she caught sight of herself in the mirror. Typical, the one time a famous actor comes calling. She combed her fingers through her hair as she ran down to let him in.

'Ah, you're in!' Terence smiled.

Lord, he might well be in his sixties but that was still one of the sexiest smiles on the Irish stage. He was dressed in a cream linen jacket and blue striped shirt, while blue jeans encased his long slim legs. The outfit was set off by a straw Panama hat. On anyone else it might have looked ridiculous, but Terence wore it with aplomb and looked every inch the handsome star he was.

'Hi, Terence.' She gestured down at herself. 'I was still in bed. Give me a second and I'll go get dressed.'

He bent to kiss her cheek. 'No need on my account, you look beautiful as you are.'

'Liar.' She laughed, but she felt herself blushing as she led the way into the drab kitchen. 'Coffee?'

'I just had one with Tara. I don't suppose you have the makings of a G&T?'

'In this house? We may not have food, milk or tea bags, but booze, always.' She took down two tumblers, made his drink and poured a sparkling water for herself.

'Thank you, darling. Let's take them outside. It's a lovely day.'

'Sure.' She opened the door and led the way out to the gazebo at the bottom of the garden. Surprisingly, it was a nice day. It was as if she had imagined the stormy night.

When they were sitting at the little table, Terence clinked his glass against hers. 'Cheers, my dear.'

'Cheers,' she said and took a sip before turning her face up to the heat of the sun. 'It is beautiful, isn't it?'

'Lovely.'

She opened her eyes and looked over to see his eyes were on her. 'You're outrageous,' she said laughing, feeling both self-conscious and flattered.

'So I'm told, but what is wrong in appreciating the beauty around you? No false modesty, please,' he reproached her. 'You're a lovely young woman. Don't pretend otherwise.'

'Not so young any more,' she said.

'There you go again.' He palmed his forehead in despair.

'Sorry, I'm just feeling a bit low. I've been wondering if it's time to give up this whole acting business and get a real job. Twenty-eight and my latest part involves eight lines.'

'When is the play on?' he asked.

'Next week and it's only a six-day run. I can't see it being picked up by any other theatre either.'

'That bad?'

She smiled. 'Dreadful.'

'Hmm. Well, that brings me to the reason for my visit. There might be a part for you in my new play, *Isabella*.'

She sat up, wondering if she'd heard him right. 'Say that again.'

He chuckled. 'Don't get too excited – you would have to audition and it's a short run too.'

'But *you're* in it,' she exclaimed in delight. Terence was rarely in a bad play and his performances attracted all the critics.

'I am, and the bad news, darling, is you would have to play

my love interest. Could you handle pretending to love an old man?'

She raised her eyebrows. 'Now who's indulging in false modesty?'

He clapped his hands and laughed. 'Touché! Beautiful and funny too. No doubt it will make my darling daughter squirm in her seat to see us schmoozing on stage, but I see it as part of my parental duty to embarrass her.'

'Tara adores you and so do I.' Zoe threw her arms around his neck and hugged him.

'And I adore you, darling. You'll have to audition for Robbie but I know that he'll love you.'

'Robbie Prendergast?' She pulled away and stared at him. Of course she shouldn't have been surprised. Terence and Robbie had teamed up on numerous productions, most of which had been successful. Lord, was she dreaming?

'The one and the same.' Terence looked at her in amusement and settled back in the chair with his drink.

'Robbie Prendergast, wow. I hope my nerves don't get the better of me.'

'You'll be fine.'

'Terence, you've made my day. Tell me about the play,' she urged him.

'It's the story of a barrister who is going through a crisis of confidence, questioning his life, his marriage and feeling old and past it.' He pulled a face. 'Not much of a stretch for me. He falls in love with his client, Isabella. She's accused of murder and he is pretty convinced that she's guilty, but despite that, he is completely besotted and obsessed with her. She plays with his feelings, leads him on and he is putty in her hands. He goes on to win the case and she walks out of his life for ever. He is devastated and then spots his wife at the back of the court and, looking into her eyes, he can see she knows. And she turns and walks away. And of course he comes down to earth with a bang and realises what his silly little crush has cost him.'

'Oh, that's so sad,' she said.

He laughed. 'He's a sad old bastard all right. The play is all about my character, his thoughts and feelings, and how Isabella makes him feel young and alive again. She is almost a silent presence for most of the play, but there is one beautifully written scene, a dream sequence, where he imagines her falling into his arms. So, lovely Zoe, could you see yourself as Isabella?'

Fingers of fear clenched Zoe's gut. She raised her eyes to his. 'Terence, what makes you think I can do this?'

'What makes you think that you can't?' he countered, holding her gaze.

'I didn't say I couldn't, but you haven't seen me act in years. How can you have such faith in me?'

'I've seen many of your performances, including the one in that appalling play about women hating their bodies.'

'You saw that?' She gasped, putting a hand to her mouth.

'I did and you carried it, Zoe.'

She didn't know what to say. His words were music to her ears. Despite his flirty nature and flamboyant compliments, she knew with certainty he wouldn't lie about her acting. 'Thank you. That means a lot to me, truly.'

'You are going to be wonderful. We will have such fun.' His face lit up in anticipation.

'I don't have the part yet,' she protested, crossing her fingers. 'I have to impress your director first.'

'Not a problem, unless . . .'

'Unless?' She looked at him, worried.

'You'll feel inhibited or embarrassed kissing your best friend's old dad.'

Zoe grinned, thinking of the women of all ages who would kill to be kissed by Terence. 'I think I'll cope.'

He drained his glass. 'Good. So, why don't I take you to dinner later and we can talk more about it and then do a read-through?'

Wow, he didn't hang about! 'Great – oh, I can't, I forgot. I'm working for Tara tonight. But it's a pre-theatre supper, so I should be free by nine, if that's not too late?'

'That's early for me,' he assured her. 'Text me and let me know what time you finish and I'll pick you up.' He stood up. 'You have my number?'

'I'll get it from Tara.'

He kissed her cheek at the door and smiled, his eyes twinkling. 'I hope this works out, Zoe. I would love to work with you.'

'And I'd love to work with you,' she assured him. 'In fact, it would be an honour.'

'Oh, please,' he groaned, 'enough of that. We're just two actors from now on, yes?'

She smiled and nodded. 'Yes.'

'Okay, see you later.' He turned at the gate, took off his hat and gave a theatrical bow before sauntering off down the road.

Chapter Four

'You're going on a date with my dad?' Tara said when Zoe called her a few minutes later.

Zoe, in bra and pants, cradled the phone between her neck and chin as she flicked through the clothes in her wardrobe. 'It's not a date, it's work. Just tell me what to wear, Tara. I never asked where we were eating and he always looks so well I don't want to let him down.'

'He'll probably take you to the Trocadero or, if there's anything decent playing at the Gate Theatre, Chapter One. He never misses an opportunity to show off his dates.'

'I told you—'

'Just teasing. Wear a little black dress and heels and you can't go wrong.'

'Okay, thanks. What time are you picking me up?'

'Five?'

'Fine, see you then. Bye, Tara.' Zoe flung the phone on the bed and went back to the wardrobe. She pulled out a knee-length dress and stepped into it. She zipped it up and frowned at her reflection in the mirror. She had lost weight and it no longer clung in the right places. That's what a diet of yoghurt and Pot Noodles did to you. She pulled the dress over her head and rummaged through her wardrobe until she found her sleeveless black mini with the scooped neckline. She'd only worn it a couple of times as it was a little tight across her stomach and hips but now – she smiled and smoothed it over her hips – it was a perfect fit. She went to the mirror. 'Oh, yeah, you look good, kid!' She twisted and turned, admiring herself. But she needed a splash of colour. A root through her drawer of costume jewellery turned up a chunky topaz choker and bracelet that brought out the golden flecks in her dark eyes. Happy that she wouldn't make a show of Terence, she hung the dress up again and went to take a shower.

As it turned out, she and Tara had cleaned up and packed all their gear in the car by eight-thirty and, after sending Terence a text, Zoe nipped into the downstairs loo to change, leaving Tara polishing the already gleaming glasses.

'Will I do?' she asked, doing a twirl.

Tara stopped polishing to look up and smile. 'You'll do.'

'Leave that, Tara,' Zoe protested. 'The place is cleaner now than when we arrived!'

'It's important to leave a kitchen spotless if you want repeat business,' Tara insisted.

'It is and you have. I've seen operating theatres less clean. Come on, I've got a date, remember?'

When they went outside, there was a taxi waiting behind Tara's van and Terence hopped out and smiled at them. 'Evening, ladies. How did it go?'

'Fine,' Tara said, hugging him.

'That's an understatement,' Zoe told him. 'They adored everything and I don't blame them – it looked and smelled delicious.'

'I doubt the restaurant we're going to will measure up.'

Tara laughed. 'I'm quite sure it will, Dad. Have a good time, you two. I'm heading home for a nice bath, a glass of wine and an early night.'

'Goodnight, sweetheart,' Terence said, and opened the door for Zoe.

'I'll call you tomorrow.' She waved at Tara before climbing in. Terence went round the other side and smiled at her as the cab pulled away.

'You look lovely, darling.'

'Thanks,' she said with a shy smile.

He held up a folder. 'I've brought the script.'

She stared at it, mesmerised.

'Zoe?'

She looked up and grinned. 'Sorry, I just can't quite believe this is happening.'

'Believe it. You have an audition in two days.'

'Two days?' She looked at him in horror. 'Oh, but that's too soon. I'll never be ready.'

His eyes narrowed. 'Yes, you will. By the time you go to bed tonight, you'll think you *are* Isabella.'

She forced herself to take slow, deep breaths. She couldn't screw this up because of nerves. She'd never be able to forgive herself and she doubted Terence would be too pleased either, having been the one to put her forward for the job.

The taxi pulled up outside a small, expensive fish restaurant in Howth.

'I thought after we've finished we could take a walk down the pier and rehearse.'

She raised an eyebrow. 'Won't it be a bit dark to read the script?'

'We won't need the script, darling. I'm going to tell you all about Isabella Shine and Jonathan Keane. Once you get a feel for their characters and understand what motivates them, the words are incidental. You will have the script in front of you at the audition and you will blow Robbie away if you can show that you "get" Isabella.' He paused in the doorway and smiled at her. 'Trust me?'

She smiled, the excitement returning. 'Always.'

The food was incredible. As each delicious course was presented, Zoe admired its beauty, marvelled at its delicacy and then, after a sip of wine, was astounded at the explosion of flavours in her mouth.

Terence smiled. 'You like?'

'I love. This is amazing.'

'I like to see a woman enjoy her food. There are too many who try to survive on lettuce leaves and cigarettes.'

'That's the acting business for you,' Zoe said, feeling defensive. She had done her share of dieting and would eat little tomorrow to make up for this blow-out. 'You have to do what you have to do to get a part.'

'Nonsense. I never did.'

She looked at his lean youthful frame, thick dark hair with just enough grey to make him look distinguished and the startling blue of his eyes. 'You never had to! You're just one of those annoying people who can eat anything and not put on a pound.'

'And you're beautiful and talented and, given the chance, I know you'll make it, Zoe.'

'I wish I shared your confidence, Terence, but I may have to throw in the towel if I don't get this role.'

He rested his chin in his hand. 'You don't walk away from acting, Zoe. If the theatre is in your blood, it's in your blood.'

'I could stay in it, just not as an actor. I was thinking of writing.'

He raised his eyebrows. 'Screenplays?'

'Maybe.'

'Does the idea excite you as much as walking out on stage?'

She thought for a moment and then shook her head. Nothing beat the adrenalin of acting. Nothing.

'Then stick with it.'

She smiled. Why was she even thinking about giving up now when he was offering her such an opportunity? 'Tell me more about Isabella.'

'That's my girl.' He pulled the script from his pocket. 'Isabella Shine is not only beautiful, she knows it and knows how to use it as a weapon.'

Zoe closed her eyes and swallowed, trying to visualise herself in the part. She was attractive, she knew, but, despite Terence's compliments, she was no beauty. Could she be so sure of her looks that she could treat this fine man with cold disdain and convince an audience? She opened her eyes to find him watching her. 'That's a tall order. It won't be easy to get that across if my part is as small as you say.'

'You will when the sad old man on stage with you reveals how besotted he is.'

He was right, she realised. Being faced with someone vulnerable and exposed who worshipped her would, of course, make Isabella feel powerful. With her sole focus on being found innocent, she would use every trick in the book to secure her freedom. If Zoe managed to assume Isabella's persona then she would no longer see the successful Terence Ross opposite her but the sad, ageing Jonathan, and she would be able to carry it off. Perspective was a wonderful thing.

She had first-hand experience to draw on too, thanks to her snake of an ex-husband. Ed had seduced her and convinced her that he loved her. He'd made her feel like the sexiest woman in the world, until she'd discovered that she was no more than his crutch to support him when his ego needed massaging. Yes, she could play this part, she decided with grim determination, and do it justice.

'Shall we read it?' Terence asked.

'Yes, please.' She shuffled closer on the banquette and he put the script between them.

Terence read the part of Jonathan while she read the wife and Isabella. They sat in silence for a few moments when they'd finished and Zoe wiped a knuckle under her eyes, hoping she didn't look like a panda. 'It's wonderful.'

It was indeed all about Jonathan and his dissatisfaction with his life. He saw Isabella in a completely unrealistic, romantic light, imagining her as his last hope of love. Isabella and his wife were incidental and yet, because of the way their parts were written, Zoe knew that this was her greatest opportunity to date.

Terence signalled a waiter. 'Cognac? coffee?' he asked her.

'Nothing more for me, thanks.' She'd had too much wine and it would be hard enough to sleep tonight without adding caffeine to the mix. It was ridiculous to be this emotional from a read-through but she had lived it, had felt Jonathan's pain and the emptiness of his life.

Terence drained his glass and held up his credit card. Once he'd paid and they got up to leave, three women stopped him for autographs. When they eventually made it outside, Zoe shot him a curious look. 'Don't you get tired of that?'

His eyes widened in surprise. 'Why would I?' He linked his arm through hers and guided her in the darkness towards the pier.

She was glad of his support. High heels and uneven cobbles did not go well together. Boats bobbed in the harbour, and gentle waves lapped the rocks. It was a beautiful night and she breathed in the sharp salty air.

Suddenly, Terence stopped and faced her. He took a step back, his expression blank, his stance formal. 'Ms Shine, are you guilty?' he asked, his voice deeper, his diction clipped.

She arched an eyebrow and smiled. 'Are you supposed to ask me that, Mr Keane?'

'You don't have to answer, Ms Shine.'

'Please call me Isabella, Jonathan,' she said, her voice husky. 'You don't mind me calling you Jonathan, do you?'

He stared down at her, his expression one of discomfort and embarrassment. 'No.'

She moved closer, put a hand on his arm and looked up into his face, thinking of a cold, bare cell, of coming out middle-aged, her looks gone, and shivered. 'I'm guilty of many things,

Jonathan,' she said, her lips almost touching his ear, 'but I did not kill Larry.'

She felt a tremor run through him and he turned his head and stared into her eyes before his gaze slid down to her mouth. She licked her lips and made no attempt to move.

Jonathan – Terence was gone – pulled back and cleared his throat. 'Good. Then why don't you tell me exactly what happened?'

'And then it cuts to Jonathan and his wife, right?' Zoe said.

'Yes. For the audition, I imagine Robbie will want us to do the dream scene. She comes to Jonathan's office in tears and he comforts her and then they kiss.'

He put his hands on her shoulders and stared into her eyes. 'Robbie and the audience have to believe that kiss, Zoe. In fact, if we do our job properly, they should leave the theatre wondering if *we're* having an affair.'

Zoe was glad that he couldn't see her blush in the darkness. She held his gaze. This is not Terence, this is Jonathan, she reminded herself. I have to make him believe I want him. He is, literally, Isabella's get-out-of-jail card. She reached up and cupped his face in her hands, gazed into his eyes and then brushed her lips against his. When he didn't move away, she did it again. Jonathan pulled her into his arms and kissed her, a kiss that spoke of passion and desperation and desire. When they pulled apart, she searched his face. He seemed perplexed. 'Not convincing?' she asked, disappointed. It had felt damn real to her.

Terence burst out laughing. 'Damn convincing. Phew! Every man in the place is going to want you. You are going to make a spectacular Isabella, Zoe.' He hugged her.

'Yes!' She punched the air and kissed him again, but this time as Zoe.

'Come on, my Isabella, let me escort you home.' Terence offered his arm and she took it.

'I'm so excited, I don't know how I'm going to sleep.'

He handed her the script. 'If you're going to be awake anyway, you may as well take this.'

She clutched it to her chest like a greedy child as they made their way back to the main road. 'I may stay up all night!'

'Why not? Sleep is greatly overrated,' he said, flagging down a taxi, 'and creativity thrives in the wee small hours.'

Zoe turned to him. He'd probably think she was nuts but . . . 'Please just say no if this is a completely crazy idea—'

His teeth flashed in the darkness. 'I love crazy.'

'Do you want to do a full read-through, I mean, right now?'

'I'd love to!'

'Shane is away so we'll have the place to ourselves.'

'Better again.' He winked.

Zoe stared at him. Oh, God, did he think she was propositioning him?

He threw back his head and laughed. 'Ah, Zoe, darling, you are so easy to wind up.'

She belted him with the folder. 'Very funny.'

'We're going to have a good time doing this,' he predicted.

She smiled. 'Yeah, I think we are.'

Zoe ached all over and her eyes burned but she was high as a kite. She'd just spent the most amazing evening with a man and there was no sex involved. The script was so powerful she felt humbled by the writer's talent. And though Terence came across as laid-back and careless, she'd just seen first-hand exactly how gifted an actor he was, and how much he demanded of himself and those working with him. Even their kiss had been dissected, examined. He had talked, explained, questioned and she had learned more in one night than in her entire time at drama school. No wonder his leading ladies fell for him – he was an incredible man. And though Terence oozed confidence and charisma, his portrayal of Jonathan Keane, a broken man at a crossroads in life and on the point of losing everything, had been completely credible and moving. It had made it so difficult for her to be the hard, cold Isabella. He had really pulled on her heart strings, made her care. So much so that she had wondered if his own bonhomie was just a mask he hid behind. But then, didn't everyone do that? Especially actors. As dawn broke, Zoe pulled off her dress and fell into bed in her underwear, just taking time to tuck the script under her pillow before falling into a dreamless sleep.

Chapter Five

Robbie Prendergast had groaned when he read the message on his phone. Working with Terence Ross was a trial at times. He had a great respect for the man but they occasionally locked horns and he had a feeling that this was one of those days. Robbie had an actress in mind to play the part of Isabella. Not only was she perfect for the role but she was experienced and had just appeared in a drama series on TV that won great acclaim. You couldn't buy that kind of advertising. And Terence expected him to ditch her in favour of a nobody? It wasn't going to happen. Robbie showered, dressed in a shirt and jeans and, pocketing his phone, he walked down into Ranelagh village, stopped to pick up a newspaper and then went into the café next door. The pretty waitress was over like a flash to take his order.

He ignored the paper and gazed out of the window, his mind still on *Isabella*. Terence knew as well as he did that they needed it to be a success. Their last two productions had been well received but they had made little money on either. And Robbie needed money. He was sure *Isabella* was a winner, that it had the 'It' factor. But to draw in the crowds, they needed a well-established actress to play Isabella. It might be a small part but it required presence and allure and Anna Kerrigan had both. But he'd get no peace unless he at least let this girl audition. That should be enough to get her into Terence's bed and then they could get back to concentrating on the play.

That afternoon, Robbie arrived at the room they had reserved in the acting school on George's Street. Though he was early, he still chalked it up as a mark against the girl that she wasn't there first. He knew he was just looking for reasons not to like her, but she was in the way of his plans, a nuisance he didn't need. He heard Terence arrive, greeting someone in the hall-way with his golden voice and warm laugh, and then there was a brief knock and the door was thrown open.

'Robbie, you're bright and early!'

'Well, I'm early,' Robbie corrected.

Terence laughed and took a sip from the styrofoam cup of coffee he'd brought in with him. 'You'll be bright once you've met Zoe. She lights up a room.'

'So why haven't I heard of her?' Robbie asked.

Terence pulled up a chair and sat down. 'She married an actor. Need I say more?'

He didn't. Robbie had seen plenty of marriages between actors fail. It had to be a very strong bond indeed to keep a couple together when they were both in a profession where jealousy and insecurity abounded. Usually, the stronger partner flourished and the other disappeared into obscurity.

Robbie leaned forward, resting his arms on his knees. 'You know I love this play, Terence, but it's crucial that we get the right woman for the part.'

'I couldn't agree more.'

There was a tentative knock on the door and Robbie gave a resigned shrug. 'Fine. Let's do it.' As Terence ushered the girl in, Robbie bent his head over his phone. It was a tactic he'd found useful in the past. It made actors nervous but good actors could channel that rather than be put off by it.

'Robbie, meet Zoe Hall.'

He looked up and locked eyes with the woman who stood with her hand held out waiting for his. He hadn't meant to stand up but he found himself on his feet and smiling. Her hand was warm and soft in his and, though he could see some apprehension in the brown eyes that were as dark as her hair, she seemed poised and confident. 'Nice to meet you,' he said, genuinely, and sat down.

'And you. Thank you for giving me the opportunity to audition. *Isabella* is a wonderful play and she is a challenging character.'

She had a good voice, deeper than most women's and yet musical.

'Right,' Robbie said. 'Let's start with the third scene, when it looks like Jonathan might be losing the case, and then a little of the dream scene.'

Zoe dropped her bag and jacket in a corner and pulled her hair up into a knot on the top of her head. She was dressed in a black top and jeans and ballet pumps. Though she had a good figure it was clear she wasn't trying to use it to get the part. Robbie was sorry that she had scraped up her lovely hair, and though it made her look sophisticated, she looked harder and less approachable. Then he realised that was exactly her intention. This woman had thought the part through. He looked across at Terence and saw the man was watching him, his eyes twinkling in amusement. Robbie remained deadpan. She'd have to do a lot more than that to win him over. He was glad he had picked a particularly hard scene for her. She had very little to say and had to convey her attitude and feelings through facial expression and body language. That was the sure-fire way to separate the wheat from the chaff. 'Ready?' he said.

'Ready.'

He watched her pull her shoulders back before swinging round and marching across the room to where 'Jonathan' sat, pretending to go through papers. She stood over him, quite close, until he sensed her presence and he jumped to his feet.

'Ms Shine. I'm glad you got here early—'

'Mr Keane, I hired you because I was told you're the best. But if that's the case, why has the prosecution produced a witness that you didn't know about?'

Her eyes were glacial as she looked at him and Robbie actually saw Terence draw back, and he wasn't convinced he was acting.

Jonathan, who had started the play as a tough and successful barrister, a chauvinist and misogynist who won nearly all of his cases, actually stammered. 'I – I have my people looking into that right now and I hope to have some information within the hour. Meanwhile, I will, of course, be objecting to the witness.'

She paced before him, anger emanating from her. Robbie

could almost see her, Garbo-like, in a pencil skirt and high heels clicking out her dissatisfaction. She stopped in front of Jonathan and held his gaze for the longest time before speaking again. 'This witness must not testify, Mr Keane. Do you understand?'

He stared back at her, nodding. 'I'll take care of it, Ms Shine.'

'Good.' Zoe – Isabella – smiled a smile that changed her into a different person entirely. She put a hand on Jonathan's arm. 'Forgive me for being so abrupt.' She paused, and when she continued there was a tremor in her voice. 'But this is a very stressful time. I'm frightened.'

Jonathan drew himself up to his full height, eager to be her protector. She looked up at him, her eyes like Bambi's, soft, trusting and beautiful.

Jonathan fawned over her, grateful for the kind words. 'I understand. Don't worry about that witness, Ms Shine. I'll see to it he never takes the stand.'

They stood silent for a second and then Terence turned round, awaiting instructions.

Robbie chewed on his bottom lip. 'Good. Now the dream scene.'

Zoe released her hair from the clip, shook it loose around her shoulders and mussed it up with her fingers. She immediately looked younger and sexy.

Terence went to the far side of the room and Robbie went over to talk to her. 'In this scene, Zoe, Jonathan is in his office, having a late-night drink, staring out of the window and daydreaming but talking aloud for the benefit of the audience. He'll be left side, front of stage with one spotlight on him.

When he has finished talking, the light will go off and in the darkness he will take his place at his desk. Then the light comes on front right and a dishevelled, upset Isabella walks in. Any questions?'

Zoe shook her head and Robbie resumed his seat.

Terence took up his place, turning his cup in his hand as if it were a glass. He said the last of his lines, sounding weary and defeated, and then visibly lit up when he remembered the feel of Isabella's hand in his, her scent and the way she'd looked at him, as if he was the most important person in the world. He would win her case and she would be so grateful, she would fall in love with him ... He went to the back of the dais.

Zoe rapped her knuckles against a chair and stepped forward, no longer the confident, arrogant Isabella but a frightened woman, beautiful and feminine in her vulnerability.

Jonathan stood up and rushed forward to meet her, frowning, surprised. 'Isabella! We didn't have a meeting scheduled, did we?'

She shook her head, hugging her arms around herself and not looking at him. 'No.'

'What is it? Has something happened?'

She shook her head. 'I can't sleep. Not tonight, not any night. I lie thinking about going to prison and, if I do finally sleep, I dream of being in a cell and wake up crying for help.' Though her voice carried clear as a bell she sounded unsure and nervous.

Jonathan put a comforting hand on her arm and, with his other, tipped her chin up so he could look into her eyes. 'Don't cry, please don't cry.'

Robbie did a double take when he saw that she did, indeed, have tears running down her cheeks. He was impressed.

Jonathan was the one in control now. He was tall and strong and he put his hands on her shoulders and gave her a confident smile. 'You're not going to prison, Isabella, I won't let that happen. I need you to be strong for me for just a few more days. Can you do that?'

She searched his face and then nodded. She gave a small grateful smile but not with her mouth, just her eyes, her expression one of total faith and adoration. Terence, ever the professional, held the moment, his eyes not leaving hers. Robbie licked his lips and when Jonathan finally dipped his head and she raised her mouth for his kiss, Robbie couldn't take his eyes off the couple. The kiss was gentle, tender and they seemed lost in each other. When Jonathan tangled a hand in her hair and pulled her closer, Robbie suppressed a groan of pure envy. The air was so charged, he was beginning to feel he was invading their privacy.

Finally, Jonathan pulled back and, with his thumb, wiped away her tears. Zoe – Isabella – turned her face into his hand, her eyes clenched shut, and kissed his palm.

Robbie sat in stunned silence. He and Terence hadn't even talked about how that scene would play out and that certainly wasn't how Robbie had visualised it, but it worked. Everyone in the theatre would believe that performance and the men would be as randy as hell and wishing they were in Jonathan's shoes.

Robbie realised that the two of them were standing watching him, waiting for a reaction – Terence curious, Zoe clearly troubled. He gave her a quick, polite smile. 'Thank you, Zoe. It was lovely to meet you. We'll be in touch.' He saw Terence open his mouth to protest but Robbie killed the words with a look.

'No problem.' She smiled but it was clear she was gutted. 'Thanks again for allowing me the opportunity to audition.'

Terence walked her to the door and kissed her on both cheeks. 'Talk soon, darling,' he said, and then came and flopped into the chair opposite Robbie, a smug grin on his face. 'Well?'

Robbie looked at him. 'You're screwing her, aren't you?'

Terence's eyes widened and then he burst out laughing. 'No, no, I'm not. She's actually my daughter's best friend, has been for years.'

It was Robbie's turn to be gobsmacked. That had been real acting? Terence was clapping his hands in delight. 'Brilliant. I love it. Didn't I tell you that she was Isabella?'

Robbie hated to admit it: the TV actress would be a much better bet from a promotional point of view, but Zoe Hall had incredible presence.

'I don't understand how she hasn't had any success,' he said.

Terence shrugged. 'Me neither. Still, you know how hard it is to break into the acting scene here, especially if you're older but with little experience. She's a far better actor than the husband she sacrificed herself for.' Terence sighed. 'That's love for you.'

Robbie shook his head. 'I don't know him.'

'You know him all right. It's Ed McGlynn. Hall is her maiden name.'

'No kidding?' Robbie had never met the guy. McGlynn was based mainly in London but was doing well enough for articles about him and reviews of his plays to appear in the Irish newspapers on a regular basis. He was considered a bit of a heart-throb and his name was often linked with beautiful actresses. Robbie didn't even know he'd been married. 'If you've known her so long, how come you're only telling me about her now?'

Terence smiled. 'I didn't see her perform until she moved back here and I didn't want to put myself in the position of giving her a break and living to regret it. But I've been keeping an eye on her progress and saw that, despite the poor roles, there was something special about her. I suppose it's in the blood – her brother's a playwright.'

'Shane, of course!' How had he not made the link earlier? They even looked alike.

'When I read *Isabella*, I immediately thought of Zoe. She's perfect for the part. Tell me I'm wrong.'

Robbie tossed down his pen and sat back in the chair with a defeated sigh. 'I want to but I can't.'

'You won't regret it. This is going to be a hit, I can feel it.'

'I hope you're right because we need one. I'm not kidding, Terence.' Robbie thought of the number of outstanding bills stacked on his hall table and the overdue rent. It really wasn't supposed to be like this, not at thirty-seven. He was well known, respected in the theatre and had even won a couple of awards, yet he was broke. That's what divorce from a greedy wife did to you.

'I'm right,' Terence said with supreme confidence.

Robbie had to smile at the rapturous look on the other

man's face. But who could blame him? Zoe definitely made an impression. He was glad other directors hadn't spotted how talented she was, that, hopefully, he would be the one to launch her career. He felt a tingle of excitement at the thought that this play might be 'the one'. *Isabella* was such a simple story but it packed a punch and Terence would be at his best, given he had hand-picked his leading lady.

'Let's go to The Shelbourne for a bite.' The actor jumped to his feet, beaming.

Robbie laughed. 'Terence, I can't afford Bewley's Café, never mind the Shelbourne.'

'My treat, dear boy. Come on. We must celebrate!'

Zoe sliced the onions as thinly as she could manage. The damn things were making her cry . . . everything was making her cry. She was so sure that the audition had gone well. She loved that play, she loved the part of Isabella and she'd been so confident that she'd nailed it. But Robbie Prendergast had seemed unimpressed and, in fact, couldn't get her out of the room fast enough. And, more telling, Terence hadn't called.

'Whoa there, Zoe. I'm feeding twenty, not two hundred.'

Zoe dropped the knife and wiped her eyes on her sleeve. 'Sorry, Tara.' She picked up her phone and checked the display, the signal and then the volume.

Tara cleaned her hands on her apron and shook her head. 'I could murder Dad for building your hopes up.'

'He didn't,' Zoe said, although he had really. She hadn't gone into great detail about the audition, she couldn't. The tears were too close, and it wasn't down to the onions. She'd been so sure she would get the part. The other night, Terence had made her feel like the most talented actress on the planet. He'd also made her feel beautiful and sexy and she hadn't felt that in years – Ed had seen to that. The wine had obviously gone to her head, though, and fooled her into thinking she was better than she was.

Tara nudged her. 'Come on, cheer up. Something might come of that play you're in next week.'

'Yeah, right.' For once, Zoe was actually praying a play she was in *wouldn't* be reviewed. She started to peel the potatoes, soothed by the monotonous chore that required no concentration.

'Why don't you come straight out and ask Shane to write something just for you?' Tara suggested.

'For a start, he's still in Spain.'

'With a woman?' Tara expertly sliced courgettes and peppers.

Zoe looked up at her friend. She was convinced that Tara still cared about Shane. She certainly showed a lot of interest in his love life. Zoe had been delighted when her brother and Tara got together, and they seemed so happy. But, out of the blue, Shane had fecked off to France, saying he had writer's block and needed to be alone somewhere that would inspire him. Zoe had figured that he'd got tired of Tara and just didn't have the guts to break up with her. Tara seemed to assume the same thing as, shortly after he left, she'd hooked up with Greg, and the rest, as they say, was history. But there had never been any bad feeling between them, quite the reverse, and Zoe wondered if sometimes Shane regretted letting Tara go.

'No woman. I think he's having a mini-breakdown.' She

confided to Tara, worried about her brother's gloomy, vacant voice on the phone. 'He was so excited about this new script and now all of a sudden he thinks it's rubbish.'

'He's always been hard on himself.'

'I know. But then you know better than anyone that depression and elation, overconfidence and insecurity are par for the course in the theatre.'

'Dad does have periods when he doesn't want to talk to a soul,' Tara agreed as she added the vegetables for the ratatouille to the smoking pan. 'Mam just heads to a health spa.'

'And Shane runs off to foreign countries.' Zoe sighed. 'I just need to keep Adam calm until he deigns to come home.'

'That's not your job,' Tara protested. 'Let Shane fight his own battles.'

'We're talking about the man who's put a roof over my head and may, out of gratitude, give me a part in his play,' Zoe reminded her.

Tara grinned. 'Two good points.'

'But it would have been great to get a decent part without my brother's help. *Isabella* is an amazing play.'

'Dad said it was just a small role.'

'It is, but a challenging one. Still, there's no point in dwelling on it. I'll just have to spend the next few weeks making myself indispensable to my brother and then beg, plead and nag until he uses his influence to get me a part.'

'That's the spirit.'

And if that didn't work out, she would just have to get a job teaching kids speech and drama. Zoe put the depressing thought out of her mind. She had to stay positive and just accept that the part of Isabella was not for her.

'It's going to kill me watching another actress in that role,' she admitted to her friend.

'Then don't go to the play.'

Zoe sighed. 'Are you mad? Of course I have to go.'

'You love torturing yourself.' Tara stirred tomatoes and herbs into the pan, tossed it with a practised hand and then started to clean down the work surfaces. 'Let's get this finished and I'll make us some pasta and we can crack open a bottle of wine.'

Zoe glanced at the clock and saw it was after five o'clock. Still no word. 'Oh, I don't know, Tara, I'm not exactly great company and I don't want to play gooseberry. Where is Greg, anyway?'

'He's at his mother's, decorating. He won't be home for hours, thank God.'

Despite her own misery, Zoe could sense Tara tense up at the mention of her husband.

'Everything okay between you two?' Previously, she'd stopped asking, as it was clear Tara didn't want to talk about Greg but felt she should enquire now.

Her friend turned her back and started to scrub pots, even though Zoe had washed them already. 'Not really. I spend my life walking on eggshells. The slightest thing seems to set him off and even when we're not rowing you could cut the atmosphere with a knife. When his mother asked him to do up her place, I could have kissed her, though I was convinced he wouldn't do it, make excuses. I don't think she needs any work done at all. She's just worried about him hanging around doing nothing all day.'

'Is he any good at decorating? Perhaps he could do that for a living.'

'He's useless and, anyway, he's a builder and a damn good one too. There's plenty of work out there if he'd just go after it.'

Zoe watched her friend take her frustrations out on the gleaming pots. 'Ed used to sulk too if he was out of work for more than a few weeks. He'd slob around the flat, unshaven, watching daytime TV.'

Tara looked up from her task. 'Greg is nothing like Ed McGlynn. That man was nothing but a selfish, egotistical bastard. The best thing that ever happened was you finally finding out what he was really like and leaving him.'

Zoe was taken aback at the venom in Tara's voice. Sure, things had turned sour with Ed but that was no reason to rubbish their entire relationship.

'That's not very fair, Tara. We had lots of good times together.'

'Please, he had the good times while you stayed home!' Tara retorted.

'What do you know about our life together?' Zoe demanded, her temper rising. 'You rarely saw him once we moved to England. How dare you make such assumptions?'

Tara straightened and gave her a piteous look. 'You seriously don't know after all these years?'

'Know what?' Zoe asked, not sure that she wanted to hear the answer when she saw guilt and remorse in Tara's eyes. Her friend remained silent but it was too late. She had something to say and Zoe knew she had to hear it. 'Tell me.'

Tara sighed. 'Ed was messing around long before you left Ireland.'

'No.' Zoe shook her head. They had been happy here, everything had been fine.

'Yes. Zoe, you must have known.'

'No,' she said again, refusing to believe it.

'And not just with one woman – there were plenty.'

Zoe raised her eyes. 'How do you know this?'

Tara sighed. 'I was at a function with Dad and I saw Ed with another girl.'

'That doesn't mean—'

Tara ignored the interruption. 'I asked Dad's then girlfriend who the girl was. Barbara was much younger than Dad and knew all the gossip. She didn't know the girl but she warned me to keep away from Ed. She said . . .'

'What?' Zoe said when Tara hesitated and looked away. 'Tell me.'

Tara sighed and looked back at her. 'She said that every time she ran into him, he was with a different woman, despite having a girlfriend tucked away somewhere, "poor cow" – her words, not mine.'

'So, it was common knowledge.' Zoe felt as if she'd been punched in the stomach. Could it be any more humiliating? But, hang on, if it was no secret, then Shane would have known about it and would have been only too happy to rat on Ed – there had never been any love lost between them. She raised her eyes to meet Tara's.

'Shane didn't know?'

Tara shrugged. 'I don't know, I rarely saw Shane in those days but I'm sure if he knew he'd have said or done something.'

'But you didn't,' Zoe said, reeling from this revelation. 'You only told me now because you wanted to hurt me.' She looked into Tara's eyes. 'How could you keep it from me? Lie to me? I thought you were my friend!' This came out in a strangled cry but Zoe felt as if her world was coming asunder. Those wonderful early days of their relationship when they had only had eyes for each other had all been a joke, a joke on her, and Tara had allowed it to happen. Her memories of those happy days were shattered. She hadn't been the love of Ed's life, he had never been faithful to her and her best friend had stood by and said nothing. 'I can't believe this.'

'Oh, come on, Zoe, as if you'd have listened. As far as you were concerned, the sun shone out of his arse. Greg said I should mind my own business and that you'd just shoot the messenger.'

'So you did what Greg told you, like a good little wife?' Zoe shook her head in disgust, tears rolling down her cheeks. 'We were friends before Greg or Ed came along. How could you betray me like that?' Tara flinched at the word. 'You were my bridesmaid. You helped me pick out the dress, you stood at the altar and watched us exchange our vows. You must have had a good laugh at that.'

'Of course I didn't!' Tara protested. 'I was miserable but I didn't know what to do. It was too late to say anything.'

'You never liked Ed.' Zoe hadn't realised it but, in hindsight, she knew it to be true.

'Not particularly,' Tara admitted. 'He loved himself more than anyone else but you couldn't see that. He changed you, took you over. He wanted to go to England, so you went. He wanted you to turn down parts because they didn't fit in with his schedule, so you did. You turned from being an ambitious actress into a bloody doormat.'

Zoe was incredulous at the bile pouring out of her best friend's mouth. The need to hit back was overwhelming. 'Ha! You can talk! One minute you were a party girl, the next you were spending your weekends in garden centres. If I turned into a doormat, you became middle-aged overnight.'

Tara's eyes widened in dismay. 'You don't like Greg?'

Zoe shrugged. 'He's okay. I just didn't think he was right for you. He was so much older and so dull.'

Tara's eyes flashed. 'Maybe he's not famous or God's gift, but he's reliable and dependable.'

'You make him sound like the family saloon,' Zoe shot back with a bitter smile.

'Well, you know what? At least he can keep his dick in his pants and, despite everything, I know that he loves me and has never been unfaithful,' Tara said, her eyes like ice.

Zoe stared at her, stunned. Finally, she found her voice. 'Yeah, you have the perfect marriage. Good for you.' And, standing up, she grabbed her bag and walked out the door. It was only when she reached the garden gate that she realised that Tara had made no move to stop her. Pulling out a tissue to soak up her tears, she strode away from the house. From now on, Tara could slice her own bloody onions.

Chapter Six

Zoe walked back into town, hoping the exercise and fresh air would calm her down and stop her heart thumping in her chest, but it didn't work. Had that really just happened? Was it all true or was Tara just exaggerating mild flirtations? But she discounted this almost immediately, remembering the expression on Tara's face when she'd spilled the beans. She wasn't sure what upset her most: the fact that Ed had made a fool of her on this side of the Irish Sea as well as the other, or that her best friend had known about it and kept it from her. Hands thrust deep in her pockets, head down to hide her tears, Zoe crossed the Liffey and made her way up lanes and alleys towards St Stephen's Green. Except for some dog-walkers, the park was quiet as workers hurried home and tourists headed for restaurants. She tucked herself into a corner of a bench by the pond, staring into the murky green water as she mulled over the revelations. How Tara could let her marry Ed, knowing what she knew, was beyond her. As she pledged herself to a man she firmly believed she would be with for ever, had others looked on with pity? And Ed? She thought about those early days in Dublin, when her feet had hardly touched the ground. They'd been madly in love, at least so she'd thought. Had it all been a lie? She had given herself to him in every way, laid herself bare to him and believed he'd done the same. The thought of him kissing and touching other women and then coming back to her bed and making love to her made her nauseous.

She became aware of a group of guys on the other side of the pond, drinking beer from cans and watching her. She dragged herself to her feet, pulled up her collar and walked quickly to the nearest bus stop. Normally when she was upset she would turn to Tara, who would feed her ice cream and comfort her. Those days were gone for good.

In the silent house, Zoe dropped her bag and slammed the door as her sadness turned to anger. To hell with *Isabella*, to hell with Ed and, she swallowed hard, to hell with Tara. She went upstairs, changed into PJs, tugged the duvet off the bed and hauled it downstairs. It didn't matter what the time of year, the house always felt cold and damp. She wasn't as keen on booze as Tara but felt the need of something to soothe her. She padded into the draughty kitchen and took a beer and crisps into the living room. As she snuggled up on the sofa, she was suddenly reminded of Sundays when she and Ed had stayed in bed all day and read the papers, ate junk food and made love. She had been so happy then but now doubted every aspect of their life together, imagining him on the phone to other women while she was in the shower, dancing with them in clubs when she thought he was working. God, had he taken any of them into their bed? She was overcome suddenly with an aching loneliness.

She decided to watch a movie, realising that if she kept going over and over things in her head she'd go insane. Though Shane was a slovenly pig in the bedroom and bathroom, his DVDs were neatly filed on a shelf next to the sofa. She swivelled it round, dismissing the crime, the thrillers, the sci-fi and most definitely the comedy – she wasn't in the mood for laughing – she wanted and needed to wallow in her own misery for a while. She finally settled on *The Big Sleep*. Bogie and Bacall were exactly what was called for, although watching the couple smoulder on screen would only make her think of Ed and, of course, Isabella. What had she done wrong in the audition? She'd have to ask Terence – she might at least learn something. But for now, she thought, reaching for the crisps and beer, she would lose herself in someone else's world.

She was woken by the doorbell – this was becoming a habit. The movie was over and she fumbled for the remote to switch off the TV. Within seconds, the argument with Tara came flooding back and she was plunged into despair once more. The doorbell rang again and she threw off the duvet, knocking off the bag of crisps and spilling beer down her front in the process. 'Shit, shit, shit,' she muttered, and crept to the window. She was in no mood for visitors. But it was Terence on her doorstep and the sight of him made her pulse quicken. Surely a personal visit was a good sign? Or was he just here to tell her she hadn't got the part and let her cry on his shoulder? Well, she'd done enough crying today. Whatever his reason for being here, she would put on a brave face. She was damned if anyone was going to call her a doormat again. She looked down at her damp PJs. It was harder to seem cool, calm and collected when you looked like shit. This man had a knack for catching her at her worst. She went into the hall, closed the door on the mess and hurried to let him in.

'Surprise!' Terence beamed. Robbie was now by his side, looking both uncomfortable and apologetic.

'Aren't you going to invite us in?' Terence brandished a bottle. 'Or do we have to drink this on the doorstep?'

It was clear that he'd had a few already.

'I did tell him that it was a little late to come calling,' Robbie said.

'Late? Late? It's not even gone ten. Lord, you young people need to stop taking life so seriously and live a little. You'll be dead long enough, buried in the stony grey soil of this great land.' He turned back to Zoe. 'Now, are you going to let us in or not? We have some celebrating to do.'

She noticed for the first time an old Audi parked at the gate. Terence was the only one who'd been drinking, at least. She suddenly realised what he'd said. 'Celebrating?' She glanced from one to the other, afraid to jump to conclusions, afraid to hope.

'The part is yours, if you want it,' Robbie said, 'and we really hope you do.'

She stared at him, dumbstruck, as much by his warm smile as by his words. Had she heard right? Really?

'Well, darling?' Terence looked at her expectantly.

'Yes.' It came out as a tiny squeak.

Robbie stepped closer, cupping his ear as a truck passed. 'Pardon?'

'I said, yes. Yes, yes and yes!' she squealed and flung herself

into his arms and then Terence's. She laughed at Robbie's startled look. 'Thank you so much. You won't regret it. I will work
my heart out and act my arse off!'

'You will,' Robbie assured her with a grin.

'Can I assume that means we may come in?' Terence gently
pushed past her and headed for the kitchen.

'Of course!' She gave a nervous giggle and stepped back to
let Robbie pass too. 'Sorry. I think I may be in shock.'

Terence had already found glasses and was easing the cork
from the bottle. 'It's not the real thing, I'm afraid.'

'I doubt I could tell the difference,' she assured him.

'Come on, let's go into the garden. You know this house
depresses me.' Terence threw open the back door.

'I was sure you hated my performance,' Zoe said to Robbie
as she took a shawl from the hook by the back door and
wrapped it around her shoulders.

'I wanted to,' he admitted. 'I had a television actress in mind
for the part and we could have done with the publicity. But
Terence is right, you're perfect in the role.'

'Thank you,' she said, realising that this man wouldn't
throw out compliments that easily.

'Come on, you two, or I'll drink all the wine,' Terence called.

'We'd better get out there.' She grinned, then grabbed a
lighter from a drawer and, leading him down to where
Terence sat, she lit the range of enormous candles around the
gazebo, before sinking into a chair.

Robbie turned to look up at the house. 'Nice place. That
brickwork is lovely. And this is a lovely road and such a great
location.'

'Yeah, I love Terenure,' Zoe agreed.

'You restored a place once, didn't you, Robbie?' Terence asked.

'Yeah.' Robbie sat down and stretched out his legs. 'I loved that house and enjoyed every minute of the renovation. But I never got to actually enjoy living there. Linda still lives there with our two kids, while I'm renting a soulless box with zero soundproofing.'

'That's rough. I'm divorced too but there were no children to worry about – we didn't even own a home. Splitting up was easy.' A lot easier for Ed, she thought, after Tara's revelations. The bastard was probably relieved when she left. She banished him from her mind. She wasn't going to let Ed spoil her celebration, or Tara either, for that matter. She looked over at Robbie and wondered why his wife had divorced him. She sounded liked a bitch, but then Zoe was only getting one side of the story. Still, it must have been hard leaving his children and the home he loved. 'Do you get to see your kids?'

'Oh, sure.' His face lit up. 'And, to be fair, it would have been madness to sell the house. We wouldn't have got a fraction of what it's worth and it's near the kids' school and their friends. My crappy flat forces me to be inventive about places to take them. It's turned into a challenge they grade me on.'

She laughed. 'Sounds like you have a good relationship. How old are they?'

'Sammy – Samantha – is fifteen and Nick is twelve.'

'Bring them to rehearsals,' Terence suggested. 'That would be an experience for them and I promise not to swear as much as usual.'

Robbie stroked his chin. 'You know, that's not a bad idea. Sammy is talking about going into the theatre. She has this ridiculous idea that it's glamorous and romantic.'

'The "yoof" of today just want to be famous,' Terence remarked with a chuckle. 'They don't seem to care how or why. But every so often you discover someone who is ready to work hard and has what it takes. Don't you, Robbie?' His eyes met and held Zoe's in the candlelight.

'Indeed.' Robbie smiled at her.

She was touched by the praise but the warm glow was quickly replaced with apprehension. As the newbie, she'd probably get the blame if the play bombed. Robbie also seemed to have his feet firmly on the ground.

'We only have a short run and we must make the best of it if we want *Isabella* extended or taken by other theatres.' He leaned forward and rested his arms on the table. 'You need to get all your contacts talking about it, Terence. We need to create a buzz to get people fighting over tickets for the opening night. I'll get working on adverts. Zoe, we'll need some photos of you and a brief bio.'

'Trust me, it will be brief,' she assured him.

Terence shook his head. 'I don't agree.'

'Oh, it will—'

'No, I mean I don't think we should draw attention to you at all in the billing.'

'Oh!' Zoe looked at Robbie, waiting for his reaction, and was filled with dismay when he nodded in agreement.

'Ah, I see where you're going with this,' he said. 'Bill *Isabella* as being all about Jonathan and play down Celia and Zoe's roles?'

'Exactly.' Terence went to refill their glasses but Robbie put a hand over his.

Zoe didn't understand their logic. She had been thrilled

when she'd learned that the third member of the cast was none other than the famous Celia O'Sullivan. Surely, Robbie should be telling everyone that she was in *Isabella*? Between her and Terence, they were bound to be invited on all the big TV shows to discuss it. What better free advertising could you wish for?

'Celia won't be impressed.' Terence's teeth gleamed in the candlelight.

'Don't worry, I'll handle her.'

Zoe couldn't help feeling disappointed. In her dreams she'd seen her name up there alongside the two veterans, albeit in smaller print. But she'd just have to take it on the chin. She had a part in a Robbie Prendergast play with Terence Ross and Celia O'Sullivan at the Abbey Theatre in Dublin and that's all that mattered. Robbie had obviously noticed she'd gone quiet.

'It's a trick we use from time to time, Zoe,' he explained. 'We give the audience only part of the story and that way on opening night there are more surprises and, hopefully, that results in more reviews and creates a buzz.'

'But the play is called *Isabella* and the story is about Jonathan's obsession with her.'

'Yes, but she's almost a figment of his imagination. The punters won't be expecting the scenes between the two of you. And that's another thing . . .' He glanced back at Terence. 'We need Gerald to do some rewrites, perhaps cut back on the amount of action in the courtroom and have another dream scene.'

Terence nodded slowly and smiled. 'You've been reading my mind.'

Robbie looked at his watch and stood up. 'I'll see if I can set up a meeting with him tomorrow. We have a lot of work to do if we want to pull this off.'

'It will be a triumph, Robbie, I guarantee it.'

'Terence, don't, that's the kiss of death.' Robbie closed his eyes and groaned, making Terence laugh. 'Zoe, I'll get a contract drawn up. Could we meet in a couple of days to talk?'

'Of course, any time,' she assured him.

She walked with him to his car, thanked him once more and returned to find a pensive Terence wandering around the garden, hands behind his back.

'You know what?' he said. 'I think that perhaps Isabella should be softer.'

She sat down, pulling the shawl tight around her. 'Wouldn't that take from the poignancy of the play?' Dear God, why was she arguing points with an old hand like Terence? Still, he'd told her to treat him as a fellow actor and so if she felt something didn't work she must say so. She'd be more apprehensive of speaking her mind to Robbie though. He had been really nice this evening but she'd seen the steely aloof side at the audition and she imagined he'd be a hard taskmaster. All the more reason to be straight with the man, and hopefully she'd earn his respect and he'd want to work with her again.

Terence was still wandering around the garden, apparently lost in thought. She wasn't even sure if he'd heard her but, moments later, he whirled round, his eyes alive.

'Wouldn't it be better if Jonathan and the audience believed Isabella was falling for Jonathan and then, bam! At the end, they discover she was just sweet-talking him to win her case?'

She shook her head. He really was something else. Did he ever switch off?

He frowned. 'You don't agree?'

'It might work but will Robbie and Gerald agree?'

'Yes, if they see the idea has merit. And if we try it and it doesn't work, fine. Let's go inside and take a look at the script.'

In the kitchen, he spread the pages between them on the table and took out a fountain pen. 'It would just need a tweak here and there. It will be more about how she is around him rather than what she says. A look, a brush of fingers, that sort of thing.'

'But do we let Jonathan and the audience find out together that Isabella's been fooling them?'

'Hmm, I'm not sure,' he admitted, drumming his fingers on the table. 'It would be more dramatic if it all came to a head at the end but then it's just another story of unrequited love.'

'Perhaps you should just tell Robbie your thoughts and let him put the idea to the writer,' she suggested.

'Yes, you're right. Do you know Gerald Spring?'

She shook her head.

'He's a grumpy old sod but a sweetheart behind it all and a little in love with me.' Terence winked at her. 'I'm sure, with some gentle persuasion, he'll agree to take another look at this. Want to try a run-through with a softer Isabella?'

'Now?'

He frowned. 'Why not?

'Why not indeed!' she said, and went to get her copy of the script. Staying up all night rehearsing with Terence was preferable to reliving her row with his daughter and Ed's despicable behaviour. The busier she was, the less chance she'd have to feel sorry for herself. And it was infinitely more attractive to become the hard, cold Isabella than to be Zoe, the girl who'd been deceived, betrayed and cheated on.

Chapter Seven

The next few days were a blur of activity with the final rehearsals for Zoe's other play. She wished it was over so she could concentrate on *Isabella* but Terence reprimanded her for her indifference.

'Play every part to the best of your ability, no matter what your personal opinion of it is.'

And so she threw herself into it and realised she was able to enjoy it more as a result. Being around Terence was an education. She'd also kept in touch with both Shane and Adam, reassuring her brother and calming his friend, pointing out that nerves were the sign of a good play and she was sure her brother would be home any day. She wasn't. Shane still sounded down and refused to discuss the play. She was dying to tell him about *Isabella*, sure that it would cheer him up, but Robbie had warned them all not to discuss it.

She hadn't heard a word from Tara and she was damned if she was going to call. She felt hurt, angry and upset that her friend had watched her being made a fool of and done or said nothing to stop it. And, yet, at the same time, she couldn't help wondering how Tara was coping with only Andrea to help. Maybe Greg would finally notice how drawn and thin his wife was and get off his arse. She told Terence about the falling-out but not the reason. It would be wrong to involve him. But Terence had dismissed the matter with a wave of his hand.

'You're friends, friends fall out. Though the timing could have been better – Greg's not much of a husband or friend at the moment.'

It was clear that he didn't have much time for his son-in-law. His words made Zoe feel guilty but this wasn't a mere tiff. It had shaken their friendship to the core and Zoe wasn't sure they'd recover from it.

And it was time to think of her own life, to focus on *Isabella*. These next few weeks could change her entire future. Despite finding out how Ed had used her, she couldn't remember ever feeling so exhilarated or alive. Maybe she didn't need a friend or a partner. Maybe she could get fulfilment from her work instead.

Zoe met with Robbie and his producer, Lauren Kelly, in a coffee shop. The first word that came to her mind as he introduced them was 'sharp'. Lauren's business suit was sharp, her thin face was sharp and the eyes that appraised her, raking her from head to toe, were sharpest of all. She was the complete opposite of Adam and looked as if she'd be more at home working in the financial industry than the frivolous world of entertainment. Zoe certainly couldn't imagine her massaging egos or dealing delicately with divas.

Once the introductions had been made, Lauren got straight

down to business. She produced the contract and quickly took Zoe through it. When she was finished, she suggested Zoe take it away with her, read it carefully and let her agent look over it. It had been a struggle to keep a straight face. Zoe was signed with an agency but she didn't have 'an agent' as such. She got calls – not many – from various faceless members of staff and she doubted checking contracts was within their remit. She wasn't sure she'd trust them anyway. She'd seen lots of contracts in her day, they were pretty standard, and this one seemed straightforward. Truth was, she would happily play Isabella for nothing. To appear at the Abbey alongside Terence and Celia and be directed by Robbie Prendergast was payment enough.

'It's fine,' she told a shocked and disapproving Lauren, signed it and handed it back.

But Robbie seemed pleased and, when Lauren excused herself to go to another meeting, he bought them both another coffee and they got down to the much more enjoyable business of discussing *Isabella*.

'Terence told me his proposed changes to the script but I'm not convinced,' he said. 'Sometimes you can overthink things. I remember how I felt when I first read the play and what made me pity Jonathan was that I knew all along that Isabella was taking him for a ride.'

Zoe thought about how she'd felt that first night Terence had taken her through the script. Robbie had a point.

'If we changed it,' he continued, 'while the ending might be alarming, the rest of the play could lose energy. I think it's a given that no matter how we play it, people will guess that they win the case.'

'True.'

'An extra dream scene is a good idea and Gerald agrees. He's working on it now. Then when he's finished, we'll have a read-through,' his eyes twinkled, 'and then you'll see the other side of Terence. Sparks will fly when he and Celia cross swords!'

She raised her eyebrows. 'Oh? But they've appeared in so many productions together and seem to get on so well.'

'Looks can be deceiving. Celia has strong opinions too, she and Terence rarely agree, but they're professionals, so we always get there in the end, usually without bloodshed.' He laughed. It was a warm rich sound that drew the attention of two women at the next table who appraised him with speculative eyes. He was attractive, Zoe supposed, in a rough-and-ready sort of way. More *Top Gear* than Top Shop.

'I'm interested in your opinion,' he said. 'What do *you* think of the play as it stands?'

She gave it careful consideration before answering. What *did* she think? 'I wonder about Isabella being so hard. If she is, something made her that way. What? If she murdered her husband, why?' She thought for a moment of Jonathan pacing her kitchen – for it was Jonathan and not Terence. He slipped into the role as easily as into a jacket. 'None of that matters if Jonathan is simply infatuated with Isabella but, if he's fallen in love with her, I think it does. I mean, you wouldn't want him falling for a monster. I think that would really bother the audience.'

Robbie sat back and folded his arms. 'I don't believe he loves her. She's come along at a point in his life when he's vulnerable. She's a fantasy, a body. It's about sex and desire, nothing more. There are two women in the play – his wife and Isabella – but the story is about him, *his* crisis. The audience shouldn't be distracted by the backstory of the women. We don't want them to *care* about either of them, we want them to live through the crisis with Jonathan. It shouldn't even matter if Isabella is innocent or not. At least not until they're on their way home. They have to get the same dose of cold water at the end that he does. The reality that, as a result of his romanticising this creature, his marriage is over and he's lost the woman he loves and who loves him.'

'That makes sense. But *does* he love his wife or is he just afraid of growing old alone?' Zoe asked.

'Does it matter? Wouldn't it be good to leave the audience wondering the same thing?'

She nodded and smiled, liking the idea of the audience going home still caught up in Jonathan's world, arguing over *Isabella* and who exactly had used who. She felt a flutter of excitement at the idea of being in a drama that would put people at loggerheads, get them arguing over the endless possibilities of the whys and wherefores. That was a play that would run and run. Stop, she told herself. Terence was right, she mustn't be distracted by the future. She had to concentrate on going on stage each precious night and giving it everything she had, absolutely everything.

How would Terence feel about Robbie's decision? She hoped she wouldn't get caught in the crossfire – she didn't want to have to take sides. It might not be a bad thing to put a little distance between Terence and herself. He called round almost every day or phoned her to meet him or sent her texts late at night. She'd caught him looking at her sometimes, a strange expression in his eyes. Was he in character already? When he looked at her, did he see Zoe or Isabella? She was about to sound Robbie out as to what Terence was usually like with his love interest but thought better of it. She hardly knew Robbie and it would be disloyal. If it wasn't for Terence, she wouldn't have got this part. With that, her phone buzzed and she glanced down at the text from the man himself.

Coming to see you in action tonight. Nervous?! Supper afterwards in Carluccio's?

'Something wrong?' Robbie asked.

She sighed. 'Terence is coming to see my play tonight.'

'So?' He shrugged. 'Despite your part being small, you put on a good performance.'

She stared at him. 'You've seen it?'

He smirked. 'I was there last night.'

Zoe digested this information, not quite sure what to say. If she had been good, why hadn't he said something earlier? She couldn't have been that impressive. She tried to keep her voice light but she was consumed with paranoia. She raised her eyes to his. 'You didn't think much of it, did you?'

He laughed. 'Of the play? God, no; dreadful and far too bloody long.'

'But what about me?' she asked in a small voice.

'I told you, you were good.'

'Sorry, I sound very needy, don't I? I suppose I'm just freaked that you were there and that Terence is coming this evening.'

'Forget Terence. He doesn't matter. Just do your job.'

She nodded again. 'You're right.'

'Of course I'm right, I'm always right. Remember that.' He grinned.

She smiled back but was wondering who would win when he and Terence came head to head over the script. And what about the writer, Gerald, whom she hadn't even met yet? And then there was Celia, who sounded like a bit of a diva. Zoe was beginning to understand why Robbie said sparks would fly.

'What utter shite,' Terence said, cheerfully raising his glass. 'Congratulations for getting through it with grace and charm.' They were sitting in the warm, busy restaurant after the play.

'Thank you, I think!' Zoe laughed. 'I'm in awe of your disguise.'

Terence was dressed in an ill-fitting drab suit, his slip-on shoes were cheap and scuffed, he wore horn-rimmed glasses and his hair was parted and greased down. No one had given him a second glance when they'd walked in and he'd mumbled his order and avoided eye contact with the waitress.

'You approve?' He gave her a wicked grin.

'I'd pass you in the street,' she assured him.

'I should probably wear it when we're out together between now and opening night,' he mused. 'We don't want to draw attention to you.'

'There's no reason for us to be out together at all,' she pointed out.

He raised an eyebrow and put a hand on his heart. 'You don't want to see me? I'm deeply wounded.'

She laughed. 'I'll see you at rehearsals and you can still come by the house.'

'Ah, yes, your wonderful abode.' He shuddered.

'If you hate it so much, I can always come to your place.'

He wrinkled his nose. 'I don't particularly want to be there either. Damn place stinks of paint. It's playing havoc with my vocal chords.'

'You have the slowest decorators in the country,' she remarked.

'I'll invite you round when it's presentable.' He poured more wine for her.

'Oh, I shouldn't—'

'Don't be silly, this is a celebration. It's the last night of that pathetic play and you were the star.'

'I was barely on stage for nine minutes,' she protested, laughing.

He splayed his hands. 'Need I say more? And now you can concentrate all your attention on *Isabella*.'

What the hell, he was right. She did deserve to celebrate and she felt more comfortable being with Terence when he wasn't being stared at. He'd taken off the spectacles and now, as he leaned towards her, she thought how ridiculously handsome and ageless he was. Was that down to his boundless energy, his fame or the fact that so many women made it clear that they were his for the taking?

'We have a lot to do, darling. It's important to me that we are convincing.'

'Me too,' she assured him.

'And you will be.'

She smiled and this time didn't object when he topped up her glass and regaled her with stories about the theatre and she told him of some of the dumps she and Ed had ended up in when they were touring England.

'Trust me, darling, I've seen my share. I remember one theatre – and I use the word loosely; it was really a hall in a
community centre – where a rat crossed the stage in the
middle of the first act. Most of the women from the first four
rows ran, screaming, for the door.'

'That must be a *very* long time ago. The women are still running but now it's after you, not away from you,' she joked.

'How very kind and so eloquently put.' He leaned his chin
on his hand and studied her.

'Could I make you run, Zoe?'

She searched his eyes, trying to figure out if he was joking,
but his expression was unreadable. How she wished she could
master that art. She wondered if he realised she was attracted
to him. How could she not be? He was gorgeous and funny
and had paid her more attention in the last couple of weeks
than anyone had in years. And his kisses ... well if that's what
he could achieve on a stage, she couldn't help wondering what
he'd be like when he wasn't acting. Oh, God, Zoe, this is your
friend's father you're fantasising about. Still, he was younger
than Jagger, McCartney and Bowie and much more attractive.
She decided not to risk making a fool of herself and grinned at
him. 'Only if you shout at me for giving a bad performance.'

He raised an eyebrow. 'I can't imagine that happening.
Coffee?' he added, as a waiter hovered.

'No, thank you.'

'Want to go home and rehearse?'

She held his gaze. 'I'd love to.'

He took her hand between his and kissed the palm, his eyes
never leaving hers. 'Then let's go.'

*

They didn't speak or touch in the taxi, which was a first for Terence. He loved to talk and his words were interspersed with a squeeze of her hand or a stroke of her hair. But tonight, he stared out of the window, seemingly lost in thought. Zoe wasn't sure what to make of his silence – wine rather than blood ran through her veins. She too stared out of the window and had to dig her nails into her palms to stop herself reaching for his hand. She couldn't believe he was having this effect on her. She'd obviously been celibate too long.

'Zoe?'

She roused herself, realising the car had stopped, and she fumbled for her keys as Terence paid the driver. Her hand shook as she put the key in the lock, and when she finally got the front door open, he walked past her towards the kitchen. She followed, stretching out a hand to switch on the light.

'Don't.' There was a full moon so they weren't in complete darkness. He turned to her and trailed his fingers down the side of her face. 'Darling.'

She leaned into his hand and closed her eyes.

'I'll take care of you, Isabella. Do you trust me?'

'Yes, Jonathan,' she said, and slid her arms around his neck. He lowered his lips to hers and kissed her. It was a light, gentle kiss, not like the passionate full-on ones of before. He pulled back and looked into her eyes and then kissed her again, and again. His lips were barely touching hers, but it was the most erotic feeling, and then his lips moved to the side of her mouth and traced feather-light kisses from there up to the back of her ear and then down her neck. Her head fell back and she clung to him for support.

'Isabella, my Isabella,' he murmured, and held her body

tight against his. She was on the point of suggesting they go upstairs when he stepped back and smiled.

'Excellent, darling. You see, wine has its uses! That felt much more natural, didn't it?'

Zoe blinked, sobering up in an instant. Grateful for the darkness, she acted for the first time that evening. 'Really? Was I convincing?'

'You've always been that but this time I felt that you were immersed in the part.'

'Thanks,' she said faintly.

'When you auditioned, Robbie assumed we were having an affair because of the chemistry between us. Can you believe it?'

She laughed with him. 'I guess that means we're doing something right.'

'Darling, your career begins with this play.'

Excitement dispelled her embarrassment as she thought of her acting finally being taken seriously. 'I hope you're right, Terence.' He held her hands and she saw her excitement mirrored in his eyes.

'I will help you in every way I can.'

She shook her head. 'Why are you being so kind to me?'

'You need someone who truly believes in you when you're starting out. I was lucky enough to have someone like that and now, Zoe, you do too. Let's say I'm repaying a debt.'

There was a wistful look in his eyes and she gave him an impulsive hug. She may not have found a lover but she'd definitely found a friend. 'I can't think of anyone I'd rather have in my corner.'

*

When he'd left, excitement gave way to misery and she cried into her pillow. She couldn't believe that she had read the situation wrong. Wine was dangerous, at least to her. She had come so close to making a pass at him. Oh, the humiliation. What would he have done, she wondered? Probably left, and how then would they have been able to play their parts? She thanked the Lord that she had copped on in the nick of time and Terence hadn't noticed anything amiss. In fact, the opposite. He'd hugged her close in the doorway and told her that she was improving every day. She hoped that she could keep that up after tonight's fiasco. What was wrong with her? First, Ed made a fool of her, now a man more than twice her age didn't seem attracted to her. He saw Isabella not Zoe. And that was fine, really. Yes, he was attractive, yes, a flirtation would be nice – she wouldn't want more than that – but the fact that she'd imagined his interest was mortifying. Concentrate on the job, Zo, she told herself, and you might finally get a lucky break. But you are most definitely unlucky in love.

Chapter Eight

Tara stood in her nightshirt at the kitchen table, kneading bread. It was three in the morning and, after tossing and turning in bed for hours, she'd decided she might as well get some work done. Once the dough was in the oven, she went to make a cup of tea, only to find the milk carton in the fridge was empty. The familiar feeling of impotent anger bubbled up inside as she thought of Greg snoring. She felt like storming upstairs, switching on the light and screaming at him. She could really understand how people went berserk with knives, rolling pins or the kitchen shears.

Tara opened their drinks cupboard, and when she realised she hadn't bought any gin, reached for the whiskey bottle and poured a generous dollop into a tumbler. She took a sip, her eyes watering as it burned its way down her throat. She went to the sink, added a dash of water and took another tentative sip. Yes, better. Sitting down at the table, she opened her notebook and checked her lists. One was of bookings – not as many as she needed, although probably as much as she could handle. The other was of outstanding bills, and cheques that had bounced. The second made her angry, not just because of the money that should have been in her account, but because she'd known some of these people for years and they knew that Greg was out of work. She wasn't usually confrontational but there was no way she was taking any more of this shit. How could people be so bloody mean when she'd given them great food for a fair price? She had been calling them every couple of weeks but now she planned to call daily – if she had the time. She yawned widely. And from now on she would demand fifty per cent in advance and increase her charges. She would also reduce portion sizes – not enough for anyone to notice – and, though she hated to skimp on quality, she'd buy generic brands of staple ingredients like flour, pasta and rice.

Tara refilled her glass, abandoned the paperwork and flopped into the old armchair by the window, tucking her feet underneath her to warm them. The sensible thing to do would be to sell the house – it would fetch a good price – but Greg wouldn't hear of it, even though she was the one paying the mortgage. If they moved just a few miles out of the city they could pick up a bigger place, maybe even on a decent plot of land, where she could have a purpose-built kitchen, somewhere to escape from Greg. Until recently, she'd have felt guilty at having such thoughts. Not any more. Tara raised the glass to her lips. Her heart hardened and her resentment increased every day. He might have thrown in the towel but she was damned if he'd take her down with him. She'd go ahead and check out properties. If she presented her husband with a proposition that would get them out of debt and relieve some pressure, then how could he say no? She'd talk to Zoe ...

Then she remembered that they weren't talking. She felt riddled with guilt at her outburst. It was bad enough that she'd told Zoe, but to do it in such a nasty way. She felt truly ashamed of herself when she thought of all the times Zo had rushed to her aid these last couple of years. Tara knew that Zoe felt betrayed and she didn't blame her. Were their situations reversed, she'd feel the same way. It was all Greg's fault. He had told her at the time that what Ed got up to was none of her business and Zoe wouldn't thank her for being the bearer of bad news. And she'd listened to him. And now he'd come between them again, although why she felt the need to defend him these days she had no idea. But, still, he was nothing like Ed. Greg had always been faithful. The family-car quip hurt but, in a way, it was true. Tara's parents had always led their own lives and, though she knew they loved her, they hadn't always been around when she needed them. Then Shane had deserted her too, just as they were getting close, just as she thought she'd found 'the one'. But Greg was as solid as a rock. She knew that she could always rely on him, that he'd always be there. Only now, his presence was suffocating and she found herself doing anything she could think of to avoid him.

She knew it wasn't his fault, knew that he was depressed. She took another drink. Why, then, was she angry with him all the time? The truth was she felt let down. He didn't seem to care about her at all. And she had given up trying to talk to him about his mental state as there was no getting through. He spent most days trailing from the bed to the sofa, venturing out only to buy a newspaper, a luxury that, stupidly, got on her nerves. Why didn't he watch the news or read it online, she felt like screaming. But she was afraid that once she started to scream she wouldn't be able to stop.

She was suddenly conscious of a smell of burning. 'No,' she wailed and jumped up to rescue her bread. It was slightly browner and crustier than it should have been but, if she sliced it thinly, she'd get away with it. She lifted it out of the oven and, in the process, somehow caught her arm on the hot rack. The shock of the pain made her drop the tray and she slumped onto the floor, trying to gather the bread up and burning her hand in the process. Tears filled her eyes as the worry, pain, tiredness and, no doubt, the whiskey took its toll. Then the smoke alarm went off and she started to laugh through her tears. How in hell could Greg sleep through this racket? He was supposed to come rushing down, worried, and then tend to her burns as he promised to go out looking for work first thing, and not come home until he got some. She dried her tears, rescued the bread from the floor and flapped a tea cloth around to silence the alarm. Despite the pain, she cleaned up the mess and restored her kitchen to its pristine state before tending her burns.

Tara had just poured herself another drink when she heard her phone beep, heralding the arrival of a text. Shane. With a sigh, she settled back in the chair to read the message.

Hey, Tara, how are you? Missing you, love to talk.

Tell me your troubles, you mean, she muttered. What was she, the Samaritans? Shane never slept well when he was working and often sent messages to her in the early hours. She rarely replied. Though it was innocuous, she knew that Greg wouldn't have liked it.

Shane, you shouldn't be texting me at this hour. You shouldn't be texting me at all!

He answered almost immediately.

You're awake! Why? Can I call?

What if Greg came down? She could always say it was Zoe. He didn't know they weren't talking. He didn't know much about her at all lately. She'd stopped volunteering information about her day and he didn't care enough to ask any more. Emboldened by the whiskey, she texted:

Okay.

Tara had only just muted the sound when Shane's name flashed up. She put the phone to her ear. 'Hi,' she whispered.

'What are you doing up in the middle of the night? And why are you whispering?' He chuckled. 'He's not in bed beside you, is he?'

'Of course not, I'm downstairs. Just having trouble sleeping. How's the writing going?'

'What writing?'

'I thought you were in Spain to work. That's what your sister said. Been telling fibs again?'

It was a moment before he replied. 'Just a little one. I need to lie low for a bit. I'm avoiding a jealous husband.'

'You're impossible.' She took another gulp of her drink, quelling a twinge of jealousy. 'What if he comes looking for you and Zoe's in that house on her own – have you thought about that?'

There was silence. He obviously hadn't. Jesus, men! 'You have to tell her, Shane.'

He sighed. 'Yeah, okay, I will. I'd forgotten what a bully you are, but a gorgeous, sexy bully.'

She grinned. 'You're not supposed to talk to a married woman like that – at least not this one.'

'I'm not talking to a married woman. I'm talking to the girl who broke my heart.'

'Rubbish,' she retorted. Broke his heart indeed. Shane had had a procession of women over the years.

'It's true, my love, my Tara, my queen. It hasn't helped that you grow more beautiful with every year that passes.'

She looked down at her old nightshirt and put a still painful hand to her unkempt hair, which she trimmed herself to save money, and felt tears well again. 'You wouldn't say that if you could see the state of me right now.'

'I would,' he said, his voice soft. 'Tell me what you're wearing.'

'A nightshirt.'

He groaned. 'Is that all?'

'Yes.' What the hell was she playing at? 'I've got to go, Shane.'

'You don't, you're just saying that because you're afraid.'

Oh, he still knew her so well. 'No, I'm tired and I'm going to bed ... with my husband.'

'There it goes, a knife straight through my heart.'

She smiled. 'Remember to call Zoe.'

'I will.'

'Good night.'

'Good night, my queen. Sweet dreams.'

She snuggled down in the chair, smiling. Shane had always been able to make her laugh, even when she was cross with him, even when she felt sad. And tonight he'd even managed to make her feel sexy. Quite an accomplishment. She felt only slightly guilty about the call. It had been innocent enough. With that her phone vibrated and she looked down to see another message.

If you were with me you wouldn't be wearing that nightshirt.
xx

Smiling, she clutched the phone to her and closed her eyes.

'What are you doing down here? The place smells like a brewery.'

She opened her eyes, shielding them against the sunshine streaming through the window, to see Greg scowling at her from the doorway. She uncurled from the chair and, in the process, knocked her phone and glass to the floor, wincing as the glass smashed. 'Damn.' She went to pick it up.

'Don't. You'll cut yourself.' He helped her out of the chair and walked her safely to the door. 'Go have a shower. I'll take care of it.'

She stood for a moment, looking at him. It had been days

since he'd touched her. Not even a brief hug, or a peck on the cheek. There was a time when he couldn't keep his hands off her. Feeling weary and defeated, she went upstairs. A little later, showered and dressed, she felt a bit better, although her head ached thanks to the whiskey. A couple of painkillers and a coffee should sort that. Then perhaps she'd make Greg scrambled eggs. It had been good of him to clean up. She should try to be nice to him and ignore his grumpiness and snipes.

Tara found him sitting at the table when she returned to the kitchen. The floor was clean and the room tidied. 'Thanks, that's great. Fancy some eggs?' She pulled out a clean apron and, when he didn't reply, she turned round. 'Greg?' And then she saw his furious, shocked expression and her phone on the table in front of him. She stared at it. Shane! The memory of their chat in the early hours came flooding back. Had Greg checked her log and seen that he'd called and texted? She stayed silent. Thanks to the alcohol, her memory of events was hazy and she wasn't opening her mouth until she knew exactly what he knew, or thought he knew.

He picked up the phone and read: '*If you were with me you wouldn't be wearing that nightshirt. xx.*'

Oh, God, she'd forgotten that bit. She gave a nervous laugh. 'He was messing. You know what he's like.'

'I don't seem to know anything. I certainly didn't know that my wife spent her nights drinking in the kitchen and texting and talking on the phone with her old boyfriend.'

'You'd know a lot more if you talked to me occasionally,' she retorted.

'That's your excuse?' His eyes flamed with fury.

'It's not an excuse. I don't need your permission to talk to anyone,' she shot back, though she knew that she was wrong to goad him. And if she saw a text like that on his phone she'd be incensed. 'I know what it looks like but, truly, it wasn't that sort of conversation,' she said, placating him. 'He'd been drinking and was maudlin, that's all.'

'And I'm supposed to accept that another man talks to my wife like that?'

'I'm surprised you even remember I *am* your wife – you're certainly not behaving like a husband.' Her head began to throb, she'd a busy day ahead and she was too tired to deal with this.

'What's that supposed to mean?' Greg glared at her.

'Look at me, Greg, just bloody look at me. I'm a wreck. I'm up all night because I can't sleep for worrying. And all day, every day, I work till I can hardly see straight because I am terrified to turn any job down. Even if a man looked twice at me, how would I have the energy or time to have an affair? And, even if I did, I doubt you would notice or care.'

'So it's my fault?'

It was the note of self-pity that tipped her over the edge. 'Yes, Greg, yes, it's your fault. We are where we are because you are drowning in self-pity, because you're too proud to go and work for someone else and because you won't sell this place because then you'd look like a failure. Well, guess what, Greg? You *are* a failure.' She snatched up her phone. 'And don't invade my privacy again. Now, you'll have to excuse me, I have work to do.'

'Don't turn your back on me,' he warned.

She did exactly that and heard his chair scrape back on the

tiles. But instead of storming out as she'd expected, he swung her round to face him and Tara had only just registered the anger in his eyes when his hand made contact with her cheek. Her head swung round like a rag doll's and she staggered. He immediately gripped her by the shoulders to prevent her from falling.

'I'm sorry, Tara, I'm so sorry.'

'Get out,' Tara said, though she saw remorse and shock on his face.

'Tara, I was angry and upset. It will never happen again.'

'Until the next time.' She put her hands on his chest and pushed him away, steeling herself against the anguish in his eyes.

'Tara—'

'Get out now,' she shouted and she thought her head might explode with pain, 'or I'm going to call the police.'

He stood staring at her for a moment, then turned on his heel and left. Tara collapsed into a chair and reached for her phone and made the call. As she expected it went to voicemail.

'Zoe, I know you're angry with me and I don't blame you but something dreadful's happened. I need you, please come.'

Chapter Nine

Zoe peeked over her script at Celia O'Sullivan. The renowned actress sat knitting in a corner of the room where Zoe had had her audition, her fingers working steadily on an unidentifiable garment. Other than a curt nod when she'd arrived and Zoe had introduced herself, Celia hadn't said a word. Snooty cow. Jonathan's wife was drawn as a cold woman until it became clear that she hadn't always been that way but had hardened as her husband drifted into his fantasy world. Zoe figured Celia wouldn't have to act at all.

She always came across as so warm in interviews and Zoe had been a great admirer, not least for the longevity of her career, and had been looking forward to working with the woman. But it was clear that Celia saw herself as being far above Zoe and it was unlikely they would become bosom buddies. But then in the acting world women could be particularly envious and spiteful. Zoe knew that, despite being an established and respected actress, Celia would look on her as someone who might upstage her. Thankfully, they had no scenes together so there was no reason why there should be any issues. Zoe would be polite and respectful and stay well out of Celia's way.

Robbie and Terence arrived together. Celia abandoned her knitting and, all smiles, stood to air-kiss both men.

'Celia, looking lovely as always,' Terence said, winking at Zoe over the other woman's shoulder. She bent her head so Robbie wouldn't see her smirk.

'You've met Zoe Hall, our Isabella,' Robbie said.

'No, she just got here. Lovely to meet you, Zoe.' Celia beamed at her.

Zoe was stunned at the woman's duplicity but played along. 'And you, I'm a great admirer of your work.'

'How kind.' Celia inclined her head.

'Right.' Robbie pulled four chairs into a circle. 'Let's get started. Gerald is running late but wants us to start without him.'

Terence and Zoe sat silently while Robbie gave an overview of the play for Celia's benefit. She interrupted occasionally, made notes on her script and, when he mentioned the dream scenes, her brows knitted in a frown but she didn't comment. As they were about to begin, a small and flustered man stuck his head in the door.

'Ah, here you are. Sorry I'm late, damn traffic.'

Robbie stood up and shook hands with him. 'You haven't missed much – we were just about to do a read-through. Let me introduce you. Terence you know.'

'I'm the one who put grey in his hair,' Terence joked.

'True, all true.' The man's voice was gruff but he actually blushed, Zoe noticed.

'Celia O'Sullivan, Gerald Spring.'

Celia offered her fingers in a majestic manner. 'Nice to meet you.'

'And you.'

'And this is Zoe Hall, our Isabella.'

The writer appraised her through rimless glasses for a moment and then gave a brief nod. 'Pleased to meet you.'

'Likewise.' Zoe took the hand he offered. She was obviously going to have to prove herself to this man. 'It's a wonderful play. I'm very excited to be in it.'

He muttered his thanks then sat down in the chair Robbie had fetched for him and pulled out a notebook.

'Do you want to say a few words before we begin?' Robbie asked the writer.

Gerald stroked his untidy beard before answering. 'Jonathan and Monica Keane have been married for the best part of forty years. They have raised three children and now there are just the two of them at home. They do their weekly grocery shopping on Friday evening. Divide Saturday between the garden and garden centre in the summer and go to an afternoon movie or lunch out in the winter. Sundays they spend time with their family. They holiday twice a year: Lake Como in June and the Bahamas in January. Were they ever really in love?' He shrugged. 'Perhaps, but now they are settled they're companions and get along most of the time. In other words, they are a very ordinary couple.'

Zoe was delighted with the picture that he painted – it brought the couple to life for her. She hoped he'd tell her something about Isabella. She glanced at Terence, who was leaning forward, his eyes trained on the writer. Celia looked somewhat bored, as, indeed, Monica might have been, and Robbie was doodling.

'But Jonathan has a health scare and, though it turns out to be a false alarm, he's suddenly conscious that the years are slipping by without him noticing. He is in every sense a success yet suddenly, he feels as if he hasn't actually lived. Enter Isabella Shine. A beautiful woman accused of murdering her husband. She is young and mysterious and he cannot figure out if she is guilty or innocent, which strangely heightens her appeal. He is spellbound. They are polar opposites. His life is calm, ordered and pedestrian, while Isabella's seems cloaked in secrets and drama. And he wants that excitement, he wants her and he can think of little else.'

When he'd finished, Celia spoke: 'And what does Monica want?'

Gerald shrugged. 'That's not really important – no offence.' He gave a nervous smile when she visibly bristled. 'We can assume that she is content with their life as it is.'

'And Isabella?' Zoe asked.

'We know nothing about her,' Gerald told her. 'She is an enigma. Aware of Jonathan's adulation, she uses all her womanly wiles to encourage him to fall in love with her and pretends that she is attracted to him too – but her only goal is to walk free.'

Terence didn't interject with his ideas on that, having already primed Zoe for today, saying that, though it was just a read-through, they should act it, vocally and visually. 'It will bring Gerald's words to life and it's important that he believes you're the right person to play Isabella. Once he is completely on side, things will run much smoother and he'll be more open to any changes we suggest.'

The opening scene was between Jonathan and Monica, giving a picture of their marriage. Monica did most of the talking, with Jonathan only half concentrating on what she was saying. Celia read it as if it were the newspaper but Terence got into the part, sighing, staring off into space, answering in a distracted, bored and sometimes irritable voice. Celia glared at him over her script. Then it was Zoe's turn. As Terence had suggested, she shut everyone in the room out of her mind and concentrated purely on Jonathan.

'Is everything okay?' she asked when it was over and there was silence. She looked nervously at Robbie but it was Gerald who answered.

'Perfect, just perfect,' he said, his eyes gleaming behind his spectacles.

Robbie gave her a nod of approval, while Celia just stared, reappraising her. Good!

By the time they were finished, Zoe felt exhausted but exhilarated.

'Thoughts?' Robbie asked, looking at each of them in turn.

'I think there should be a lot more interplay between Jonathan and Monica,' Celia said.

Terence nudged Zoe and she had to hide her grin behind her script.

'No disrespect intended, Gerald,' Celia continued, 'but the audience need a clearer picture of their marriage.'

He nodded, but neither agreed nor disagreed.

'That wouldn't work,' Terence said. 'If we go down that route, the audience will start to feel sorry for Monica when they should only be thinking about what Jonathan is going through.' He looked to Robbie for support.

'I have to agree,' Robbie said, and Celia pursed her lips. 'The strength of this play is that the audience is embroiled in Jonathan's thoughts. It's what makes the final scene so powerful. Isabella has disappeared, just like the dream she actually was, and the real woman he loves and who loved him is revealed but it's too late, he's lost her.'

'I'm afraid it wouldn't work if the audience pitied Monica,' Gerald chimed in. 'They need to feel ambivalent towards her.'

Zoe remained silent. She knew her place, and anyway, a contribution from her was unnecessary. Celia wouldn't win this battle.

'I love the ending, don't you, Celia? It's powerful,' Terence said, turning on the charm. 'I can imagine Monica watching everything play out, seeing her husband for the pathetic creature he's become and walking out on him.'

'It's brilliant,' Robbie agreed.

'Wonderful,' Zoe said, nodding.

Somewhat mollified, Celia inclined her head in agreement. 'It should be quite emotional.'

'About Isabella,' Terence started, and Zoe studied her fingers, knowing what was coming next. No doubt, Robbie did too. 'I love how you've written her, Gerald, and you know I fell in love with this script the moment I read it, but I wonder ... do you think it might add some intrigue if the audience also think that she's falling for Jonathan?'

Celia gave a bark of laughter. 'Oh, please, that's ridiculous.'

'I don't think that would work, Terence,' Robbie said, but looked at the writer. 'I wonder, would it be better though if Isabella wasn't quite as calculating but was actually oblivious of Jonathan's feelings for her. After all, in her eyes he's an old man.'

Celia snorted but Terence smiled, unperturbed.

'Would it help if we read it again and I play Isabella as a nicer person and see if it works?' Zoe offered.

'Good idea.' Robbie gave a nod of approval, Terence beamed at her, Celia sighed and Gerald gave her a grateful smile.

'I admit it, Robbie. Isabella is best as a desperate woman, unaware of the extent of her charms and indifferent to the effect they are having on Jonathan.' Terence tossed his script on the floor and made a small bow to Gerald. 'Let me buy you all a drink now we're done,' he offered.

'Thank you, darling, but I have another appointment.' Celia turned to offer her cheek to Robbie.

'Thanks for coming, Celia. I'll be in touch when Gerald has made his revisions, but it will probably be same place, same time next week.'

'See you all then,' and with a general wave of her hand she left the room, her multicoloured scarf fluttering behind her.

'Thank God she's gone,' Terence muttered. 'That woman could sour cream with a look.'

'She's an excellent actress and that's all that matters,' Robbie said.

'True.' Terence slung an arm around Zoe and kissed her cheek. 'So, my Isabella, shall we?'

She caught Robbie looking and slipped out of the embrace under the guise of collecting her bag and checking her phone. 'Hang on a sec,' she said when she saw there was a voicemail, and crossed the room so she could hear it.

'Come on, Zoe, we're dying of thirst here,' Terence urged, heading out the door.

Zoe stared at her phone. 'Sorry, I can't join you. Something's come up.'

Robbie looked at her, frowning. 'Is everything okay?'

'No, I don't think it is.'

Zoe sat in the passenger seat of Robbie's car trying to figure out what could have happened to make Tara call her. Her message had sounded so desperate. Obviously, it was nothing relating to her parents. Terence was now sitting in some cosy pub with Gerald and, if there was anything wrong with Vivienne, Tara would have called her dad. It had to be something to do with Greg. She looked across at Robbie, driving, who, back at rehearsals, had immediately offered her a lift when he'd seen the worried expression on her face.

'Do you mind?' She held up her phone.

'Of course not.'

Zoe dialled, but it was several rings before Tara picked up, and, even then, she could hardly hear her. 'Tara? It's Zoe. Are you okay?'

'Think so.' Her voice was thin and wobbly.

'Are you ill?'

'No, well . . . no. Look, I don't want to talk on the phone.'

'That's okay. I'm on my way over right now.'

'Thanks, Zo,' Tara said, sounding tearful.

She put the phone down and Robbie glanced over. 'Terence's daughter? Sorry, but I couldn't help overhearing.'

'Yes. She sounds awful and it must be something serious for her to call me. We had a big row recently, a bad one.'

'Strange that she didn't call Terence or Vivienne,' he mused.

'Yes. Oh, it's the next left and immediately right, first house on the left.'

Soon, he was pulling up outside Tara's house. 'Would you like me to wait?'

'No, I think I may be here for quite a while. Don't mention this to Terence, will you, Robbie?'

'Of course not.' He looked offended that she had even asked.

'Thanks.' She smiled and hopped out, waiting until he'd pulled away before walking up the narrow path. She was relieved that Greg's car wasn't in the drive. It would be easier to talk if he wasn't hovering in the background. Zoe rang the bell and a few moments later heard Tara shuffling down the hall. She opened the door a fraction.

'You can let me in, Tara. I promise not to hit you,' she joked.

'Glad to hear it.' Tara opened the door wide and stepped back.

'Oh, my God.' Zoe did a double take at the angry red welt across her face and the small open wound at the corner of her mouth. 'What happened?'

Tara's eyes filled with tears but she said nothing.

'Greg?' Zoe said in disbelief. Tara gave a brief nod before falling into her arms.

When Tara was calmer, Zoe settled her in the armchair by the window and made a mug of sweet tea. She was about to add a dash of brandy but noticed that her friend already had a drink. Tara sat, curled in the foetal position, staring blindly out into the garden.

'Tell me what happened.' Zoe handed her the tea and pulled up a chair.

'He found a text on my phone from Shane and went ballistic.'

Zoe groaned. It would have to be down to her brother. 'Shane sent you a text? Why?'

Tara shrugged. 'He does from time to time.'

'And what on earth was in the text that caused Greg to do that? Not that I'm excusing him,' Zoe assured her.

'I haven't been sleeping so sometimes I work instead – there's always so much to do. Shane sent a text and when I replied immediately – he asked could he call and I said yes.' Tara held up her glass. 'I was feeling a bit low myself and I'd had a couple of these so I don't remember much but Shane was saying he missed me, silly stuff like that, and asked what I was wearing.' She shot Zoe a guilty grin. 'He always asks me that. I told him a nightshirt and said goodbye. He sent another text along the lines that I wouldn't be wearing it if I was with him.'

'And Greg saw it,' Zoe guessed, shaking her head.

'Yeah and we started to argue and things I'd been holding in for months came gushing out and' – she shrugged – 'he lost it and slapped me.'

Zoe was still distracted by the fact that Tara and Shane kept in touch, and in such an intimate way. She'd often wondered would her brother and best friend have got together if Greg hadn't happened along. Had Greg wondered the same and jumped to conclusions when he read the texts? Not that it gave him an excuse to hit Tara. How could he? Tara was like a tiny elf beside him and he must have used some force to cause such a mark. Zoe knew that she'd be tempted to whack him back herself if he was here; she was certainly angry enough. She was trying to keep a lid on her temper for Tara's sake. Her sounding off wouldn't help matters. 'Where is he now?'

'No idea. I told him to get out or I'd call the police. I could see that he was sorry the moment he did it, but Shane always told me that if a man does it once he'll do it again.'

'Shane said that? When?'

'Oh, I don't know.' Tara shook her head. 'Years ago.'

Zoe let it go, though she wondered what had made her brother say such a thing. Had one of his married women had a similar experience? 'Are you saying that you won't take him back?'

Tara put her face in her hands and then yelped in pain.

'Hang on.' Zoe went to the freezer for an icepack.

'Thanks.' Tara took it and held it against her cheekbone. 'I don't know what to do. I know he feels terrible about what he did, but how can I feel safe with him now? I never thought he was capable of hurting me.' She gave a thin smile. 'I suppose that puts Ed a notch ahead after all.'

Zoe ignored that. 'You could report him, even get a barring order if it would make you feel safer.'

'No.'

'Someone should tackle him about what he's done,' Zoe said, exasperated. 'He can't just get away with it.'

'I'm not calling the police, Zo; now please, leave it.'

'Sorry.' Zoe patted her hand. 'I just feel a bit helpless.'

Tara summoned up a smile. 'I called and you came. That helped.'

'Of course I came.' Zoe could understand Tara feeling torn: it was a difficult situation. 'For the record, I do think it was a one-off. Greg loves you, Tara, I know he does. Why don't you tell him that if he wants to stay he'll need to get help, go on some sort of anger-management course or something?'

'Maybe.'

'And he has to help run the business too. You look exhausted.'

'I know. And how can I go into people's houses looking like this? I had a lunch today and had to call to cancel. They won't be using me again, that's for sure.'

'When's your next gig?'

'Tuesday.'

'I'll be free. I can help with that.'

'Oh, I'm sorry, Zoe, I haven't even asked how your play went, or apologised ...'

'Forget it. We'll have plenty of time to talk. Would you like me to call Greg and suggest he stay with his mother for a couple of days and give you a chance to think?'

'But he'll need clothes and his shaving gear—'

'We can go out for a while and he can come get whatever he needs.'

'Duh?' Tara gestured to her face.

Zoe chewed her lip. 'We could go for a walk on the beach later this evening when the sun's going down. No one will notice you. I'll tell Greg to come and pack a bag while we're out. How does that sound?'

Tara nodded and gave a grateful smile. 'Sounds good.'

Though it was still the early days of May, there was some light left in the sky and a mild gentle breeze lifted Zoe's hair from her shoulders as they walked. The water lapped the shore and the air was clear and fresh. Nothing relaxed her like a walk on the beach. She sneaked a look at Tara. With a scarf muffling the lower part of her face, head bowed and hands dug in her pockets, she looked anything but relaxed. 'Are you okay?'

'Sure.'

'What are you thinking about?'

'How much we'll get for the house and where I could find a cheap and convenient place to rent. I'll call an estate agent tomorrow and get the house valued.'

Zoe stopped and looked at her. 'Really? That's it? You're going to leave Greg?'

Tara kept walking. 'That's it.'

'You probably shouldn't make such big decisions right now.' Zoe hurried after her. 'You're in shock.'

Tara peeked at her in the gloom. 'Earlier you said I should report my husband to the police and get a barring order!'

'Just to make you feel safe until he sorts himself out and you feel that you can trust him again. Reporting him would teach him a lesson and make him realise that he can't get away with that kind of behaviour. But giving up on your marriage, just like that—' Zoe clicked her fingers and then shook her head.

Tara gave her an incredulous look and her voice was hard. 'Are you seriously giving me advice on marriage?'

The reference to Ed stung but Zoe bit her tongue. Tara was upset and she shouldn't overreact to anything she said. Her silence prompted Tara to put a conciliatory hand on her arm.

'That was below the belt, sorry. But I'm not like you, Zoe. I won't let him hurt me again.'

'What do you mean? I left Ed as soon as I knew what he was up to,' she protested, feeling under attack again.

'Did you? Are you telling me that up until that night when you saw him with that woman, you thought he had always been faithful?'

Zoe sighed. Tara was right. She had suspected that Ed had messed around a little but she had been unable or unwilling to deal with it. She was glad the light was failing and it was too dark for Tara to see the truth in her eyes. 'Let's not get into all that again. If you're serious about selling up, you're going to have to talk to Greg sooner or later. I don't know how the whole separation and divorce business works over here, and things were much more straightforward for us – there was no house to argue about. I wish I knew someone in family law that could advise you. Perhaps your dad does. He knows so many people—'

Stopping, Tara rounded on her. 'Greg hit me, just a few hours ago. Do you really think I can focus on any of that right now?'

'Sorry, no. of course not. Sorry—'

'No, I'm sorry. You're just trying to help and I'm being a bitch.' Tara sighed and carried on walking.

Zoe fell back into step beside her. 'Will you at least tell your dad?'

'Absolutely not. I don't want anyone to know about this, especially my parents.'

Zoe looked at the obstinate set to her jaw and decided to pull back. 'Fine, whatever you want. I won't tell a soul. It's just that I seem to be irritating you more than helping.'

'You're not, Zoe. I just need time to think before I face people, Greg included.'

'Of course.' They carried on walking in silence. Zoe knew there was no point in trying to talk to her when she was like this. It was the same when Tara catered an event. She planned it down to the last detail and focused on her mission until it was completed – always successfully. She never stopped going. Even on a quiet day, Tara found work to do. Perhaps that's why Greg hanging around doing nothing irritated her so much.

But Zoe realised it was silly of her to try talking sense to Tara today. Greg had hit her. The safe, dependable, boring but gentle giant wasn't so gentle after all. Zoe shivered. Who'd have believed him capable? It seemed so out of character. She could murder Shane for sending that text. What the hell was he thinking? He probably wasn't, she realised. He was so caught up in worrying about his bloody play that it wouldn't have occurred to him that calling Tara and sending her naughty texts in the middle of the night probably wasn't such a good idea.

She glanced over at Tara, who was lost in her own thoughts. 'Why don't you get away for a few days? You could visit your mother in London. The break would do you good and give you some breathing space.'

'Ha, spending time with Vivienne is never a break, trust me. Anyway, I have events scheduled. I can't let my clients down and I need the money. To be honest, I'm better off if I'm kept busy. When I have nothing to do but worry, that's when I crack up.'

Zoe slipped an arm through hers. 'We should turn back, it's late.'

'Yeah, and cold.' Tara shivered.

'Come on, then, let's go home and have a hot whiskey.'

'That sounds good. Thanks, Zoe. And about Ed—'

'Forget Ed. I'm just glad we're talking again.'

Tara squeezed her arm. 'Me too.'

Chapter Ten

The damn lift was out of order again. Celia climbed the stairs and dropped her bags by the door of her apartment while she rummaged for her keys. She smiled as she heard mewing and scratching on the other side of the door. 'Yes, Ophelia, Mummy's home and I have something nice for you.'

She carried the supermarket bag into the kitchen, the cat weaving in and out of her legs. 'Now are you really happy to see me or are you just after the goodies, hmm? Perhaps it's just as well you can't talk and I can fool myself.' She opened the bag of fish pieces the fishmonger had thrown in for free along with her own dinner of sea bass.

She set the cat's food down on the floor, refilled the water dish and put on the kettle, before going into her bedroom to change into her kaftan. After making a cup of tea, she carried it into the sitting room and settled down in her chair that looked out onto the small patio full of pot plants and hanging baskets. It was a nice evening and the sun had turned her sitting room into a positive greenhouse. It was almost possible to forget the littered street below and the general grubbiness of the apartment building. Her thoughts inevitably turned to her beautiful house in Dalkey with its enormous garden and views over Dublin Bay. It was a far cry from her new home. Ha, Waterside. She had laughed at the name. The nearest river was the Liffey and that was a good ten-minute walk. Perhaps it was in honour of the way the road flooded whenever there was a drop of rain. Still, she had her mementoes and photos around her and, when she closed the door on the world, she was happy enough. Despite still being a jobbing actress and her modest lifestyle, Celia had learned to be careful with her money and had started to squirrel some away for a rainy day. She had to. What if she got sick and couldn't work? How would she pay hospital bills and who would take care of her? Certainly not her son. She felt the familiar feeling of despair and failure when she thought of him.

Albie was nothing like his father. Albert had been a kind and loving man who had taken care of her and their son. It had been devastating to lose him at just fifty-nine. The heart attack was massive. His secretary told her he was probably dead before he hit the ground. Life was so cruel. Not only had she lost the love of her life but she'd been left to cope with their already wayward son.

Albert Junior had been a miracle baby. They had longed for a child, but had given up hope after years of trying. And then, at thirty-nine, Celia had discovered she was pregnant. It was like a gift from God. They had both been thrilled. Celia, who had always been the consummate professional, bowed out of a production of *She Stoops to Conquer*, terrified that any exertion or stress might hurt the baby. Instead, she lay on the sofa or sat in the garden that long mild summer of her pregnancy, knitting cardigans and mittens and booties in the softest wools of green and lemon and white. Albert treated her like a delicate piece of china, hiring a housekeeper, who made sure she didn't lift a finger and tempted her with tasty, nurturing meals that would build her strength. The decorators came and she chose wallpaper with a tiny green-and-gold flower and had curtains and sheets made to match. The cradle and cot, magnificent creations, came from Albert's sister and had served two generations of O'Sullivan babies. No child had ever been awaited with such love and longing.

It was a stormy, wintery day when Albert Joseph O'Sullivan finally entered the world after nearly thirty hours of labour. Celia had been tearful and scared; it was almost as if he didn't want to come out. When the nurse finally placed him, wailing, in her arms, his face was red, his eyes scrunched shut and he waved angry little fists in the air.

Celia had often wondered about that over the years. Despite their love, despite showering Albie with toys, he had always thrown tantrums, always wanted more. But what she had found hardest was he seemed to hate her to kiss or cuddle him. She felt guilty about how much she enjoyed it when he went through the usual childhood ailments and, too weak to fight her, would lie quietly as she rocked him in her arms and sang to him.

Yes, of course she'd spoiled him. How could she not? She'd have done anything to make him smile, to win even the briefest hug or kiss. Albert had teased her about her golden boy. Did he realise how hurt she was by her son's lack of affection? She thought so. They never talked about it but, the more that Albie rejected her, the more loving and kind Albert became. While she knew he loved their son, as the years passed he grew stricter with Albie and admonished him when he was cheeky or disrespectful to her. Albie pretended remorse but once they were alone his sly grin and bad behaviour returned.

She had hoped Albert's death would, at least, bring them closer but her son, then nineteen, had seemed indifferent to his father's demise. Free from the only disciplinarian in his life, he dropped out of university and turned into a troublesome layabout who spent his days in bed and his nights God only knew where. When she tried to remonstrate with him or threatened to cut off his allowance, he would just shrug and say if she did, she'd never see him again and, realising he probably meant it, she would back down. Occasionally, he found work, though he seemed incapable of holding down a job. He'd brought girls home from time to time and Celia's heart would swell as he became a different person in their presence: the perfect son. He'd boast about his wonderfully talented mother, show off her awards, rave about her cooking and generally make Celia blush like a young bride. The first time she'd allowed herself to believe he was changing, maturing, but soon realised it was all an act and he was using her to suit his own ends.

Now if she glimpsed him in the audience during one of her plays, her heart didn't soar, she just wondered what he was up to. She'd found out the hard way that Albie always had an agenda. If he phoned or called in, she tensed up, knowing that he was after something. Not that she had much left to give. She looked around at the sparse decor and cheap furniture. The only precious things she owned were her mementoes of the theatre, family photos, the jewellery Albert had bought her and, of course, her beloved Ophelia. Albie's girlfriends always seemed startled by her humble lifestyle and she would feel her face flame in embarrassment. But Albie would laugh, roll his eyes and make some comment about the eccentricities of theatre folk. And, whether out of pride or shame, Celia would laugh with him and hold up her hands as if she really was living in this tiny flat in a dubious part of Dublin out of choice.

Ophelia hopped up onto her lap and licked her cheek with a loud meow. Celia smiled and stroked her silken coat, grateful for contact and the warmth of the little body pressed against her. She hadn't understood the value of human contact until it was gone. She was a relatively young woman when Albert had died, but never even considered replacing him. It was just as well. She would feel so ashamed if anyone else knew what her son was really like. But although she didn't crave company, she still missed Albert every day.

She remembered how she'd cried when her housekeeper had changed the pillows in her marital bed, not knowing how, in those early days after Albert's death, Celia had buried her face in them, inhaling deeply, desperate for any sense of her husband's presence. And then, when she thought things couldn't possibly get worse, Albie demanded his share of the inheritance, forcing Celia to sell her beloved home. At first, she'd rented a small house nearby but she couldn't bear the pitying looks from their circle of friends, and moved into the city on the pretext of feeling isolated. Her son's behaviour had taught her that she needed to protect herself and so she had bought this place. It didn't seem so bad empty and the agent had told her that the owner of the building had plans to renovate and, given its central location, it was bound to appreciate in value. It didn't. She cried the day she moved in, on discovering the bed she'd shared with Albert was far too big for the bedroom. Most of her furniture was too big and she sold anything that Albie hadn't claimed for himself.

There was so little left of her life with Albert that she treasured the couple of home videos in which he featured. She played them when the loneliness got too much to bear, just to hear the sound of his voice and wallow in the depths of his dark eyes. She'd stare like a starved animal at the arms that had enfolded her, the hands that had touched her and the fingers that had laced through hers.

Would it have been easier to lose him if he had been elderly rather than healthy, vibrant and strong? Yes. They would have grown old together, taken pleasure in simple things, and nursed each other through their ills. She missed being cared for and being the centre of someone's world. She missed how he'd make her his special honey-and-lemon concoction when she was croaky before a performance and how he'd always be waiting to take her home afterwards. No one would ever love her the way Albert had.

Celia kissed Ophelia and, setting her down on the floor, went to make some supper. She crisped the skin of the fish in the pan and microwaved some frozen greens. One glass of white wine completed her meal. She sat at the small table as she always did. She would never give in to a tray on her lap or eating in bed. As long as she was able to get up in the morning, she would maintain some standards. She was about to eat but froze, the fork halfway to her mouth, when the phone rang. She didn't bother answering. These days she let the answering machine pick up her calls and just listened. Though that meant the cost of a call back, it gave her time to come up with an appropriate answer. She didn't own a mobile phone. She didn't want to be that accessible or be constantly pestered with texts and voicemails from Albie making more demands. By confining him to the house phone, she could buy some time, pretend she was out with friends, at rehearsals or shopping. The phone beeped and she heard the rich tones of her sister-in-law's voice.

'Celia, it's Martha. I hate talking to these things. Aren't you there?' She waited a moment. 'Obviously not. Well, the thing is, Thomas is going into St Vincent's Hospital next week for his hip replacement and I wondered if I could stay with you for a few days. Oh, I hate these damn machines. Call me and let me know. Bye-bye.'

Celia sat back in her chair and closed her eyes. She had become an expert in keeping people at a distance, but she couldn't say no to Albert's only sibling. How was she going to explain her tiny flat? When Celia had told her the address of her new home Martha had queried the questionable area. 'It's got excellent security and it's in the city centre, so I never need to take taxis. I've never felt safe alone in a taxi,' Celia had told her. 'And Albie is always in and out, keeping an eye on me.'

She doubted Martha swallowed any of it but at least she hadn't pursued the matter. But Celia knew that if Martha saw this place, she'd demand an explanation. Albie was another topic Martha was curious about. She was always asking about him, trying to pin down exactly what it was he did for a living. 'Oh, something in finance,' Celia would say airily. 'I don't begin to understand what. But he seems to be doing very well for himself.'

Ophelia meowed at her feet, her green eyes on the dinner plate. Celia set it down on the ground. 'Help yourself, darling. I've lost my appetite.' She took her wine and went back into the sitting room. She would have to come up with some tale about losing her money. She could blame it on a bad investment; that wasn't so incredible these days. And Martha would understand why pride had kept Celia from sharing the news of her change in circumstances. She had a spare bedroom, although it was more of a large closet she used for storage. But there was a small divan that Albie tumbled into when he was too drunk to find his way home to his own place in the suburbs. Celia would have to give it a good clean and airing and perhaps buy some cheap curtains and a new duvet cover to make it look cosier. She would make Martha as welcome and comfortable as possible. She owed it to Albert.

Celia expected a cheque next week, an advance on *Isabella*, which would allow her to finance Martha's visit. She'd planned to pay some bills with that money and buy some new clothes but hopefully more money would follow. It was a good play and there was no reason why it shouldn't run for a few more weeks and be picked up by other theatres. And she was confident that Robbie Prendergast would still want her in the wife's role. Her name still counted for something in the business.

Everything would be fine as long as Albie didn't make an appearance during Martha's visit or, if he did show up, he behaved. Perhaps she should call him and let him know his aunt was coming to visit, but that could work against her.

Depending on his mood, he might arrive in a suit with a bouquet, or turn up unshaven and drunk and go out of his way to humiliate her. One thing was for sure, if she asked him to be nice to his aunt, he would expect some sort of payment in return. No, it was better to take her chances and put her acting skills to good use.

Celia went into the kitchen to clean up after Ophelia and opened a window to rid the small flat of the smell of food and let the cat out for its evening prowl. Then, fetching her knitting, she put on the radio and settled back down in her chair. The soothing sound of the needles clicking allowed her to let go of the present, and she drifted back to the happy days when Albert was alive. Perhaps her life now was the price she had to pay for the wonderful years they'd shared. If so, it was a price worth paying. Albie could rob her of everything but no one could take away her cherished memories.

Chapter Eleven

Adam let himself into the house, tossed his jacket on the sofa and went to get himself a drink. He was glad he'd driven tonight. If he hadn't taken the car he'd have finished the first bottle of wine before the food even arrived. There were some girls who were strictly one-nighters and it turned out that Melanie fell into that category. She had seemed like a nice girl when they'd met and so he'd asked her out. But this evening she'd droned on and on about her favourite soap opera and who should win *Big Brother* until he'd almost lost the will to live. She'd killed off any desire in him and he couldn't get away from her fast enough.

He wished someone would explain where he was going wrong. Of course, like all men, he'd sometimes asked a girl out purely because she had great legs or enormous boobs, but he was a man now, not a boy. When he was attracted to a woman he talked to her for a while, made sure that she got his sense of humour, checked they had something in common and whether she had any baggage in the shape of a bitter ex-husband or kids. He couldn't imagine being a dad, so taking on another man's kids was definitely a step too far. Even when he found reasonably normal girls, they always wanted to know about his childhood and his family and he'd clam up and that never went down well. So despite his best efforts, he struck out every time.

His phone chirruped and he pulled it out of his jeans pocket to read the text. Zoe. He sighed. Now there was a woman who never bored him, but he didn't have the guts to approach her, knowing a rejection would be torture. He read the text.

Hi Adam. Just wondering if you and John are happy with the script Shane emailed to you, Z.

Oh well, it was hardly likely to be a message asking him out. He hadn't even looked at Shane's manuscript. He trusted Shane's work, he consistently produced good plays, but his first draft never turned out to be the final one. Once rehearsals began, it would change, so he never bothered reading the first draft. All that mattered to him was that there *was* a script.

Hi Zoe. Haven't read it or passed it on to John yet. He's busy in Belfast. Waiting for him to make contact first. How are you?

He went to get another beer as he waited for an answer. He was just sitting down when it came through.

Busy with rehearsals for a new play and enjoying. Take care. x

'Ah, if only that were a real kiss,' he said, but keyed in:

Glad to hear it. x

She hadn't mentioned how Shane was doing and he didn't see the point of asking. He probably had more of an idea than Zoe did as to how her brother was.

Shane was prone to mood swings, sometimes thrilled with his writing and sometimes describing it as total rubbish, but Adam sensed there was something darker going on this time. It reminded him of Shane's first day at school. For all his bravado, he had looked like a scared, skinny kid in his over-sized uniform, but it was his eyes that Adam remembered most. They were dark, haunted, as if he had just seen something terrifying, and, of course, he had. It wasn't too long before Adam looked in the mirror and saw a similar expression in himself.

He had just turned fourteen when he came home from school one day and found his mother conked out on the kitchen floor. He'd dialled 999 and the ambulance crew told him he was a great lad and had saved his mother's life. She'd been in hospital for a couple of weeks and he'd had to stay with a neighbour, despite protesting that he was old enough to look after himself. Of course, they didn't know that he'd been doing that for a long time, and looking after his mother too.

Mum had been having problems for years. She could go for weeks, sometimes months, and be grand and then she'd start to get agitated or hyper and he'd know it was only a matter of time before he'd come home to find her perfectly calm, almost in a dreamlike state, and her speech a little slurred. When she was in that state she slept a lot and forgot things. Sometimes it was a cake in the oven, or that she'd left her keys in the door.

She'd forget to lock up at night or would leave the lights on and, once, she'd gone to bed and left a cigarette smouldering in the ashtray. That had scared the shit out of him. He imagined waking up with his room full of smoke and burning to death. From then on, every night, once she was safely in bed, he'd tiptoe past her room and check everything was as it should be. Only then would he be able to sleep.

When he went in to see his mother in hospital, a doctor took him to one side and explained that she was addicted to prescription drugs. He'd felt so bloody angry. All the fear and worry he'd gone through was her fault, not some mystery illness. And yet, when she put her arms round him and cried and said she was sorry, he'd held her and told her it was okay.

When he returned to school a few days after the 999 call, it was clear from the whispers and the shocked, wide-eyed expressions that everyone knew about the ambulance incident. He felt embarrassed and angry and ashamed and he avoided everyone. But Shane wouldn't be brushed off, and took to sitting next to him in class or wandering over at lunchtime and asking him did he fancy having a kick-about. Shane asked no questions, gave no advice but became a silent wall between Adam and the rest of the world and their friendship was sealed.

Years later, when Shane urged him to come to Dublin, he'd refused. How could he leave her?

'Do you plan to put your life on hold for someone who doesn't want to be helped, who loves drugs more than her son?' Shane had asked.

That hurt, really hurt, but Adam knew that Shane was right and so he'd left his mother before she could leave him.

He and Shane never talked of those days but they both still bore the scars. So while Adam was pissed off with Shane for leaving him high and dry, he was also worried. His instincts told him that something had happened to send Shane back into his past. It would account for the sudden departure. He wouldn't want Zoe to see him low. He'd always tried to protect her, successfully too. Adam was glad that she'd been too young to truly appreciate the tragedy, and quickly fitted into her new home and school. It would be awful to see the same pain in her eyes and heart-breaking to see anything take away that beautiful smile and earthy laugh. And yet, he felt sorry for Shane carrying his burden alone. God, life was complicated when you loved someone. Which reminded him of his promise to Shane, that he would keep an eye on Zoe. He'd drop over in a couple of days, he decided, only too glad of the excuse.

Zoe wandered up and down the supermarket aisles, preoccupied with the thought of playing Isabella but distracted, worrying about Tara. She had been about to tell Shane off for sending that text but stopped herself in the nick of time, remembering Tara's warning that she was to say nothing to anyone. Which was all very well, but that was two weeks ago now and there was no sign of Tara doing or saying anything.

'It's not your business,' Tara had said when she tried to tackle her. 'I know you mean well, Zoe, and I really appreciate your support, but I have to do this my way.'

Tara's cheek had healed and she no longer needed the concealer that Zoe had carefully applied each time they were going on a job, but the deeper pain obviously remained. Greg had stayed away, as agreed, but had sent Zoe texts asking if there was any chance of Tara meeting him somewhere to talk. Tara would just shake her head. 'I need to be really strong before I see him,' she'd say, her eyes bright with tears, 'and I'm not there yet.'

Zoe was grateful that Terence lost himself in his work and was so focused on her and the play that he hadn't seemed to notice anything amiss. When eventually this all came out, Zoe hoped that he'd understand why she hadn't told him. For now, her days were split between father and daughter and she didn't discuss one with the other.

Glancing at her watch, Zoe realised she'd better get a move on or she was going to be late. She was shopping for dinner with Terence – he was cooking. She had offered to order in something but he'd shaken his head in disgust.

'Fast food is only marginally better than your cooking, darling,' he told her and gave her a list, which of course she'd left behind and she couldn't even call him as he was on a flight home from London. Zoe put duck breasts and baby new potatoes into the basket, but she couldn't remember what else he'd asked for. She drifted round the vegetable section and her eyes lit up when she saw spinach. Yes, that had definitely been on the list. Now for the sauce. Orange usually went with duck but Terence had asked for some other fruit. She opted for plum sauce and redcurrant jelly and bought some port for good measure, remembering that Tara used it in her duck sauce. Terence was seeing to the wine but, with the crème brûlée and blue cheese that she'd bought for afters, she figured he'd be happy enough.

*

'Plum?' Terence looked at her, eyebrows raised. 'Did I *say* I was cooking Chinese-style? And you forgot the mustard, but' – he held up the port and smiled – 'you made up for it with this.'

'Want me to help?' Zoe asked.

'Does my daughter let you cook?'

'No.'

'Need I say more?'

She swatted his butt. 'I'm not that bad. I never poisoned you.'

'No, but I think you may have given me an ulcer.'

'Don't worry, I keep a good stock of antacids,' she said, laughing. 'Do I have time for a quick shower?'

'Yes, run along and make yourself beautiful. I think I'd like to dine with Isabella.'

'Isabella, Isabella, always Isabella,' she complained, but went upstairs smiling.

Out of the shower, she put on a vest and pants and then the burgundy pyjamas Terence adored – so Isabella! Lightly drying her hair, she left it loose around her shoulders, lined her eyes with kohl and applied a touch of lip gloss, before going back downstairs to join him.

'Something smells good.' She came to a halt in the doorway at the sight of Adam standing in the centre of the kitchen. His stunned gaze travelled from her still damp hair down to her bare feet and then to Terence, who was turning the duck breasts in the pan.

'Adam, hi!' Zoe said, looking searchingly at Terence.

Terence shrugged. 'He said he wanted to see you. Wouldn't take no for an answer.'

'I just dropped by to check on you,' Adam replied.

Terence crossed the room to get the pepper, pausing en route to kiss Zoe's cheek. 'She's wonderful.'

Zoe laughed and pushed him away, her eyes boring in to his. 'Stop messing about,' she said through gritted teeth and turned to Adam. 'Good timing. We were just about to eat. Will you join us?'

Terence glared at her. 'We're eating in the garden.'

Zoe followed Adam's glance and sighed when she saw that the table under the gazebo was set for two with a white cloth, their best glasses and a single red rose in a vase.

'No, thanks. I don't want to interrupt.'

'You're not interrupting.' She hated the way he was looking at Terence, his disgust barely concealed, and when he glanced back at her, she felt as if she needed another shower. She wanted to explain they were working together but, thanks to Robbie, she couldn't even do that. She offered Adam a lame smile. There really was no explaining why a handsome, well-known, ageing actor was cooking her dinner and why she was dressed for bed. 'Any news?' she asked.

'No, as I said, I just dropped in to check on you. I'll leave you to enjoy your dinner.'

'You're sure you won't join us?' She waited for Terence to echo her invitation but he kept his back to them, the clearest 'Fuck off' signal he could give.

'Quite sure,' Adam said, and went back into the hall. 'Bye, Zoe.'

Once the front door had closed, Zoe whirled round to confront Terence. 'What the hell are you playing at? What must he have thought?'

'No idea but I imagine he enjoyed the view.'

Zoe followed his eyes and saw that the top button of her pyjamas was open, revealing far too much. She fumbled with the button. 'Oh, God. We're supposed to be keeping our heads down and Adam thinks he just walked in on an orgy.'

He raised an eyebrow. 'There are usually more than two in an orgy, darling. I would have thought you'd have learned that from your ex.'

She flinched. That barb was far too close to the truth for comfort.

Terence's eyes filled with remorse as he smoothed her hair back from her face. 'I'm sorry, sweetheart, that was unkind.'

'It's okay.' She found it impossible to stay mad with the man. 'It's just that I don't want Adam or anyone else thinking that I'm your new girlfriend. I have to be more than some famous actor's latest woman.'

'But I'm cooking you dinner,' Terence complained, although there was mischief in his eyes.

She smiled. 'I'm serious. It will completely undermine me if people think that I only got the part of Isabella because I was sleeping with you.'

'What utter nonsense,' he said, turning back to the pan. 'Anyone who sees the play will know you got the part because you're damn good. How many times do you need me to tell you that? Anyway, you should be thanking me for scaring him off.'

'I should?'

'You must realise that he wants you.'

'Rubbish. I've known Adam most of my life – he's like another brother.'

'Ha! Trust me, he doesn't see you as a sister.'

'He's just being protective. Shane will have asked Adam to keep an eye on me while he was away. He worries about me and, frankly, he would be very worried if he thought I was sleeping with a, well . . .' Zoe petered out, embarrassed.

Terence groaned. 'An oul' fella,' he said, finishing the sentence for her.

'Sorry,' she said, relieved that he didn't seem remotely bothered. 'And I'm sure you're wrong about Adam. Either way, I can assure you the feelings are not returned.' But she hoped he was reading it wrong. It would be so bloody awkward if Adam made any sort of approach and she had to turn him down. Maybe it wasn't such a bad thing that he'd found her with another man after all. 'Is the food nearly ready? I'm starved.'

'Nearly.' Terence took the duck out of the pan and quickly got to work on the sauce. 'Glad you're not smitten, darling. Adam's not the one for you. Now make yourself useful and open the wine.'

Chapter Twelve

'Do you ever sleep?'

Shane looked up at the girl standing in the doorway, who was wearing only a shirt. He'd picked her up last night. Actually, she'd picked him up, now that he came to think about it. For a change, he hadn't been flirting but was lost in thought, doodling on the pad he'd brought with him in case inspiration struck. It hadn't. She was a barmaid, English, working in Nerja for the summer to help finance her way through university, and she made no secret of the fact that she fancied him. He was mesmerised not only by her generous breasts and perfect teeth, but by how sure of herself she appeared to be. She chatted away about university and the future she'd mapped out for herself. He was charmed by her extrovert nature, amused by her naivety and impressed by her determination. 'What do you do?' she'd asked. 'I'm a writer,' he'd told her. That had thrilled her, turned her on. She didn't seem bothered that he was almost twice her age and when, half-cut, he'd asked her back to the villa, she'd smiled and said she'd go and get her toothbrush.

As soon as she was asleep, Shane had gone into the kitchen to make coffee and sit at the breakfast bar, staring at the blank screen of his laptop. He wasn't sure how long he'd been there when she came looking for him.

'Working?' she asked, leaning over his shoulder. He felt her breasts pressing against his back, reigniting his desire for mindless sex.

'Does it look like?' He whirled the stool round, capturing her between his thighs and slipping his hands under the shirt to caress her firm, young body.

Her eyes gleamed in the half-light. 'I should go.'

'Don't,' he said, following his fingers with his mouth.

She groaned and held his head against her chest. 'I have to work in two hours.'

He drew back in confusion. 'In the bar?'

'No, mornings I work in a launderette.'

'You work too hard,' he said, returning his attention to her breasts.

'I finish at two and I'm not due in the bar until six,' she murmured, arching herself against him.

'Siesta time?' he asked.

'I live in a very noisy part of town, so I don't get to sleep much in the daytime.'

He looked up into her face. 'You could come back here instead, but I can't guarantee you'll get any sleep.'

'I'll risk it.' She kissed him and moved out of his arms, turning in the doorway, her teeth flashing when she smiled. 'And the name's Penny.'

'I knew that,' he lied.

'Sure you did.'

Minutes later, he heard the door close and he was alone again with his thoughts. Feeling the room close in on him, he went out onto the impressive patio and, lighting a cigarette, watched the town awaken, the sounds of delivery trucks and bin lorries drifting up to him on the still morning air. The bakery would be open soon. It was a pleasant gentle stroll down a winding road but a steep hike back. Diana had said he was welcome to use the moped in the garage but he was happier to walk or take the bike, getting sadistic pleasure in conquering the punishing slopes, the road dust sticking to his skin, slick with sweat. He'd shower and lounge around the pool, trying to pretend that this was just a holiday and that in a couple of weeks he would return to Dublin and carry on as before. Then he'd imagine looking into Zoe's eyes, those trusting eyes, and seeing the disbelief, grief and then the anger that would inevitably follow. She'd hate him, perhaps refuse to ever see or talk to him again. How could he live with that? But how could he live with himself if he didn't tell her the truth? He went back inside in search of his phone. When he switched it on, there were several texts and a voicemail. He shivered when he saw yet another message from Rachel.

Shane, I'm worried about you. Is everything okay? Please call me.

He wished she would just leave him alone. The girl was a constant reminder of everything he wanted to forget. If it wasn't for her, he wouldn't be in this state and might have gone through life in blissful ignorance. But he was kidding himself and being unfair to Rachel. The truth had always been lying dormant in some dark recess of his mind. He remembered how, long ago, when he'd first picked up a pen to write down his story, the words had gushed out, he couldn't stop them but just vomited them onto the page. He'd crammed notebook after notebook in barely legible scrawl, his wrist aching from the frenzied pace. He hadn't slept or eaten until he was finished and then he had locked the notebooks away and never looked at them again. Why? Because he was afraid to probe, afraid to confront the truth. Neither could he bring himself to throw them out. He'd heard that there was a darkness in all writers and he'd allowed himself to go along with that theory. He was a moody, crazy, paranoid writer, that's all. His thoughts returned to Rachel. It wasn't her fault that he was in this mess; she was just the catalyst. He had treated her very badly, not even considering how she must be feeling. Leaving her had been thoughtless and cruel but he hadn't been thinking straight. He'd just panicked. He sent her a text:

Sorry I haven't been in touch, Rachel. I'm fine, hope you are too. Will call in a few days. x

Next, he played the voicemail. It was from his sister and her voice rang out clear and happy.

'Hey, Shane, I see you're still ignoring poor Adam but there's no need, it's good news. Apparently, John is so busy in Belfast that Adam hasn't even sent him the script yet so it looks like you'll have plenty of time to get the ending just the way you want it. Hope you're back in the zone and taking some time to soak up some of that Spanish sun. Mind you,

Dublin is like the Riviera at the moment. Keep in touch, byeeee.'

He grimaced at the affection in her voice, the love that he didn't deserve and would lose when she knew what he'd done.

He ignored the other messages and sent a text:

Are you awake?

Less than a minute later he got a reply:

Yes

Talk? he typed and held his breath as he waited for an answer.

Okay.

His pulse quickened as he pressed the call button. 'It's early. Are you making bread again?' he asked.

'No.'

'So what are you doing?'

'Just thinking. You?'

'Same.' He went back outside and settled down to watch the sun creep slowly over the horizon.

How he wished Tara was here watching it with him instead of in her cosy little home with Greg. 'Are you sure this is okay? I don't want to upset the marital bliss.'

She laughed. 'You already have, I'm alone.'

He listened as she told him what had happened as a result of his previous text, his fingers clenching into a fist as he thought of what he'd like to do to Greg Coleman. How could a man that size hit a tiny little thing like Tara? It was nauseating and it was all Shane's fault. 'I'm so sorry,' he said when she fell silent.

'If it hadn't been your text, something else would have set him off, Shane. He's been spoiling for a row for weeks.'

'A row is one thing, hitting you is a completely different matter,' he raged.

'It was a slap.'

'He shouldn't have done it,' he insisted.

'No.'

'I'm sorry that I was the one who tipped him over the edge.' She sounded so sad and miserable, he wished there was something he could do, even if it was just to hold her in his arms as she cried. 'What will you do, Tara?'

'Move on,' she said without hesitation.

He was startled by the hardness in her voice and a little shocked. And, God forgive him, a little hopeful. 'Don't believe you,' he said. 'You're just in shock.'

'I mean it. You were the one who told me if it happens once it will happen again.'

'I said that?' Shane said, surprised. He must have been drunk.

'You did.'

'Well, that's true if the man tries to pretend it never happened. But if he's sorry and gets some help controlling his temper, then it's different. Come out here for a few days. The break will do you good and give you time to think.'

'Won't your girlfriend mind?'

He banished the memory of Penny even though her scent was still on his skin and she would return to his bed in just a few short hours. 'There's no girlfriend. Come and stay, Tara. I'll behave myself,' he promised. 'I just want to look after you.'

'Isn't it enough that you're already in trouble with one husband?' she teased.

'But Greg's not going to be your husband for much longer,' he reminded her. 'You're free to do what you like now.' Despite everything, he couldn't suppress the hope bubbling up inside him. 'Have I mentioned I want to kill him? Your dad must be livid.'

'Only you and Zoe know. Well, I suppose Greg might have told his mother.'

Shane snorted. 'I sincerely doubt that. It's not something to brag about.'

'True. She'd probably throw him out if she knew.'

'Why the secrecy?'

'I just need time to decide exactly what I want before everyone starts sticking their oar in.'

'Oops, sorry.'

'I didn't mean you, Shane. I didn't have to tell you. Just like I didn't have to answer any of your texts or agree to talk to you on the phone.'

'Why did you, Tara?' He held his breath as he waited for her answer.

She sighed. 'I suppose I wanted to remember what it felt like to be attractive.'

It wasn't the answer he'd hoped for but what had he expected her to say? That she loved him and was sorry she hadn't waited for him? 'Always happy to tell you how gorgeous and sexy you are, darling,' he said, injecting his voice with a cheer he didn't feel.

She laughed. 'Thanks, I'll remember that. I'd better go and shower and get to work. Life must go on.'

'Must it?' He closed his eyes and imagined her in the shower. 'Call any time you need an ear and if you don't, call anyway. I'm always happy to talk dirty to you.'

She laughed. 'Bye, Shane.'

'Bye, sweetheart.' He went back into the apartment and headed for the shower himself. Maybe if he closed his eyes he could pretend for a moment that she was with him. Poor Penny. He knew when she was back in his arms that it would be Tara he'd be thinking of. But then she would probably be fantasising that he was Justin Bieber. He undressed, turned on the water and examined himself in the mirror. The scars on his torso were now thin silver lines and even the new bruising across his chest had mellowed to shades of yellow and purple. How quickly the body healed yet the mind never did. It continued to function, to carry out the normal day-to-day routines of life on auto-pilot, requiring little actual thought. But the part of the mind that held the emotions and memories was like a bubbling cauldron that from time to time spilled over, cruelly scalding everything in its path.

The mirror steamed up and he got into the shower. He pondered on the fact that John hadn't read his play yet. It wasn't too late to revert to the realms of fiction. If he wanted, he could leave the past alone, keep his secret and hold on to his sister. He thought of how he'd love to be able to confide in Tara. It might distract her from her own problems. It also might mean she would never talk to him again. Fuck it, there was no way this could end well. A towel wrapped around his waist, he went back out to the kitchen. Armed with a bottle of tequila, his cigarettes and a pad and pencil, he went outside and sat down at the patio table. He drank two shots before he started to write, forcing his mind back into the past. When he'd woken from the nightmares he'd drank to forget but now he was going to drink to remember, to face up to it. He paused from time to time, to light another cigarette, have another drink or wipe tears from his eyes. As he wrote, his fears and guilt turned to anger and he embraced it and wrote on.

He was slumped across the table, sleeping, when he heard Penny call his name. She appeared around the side of the villa and looked from the half-empty bottle to the notebook and the overflowing ashtray.

'Looks like you started the party without me.'

'I'm not sure I'm up to partying,' he said, reaching for his sunglasses.

'The water looks lovely. Mind if I take a dip?'

He shrugged. 'Go ahead.'

Slowly, she peeled off the tight top and cut-off jeans and then, her eyes on his face, stepped out of her flimsy lace bra and pants and made a perfect dive into the pool, squealing at the cold.

She struck out across the pool and then bobbed up at the other side. 'Come on in, the water's lovely.'

Laughing, he stood up, letting the towel fall, and went in after her.

Chapter Thirteen

Robbie threw up his hands in despair as Celia fluffed her lines again. What the hell was wrong with the woman today? It wasn't as if there was that much to remember. 'Let's take five,' he said, and turned away to check his mobile.

Terence was immediately at his side. 'The bloody woman is losing it,' he muttered. 'I think she's on the sauce.'

'We all have off days,' Robbie said, unwilling to be drawn into one of their tiffs.

'She has more than most. Zoe, darling, want to grab a coffee?'

She was tapping away at her phone. 'No thanks.'

Terence frowned. 'Robbie?'

'No thanks.'

'Right,' Terence said, looking put out, and left the room alone.

Robbie went over to Celia. The woman was bent over her knitting but her fingers were motionless. He glanced up and caught Zoe's eye.

'There's no damn signal in this place,' she said, thankfully taking the hint, and headed for the door. 'Back in a mo.'

When the door closed on her, Robbie sat down beside Celia. 'Is everything okay, Celia?'

She looked up, her eyes bleak, and gave him a weak smile. 'Fine, darling, why do you ask?'

'It's just you seem distracted. Is it the play or' – he smiled – 'is it Terence?'

'No, no, I can handle him, don't worry,' she chuckled. 'To be honest, I just didn't get enough sleep last night. Apartments are wonderful when it comes to security, but not so good when the neighbours are noisy.'

'Ah, I see. I suffer the same problem from time to time. Why don't you head home and get some rest?'

'Oh, no, I'll be fine.'

'Please, Celia. I was planning to wrap up in an hour anyway.'

'Well, if you're sure—'

'I am.'

She packed away her knitting, and pressed her powdered cheek to his. 'Thank you, darling. See you tomorrow.'

She had just left when Zoe returned. 'Is everything okay?'

'Yeah, fine. Turns out Celia just didn't get much sleep last night, so I sent her home.' Zoe said nothing and he looked up to see her staring at him, hands on her hips. 'What?'

'You believed her?'

'Yeah, why not?'

Zoe shook her head. 'I just don't buy it. Usually, you know she's arrived as soon as she's in the building, but today, she was as quiet as a mouse.'

Robbie frowned. He hadn't noticed, but that was proof in itself that Zoe was right. Celia's voice always carried and you could usually hear her calling out 'Good morning's and hear that tinkling, false laugh long before she came into view.

'Perhaps it's a health issue or family stuff,' Robbie said now. 'Maybe you could have a word?'

'Me?' Zoe looked at him as if he'd lost his mind. 'You must be joking. She'd stab me with a knitting needle for having the audacity to address her.'

He chuckled. 'That's not true – she's definitely warming to you.'

'From frozen to chilled,' Zoe agreed. 'Seriously, Robbie, I'd like to help but—'

'I really would appreciate it.' He adopted a plaintive pose. 'You don't want the play to be held up because she goes off the rails, do you?'

'Fine, I'll ask, but don't blame me if Isabella ends up in A&E,' she warned, glowering at him; but he could tell she was enjoying the sparring as much as he was.

'Off you go then.' He jotted down the address and handed it to her.

'Now?'

'No time like the present. I can go through the solo scenes with Terence.'

Zoe chewed on her lip, looking worried. 'Is it not a bit intrusive to go to her home?'

'I'm sure it will be fine. If she's telling the truth, she'll be fast asleep and won't even hear the doorbell.'

'And what do I get in return for this favour?' she asked, her eyes twinkling.

He held her gaze. 'I'll buy you dinner?'

She looked surprised and he thought he'd pushed his luck.

He was on the verge of passing it off as a joke when she finally answered.

'Where?'

'You pick,' he said, now fervently hoping that Celia would let her in.

She grinned. 'I hope you've got a suit.'

He gave an exaggerated groan. 'Now I'm praying that Celia's asleep. Please remember that I've two children to support.'

Her smile faltered for a moment but then her eyes lit up. 'Bring them along, I know just the place.'

Damn, that wasn't exactly what he had in mind. 'Sorry, school night, their mum wouldn't allow it.'

'Ah, right. Never mind. I doubt you'll lose the bet anyway but I'll give it a shot.' She slung her bag over her arm and was just leaving when Terence arrived back.

'Are we done?' he asked, putting an arm around Zoe in such a familiar way that Robbie wanted to punch him. What was wrong with the man? Terence flirted with everyone and Zoe was a free agent. But there was no denying that he was attracted to her, big time.

'We are, you're not!' Zoe gave Terence a peck on the cheek and danced away. 'See you tomorrow!'

Robbie grinned at the perplexed look on the actor's face. 'Right, Terence, let's get to work.'

Zoe looked at the address and then at the apartment building in front of her and clutched her bag tighter against her as some kids in hoodies mooched past. Robbie must have given her the wrong address. As she was about to call him, the front door opened and a guy around her own age held the door for her, his lecherous gaze travelling the length of her body, coming to rest on her breasts.

'Haven't seen you around before,' he said, and she recoiled from the smell of booze.

'Just visiting,' she mumbled, trying to slip by him without touching. She kept her eyes down and regretted it when she saw the fly of his dirty jeans was open. This just had to be the wrong address. She kept moving and hit the button for the lift.

'I hope you come again' – he grinned at her – 'and again, and again.'

She abandoned the lift and scarpered up the stairs instead, his laughter following her.

'You would have to live on the fourth floor, Celia,' Zoe muttered, breathless as she rang the doorbell of apartment 4B.

'No more! Go away, leave me alone!' Celia called, sounding frightened.

'Celia? Celia? It's Zoe Hall. Is everything all right?'

There was total silence. 'Celia, I met a man in the lobby. Did he break in? Are you hurt?'

Still silence. Zoe was pretty sure that Celia was okay, but she wasn't leaving here without knowing for sure. 'Okay, I'm calling for an ambulance and the police,' she said loudly.

Immediately, the door opened a crack, the safety chain on, and Celia peered out at her. 'For goodness' sake, there's no need for that. I'm absolutely fine.'

She didn't look it. Despite the make-up, she was white as a

sheet and her normally neat bun was lopsided, stray hair loose around her face. 'Then why were you so afraid to open the door? Who were you telling to leave you alone?' Zoe wasn't about to leave because the woman didn't like her and was too proud to ask for help.

Celia shook her head, looking confused. 'That wasn't me – it must have been the woman in the next apartment. She's a bit odd. Did you want something?'

'No, Robbie said you weren't feeling great so I thought I'd drop in on my way home and see if you needed anything.'

The woman's expression softened a little but she shook her head. 'No, thank you, darling, but that was very thoughtful. Now, please excuse me, I was resting when you called.'

'Sorry I disturbed you. See you tomorrow.'

'Goodbye, dear,' Celia said, and prompty shut the door in her face.

As Zoe waited for the lift, the door next to Celia's opened and a couple emerged and smiled at her. The man nodded towards Celia's apartment. 'Is everything okay?'

'We heard the shouting,' the woman whispered as they all stepped into the lift and Zoe pressed the button for the ground floor.

'Shouting?' Zoe asked. 'She told me everything was fine but I'm not sure I believe her.'

'She keeps herself to herself. Won't take help from anyone,' the man said, shaking his head. 'But I tell you, if a son of mine treated Betty like that, I'd report him myself.'

Zoe stared at him. 'I met a man in the lobby. He seemed a bit ... strange.'

'Big lad with dark hair, scruffy-looking?'

'Pat!'

He shrugged. 'Well, he is.'

'Sounds like the same guy. That's Celia's son?' Zoe couldn't believe it.

'Yes, God love her. And we don't mean to eavesdrop but the walls are very thin,' the woman – Betty – said. 'He's always pestering her for money.'

The doors opened and Zoe was relieved to see that the lobby was empty.

'Someone needs to sort him out.' The man – Pat – looked at Zoe as if expecting her to take on the job.

'I'm afraid I hardly know Celia. We've just started working together and she left early today, so I stopped by to check she was all right.'

'Well, she's not,' Pat said.

'There's not much this poor girl can do about it,' Betty reprimanded him.

'Hasn't she any other relatives?' Zoe asked, feeling helpless and uneasy.

Betty frowned. 'I don't think so; she very rarely has visitors.'

Zoe didn't have a clue what to do but she felt she had to do something. 'Can I leave my name and number with you? Maybe you could call me if you're worried about her?'

'Of course you can.' Pat nodded his approval and, whipping out his phone, added her details to his contact list. 'Well, it was nice to meet you, Zoe.'

'You too.' She shook hands with them both. 'I'm glad that at least Celia has good neighbours.'

*

On the bus home, Zoe replayed the events in her head, from her surprise at Celia's humble home – hadn't she read that the acclaimed actress lived in one of those splendid seafront properties in Dalkey? – to the encounter with that awful man who turned out to be Celia's son! And, then, the undoubted fear in Celia's voice when Zoe had rung the doorbell. Zoe might have swallowed Celia's line if she hadn't met her neighbours. Now she felt as if she had stumbled on a crime scene. She sent Robbie a text:

What time are you picking me up?

It was a simple question but could be interpreted as flirty. If she'd misread the signs and the twinkle in his eye earlier, then it would go over his head.

He replied within moments:

Knew you could do it! See you at seven. ☺

She smiled, although her visit hadn't really achieved much. Still, if she hadn't gone, she wouldn't have found out about Celia's son. She hoped that Robbie had some ideas as to what, if anything, they should do, because she was at a loss.

Her thoughts turned to the evening ahead and she felt a flicker of excitement. She liked Robbie, really liked him. He wasn't a rogue or a charmer or a fashion icon like Terence; in fact, he made no effort to impress anyone. But he had a quiet, dry sense of humour that she enjoyed. He didn't talk for the sake of talking and silences didn't bother him. As a result, when he did speak, people listened. And she loved his laugh to the extent that she found herself trying to prompt it just to see his broad grin, those hazel eyes twinkle, and hear his deep, rumbling chuckle. She imagined he was a great dad. He was always talking about his kids and he seemed to spend lots of time with them. Stop building him into some sort of god, she told herself. He's just a nice guy. And it wasn't as if this was a date. Although, she was pretty sure that he liked her too. She'd seen Robbie's frown when Terence cuddled up to her and she had taken to avoiding those displays of affection in front of him, wanting to make it clear that there was nothing going on.

Mindful of Robbie's financial pressures, she'd decided to take him to the local Italian restaurant. The menu was short but the food was good and the prices were reasonable. After trying on and discarding a number of outfits, she settled on a white sleeveless top, tight black jeans and black stilettos. She pulled her hair back into a ponytail, carefully applied her make-up and added huge silver earrings, bangles and a pendant that dipped into her cleavage. She studied her image, happy with the effect. It was the sort of look that would work in a top-class restaurant or the local pub. Perfect.

She had just come downstairs when the doorbell rang. He was early. Still, at least on this occasion she was presentable, she thought, and she went to the door, smiling.

'Hello, Zoe.'

She froze when she saw the man standing before her and then her heart started to hammer in her chest. 'What are you doing here, Ed?'

He hadn't changed at all, was handsome as ever, and his smile was confident and relaxed.

'Well, that's not a very warm welcome,' he reproached her. 'I just dropped by for a chat.'

She glared at him. 'You should have called first. It's not convenient, I'm going out.'

His eyes appraised her and he nodded. 'I can see that. You look great, darling.'

'Just tell me what you want and go, Ed,' she said, hating the tremor in her voice. Out of the corner of her eye, she saw Robbie's car pull in behind Ed's flashy red sports car.

'I just thought you should know that I'm moving back to Dublin.'

'Why?' She stared at him in dismay. With them both working in the theatre, that meant their paths would cross. God, she might even end up having to work with him.

'Lots of reasons,' he said with a vague shrug.

'Need to be a big fish in a small pond?' she jeered. 'Disappointed that you haven't landed that movie role yet?'

His lips twitched and there was a triumphant look in his eye. 'Actually, I have. That's one of the reasons I'm coming back. It's being made here.'

She was saved from having to respond to this annoying piece of news by the sight of Robbie walking up the path, and what a sight he was. Wearing a beautiful pale grey suit with an open-necked blue shirt, he looked incredibly handsome and, as he drew nearer, she was delighted to see he was at least three inches taller than Ed.

'Hello, darling.' Robbie smiled directly into her eyes and she realised that he knew exactly who Ed was. Ignoring her ex, he leaned down to kiss her cheek.

'Hi,' she said, wanting to throw her arms around him, as Ed

stood up straighter, his eyes widening as he registered who the man kissing his ex-wife was. 'Robbie, this is—'

'Ed McGlynn.' As he stuck out his hand, Ed watched Robbie's face, waiting for him to react.

Robbie shook it but, to her delight, showed no sign of recognition. 'Robbie Prendergast.' He looked back at Zoe. 'Sorry to hurry you, sweetheart, but we're running a little late.'

'I'm ready to go,' she assured him, and went to the hall table to get her bag and wrap. 'Sorry, Ed, but as I said, you really should have called first.'

Ed looked properly pissed off. 'Fine. How about lunch tomorrow?'

'No, I don't have anything to say to you. If it's a legal matter, call my solicitor. Goodbye, Ed.' She closed the front door, took the hand that Robbie was holding out to her and swept past him.

'Well played,' Robbie murmured as he opened the passenger door for Zoe and went round to climb in beside her. 'Are you all right?' he asked as he pulled out of the parking space.

'Yes,' she said, though she was shaken by the encounter with her ex-husband. 'It was just such a shock to see him on my doorstep.'

Robbie put a hand over hers and squeezed it. 'He must be feeling a total idiot for letting you go.' He smiled over at her. 'You look amazing, Zoe.'

'Back at ya.' She turned in the seat to admire him. 'I thought it was James Bond coming to my rescue. As for Ed, he says he's moving back to Ireland, and the bastard's going to be in a movie they're making here. I did want to know all the details, but I was damned if I was going to ask. I wasn't going to feed his ego.'

'It seems big enough,' Robbie agreed.

She laughed. 'He was disgusted that you didn't acknowledge him. Thanks for that. He knew who you were, that's for sure.'

'He'd be waiting a long time for me to lick up to him. I can find out more about this movie for you, if you like.'

'Yes, please.' Zoe shot him a grateful smile. Wow, he really did look gorgeous. 'I'd just like to know where he'll be based so I can keep my distance.'

'Wouldn't you like him to be in town to see your rave reviews for *Isabella*?'

'Now who's tempting fate?' she teased. She did like the idea of her husband being around if indeed she was a success. 'It would be nice but it would pale against his achievements.'

'Don't put yourself down. He's a good actor but he's not a great one. For my money, you're better.'

She blushed. That was quite a compliment from a director of his standing. 'I don't know what to say.'

He grinned. 'You could tell me where we're going and that way I can stop driving around aimlessly.'

She laughed. 'I hadn't noticed. I was going to take you to a nice little place in Terenure that's quite good but it's very casual and it seems a shame to waste that suit.'

He laughed. 'True, you never know when you'll see me in one again. Will we head into the city and wander? I'm sure it won't be that difficult to get a table somewhere on a Tuesday evening.'

'Fine by me.' She sat back in her seat, feeling happy and in control. If when Ed had dropped by and she'd been a mess, or Robbie hadn't arrived, she knew that her mood would have been quite different.

'I should take you to Trocadero's and show you off,' he remarked as they strolled through Temple Bar, 'but we'd be sure to meet people from the theatre and I'm not in the mood for more company, are you?'

'No, I've got all the company I need,' she said, meeting his eyes. 'And the last thing I want is to bump into Ed. He always goes where he will be the centre of attention.'

He took her hand. 'I think I know just the place.'

Chapter Fourteen

When they had ordered, Zoe looked around the warm restaurant. It was in a basement, low-key and far too dark and small to attract anyone wishing to be noticed. It was also very cosy and romantic. Was that intentional? 'The perfect spot and reasonable too.'

He looked at her, frowning. 'Are you calling me a cheapskate?'

'No, of course not—' she started and then saw him grin. 'I fell for that.'

Robbie broke off a piece of his bread roll, slathered it with butter and took a bite. 'When did you and Ed last meet?'

She put her head on one side and thought about it. 'It must be four years ago. Shane and I went over to pick up some things from the flat.'

'And have you kept in touch?'

'God, no. I've had as little to do with him as possible since the day I left.'

'It ended badly? Sorry, that's a very personal question.'

'It's okay. He was playing around and' – she swallowed –

'I've recently heard he was unfaithful all the way through our relationship.'

'He's an even bigger idiot than I thought, then.' Robbie shook his head. 'Sorry.'

'It's fine. It was a long time ago.' She looked up at him and smiled. 'But I am so glad you arrived when you did today. Now Ed will think either I'm dating the great director Robbie Prendergast or I'm working with him.'

'Which would you prefer?' he asked.

She held his eyes, not quite sure what he wanted to hear. 'Either would be good.'

'Did your brother approve of Ed?'

She was a little disappointed he'd changed tack but went along with it. 'Not at all. He did everything he could to break us up. I should have heeded his warnings but I was young and, the more Shane put Ed down, the more it pushed us together. When I moved to London with him, Shane wouldn't take my calls for weeks and he didn't come to my wedding.' She was surprised to feel tears prick her eyes. She swallowed them back and took a sip of wine.

'You seem very close.'

'We are but then there's only the two of us.' She felt guilty, as always, for not thinking to mention Gerry and Hannah but they'd never really felt like family, that was the truth of it. 'So, what about you, what's your divorce story?' she asked.

'Nothing as dramatic. I met Linda at school, we started dating and then, just after we left school, we found out that she was pregnant with Samantha and I asked her to marry me.'

'Were you in love?' she asked.

He scratched his head. 'I don't think we knew what love

was. We were having fun and were so shocked by the pregnancy and afraid of the reaction we would get from our parents – particularly hers – marriage just seemed the obvious and easiest solution. We got on very well, so it didn't seem like too much of a hardship to set up home together. But sleepless nights, mortgages and bills test the best of any relationship. When our son Nick started school, Linda got a secretarial job and she seemed happier. Life had finally settled down for us. That's when I found this amazing little house that was in need of complete renovation and going for a song. Linda was happy to go along with it once it was clear that she had no intention of helping, or moving into a building site. That suited me, to be honest.' He pulled a face. 'By then the less time we spent together, the happier we both were. But once we had moved in and I had no project to keep me out of her hair, things started to go downhill. We tried to hide it from the children, but it wasn't a large house and they were getting older and smarter and became aware of the tension.' He sighed. 'And so we agreed that it would be best to separate before it became acrimonious.' He shrugged. 'We get on quite well now and the kids seem happy.'

'I'm glad but, as it was a mutual decision, it doesn't seem fair that you had to leave your children and the house you had put so much work into.'

'Life isn't fair. But who knows, on the back of the success of *Isabella*, I may be able to build a mansion.'

'Huh, no pressure then!'

He smiled. 'No pressure.'

'Are you happy with the way it's going?' Zoe asked, searching his face for any signs of concern.

'Absolutely. It's been plain sailing until today. By the way, is Celia okay?'

'Oh, Lord, with Ed and everything I completely forgot about her. The answer is no, Robbie, I'm afraid she may be far from okay.' She went on to tell him of her visit.

'That's odd,' he said when she was finished. 'Celia's always boasting about Albie and how he spoils her. It can't be the same guy.'

'The neighbours seemed quite certain of it and they're a nice couple. Having said that, they're going by what they hear through the wall. The apartment block is very basic, not at all the sort of place you'd imagine her living.'

'Nothing is ever quite as it seems, is it?' He gave a sad smile. 'But whatever's going on, she clearly doesn't want people to know.'

'There must be someone she'd talk to. She seems to have a soft spot for you.'

Robbie shook his head. 'I'm a director and she's an actress and a professional. Of course she treats me better than her fellow actors, but I know as little about her as you do. Other than that she adored her late husband and has never done anything but praise her son.'

'She is an award-winning actress,' Zoe reminded him. 'And what woman would want people to know her only child is a bully?'

'Exactly why broaching the subject would only embarrass her.'

'But if he is extorting money from her, we must do something.' Zoe couldn't believe that she was so concerned about a woman who barely acknowledged her presence. But Celia had sounded so frightened that Zoe couldn't get it out of her mind. She didn't particularly like the woman but when she thought of the sleazeball she'd met in the lobby – Celia's son, it seemed – Zoe found it hard to turn her back on the woman. There was something nasty, even sinister, about the guy and she'd felt genuinely nervous and intimidated by him.

'I'll try to figure out a way to bring it up. For now, I think it's best you pretend that you've accepted her explanation and forgotten all about it.'

'I seem to spend more time acting off stage than I do on,' Zoe complained, half jokingly.

'I think that's a little thing called "life".' Robbie chuckled.

'How did you end up in this business?' Zoe asked, changing the subject. Their starters arrived and looked delicious. Goat's cheese salad for her and mussels for him.

'The usual way,' he said with a grin. 'I was a frustrated writer and when no one showed any interest in my plays, I decided to direct and produce them myself.'

She looked up in surprise. 'I didn't know that you wrote.'

He pulled a face. 'I did but not very well. My work made Greek tragedies look like slapstick.'

She laughed. 'I'm guessing this started in your teenage years.'

'Yep.'

She smiled. 'I used to write poetry that made Emily Dickinson seem cheerful.'

'All a necessary part of growing up, I think. But though I wasn't a great writer, I was able to spot a good script and, when I was reading it, I could visualise exactly how it would work on stage. My first production was at university. A guy I hung out with was always writing, tomes of stuff. Deep, meaningful, heavy, you know the sort.'

She nodded, smiling.

'I challenged him to write three twenty-minute plays, one happy, one sad and one comedy, and we would put them on in rag week.'

'Did he do it?'

'He did. It was the most irritating, stressful and wonderful project and that was before we got the other actors on board.'

'You acted?' She smiled, trying to imagine it.

'Don't sound so surprised,' he said, trying to look offended. 'I wasn't that bad and Morgan was amazing.'

'Not Morgan Kavanagh?' She stared at him. The famous movie actor was now one of Ireland's greatest success stories.

Robbie nodded. 'He had ambitions to be a history professor but that all went out of the window after the reception our plays got. We were both bitten by the bug.'

'Were you never tempted by cinema?'

'I was, but you needed to be in Hollywood to get anywhere when I was starting out and, remember, I had a wife and child. It just wasn't possible. Anyway, I'm not sure I'm cut out for the movie industry. I love the immediacy of the theatre. I like that it's live, that it can be different every night, and I get a kick out of seeing the audience reaction. Well' – he laughed – 'most of the time. How about you? Did you always want to act?'

'It was a dream but it never crossed my mind that I could. It was only when Shane went to work at the Gate and I got to see live theatre that it actually seemed possible. Shane insisted I go to drama school, which was one of the happiest times of my life. I started to get small parts quite quickly and then I got together with Ed and, as Shane would say, I threw away my career.' She smiled.

'Do you regret it?'

'Marrying Ed?' She thought for a moment. Her answer a few weeks ago would have been no, that before things turned sour she and Ed had been in love and happy, but since Tara's revelations it felt as if it had all been a joke and she'd been the butt. 'Yes, I regret it. He wasn't worth the sacrifice.'

'I won't argue with that. How do you feel about touring?'

'It would depend on the play, Robbie,' she said, wondering was this a trick question. 'I'd certainly be happy to tour with *Isabella*.'

'Always be choosy,' he advised. 'Don't take a job just to eat. And be careful with your money. So many actors go crazy when they first get success and flash the cash without realising what a fickle industry it is.'

'Believe me, I know. I've been through it all with Ed,' she assured him. 'And Shane and I were brought up to respect the value of everything.'

'You had strict parents?'

'No. Mam and Dad died in a car crash when I was seven.'

'That's sad; I'm sorry.'

'Thanks. We were raised by my father's brother and his wife and let's just say, they were frugal.' She smiled.

'You must have really missed your parents.'

He covered her hand with his and she liked the warmth of his touch and the compassion in his eyes. 'It was tougher on Shane. He was old enough to appreciate the horror. I think what I found hardest was that no one would tell me what was going on. Daddy had dropped me off at a birthday party and, when it was over, he didn't come to collect me. Laura's mother phoned my house and then, after a while, told me that, as a special treat, I was staying the night. But that didn't make sense. Mam and Dad knew that I was never able to sleep without my doll and blankie. Whenever we went on holiday, they came too.' She smiled at Robbie. 'So, naturally, I burst into tears and said I wanted to go home, but no one listened. Of course, I couldn't sleep and ended up spending the night on the sofa with Laura's mum.'

'What happened the next morning?'

'I sat at the window watching for Daddy but then a police car pulled up outside and our neighbour, Mrs Doyle, and another woman got out. I knew then something was wrong. Laura's mum kept her arm round me as Mrs Doyle told me that there had been an accident and that Mam, Dad and Shane were in hospital.' She paused, swallowing her tears, and Robbie took her hand in both of his. 'They said I wasn't allowed to see them but that the doctors were doing their best to make them better. Mrs Doyle took me to her house and then, later that day, Shane arrived with our uncle and aunt. I kept asking about Mam and Dad but they wouldn't answer. When we were left alone, Shane told me that they were dead and he held me in his arms and we both cried. But I still don't think I understood. You see, I never saw their bodies, just these boxes being put in the ground. Everyone was hugging me, patting my head. I was the centre of attention. It only really hit home that my life had changed for ever when my aunt packed up all our belongings and we went to live on their farm in Meath. Not only had we lost our parents but also our home, our friends, our schools. It was such a shock and I was scared and upset. But at least I had Shane. Although the poor guy seemed oblivious of everything going on around him.'

'In shock,' Robbie surmised.

Zoe nodded. 'Yes. Gerry and Hannah were – are – good people, but they didn't have children of their own and hadn't a clue how to handle us. It must have been daunting to suddenly find themselves the guardians of two kids. They enrolled us in the local schools and gave us jobs to do around the house and farm – that was a shock! But they never talked about Mam and Dad. There weren't even any photos around the house. I think they thought it was best for us if we forgot them, but of course, we didn't.'

'My God, you've both been through so much.' He stroked her hand, almost absently.

'It was fine after a few months,' Zoe assured him, realising what a bleak picture she was painting. 'The farm wasn't far from the town and I made lots of friends in school. It was a completely different way of life and we had a lot of freedom. But Shane didn't settle in as well as I did. He couldn't wait to get back to Dublin and he left as soon as he finished school.'

'You must have missed him.' He stroked her hand.

'Yes, but I went up to see him all the time and then when I left school I moved in with him.'

'Didn't your aunt and uncle mind?'

'Do you know, I think they were relieved to get back to their own lives. I don't mean that in a bad way, but they never wanted children. It was good of them to take us in and raise us. I'm sure they could have refused and we would have ended up in a foster home or even been separated.' She shivered at the thought.

'That's quite a story. No wonder you and Shane are close. I grew up on a farm too, on the outskirts of Galway City. And I have one brother. Jack took over the farm when Dad retired a couple of years ago. Now my folks spend their time travelling, making up for the years they were chained to the land.'

'That's lovely.'

He nodded. 'Yeah, they seem happy.'

'And your wife was a neighbour?'

'Yes. We went up to university the same year and that was when we suddenly had all this freedom and' – he rolled his eyes – 'it proved too much of a temptation and we were unlucky. Or' – he smiled – 'that's how it felt back then. But, had we behaved ourselves we wouldn't have Samantha and I can't imagine life without her.'

'Things have a way of working out,' Zoe agreed. 'I'm glad that Ed and I didn't have children. I think I would have found it hard to maintain a civil relationship with him after the way he behaved. I'm not sure that he's parental material anyway.'

Robbie released her hand as their main course arrived and, as they ate, they continued to chat about everything under the sun. Zoe couldn't help contrasting Robbie with Terence. She was immensely fond of Tara's dad, he was wonderful company, but, she realised, their conversations began and ended with the theatre, with *Isabella*.

'Do you think Terence is happy?' she asked Robbie.

He held her gaze, his eyes thoughtful. 'He certainly has been since you came along.'

She shook her head and smiled. 'There's nothing going on between us, I assure you.'

'Really? You spend a lot of time together.'

'He's taken me under his wing, wants this to be my big break. To be honest, I've learned more about acting in the last few weeks than in all the time I've been in the theatre.' Robbie was silent, but it was obvious that he had something to say. 'Come on, spit it out.' She gave him a smile of encouragement.

'It's not really my business ...'

'Please.'

He put down his knife and fork and leaned closer. 'Terence is inclined to become obsessive about whatever he is working on. He almost lives the part, day and night, for as long as he's playing it. In his head you are actually Isabella right now. For a director it's a dream – you've seen him perform so you know how good he is. But when it's over some actresses have found the sudden loss of all that attention quite upsetting.'

'You don't have to worry about me, Robbie,' Zoe told him. 'I'll admit, initially, I was a little starstruck but we're just close friends who want to make this the best play that we can, that's all.'

He visibly relaxed. 'Good. I didn't want you to get hurt again.'

'Is that all?' She looked at him, hoping that she wasn't imagining how special this evening felt. They were so relaxed together and yet she was so conscious of him, watching his long fingers trace patterns on the tablecloth as he talked and catching him observing her from time to time, his expression intense but inscrutable. Perhaps it was all in her head, but she was done with dreaming. She needed to know if Robbie was attracted to her and if not then she would spend the rest of the evening laughing and joking with him, giving the performance of her life. Then she would tuck her heart safely away and not risk any further damage.

He returned to stroking the back of her hand, his eyes never leaving hers. 'I have to admit, watching him touching you and holding you at every opportunity makes me uncomfortable.'

'Why?' she asked, determined to make him spell out his feelings so that she knew exactly where she stood.

'I'm envious.'

That wasn't the word she had wanted to hear. She kept her expression neutral. 'Of his way with women?'

'No!' He shook his head, looking confused. 'I don't want to be like him. Dear God, just watching the pace he goes through life and women exhausts me. I was envious that he had focused his attentions on *you* and, I thought, with some success. And sitting through rehearsals every day, watching him kiss you so bloody thoroughly has been a little hard to stomach.'

Her pulse quickened at his words and she smiled. 'Is that a long-winded way of saying you like me?'

His eyes twinkled. 'I suppose it is.'

'Why didn't you just ask me out?'

'As I said, I thought Terence had beaten me to it. The three of us have to work together and it's been going so well, I couldn't risk upsetting that dynamic just because I fancied the leading lady.'

Finally, he'd said it. She beamed at him. 'I don't think you need to worry about the dynamic.'

'Does that mean if I asked you out on a date you would say yes?' he asked.

'So this isn't a date?'

He gave a sheepish grin. 'I suppose it's a sneaky date. I hoped that after we'd spent some time together you might warm to me and forget Terence.'

Zoe leaned closer. 'Forget who?' she murmured.

His eyes focused on her mouth before returning to meet hers. 'Would you like to see the dessert menu?'

'No, thank you.'

He threaded his fingers through hers. 'Then would it be okay if I took you home? I want to kiss you ... a lot.'

'That would be very okay,' she said, her heart pounding in her chest at the desire in his eyes.

They left the restaurant, Zoe acutely conscious of Robbie's hand on the small of her back. Outside, he pulled her into a doorway.

'I'm sorry but I can't wait,' he said and lowered his mouth to hers.

She clung to him and responded, her passion matching his. This wasn't the practised, seductive kiss that Terence excelled at. This was sweet and tender and much more intimate. When they broke apart, she saw her surprise mirrored in his eyes.

'I think I need to do that again,' he said, cupping her face in his hands.

Zoe was oblivious to everyone and everything, completely losing herself in this kiss that she never wanted to end. They were so close she could feel his heart beating; she wondered whether he could feel hers. She felt almost shy when he drew back and looked at her, knowing that the effect he was having on her must have been written all over her face. But he was looking at her in wonder. He took her hand, kissed it and, without a word, led her back to the car, glancing down into her face every so often and smiling. She squeezed his hand and smiled back. It was crazy, they were like a pair of teenagers. When they got to the car, he pressed her up against it and kissed her again, and she wrapped herself around him, savouring the taste and smell and feel of the man. On the way home, he kept glancing over as if to reassure himself that she was really there. She put her hand over his and smiled at him in understanding. She couldn't believe this was happening either. Yes, she had felt a growing connection between them but she hadn't expected the lightning bolt that struck when he kissed her.

'We're here,' he said unnecessarily as he pulled up outside her house. They looked at each other, before hopping out of the car and hurrying up the path.

All fingers and thumbs, Zoe tried to get the key in the door, but even then, when she pushed on the door, it wouldn't budge.

'Weakling.' Robbie chuckled. 'Here, let me.'

She stood close to him as eventually the door gave way and then shrieked as water came rushing out around her ankles. 'What the hell!'

'You must have left a tap running,' he said, pushing the door against the current to reveal the hall and the kitchen beyond under at least six inches of water.

'Oh, Robbie, your suit!'

He quickly jumped back and began to take off his trousers.

'What on earth are you doing?' She put a hand over her mouth to smother her laughter. God only knew what the neighbours made of the comings and goings in this house.

'I have to get in there and stop the flow and this *is* my best suit.' He handed her his jacket and trousers and stepped back into the flow, wearing only his shirt and boxers. Zoe piled his clothes carefully on the table before kicking off her shoes, rolling up her jeans and following him inside. He was standing in the doorway of the kitchen, shining the torch on his phone up at the ceiling. She looked up and gasped at the gaping hole.

'Oh, my God, what happened?'

'Is the bathroom straight above?' he asked.

'Yes.' Zoe turned to go upstairs.

'Hang on, where is your fuse box? Water and electricity aren't the best combination.'

'Oh, Lord, you're right, it's out here.' She waded back down the hallway to the cubby hole behind the front door.

'Be careful,' he cautioned.

She pulled down the main switch and let out a sigh of relief when there was no flash or bang. Robbie led the way upstairs and paused in the bathroom doorway. Zoe peered over his shoulder, frowning at the debris all over the floor. 'What the hell is that?'

'I'm guessing your boiler blew up,' he said, shining the light on the open door of the airing cupboard.

She stared at the hole in the tank and the sodden clothes around it. 'Damn thing has been making weird noises and acting up lately.'

'How old is it?' He switched off the valves to stop any more water coming from the tank in the attic into the boiler.

'No idea. Probably as old as the house.'

He shone the light around. 'It looks like the main damage is confined to the bathroom and kitchen. You'll have to call the insurance company in the morning and get some builders' quotes and you'll have to move out for a while.'

'Move out?' she echoed. The thought hadn't occurred to her but of course he was right. If she had no electricity or plumbing she didn't have much choice.

'You can stay at my place tonight. I'm not trying to take advantage of the situation,' he assured her. 'I have a spare room.'

'That's disappointing.' She grinned up at him and he immediately enfolded her in his arms and kissed her. She was acutely conscious of his state of undress and couldn't imagine being able to sleep knowing he was in the next room.

'Why don't you pack a bag and I'll hold the torch for you? Then I'll sweep out the water from downstairs.'

It was a couple of hours before they finished cleaning up the worst of the mess. 'It's a clear night and there's a good breeze. We should really leave the windows and doors open to try and dry the place out,' Robbie said.

'Perhaps I should stay and do just that.' Exhausted, Zoe was already resigned to the fact that their evening wasn't going to end the way she'd hoped.

'I'm not leaving you here alone with the doors open,' he protested.

She smiled. 'You could always stay.'

'In the spare room?'

'The bed's not made up and all the linen was in the airing cupboard, I'm afraid. You'd have to bunk in with me.'

'Do you trust me?' he asked, linking his arms loosely about her.

She yawned. 'I think we're both far too tired to get up to anything.'

'I can't make any promises,' he murmured into her hair.

She shivered and nestled closer to him. She didn't mind if they just kissed or lay in each other's arms. In fact, it was a very attractive thought, very attractive indeed.

Zoe woke the next morning, conscious of two things: a stench of damp and a warm arm wrapped round her. She smiled as she remembered stripping down to her underwear and huddling under the duvet with Robbie, kissing and whispering, laughing at the situation they'd found themselves in. And while she'd been conscious of his body against hers, she had felt relaxed and safe. As their eyes grew heavy, Robbie went down to close and lock the doors and, though she had tried to stay awake, that was the last thing Zoe remembered. She wondered if he'd been disappointed. Reluctantly, she dragged her mind and body fully awake, reached for her phone, which had only the tiniest bit of power left in it, and sent her brother a text, giving him a brief summary of events, asking where he kept the insurance papers and if he knew any plumbers or builders.

'Morning.'

She turned to face Robbie. Tousled and sleepy, he looked more gorgeous than ever. She put a hand to her hair, doubting she looked quite as sexy. 'Morning.'

He looked at his watch and jerked up in bed. 'Shit, I have to go.'

She tried to hide her disappointment. 'Oh, okay. Thanks for the help last night.'

He looked at her, puzzled. 'I won't be long. It's just it's my turn to do the school run.

172

She felt both relieved and guilty. 'You shouldn't have stayed over.'

'No, it was the right thing to do. The quicker the house dries out the less damage will be done. Besides' – he dropped a kiss on her hair – 'I can't remember the last time I slept so well.'

'I slept great too,' she said, surprised.

He got out of bed and looked around for his clothes.

'Damn, I can't have a wash.'

'I think your suit's downstairs on the hall table.'

'Oh, right, thanks.' He ran down to get it and returned, shrugging into his shirt. 'I'll call back for you after I've dropped the kids and take you to my place and you can shower and charge your phone.'

'Perhaps I should stay here and open the doors again.'

He shook his head. 'We can come straight back after we've had some breakfast.'

'You don't have to do that—'

'I know.' He bent to kiss her on the lips and groaned. 'You taste lovely and look as sexy as hell.'

'And you obviously haven't woken up yet,' she said laughing, but her heart soared at the desire in his eyes.

'I'm wide awake, I assure you.' He kissed her again and left.

Chapter Fifteen

Zoe was dressing when her phone rang. It was Shane.

'What's going on? Are you okay?'

'I'm fine. I wasn't here when it happened but it seems the boiler blew up. I came home to a paddling pool in the hall.'

'It came down the stairs?'

'No, the ceiling gave way under the weight of water. The bathroom and kitchen are a mess but everywhere else is fine. Good thing you never bothered carpeting the hall.'

'Shit, I'm sorry you had to deal with that alone.'

'I didn't, I had a friend with me.'

'A friend, eh? Anyone I know?'

She could hear the smile in his voice. 'Never you mind.'

'The insurance papers should be in the top drawer of the cabinet in my study, but I'm not sure we'll be covered. That boiler must be ancient and I think there's something in the policy about wear and tear. As for getting quotes, the only person I can think of is Greg Coleman.'

'I can't call him!' Zoe exclaimed, belatedly remembering Shane didn't know the situation. Damn it.

'I know what he did, Zoe. I talked to Tara.'

'Then you also know that you triggered it with your silly, selfish bloody texts,' she said, unleashing the fury she'd felt at his thoughtless behaviour.

'Trust me, nothing you can say can make me feel worse than I do already. Greg mightn't want to help me, but he'd help you just to get back in Tara's good books, and wouldn't it be better if he got the money rather than a stranger? From what Tara's told me, they need the cash. And, who knows, doing a bit of real work might pull him out of this stupor he seems to be in. I may be to blame for a lot of shit in this life, but that's one thing you can't pin on me.'

'What shit?' she asked, bemused.

'Nothing, never mind,' he muttered. 'Just talk to Tara. If she thinks it's a bad idea then I'll find someone else. Now, what about you? You can't stay there. You could stay with Tara. I'm sure she'd welcome the company.'

'Don't worry about me. I'll figure something out. But you need to come home, Shane. Someone is going to have to oversee all this.'

'But I'm not ready. I'm still working on an ending.'

She heard panic in his voice but ignored it. She couldn't keep mothering him. 'And I've just started rehearsals on another play, Shane. I spent half the night sweeping water out of your house and now have to chase up the insurance and plumbers and builders. You can't just walk away from your responsibilities any time you feel like it. You've been in Spain long enough to write a dozen plays. You'll have to finish it in Dublin.' Again there was silence so long she thought they'd been cut off. 'Shane?'

'If Greg is doing it then it's hardly a good idea for me to be around, is it?'

He had a point there. 'Then maybe we shouldn't use Greg. I just can't take this on, Shane.'

'Okay, calm down. Call me when you have more news and I'll sort something out.'

'Promise?'

He sighed. 'I promise.'

Celia finished putting the CDs back in the unit and looked around. Apart from the stain on the carpet where Albie had knocked over her coffee, the place looked fine again. Of course, if anyone were to turn over the seat cushions, they'd see the rips where he had hacked into them with a penknife in search of the money he was so sure she was hiding from him. Her eyes went to the stain and she thought of the wild look in Albie's eyes. He had been such a gorgeous child but his handsome features were hidden now under bloated grey skin, though he wasn't yet thirty.

Ophelia appeared at the window, pawing to get in. 'Traitor,' she reproached the feline, but opened the window and took down a tin of cat food. Whenever Albie appeared, Ophelia disappeared. Celia's father always used to say that you could trust an animal's instincts. The thought that the cat was wary of her son brought tears to her eyes. This was the first time she had felt really afraid of him yet she didn't think that he would actually hurt her. She was his mother and his cash cow. *But are you worth more dead than alive?* Two days running he'd harrassed her. What would he do if he came back a third time? She banished the silly thought and set the bowl down for the cat, stroking its soft coat as it ate. 'You have the right idea, darling. Look out for yourself – no one else will.'

Zoe's anxious face came to mind as she went into her sitting room and settled down with her knitting. Thank God she hadn't arrived ten minutes earlier. The thought of Zoe and Albie coming face to face made her shudder and she was immediately filled with guilt at being ashamed of her own son. But sometimes she was actually glad that Albert hadn't lived to see the terrible person he'd become. Every time she saw him, Celia searched for some redeeming feature and could find none. Had she been too old to bear a child? Had that resulted in some abnormality that made her son so hard and unfeeling? Or had she, as Albert thought, simply spoiled him to the point where he expected love and support without giving any in return? She'd hoped that, as an adult, when he had a responsible job, he would change. Though he was an average student in most subjects he excelled at maths and she'd had high hopes for him. While he picked up a job quite quickly, he'd been let go at the end of the probationary period. And that seemed to be the pattern: he would be hired but let go after a short time. When his employers got to know him, she surmised, sad and embarrassed at the thought. Given his frequent visits lately, his dishevelled appearance and demands for money, Celia suspected he was unemployed again.

The intercom buzzed and she froze, but common sense told her it wouldn't be Albie. He never even had the decency to knock on the door, but using his key would arrive unannounced. How she wished she had never given him a key.

Celia hoped it wasn't Zoe back to poke her nose in where it wasn't wanted. How stupid she had been to think Zoe was Albie, to cry out like that. But he had scared her and she hadn't been thinking rationally. The buzz came again and she answered for fear that it might be Robbie Prendergast. The last person she wanted to alienate was her director. She couldn't afford to.

She crossed the room and pressed the button. 'Yes?'

'Celia, it's Martha.'

'Oh! I wasn't expecting you until tomorrow.' Celia patted her hair and looked down to check her dress was presentable. It had seen better days but Martha would be too busy worrying about her husband and gawking at the flat to register what Celia was wearing.

'Thomas got bumped up the list. He's being operated on first thing. Are you going to let me in?'

'Oops, of course, sorry,' Celia trilled and pressed the button to admit her sister-in-law. 'Take the lift to the fourth floor, Martha. I'm in 4B.' She quickly adjusted a few cushions and moved the footstool over the coffee stain. She was standing at the hall door when the lift opened and Martha stepped out, holding her nose.

'I think something died in there,' she remarked as Celia hugged her and took her bag.

'The lady on the second floor has an incontinent poodle.'

'Madness having a dog in an apartment.'

'You look wonderful, Martha,' Celia said and she did. A shorter, older, female version of Albert, she was a thickset woman who always wore suits. Her hairstyle was severe but her lively dark eyes softened the look. Celia watched her take in her surroundings, unable to hide her dismay and concern. 'It's basic but it's home and it suits me,' Celia said, answering the unasked question. 'Is Thomas settled in okay?'

'I don't really know. He was brought up earlier today by ambulance and when I phoned, the surgeon was with him.'

'Is he nervous?' Celia asked, going into the tiny kitchen to put on the kettle.

Martha followed her, eyes taking in everything. 'No, he's relieved that it's finally happening.'

'I believe it's a very straightforward operation.'

'Apparently. How's Albie?'

'Very well indeed. He was here yesterday – he's always dropping in and out to check on me. I tell him there's no need but he worries about me.' Mortified by the disbelief in Martha's eyes, she turned away and reached up to take the biscuit tin down from the shelf. What did Martha know or suspect, and how? Celia had worked hard to isolate Albie from both family and friends. In fact, she was quite sure that the last time Martha had seen her son was at Albert's funeral.

'I'm glad to hear he's changed,' Martha said. 'I know Albert used to get very cross at the way he treated you.'

It required all of Celia's acting skills to hide her shock, but she could do nothing about the flush of her cheeks. What had Albert been thinking telling her that? They had been private people; they dealt with Albie's issues alone. Or didn't deal with them. 'I don't know why he would have said such a thing.' She shook her head, smiling. 'Oh, it was probably when I was nagging him to study for his exams. Albie was a typical teenager, hated putting in the hours.'

Martha settled her ample bottom on the sofa and, grimacing, tucked cushions behind her back. 'What is going on, Celia? Why on earth are you living in this place?'

'I told you, I like living in the city. It's not as lonely and I can walk everywhere.'

'You're broke, aren't you?' Martha said, never one to mince words.

Celia shrugged. 'I don't have much but my needs are few. I get by very well, very well indeed.'

'But I don't understand – you should be comfortably off – Albert was always so careful with his finances and you must have got a good price for the house.'

'We did.' Celia felt on safer ground as she went into the piece she'd rehearsed. 'But I've never been good with money – Albert took care of all that. When he died, I hired an accountant a friend had recommended and let him handle all my finances.'

Martha lowered her tea cup. 'He robbed you?'

Celia shrugged. 'Possibly, or it may have just been incompetence. He's under investigation.'

'Then you should be compensated – thank God for that.'

'Not necessarily. He seems to be broke or he's put the money somewhere they can't find it.'

'But he should be jailed!'

Celia was glad to see Martha outraged, which meant she was swallowing the story. 'He may well be, but that won't help me. Not that I need help, Martha, really. I have Albert's pension and happily I'm still working. I'm in rehearsal for a new play that I sense may go the distance,' she added, ignoring Robbie's direction to keep quiet about *Isabella*.

'But have you enough for this place? For electricity? And what if you get sick?'

'You're very cheerful,' Celia teased.

'I know what I'm talking about,' Martha assured her. 'Thomas has been on sick leave for months because of that damn hip.'

'This apartment is paid for and I have plenty to cover the bills, and if I got sick, Albie would look after me. He's changed, Martha.' *For the worse*, she added in her head. 'He's an adult now and very thoughtful and kind.'

'And so he should be.'

'Will I call a taxi to take you to the hospital?' Celia offered, already feeling claustrophobic. Whether or not there were rehearsals, she planned to stay out of the apartment as much as possible during Martha's stay. The woman was as smart as her brother had been and, no matter how good an actress Celia was, she was afraid of slipping up.

'No, I'll take the bus,' Martha said.

'Would you like me to come along?'

'No thanks, dear. I think tonight he'll want to rest. I won't stay long. Visit him after the operation – he'd love to see you then.'

'I'll have some dinner ready for you when you get home.'

'Just something light. I don't eat much in the evenings.' Martha heaved herself off the sofa. 'Could I freshen up?'

Celia stood up too. 'Of course. I'll show you your room. There's plenty of hot water if you want to take a bath or shower.'

She opened the door of the spare room and watched, humiliated, as Martha's eyes widened. Celia had done her best to make it more comfortable but the new cover and curtains didn't hide the damp patches on the wall, the mould around the window or the flutter of the curtain in the draught. Thank God it was summertime. Martha would freeze otherwise.

'Oh, Celia.' Martha looked at her, tears in her eyes. 'Albert would be so upset to see you living like this. When I think of your lovely home and garden in Dalkey.'

Celia fought hard to hold back her own tears. 'But, Martha, I'm ten minutes' walk from Stephen's Green and I don't have to weed flowerbeds or mow the lawn,' she joked.

Martha cracked a smile but her eyes were still sad. 'You know we'd love to help but with Thomas and his silly hip the future is uncertain—'

Celia held up a hand to stop her. 'Put that thought right out of your head. I am fine. You mustn't worry about me – I am perfectly content. Of course I still miss Albert but I have my work, I have my son and I have Ophelia. I quite like the simple life.'

'You never were one for parties,' Martha acknowledged, sitting down on the hard, narrow bed and dabbing her eyes. 'But you need your comforts as you get older.'

'Albie has plans to put in double-glazing and to upgrade the central heating but I think I'm better off with a hot-water bottle and a nice cup of tea. That recycled air plays havoc with my vocal cords.'

'You're a stubborn woman,' Martha told her. 'Let him look after you. You looked after him long enough.'

'Someday he'll have his own family to look after and he'll need every penny to do it,' Celia pointed out.

'Is there a woman on the scene?' Martha asked.

Celia smiled. 'I think there might be. I do hope so. I would love to see him settled. Anyway, I'm standing here nattering and keeping you from getting ready. The bathroom is right next door and I've left out towels. Call if you need anything else.'

'I will. Thanks, Celia.'

By the time Martha had gone, Celia's nerves were in tatters. If she was like this after a couple of hours, what would she be like by the time her sister-in-law went home? She set off for Moore Street to do the shopping she'd planned to do the following morning. Thank goodness that Martha hadn't made her unexpected arrival last night and seen the state of the apartment after Albie's visit.

Celia stocked up on fruit and vegetables, bought some fish for supper and lamb pieces for a shepherd's pie for tomorrow's meal and then threw caution to the wind and bought a couple of bottles of wine. Martha liked a little tipple and Celia didn't want her thinking that she was completely destitute. And if she were to carry off this charade for a week, maybe more, then she'd probably need sustenance herself. She prayed fervently that Thomas would make a speedy recovery.

Chapter Sixteen

Tara scraped her hair back into a bun and stared at her reflection. She looked and felt years older. Her skin was grey and her eyes were ... dead. She turned away from the mirror and went downstairs to start work. Finally she had the house to herself and could cook and bake whenever she wanted without Greg shuffling into the kitchen looking for food, but the house seemed very quiet without him. Especially at night. He sent her texts every couple of days, asking her to meet him or, at least, to talk to him on the phone. He even volunteered to go to a relationship counsellor if she felt nervous of meeting him alone, but the thought of discussing their problems in front of a stranger didn't appeal to Tara at all. She still hadn't told her parents what had happened and, thankfully, Zoe had stopped quizzing her about it. In fact, Zoe had been great. She helped out whenever she could and chatted about everything under the sun except Greg, and that suited Tara just fine. But she still would gently nudge Tara from time to time to at least let Greg know where he stood. She hoped Zoe wouldn't start going on about it today: she wasn't in the mood.

*

But when she arrived, Zoe had more pressing matters on her mind. Tara made a pot of tea and listened aghast as her friend told her about the flood. 'That's terrible. Did you call Shane? Is he coming home?'

'Of course I called and I told him to come home but I'm not holding my breath. I'm meeting an assessor from the insurance company at the house this morning and then I need to find someone to do the repairs and redecoration. I'm furious with Shane. I have enough on my plate at the moment and what do I know about plumbing? I'm way out of my depth.' She pulled a face. 'No pun intended.'

Tara digested this. She figured that Greg would do anything she asked him to right now, but was it a bit cheeky to ask him to help out Shane after the texting business? No, she decided. It had all been innocent, despite what he thought, and it was Zoe he'd be helping. 'Want me to call Greg? I'm sure he could recommend someone reliable.'

Relief flooded Zoe's face. 'Would you? I'd really appreciate it.'

'No problem,' Tara said. It was the least she could do for Zoe, but her stomach churned at the thought of talking to Greg. 'And you can move in here until it's all sorted. It would be fun.'

'Er, well . . .' Zoe's eyes twinkled.

'What? Have you met someone?' But she hadn't been out with a guy in months, or at least she hadn't mentioned anyone.

'I've moved in with Robbie.'

'Robbie Prendergast?' Tara asked, stunned.

'Yes.'

'Moved in as "in", he's putting a roof over your head for a while?'

'Sort of.'

'Zoe! What's going on?'

'Well, I suppose we're an item. It's only just happened really. He was with me when I got home last night. He was great, took off his suit and got stuck into the cleaning.'

'Did he indeed? I bet that was a sight to behold,' Tara teased, and Zoe actually blushed.

'He is easy on the eye,' she agreed.

Tara was thrilled to see her friend so happy. 'I'm delighted for you, Zo, but is moving in with him such a good idea? It's early days and you don't want to look too eager. Besides, you have to work together.'

'I'll only stay until the repairs are done, and believe me, I know how crazy this is, but it feels right, you know?'

Tara felt a lump in her throat and nodded. She knew. 'Just remember, if it doesn't work out, you're welcome to bunk down here.'

'Thanks, darling.'

'I think I'll send Greg a text. That way if he doesn't want to help Shane out it will give him time to think up an excuse.'

'Good idea.'

Tara tapped in the message.

Hi Greg. Zoe needs help/advice re house. If u call when suits, I'll fill u in.

He rang almost immediately and Zoe put a supportive hand on Tara's arm as she took a deep breath before answering. It would be the first time they'd talked since the day he left. 'Hello?' She hated the tremor in her voice and him for putting it there.

'Hi, Tara, how are you?'

'I'm okay.'

'I've missed you.'

She ignored that and explained why she had wanted to talk to him.

He was silent for a moment. 'Give me Zoe's number and I'll arrange to meet her at the house and take a look.'

She rattled off the number. 'Thanks, Greg.'

'Tara, talk to me, please? Meet me for a coffee somewhere, I don't care where, but we must talk.'

'I'll get back to you. Bye.'

'That can't have been easy,' Zoe said as Tara put down the phone. 'Thank you.'

'No problem. He says he'll call you to arrange a time to go and assess the damage.'

'Great. Oh, I almost forgot. I have more news!' Zoe shook her head. 'Yesterday was quite a day. You'll never guess who turned up on my doorstep.'

'Who?'

'Ed.'

Tara stared at her. 'My God. Why? What did he want?'

'To let me know that he's back in Ireland.'

'For good?' Tara asked.

'I'm not sure. He says he's doing a movie here.'

'Huh, so he finally made the big league; there's no justice. God, he's not the lead, is he?'

'I don't know anything more. I was waiting for Robbie to arrive to take me to dinner when he called.'

Tara grinned. 'Please tell me that he met Robbie.'

Zoe nodded, her face lighting up. 'It couldn't have worked

out better. Robbie arrived looking amazing in a gorgeous suit, and he pretended not to recognise Ed. I introduced them and Robbie swept me away, leaving Ed with his mouth hanging open.'

'Ha, fantastic. So, is he going to call back?'

'He wanted to have lunch today, but I told him I wasn't interested.'

'I'm impressed! Well done.'

'I'm not sure I'd have been as cool if I was on my own.'

'Well, you weren't. And Robbie Prendergast put on a suit to take you to dinner? He *must* fancy you!'

Zoe beamed. 'You know, I think he does.' She glanced at her watch and hopped to her feet.

'I'd better get over to the house. I don't want to miss the insurance man.'

'Let me know how it goes,' Tara called after her as Zoe left, and went back to chopping vegetables.

She was happy for Zoe. Her dad had worked with Robbie many times and she knew that he was a decent guy, nothing like Ed McGlynn. Or Greg for that matter. Robbie was self-effacing but exuded a quiet confidence. He was the stable factor that Zoe could do with in her life. Tara went through her tasks in her usual methodical way. When she had prepared as much as she could for the baby-shower party – when had Ireland adopted all these American traditions? – she started to clean up. Next to pounding dough, cleaning was her best stress-buster. She washed, scoured, scrubbed and polished until she was exhausted and the kitchen was spotless – she could clearly see her reflection in the worktops and glossy white doors. Her hands were red and she was breathing heavily and sweating. After she'd put all her cloths and her apron in the wash and set sponges and spatulas to sterilise, Tara poured herself a large glass of wine, took it upstairs, and ran a bath. As it filled she got the nailbrush and scrubbed under her nails before stripping off her clothes and lowering herself into the foam. She raised the glass to her lips. So what that it was only lunchtime? She'd been on the go since seven and she wouldn't be driving until five. It was a damn miracle she was able to stop at one.

Zoe wasn't sure how she was going to handle this. It had seemed like a good idea to ask for Greg's help but, when he arrived shortly after the insurance man had left and held out his hand to shake hers, all she could think of was it slapping Tara, leaving her cut and bruised. He lowered it and looked down at his feet. He looked so inoffensive and quiet and, yes, boring. It was hard to imagine him in a rage. Though built like a rugby player, Greg looked much older than his thirty-eight years, in his baggy jeans and old sweatshirt. His greying hair looked like it hadn't seen a brush in some time. In other circumstances she'd probably have felt sorry for him, but not any more. She couldn't even raise a smile.

'Thanks for coming. Greg,' she said, her voice stiff.

'Sure,' he mumbled and followed her inside. 'Has the risk assessor been out?' he asked.

'He's just left. He didn't say much so I'm not sure where we stand.'

'Can I take a look at the bathroom?' he asked.

'Please.' She waved a hand towards the stairs and prayed he would recommend someone else for the job. Now that she'd come face to face with him, she wasn't sure that she could handle being around him. She had been pushing Tara to talk to Greg, to give him a second chance, but what if Tara took him back and he hit her again and kept hitting?

'I'm just going up to the attic to check the tank,' he called out.

'Okay!' She went outside, to sit on the front step and await the verdict.

'It's not as bad as it looks,' he said a little while later, his voice coming from directly behind her, making her jump. She scrambled to her feet as he turned away, shaking his head.

'I'm not some kind of monster, Zoe.'

'Aren't you?' she blurted out.

'You don't know what it's been like.'

'I don't need to.'

Greg turned to face her, his expression tortured. 'You don't know,' he repeated.

'I know you hit her,' she retorted, angry at him daring to defend himself. But what was she doing taking him on? What was to stop him giving her a slap too? She backed away into the driveway so that if he did try anything a neighbour would be bound to see.

His eyes widened as he realised she was afraid of him and he flopped down onto the step. 'I don't believe this. I won't lay a finger on you, don't worry. I never intended to touch Tara, but she'd been pushing and pushing and something snapped.'

'Yeah, probably her neck. Look at the size of you! Hitting Tara, is like hitting a child.'

He looked up, his expression hardening. 'There's nothing defenceless about Tara.'

Zoe came closer, hands on her hips. 'What's that supposed to mean?'

'She's a lot tougher than she looks.'

'She's my friend, I know what she's like. And if she wasn't as strong as she is, you probably would have lost your home by now.'

Greg stood up and headed for the car. 'I'll put some figures together and come back to you,' he said over his shoulder.

'Don't put yourself out,' Zoe muttered as he got into his car and drove off.

The tension of her day disappeared as Zoe relaxed in Robbie's bath while he cooked dinner. She smiled at the sound of him whistling along to a song on the radio. It was hard to believe that they only got together yesterday and that she was going to spend the night with him in his house; and, though he had told her there was no pressure, she had no intention of using the spare room. Last night, Shane's house might have been cold and damp but she'd felt ridiculously content and secure in Robbie's arms and she wanted to lie in them again tonight. Despite the steaming water, she shivered with excitement at the thought of him making love to her. She had expected some awkwardness this morning but, true to his word, Robbie had called back to collect her after the school run, and once she'd washed and changed, they'd gone for a lazy breakfast and then he'd dropped her at Tara's before going on to meet Gerald. It had seemed so natural and relaxed, as if they had been dating for months.

She stepped out of the bath, wrapped a towel around herself and then massaged in the expensive scented moisturiser that Tara had bought her for Christmas. She put on her prettiest pyjamas, not the sexy sort Isabella would wear. But tonight, she wanted to be Zoe, just Zoe. She dried her hair and went out to join Robbie in the kitchen.

'Hey,' she said, feeling suddenly shy.

He looked round, his eyes darkening as they raked her from head to toe. 'I'm not sure about the food but *you* certainly look good enough to eat.' He pulled her into his arms and buried his face in her neck. 'You smell good too.'

Zoe snuggled closer and raised her mouth to his. She would happily forego dinner and drag him straight to bed, craving the feel of his bare skin against hers. But she was touched that he had gone to the trouble of cooking for her and they had all evening, all night, and, hopefully, many nights to follow.

When they broke apart, she licked her lips. 'You taste of wine.'

'You taste of more.' He poured her a glass. 'I'm afraid I'm not a very adventurous cook. It's just steak, onions and salad.' He tossed the meat into the smoking pan.

'It sounds like a feast,' she assured him. 'I'd have offered to cook for you but Terence says I'm useless.'

He frowned. 'You've cooked for him.'

She leaned against the counter and took a sip of wine. 'Only once. After that, he insisted he'd cook or we would eat out.'

His frown grew deeper. My God, he was jealous! And while

that delighted her, she knew she had to reassure her. The last thing she wanted was to come between the two men. She reached up to kiss his cheek. 'We eat together, we talk and we rehearse. That's all, Robbie.'

He flicked the steaks over. 'I believe you but I still don't like it. He's so proprietorial around you.'

'Both you and Tara told me he's like that with all his leading ladies,' she reminded him.

He grimaced. 'Yeah, well, it's not as easy to handle when y*ou're* the lady involved.'

'How do you know that I'm a lady,' she murmured with a mischievous smile.

'Keep looking at me like that and you won't get fed,' he warned, pulling her in for another kiss.

She wound her body around his. 'I'm in no hurry to eat.'

He raised an eyebrow. 'No? Then perhaps we should do something to whet your appetite.' And, putting the lid on the pan, he switched off the hob and led her towards the bed-room.

It was almost eleven when they finally sat down in the candle-lit kitchen and tucked into steak-and-salad sandwiches.

'I doubt this dinner comes up to Terence's standards,' he said, with a lopsided grin.

'Oh, I don't know. It's very tasty and the starter was truly incredible,' Zoe said with feeling. Her body glowed from their lovemaking and, as she watched him lick his lips, she had a sudden craving for afters.

'I find it hard to believe that we've only just got together, we seem to . . .' he searched for a word.

'Fit.' They said it together and then laughed, delighted with themselves, caught up in the wonders of new love.

'This tastes damn good.' Zoe munched on her sandwich, her eyes never leaving his. His hair was tousled, there was a tiny bit of sauce on the corner of his sexy mouth and he was looking at her as if he wanted to devour her. It had never been like this with Ed. Yes, it had been passionate but, with Robbie, there was something more, something different that she couldn't quite define. He was gentle, tender and considerate and – then the word came to her – respectful. In the short time she'd known him and throughout these intimate couple of days, he had shown her nothing but respect and that meant more to her than flattery or flowers.

After they cleared up, they went back to bed and talked about their lives. Zoe told him about her parents, recalling her few childhood memories and Robbie, his voice full of pride, told her about Samantha – Sammy – and Nick and how they'd changed the way he looked at everything. And then he made love to her again, slowly, almost reverently. As she drifted off to sleep, Robbie spooning her, his arm around her waist and his steady breath on her cheek, she relaxed into him, feeling as if she had finally found home.

The next morning, back at Shane's, Zoe went from room to room, gathering belongings she wanted to take with her. Her mind wasn't fully on the task. All she could think of was

Robbie and the magical night they'd spent together. She filled a suitcase and an overnight bag and was about to phone for a taxi when the doorbell rang. It couldn't be Greg back, surely. No, probably Terence. He'd called a couple of times and left messages but she hadn't had a chance to get back to him. But when she opened the door, a girl on crutches gave her a shy smile.

'Hi, you must be Zoe, I'm Rachel. Is Shane in?'

Zoe took in the scar that ran from the girl's eye to her chin, the bandaged arms and the leg in plaster and wondered how the girl had managed to make her way here.

'My dad's waiting in the car,' the girl said, obviously seeing Zoe's puzzled expression. 'I'm just out of hospital. I wanted to check on Shane. I haven't seen him since the accident and I was worried.'

Zoe stared at her, stunned, her heart sinking. 'Please, come in.' She took the girl into the sitting room and, as Rachel carefully lowered herself onto the sofa, Zoe propped cushions behind her to try to make her more comfortable.

'Thanks.'

Zoe sat next to her. 'I'm sorry, I can't even offer you tea. We had a minor flood and the water and electricity is switched off. I was just leaving. I'm staying with a friend.'

'Isn't Shane here?'

'No, he's in Spain. This is the first I've heard of an accident. Is my brother okay?'

The girl reached out to squeeze her hand. 'Oh, I'm so sorry! Yes, he's fine, some cuts and bruises but that's all, thankfully.'

'What happened?' Zoe asked, her concern for her brother rising.

'It was my fault. I was driving too fast and a cyclist came out of a side road and I swerved to avoid hitting him and lost control and we ended up in the ditch.'

'Oh, God.' Zoe cradled her arms around herself, her heart racing. It felt like history was repeating itself.

Rachel looked worriedly at Zoe. 'Are you okay?'

'Yes, please go on.'

'We met at a party and were on our way back to my place, but I wasn't drinking, honestly.' She sighed. 'I was just a bit distracted.'

Zoe could imagine exactly how distracting her brother would have been when he was with such a pretty girl.

'I blacked out and didn't come to until the next morning. I was frantic to know if Shane was okay. Nobody seemed to know where he was. Finally, a doctor told me that he had discharged himself once they'd treated him.'

'When did this happen?'

Rachel frowned, thinking. 'It would have been the eleventh, it was a Wednesday.'

The day before Shane had taken off for Spain. Zoe had left the house the next morning, assuming he was fast asleep, but he'd actually been in hospital. And he'd called her later in the day from the airport.

'I rang a few times, left messages, and eventually he sent me a text saying he was okay and he'd call me in a few days but he hasn't.' Rachel raised her sad eyes to meet Zoe's. 'I can understand him being angry with me but I just wanted to apologise.'

'I'm sure that he doesn't blame you,' Zoe assured her. 'Truly. The thing is, Shane was in a car accident many years ago and both our parents died. I'm guessing this brought it all back to him and that's why he freaked out.'

Rachel's eyes widened in horror. 'Oh, wow, the poor guy. No wonder he didn't want to talk to me.'

'I doubt he was capable of talking. He was probably in shock, perhaps he still is. Don't blame yourself in any way, Rachel. How wonderful that you reacted so quickly or that cyclist might have been injured or even dead now.'

'That's what Dad says.'

'Your dad's right. Now go home and stop worrying. I'll take care of Shane.'

She didn't have to think about it. There were no choices to be made. After Rachel had left, Zoe called a cab and went to Robbie's flat and, telling the driver to wait, she let herself in with the key he'd presented her with a few hours earlier. She gathered her belongings and paused, wondering whether to leave a note or call him. She decided on a note, unable to deal with questions. She left the key next to the note and, going back out to the cab, directed the driver to Tara's house.

Zoe had already called her friend so, when the taxi pulled up outside the house, Tara hurried out to help her with the bags. 'Pay the driver and let him go,' she told Zoe. 'I'm taking you to the airport.'

*

At the kitchen table, Zoe drank the coffee Tara put in front of her. 'It makes sense now, doesn't it?'

'Yes,' Tara agreed, 'but I'm sure that Shane will be fine. He sounded okay on the phone.'

'He said he'd gone because he was struggling with the play.' Zoe shook her head. 'Why didn't he tell me the truth?'

'Because you're his little sister and he doesn't want you worrying about him.' Tara grinned. 'He told me he was avoiding an irate husband. What's the story with Rachel? Is she his girlfriend?'

'No, not at all, they'd just met and were going back to her place.'

'Have you told him you're coming?' Tara asked.

'No, I'll call him from the airport.'

'And what does Robbie think of all this?'

Zoe sighed. 'I couldn't go into it all, Tara, so I took the coward's way out and left him a note. He's going to be furious with me for walking out on rehearsals. Your dad, too, for that matter.'

'You'll probably be back in a couple of days and everything will be fine.'

'Oh, shit, I forgot all about the damn house.' Zoe dropped her head in her hands, feeling suddenly drained and emotional.

'Leave the key with me,' Tara said. 'I'll make sure that Greg sorts it.'

Zoe looked at the steel in her friend's eyes and was reminded of Greg's comment that she wasn't defenceless. 'We had words,' she admitted.

'About me? Oh, Zoe.' Tara sighed. 'You should have stayed out of it.'

'I intended to but when I saw him I couldn't stop myself. Don't deal with him if you find it too hard. I don't want him upsetting you any more than he has already. It's only a bloody house. It can wait until I get back. Frankly, it's the least of my worries.'

'Forget Greg, and the play and Dad and Robbie, Zo. You've got your priorities in order. Shane needs you, it's that simple.'

Zoe nodded. 'Yes, you're right, it is.'

'Have you booked a flight?'

'No, I was going to wait until I got to the airport.'

'Madness. It's coming into holiday season.' Tara opened her laptop and within twenty minutes had booked Zoe on an early-evening flight to Málaga.

Tara unloaded the bags from the back of the van at Departures and turned to give Zoe a hug. 'Give him my love.'

'I will.'

'What do I tell everyone?'

'The truth.' Zoe looked at her. 'Tell them Shane needs me.'

Chapter Seventeen

Shane didn't hear the phone the first couple of times. He'd fallen asleep at the patio table, the ashtray and empty tequila bottle glowing in the dim light from his laptop. The phone rang again and he winced at the noise. He glanced at the screen and answered immediately when he saw it was his sister. What on earth would she be doing calling at this hour?

'Zoe? Is everything okay?'

'I could ask you the same question but right now I just need your address.'

'My address? Why?'

'Because I'm at Málaga Airport.'

'What? Why? I don't understand.'

'Rachel came to see me.'

For a moment, he couldn't even remember who Rachel was and then it all came flooding back. He called out the address and gave her directions and then went to make up another bed, sober now although his head ached. He felt relieved that Zoe was here and terrified too. He wondered what to tell her.

Now she'd met Rachel, she'd have figured out why he'd done a runner. At least she'd think she had. He was touched that she had got straight on a plane. He poured himself another drink, lit a cigarette and went back out to sit on the patio to wait. From here he'd see the car snaking its way up to the house. His phone beeped and he went back inside, smiling when he read Penny's text.

I've finished work early and fancy some skinny-dipping. x

The girl was insatiable. She came up to see him a couple of times a week and was naked within seconds. She had no inhibitions and seemed to want nothing from him other than sex, and he was happy to oblige. Reluctantly, he tapped in his reply:

Sorry. My sister is visiting. I'll call you. x

Any other woman would think that was a brush-off and go into a sulk but not Penny:

No prob. Bring her into the bar tomorrow. Nite. x

When he went back outside it wasn't long before Shane saw the lights of the taxi as it weaved its way up the hill. He went to the front of the house to switch on the porch and garden lights and stood, smoking, until the car turned into the driveway. He ground the cigarette out in a flower pot and went to greet his sister. Despite his fear and anxiety, he couldn't but be pleased to see her and, crushing her in his arms, he lifted her off her feet. 'Hey, Zo.'

When he put her down, she looked up and met his eyes. 'Glad I'm here?' she asked.

'Definitely,' he said and meant it. He paid the driver and carried her bag into the house.

'Want a drink or are you ready for bed?'

She tossed her jacket on a chair and wandered round the room. 'What do *you* think? I didn't come here to sleep. Nice place, Diana did well for herself. If I was her, I'd be out here every chance I could get.'

He opened some wine, smiling at her rather obvious way of asking when he was coming home. 'She's spoiled for choice. Apparently, the family is in Australia at the moment.'

Zoe wandered out onto the patio and gasped at the pool, the panoramic view of the twinkling lights of Nerja below and the moon on the water in the distance. 'I can see the attraction. Are you writing?'

Shane took her glass out to her. 'Yes and no. I'm at a point where the story could go in one of two directions and I can't make up my mind which way is best.'

'Want me to read it?' she offered.

He pretended to think about it and then shook his head. 'Not yet.'

She stretched out on one of the cushioned loungers, kicked off her shoes and looked up at him. 'Tell me about the accident.'

'Which one?' He refilled his glass, before sitting down, glad of the gloom that hid the pain in his eyes.

'Either, both.' She shrugged. 'Your call.'

'Poor Rachel. Is she okay?'

'She just got out of hospital. She has a broken leg, injuries to her arms and a nasty scar on her face.'

He shivered. 'I did go and see her before I left, Zo, honestly, but she was asleep and they told me that she was going to be fine.'

'The accident, Shane,' his sister prodded gently.

'Just like the first time,' he told her, 'it all happened in the blink of an eye, and yet in slow motion. She was giggling and chatting and one minute we were driving along this quiet stretch of road and the next thing this guy on a bike appeared out of nowhere. She swerved to avoid him and we went off the road. At first, I was shaken, didn't really know what the hell had happened. I remember thinking how quiet it was and then I looked over and saw her.' He shuddered and reached for his glass, remembering the red blood against the white skin pressed at an awkward angle against the dashboard. 'I thought she was dead. I talked to her but she didn't respond and I knew that I wasn't supposed to move her. I probably wouldn't have been able to anyway – the car was on its side, the passenger side. The only way out was if I climbed over her and that didn't seem like a good idea. I don't know how long it was, probably only minutes, but I heard voices. Someone called down that help was on its way. I must have passed out then because the next thing I remember I was being lifted into the ambulance.'

'How come no one called me?' Zoe asked, shaking her head. 'Isn't it the norm to call the next of kin?'

'Because I was conscious, they asked me who they should call. I said there was only you and that you were in London on business and it would be ridiculous to phone you when I was obviously fine.'

'Jeez, Shane!'

He shrugged. 'I didn't want you to get a call like that. I was kept in overnight, just to be on the safe side. We were both lucky to be alive. When I got home, you'd gone out.'

'I thought you were asleep in bed. You should have called me.'

'I wasn't thinking straight. Seeing Rachel like that brought everything back and I fell to pieces. I had to get away. I called Diana. I knew she had a flat in London that she wouldn't mind me using for a couple of days. I told her it was writer's block and she suggested I come here instead.'

'But it's not about the writing at all, or the crash with Rachel, for that matter. It's about Mam and Dad, isn't it?'

'Yeah.' He got up and walked to the end of the patio and lit a cigarette. How could he explain to her the thoughts that haunted him, the ones he tried to escape in the curves of Penny's luscious body and which returned every time he closed his eyes or tried to write? He wanted to write fiction but the truth kept getting in the way. It terrified him and he ended up walking the streets of Nerja or sitting in a bar, or having sex or swimming lengths of the pool until he slept from sheer exhaustion.

Conscious that his sister was waiting for an answer, he came back and sat down. 'When I looked at Rachel, all I could see was Mam.'

Zoe put down her glass, dropped to her knees and rested her head on his lap. 'I wasn't much use to you then but I'm here for you now, Shane. Let it out. Tell me. Please?'

He stroked her hair, tears filling his eyes. 'I'm sorry, Zoe, I'm so sorry.'

'Hush, there's no need to be sorry. Everything will be okay.

We can talk about it all, get everything out in the open. You'll feel better then.'

'Will I?' he said, wishing he could believe it.

She looked up at him. 'I won't leave you until you do.'

His stomach heaved at the love and trust in her eyes but he forced himself to smile. 'Okay then, but first let's get hammered.'

And they did. At seven the next morning, Zoe dragged herself out of bed and went into the kitchen in search of water. She found a jug and a glass and carried them out onto the patio, setting them down on the table before going to lean on the wall and look out on the incredible view. If she lived here she figured she'd never stay indoors. She eyed the pool. It looked deliciously inviting but she decided to wait until the sun came up and it was warmer before she braved the water.

Her thoughts turned to last night and the conversation with her brother, who seemed at once so strong and so fragile. She knew that he was keeping things from her, trying to protect her as he had all her life, but it was time to put an end to that. She had no intention of leaving here until he spilled his guts. Depression had always dogged him and she was convinced it was because he wouldn't discuss the accident. The fact that Gerry and Hannah had never talked about it didn't help, although she knew they'd meant well. Poor Shane. He was so handsome and talented and clever and funny and yet he had never had a proper relationship. She was convinced that all his problems and moods were because of the crash that had robbed them of their parents and she was determined to get to the bottom of it once and for all. She'd have to tread carefully, though, let him set the pace. If she pushed him too far, he might withdraw even more.

When he had steered her unsteadily towards her room in the early hours, hugged her and said he was glad she'd come, she figured he meant it. She might not get to play Isabella, she might be letting down Terence, who had been so generous with his time and taught her so much, and as for Robbie . . .

This time yesterday, she was curled in his arms, thinking that finally she had met a man she could be happy with. And she'd run out on him. He would be hurt and angry but she didn't have the time to explain her family's history and balked at putting her fears into writing. She didn't have to do any of that with Tara. Her friend understood Shane and knew exactly why Zoe needed to be with him now. But she didn't have any idea how long this would take, and so it would be best if Robbie found another actress to play Isabella. She didn't want to string him along with promises she might not be able to keep. God, it was a mess but she honestly couldn't see what other choice she had.

She watched the sun's rays peep over the horizon, casting an orange glow over the water. As the light improved, she looked around her and marvelled at how sumptuous the villa was. Trust Shane. When he had a breakdown he did it in style. Not for him some squalid back-street bedsit, but a five-bedroom luxurious villa with breathtaking views and fitted out with the highest-quality furnishings. The patio was surrounded by colourful flowerbeds that must cost a fortune to water, and the garden furniture was upholstered in soft cream leather, the frames made of wrought iron that probably weighed a ton. The pool itself was a work of art: there was a very sexy mural of a mermaid on the bottom that bore an uncanny resemblance to Diana. How did Shane not only manage to bag women like that, but remain friends with them? He almost always ended the relationships, yet none of the women seemed bitter.

And how could he be such a sad soul when he was surrounded by such love? It was almost as if he was waiting for it to be whipped away or another catastrophe to befall him. Zoe wondered if she was meddling in something that was beyond her. The responsibility of getting this right overwhelmed her. Just listen to him, she told herself, and take it from there.

Zoe was in the pool, slightly less hungover having done a few lengths, when Shane appeared in shorts and sunglasses. She bit her lip when she saw the scars on his chest, old and new.

'Morning,' he said, sitting down on the edge and dangling his feet in the water.

'Hi. Do you feel as lousy as I do?'

'Worse, I imagine.'

She smiled. 'Will I make some breakfast?'

'I've very little in. How about coffee and then we can go into town and get a nice greasy fry-up and pay a visit to the supermarket to stock up?'

'Sounds like a plan,' she agreed. But afraid they would lose the closeness of last night, she added, 'Still glad I came?' She couldn't see his eyes behind the mirrored frames but the smile was genuine.

'I'm delighted you're here.'

He warned her about the hill and offered to take her into town on the moped, but she knew that would be tough for him so she settled for the bikes. Still, it was a good sign that he'd been willing to drive so soon after the accident. It was a perfect morning and as they free-wheeled down into Nerja, Zoe forgot about her brother's troubles and the chaos she'd left behind in Dublin, and savoured the sea air and sun on her face. They ate breakfast in comfortable silence, sitting outside a café in the square, people-watching, and Zoe felt the tension drain from her body.

When they'd finished, Shane led her a few minutes along the coast and down a narrow path to the most beautiful cove with only a handful of people. They left their bikes against a rock, took off their shoes and walked along the beach through the surf.

'It's perfect here,' she said.

'Yes.' He skimmed stones across the water.

'But you can't stay. At least, not like this.'

He looked at her. 'Like what?'

Zoe looked up at him. 'Hiding.'

He said nothing and they kept walking and then he started to chuckle. 'Remember when Mam took us to Galway for a week? The weather was lousy but we still spent all our time on the beach.'

She laughed at the memory. 'She sat huddled on a blanket with her coat on and we were dodging the waves.'

'And the sandwiches really were *sand*wiches.'

'Ugh, yeah, gritty banana, I remember. How come Dad wasn't with us?' she asked. Her memory was hazy. She couldn't have been more than five.

'He was probably at work.'

'I remember so little about them,' she said, feeling sad. 'Especially Dad. I suppose it was because Mam was at home with us all day.'

'And often he didn't come home until after you were in bed.'

'Are we like either of them?' she asked. Any of the family photos they had were mainly of her and Shane, taken on holidays, birthdays or at Christmas.

He looked at her and smiled. 'We have Mam's eyes and you sometimes hold your head in the same way as she did. I'm afraid I have Dad's moodiness and temper.' He stopped to collect more stones.

'Mam could be pretty moody too, couldn't she? I remember her being great fun some days and others she'd stay in the bedroom and leave you to mind me.'

He glanced at her. 'You remember that?'

She nodded. 'Was she sick?'

He skimmed a couple more stones before replying. 'Migraine, I think. Any news from Gerry and Hannah?'

'No.' Zoe pulled a face. It had been a while since she'd been to visit. 'I'll go and see them when I get back. Life's been so hectic lately.' She looked at him. 'Come with me?'

He laughed. 'That's a trick question.'

'I'm not trying to trick you, Shane.'

'I know.' He stopped and frowned. 'Aren't you in a new play? Should you be here?'

'The writer had some changes to make so we're on a break,' she fibbed. He'd enough to worry about and she didn't want him trying to talk her into going home.

'So life is hectic. Why?'

'Well, there was that other play I was in and I've attended some auditions and I help Tara out as much as I can.' They reached the far side of the cove and she sat down on a rock.

He dropped down onto the sand and sat cross-legged in front of her. 'Is she okay?'

'Not really.'

His face darkened. 'I could kill that bastard, I really could. After all that she's done for him, all she's put up with. Has the man no idea how lucky he is?'

'He always seemed so quiet and inoffensive.'

'Until he hit her. Is she going to stick to her guns, do you think, and divorce him?'

Zoe heard the hopeful note in his voice. 'You still love her, don't you?'

He said nothing, just started drawing patterns in the sand with his finger.

'Is she the reason you've never settled down with anyone?'

He shrugged. 'Maybe I'm just not the settling down kind.'

'I could never understand why you fecked off to France that time. If you'd stayed in Dublin, Tara wouldn't have met Greg or, if she had, she wouldn't have given him a second glance.'

He looked up at her. 'You think so?'

'Yes, I do. You were a great couple.' She stared out to sea for a moment before speaking again. 'Ed is back in Dublin. He came to see me.' Even behind his sunglasses, she could see Shane scowl. 'He's going to be in a movie.'

'What did he want?'

'To talk.'

He pushed up his glasses and glared at her. 'You're not getting back with him?'

'Of course not. Did you know he was seeing other girls before we left for London?'

'What?' Shane's eyes filled with fury. 'No, of course not! If I'd known, do you think I'd have let you go off to England with him? Piece of shit. I suppose I shouldn't be surprised. I'll never understand why you were so besotted with the guy.'

'Come on, he's gorgeous and I was flattered too, I suppose.'

'You're gorgeous,' he said, frowning. 'Inside and out, and you certainly couldn't describe Ed that way, two-faced fucker. Who told you about his carrying-on in Dublin?'

'Tara. She knew all along.'

'What?' He seemed shocked by that. 'And she never told you?'

She shook her head. 'We had a terrible row. We only made up because of what happened with Greg. It didn't seem as important after that.'

'But why would she let you marry Ed?'

'She said Greg told her to mind her own business.'

'I suppose it's understandable that she listened to him. She was only a kid and he was so much older. She seemed to go along with whatever he said.'

Her ears pricked up at this. 'You noticed that too?'

'Sure. Don't you remember how she stopped hanging around with us? They were always doing things with Greg's family or friends.'

'True.'

He looked at her. 'How did you feel, seeing Ed again, having heard all that? Did you let him have it?'

Zoe smiled. She'd wondered so many times what she'd do if Ed ever turned up and begged her to take him back. Would she be strong enough to resist or would she fall for his bullshit all over again? Then when Tara dropped her bombshell, she'd imagined tearing strips off him. But when he'd stood before her that day, she realised none of it mattered. She felt nothing for Ed McGlynn any more, nothing at all.

'It was a bit of a shock when he turned up but, you know, I was fine. The conversation lasted less than five minutes. I was on my way out.'

'Good.' He nodded in approval. 'He's a bad lot. God, I was so mad with you when you went to London.'

'Trust me, I remember,' she assured him. 'Let's not go there.'

'Agreed.' He glanced at his watch. 'We'd better get down to the supermarket – they'll be shutting for siesta time soon.'

She groaned. 'I just remembered that hill.'

He laughed. 'But at the top is a nice, cool pool and some very comfy sunbeds.'

'If I make it that far,' she said, and followed him back across the hot sand.

Chapter Eighteen

'What do you mean, she's gone away?' Terence bellowed, unable to believe his ears. His words reverberated around the rehearsal room as he glared at Robbie, waiting for some kind of explanation.

'What I say,' Robbie replied. 'I called Anna Kerrigan's agent to see if she is available. If not, I'll get Lauren to set up auditions.'

'Now hang on a minute, Robbie. There's no need to be so hasty. When will she be back? I'm sure we can move things around to accommodate her. She wouldn't have just abandoned us.'

'That's exactly what she's done,' Robbie said, his voice like ice. 'She said she had no idea how long she would be away and it would be best if we replaced her.'

'It is rather odd,' Celia remarked. 'She seemed elated to have got the part.'

'She was,' Terence agreed, surprised and grateful for the support. 'There must be a very good reason for her absence. Let's not rush into anything. She is so perfect in the role. No one will play Isabella as well as Zoe.'

Celia rolled her eyes. 'It was very unprofessional of her to walk out without giving some notice. Even if she comes back, how do we know we can trust her not to do it again?'

So much for the support. Terence glared at her before looking back at Robbie. 'Give me a moment.' He waited until he was outside the building before dialling Zoe's number. It went straight to voicemail. 'Zoe, darling, what on earth's going on?' he said, trying to keep the anger out of his voice. 'Call me as soon as you get this.' He rang off and dialled again. 'Tara, do you know where the hell Zoe is?' He heard her sigh.

'Yes, Dad. She's in Spain with Shane. He's not well and she's gone to look after him. She left Robbie a note explaining all this.'

Terence hesitated for a moment. 'Is it serious? Is he dying?'

'No, nothing like that—'

'Then she has no business being there. Tell her to come home at once.'

'That's not going to happen, Dad. She'll stay as long as Shane needs her.'

'This is unforgivable.' He hung up and stood for a moment, trying to regain his composure. He felt angry, disappointed and, yes, betrayed. He went back up to the room but said nothing until Celia had left.

'I talked to my daughter. She seems to think that Zoe has very good reasons for her behaviour. Zoe's brother is sick but it doesn't seem to be a physical problem.'

'I gathered as much but it doesn't change things, Terence. We must find someone else to play Isabella.'

Terence went over it again and again in his head. Zoe had been living to play this part. Only something really serious would make her rush off to Spain. The fact that Tara was supporting her friend confirmed that. Only his daughter didn't know everything. He looked at Robbie. 'I need to talk to Tara again. Because you told us all to keep quiet about *Isabella*, she doesn't realise this play could change the course of Zoe's career.'

'I'd forgotten about the gagging order,' Robbie admitted, 'but I don't see what difference it makes. Zoe knew what she was doing. She was crystal clear, Terence. Her brother had to come first.'

'Which was incredibly unselfish given what she was prepared to give up for him,' Terence pointed out. 'Let's wait just a few days before rushing into replacing her, please?'

Robbie sighed. 'Okay, then, but I wouldn't get your hopes up. If this is a mental-health issue, there's no knowing how long it will take.'

'All I'm asking is that we give her a week or two. We owe her that, surely.'

Robbie met his eyes, looking slightly ashamed of himself. 'Yeah, I suppose we do.'

Tara lifted the last batch of scones out of the oven, left them to cool and took a large glass of wine into the garden. She sank into the deckchair and kicked off her sandals. As she took a sip, she spied her flowerbeds and herb garden with a critical eye. They badly needed weeding and watering but she could only do so much. Her phone beeped and she reached into the pocket of her apron to see who wanted her now.

New tank and boiler installed. Tiler coming tomorrow. G.

She sighed. Her husband felt this need to keep her informed of every single step of the renovation and she really couldn't care less.

Grand, she typed back, pressed Send and took another drink. Having to communicate with him at all put her on edge but she'd promised Zoe. She figured she owed her friend for not having told her about Ed's womanising and for her being such a support when Greg had ... she stopped, she didn't want to go there.

There was a knock at the front door and, though she wasn't in the mood for visitors, the thought that it might be work-related propelled her out of the comfortable chair. She went back into the house, headed down the hall, barefoot, and opened the door.

'Hello, stranger.'

'Hi, Dad.' She returned his kiss and tried to look pleased to see him, but she suspected he was here to rant about Zoe's desertion again.

'You look terrible.'

'Thanks.' She fetched him a glass of wine and led him outside.

'Any news?' he asked.

'If you mean have I been talking to Zoe, no.' She felt irritated by her father and his beloved play. He didn't live in the real world at all. Immaculate in a casual blue shirt – he always wore blue or white, blue to complement his eyes and white to show off his tan – beige chinos and deck shoes, he looked young and healthy and vibrant, none of which she felt at the moment.

He wandered around her little garden, bending to sniff the

thyme before coming back to join her. 'Where's Gregarious Greg?'

At least she could answer that honestly. 'He's working on Shane and Zoe's house.'

Terence frowned. 'Doing what?'

She explained about the accident and subsequent damage and how Greg was sorting it all out. 'I'm surprised Robbie didn't mention it,' she said.

'What's Robbie got to do with it?'

'He was with Zoe when it happened.' She saw the surprise on his face. 'You didn't know they were seeing each other?'

'No, I didn't. Is it serious?'

She suppressed a smile. He was always so possessive about his leading lady. 'I've no idea, Dad. I mind my own business. You should try it sometime.'

He gave her a knowing look. 'Oh, please, don't be so prim and proper. I've no doubt she told you every last detail and you loved every minute of it.'

She shook her head, laughing. 'You can pry all you like, I'm saying nothing.'

He smiled. 'It was worth a shot. But that's not why I came over.'

'No?'

'We need you to talk to Zoe about the play.'

'Oh, Dad, she has more on her mind than some stupid play.'

'What exactly is wrong with Shane, Tara?'

'I don't know the full story, neither does Zoe. That's why she had to go out there. She's the only one he has.'

He leaned forward. 'Darling, there's something you don't understand. Zoe has a very big part in this play. We need her.'

'Oh, please, there are actresses queuing up to play opposite you.'

He smiled. 'Thanks for the compliment but that's not the point. Zoe is good. No' – he shook his head – 'she's not good, she's great. And this play is great. And it could launch her career big time.'

Tara stared at him. 'But why didn't she tell me that?'

'It's a marketing strategy. We want to keep much of the play, and Zoe's part in it, a secret until opening night, so we agreed not to talk about it outside the rehearsal room. The thing is, darling, even if Robbie is mad about the girl, he can't hold the part open for her indefinitely. If we have to find another actress, then we will.' He shrugged. 'But if Zoe doesn't play the part of Isabella, it will be the biggest mistake of her professional life.'

'Seriously?' Tara said, struggling to take this in.

'Could she not bring him back here?'

'Dad, I don't know.'

'If you call her, will she talk to you?'

Tara nodded. 'Yes, yes, she will.'

'Then tell her that we're not mad with her and we will do our best to stall until she gets back, but she has to keep in touch and give us some idea of a timeframe.'

'Okay.'

'And talk to her about bringing Shane home. If he needs medical help, it would make much more sense if he got it here.'

'I agree. But she can't exactly force him.'

The doorbell rang and Tara groaned. 'Sorry, I'll get rid of whoever it is and be right back.' Putting down her glass again, she went back into the house to open the front door.

Greg's mother gave a nervous smile. 'Hello, Tara.'

Instinctively, she put her hand to her cheek and the woman flinched.

'Can I come in? I won't stay long.'

She was already in the hall before Tara had a chance to protest. 'Look, Connie, this really isn't a good time.'

'There'll never be a good time but I have to say my piece; I need to get this off my chest. Greg is heartbroken. He is sorry and ashamed for what he did but—'

'But?' Tara shook her head, incredulous. 'Are you going to make an excuse? Tell me he had a good reason?'

'No, of course not. What he did was wrong and I would never defend it. But he's my son and I know him and I know if you give him a chance he will never do it again.'

'Do what again?' Terence stood in the doorway of the kitchen, his face like thunder.

Tara closed her eyes. Her life was turning into a soap opera. 'Let's sit down,' she said, and led the way into the sitting room. Connie sat silently while Tara brought her father up to date.

'He can't get away with this. You need to phone the Gardaí,' Terence exclaimed, glaring at Greg's mother.

'No, Dad. I told him to go and he did and that's an end of it.'

'But he loves you, Tara, and you love him, I know you do,' Connie protested.

'That doesn't mean I am willing to be his punchbag.'

'Damn right,' her dad growled, jumping to his feet and going to stand by the fireplace.

'He's willing to do whatever it takes to win your trust back, Tara.'

'Then tell him to get a bloody job,' Terence said. 'I've watched Tara work round the clock for months now while Greg just sits on his arse. She has supported him in every way since his business collapsed and what thanks does she get? A smack across the face from a man three times her size. He makes me sick. He's not a man at all.'

'Dad, stop.' Seeing Connie's stricken expression, Tara moved closer on the sofa and put an arm around the woman.

Terence sighed. 'I apologise, Mrs Coleman, but this has come as quite a shock. As a parent, I'm sure you can understand my feelings.'

Connie nodded and dabbed at her eyes with her handkerchief. 'I feel ashamed of him but he's my son and I love him.' She looked from Terence to Tara. 'Please just meet with him. You could come to the house, I'd be there.'

'I'll think about it,' Tara said, feeling cornered.

Connie squeezed her hand and stood up. 'That's all I ask. Thanks at least for listening.'

Tara showed her mother-in-law to the door and watched her walk away, shoulders slumped. She felt her dad's hand on her shoulder. 'Are you okay, darling?'

Was she? She wasn't sure.

'Would you like me to make you some tea,' he offered.

'Forget the tea. Let's finish the wine.' She led the way back out to the garden.

He emptied the remains of the bottle into their glasses and handed her one.

'Here's to those who wish us well ...'

'And those that don't can go to hell.' Tara raised her glass to his and took a long drink.

'I think I should pay Greg a visit.'

'No, Dad. This is between him and me. You'll only upset Connie if you go over there; the poor woman's been through enough.'

'Fine. Have you told your mother about this?'

'No, of course not.'

'Why of course not?' Terrence asked.

She put her glass down, shrugging. 'If I didn't tell you, why on earth would I tell her? What's the point when she's not even in the country?'

'But you told Zoe, didn't you?' Her father shook his head. He looked hurt.

'Only because I knew she wouldn't go round there and beat him up. Although she was all ready to have him arrested.' Tara smiled.

'I wish she had,' he retorted.

'Yeah, that would be great for business, a squad car coming to my door and hauling off my husband.'

'No such thing as bad publicity,' he quoted, but he wasn't smiling. 'Look, darling, all I'm saying is that maybe he needs to be taught a lesson. He's been behaving very badly for a long time now but this was a step too far. He can't just lash out when he wants.'

'Which is why I threw him out!' she snapped.

'Hey, calm down. I'm on your side, remember?'

'Sorry.' She reached for her glass and drained it.

'That's okay, you're tired and you've a lot on your mind and far too heavy a burden on your shoulders.'

She felt tears well up at the kindness in his voice.

'Let me take you out to dinner; that will cheer you up.'

Tara shook her head. 'I'm a mess.'

'Nonsense, you look lovely.'

'Thanks, Dad, but I'm just not up to getting dressed up and going to an expensive, fancy restaurant where you'll be pestered by frustrated women.'

'Then we'll go to a cheap, dodgy restaurant and I'll wear a disguise.'

She smiled. 'Don't be ridiculous.'

'Oh, come on,' he wheedled.

'I don't know—'

'Is there any more wine?' he cut in.

'No, afraid not.'

'Yet another good reason to go out.'

She grinned. 'Okay, fine, you've talked me into it.'

Chapter Nineteen

Knowing that sexy Penny had stayed over, Zoe crept out of the house, took the bike and headed for the beach. She resented the girl hanging around. She wanted Shane to herself. Every time he seemed about to share his thoughts with her, Penny would arrive unannounced or call, inviting them down to the bar for Happy Hour or to a party full of ex-pats or penniless students and Shane was only too willing to go. It was weird. He was obviously depressed but seemed to need to be on the go all the time. Zoe wasn't sure if he was trying to escape her or himself. She'd waited for him to open up to her but it wasn't happening, so she would have to confront him. Whether he liked it or not, they would talk today. She pondered asking Penny to back off for a couple of days, but if Penny said something back to Shane, there was no knowing how he'd react. She'd just have to watch and wait and pick her time.

She locked the bike to a railing on the seafront and scrambled down the slope. She had worn her bikini under her top and shorts in case she was tempted to take a dip, but right now she just felt the need to walk and breathe in this wonderful air. Perhaps she should thank Penny for forcing her out at this hour. There was hardly anyone about and the only noise was the waves gently lapping the shore. It was a romantic setting, perfect for couples in love.

Her thoughts inevitably turned to Robbie and the memory of their night together. It had been so special but she was beginning to wonder if he felt the same way. He'd only tried to contact her twice and both voicemails were frustrated and angry and gave the impression that he was more worried about her abandoning *Isabella* than leaving him. She had no right to expect him to understand or like what she'd done, but it hurt that he'd given up on her so easily. What do you expect? she asked herself. For him to jump on a plane and beg you to come back? He didn't even know where she was. Terence too seemed to have abandoned her. She hated the thought of having disappointed him. Tara was the only one who had left a message, asking her to call.

The sun was well above the horizon now and people were drifting down to the cove, mainly parents with young families who hadn't been up partying half the night. She stood up, wriggled out of her clothes and went to the water's edge. After splashing water over her skin to prepare herself, she waded out until she was waist deep, and dived in. The shock of the coldness was refreshing and, when she came up, gasping for air, she was smiling. She swam across the cove and then floated on her back and stared up at the one fluffy white cloud in the sky, the water cushioning her, lulling her into a more peaceful and optimistic state of mind. She turned onto her stomach and headed back to the shore at a leisurely pace. By the time she'd reached her bike, her bikini was almost dry and she dressed and pulled her damp hair up into a knot before heading up to the square. She found a table outside her favourite café and sat down to enjoy breakfast in the sun. When she'd finished, she ordered another *café con leche* and called Tara.

'Hello?'

Zoe checked her screen. Had she dialled the wrong number? Nope. 'Tara? Are you all right?'

'Yeah.' Tara gave a loud yawn and then a groan. 'Sorry, late night and too much wine ... Zoe? Is that you?'

'It's me.'

'I'm so glad you called, Zo.'

'Why, what's wrong?'

'Nothing at all. First, give me a chance to wake up and tell me about Shane.'

Zoe took a sip of coffee and stared out across the square. 'There's not much to tell. Yes, as I guessed, it was the accident with Rachel that triggered this episode. It brought back some bad memories about Mam and Dad but he hasn't given me any details. I hope to get him on his own later and try to draw him out.'

'Alone? Who else is there?'

'Ah, he's taken up with an English student who's working in the local bar.'

'Huh, so much for inviting me out there. That would have been very cosy,' Tara muttered.

'I think they just met a couple of days ago,' Zoe said hurriedly. 'It's nothing serious. He's just looking for ways to keep me and his memories at bay. What's your news?'

'Dad was asking about you. He says you must come home.'

Zoe groaned. 'You know that I can't, Tara. Is he disgusted with me?'

'He was but he's calmed down now but – hang on.'

Zoe heard rustling and then Tara talk to someone else, a man. Crikey, was Greg back? Surely not.

'Zoe, what on earth are you playing at?'

'Terence!'

'Do you realise that you are screwing up the greatest opportunity of your life?'

A slight exaggeration but he would never normally speak to her like that so he must be upset. 'I'm sorry, Terence. I would never have done this if I didn't think I had to.'

'How long do you expect to be in Spain?'

'I can't say.'

'Sorry to be blunt but what exactly is wrong with your brother? Why all the mystery? Is he in trouble of some sort?'

Zoe hesitated for a moment before deciding to be honest. 'Yes, he's in trouble and I'm the only one who can help him.'

'How are you going to do that?'

'By being here.'

'Bring him home. Then you can be with him and do your job too,' he said, sounding totally frustrated.

She didn't think that was going to happen anytime soon, but she decided it was best to placate him. 'I'll try, Terence.'

'You must. I've talked to Robbie and he's willing to delay production for a short time.'

'He is?' She had imagined him in a fury and was touched that, despite her running out on him and the show, Robbie was ready to give her another chance.

'But you must keep in touch and let us know what the situation is.'

'I'll do that, I promise.'

'Good. Take care, darling. I'll put you back on to Tara.'

'Close the door on your way out, Dad,' Tara called. 'Okay, we're alone now. Sorry about that. I didn't hear him come in and he just grabbed the phone when he realised it was you.'

'How come he's there at this hour?'

'He stayed over. He was here yesterday when Greg's mum arrived to plead his case.'

'So he knows?' Zoe asked.

'He does.' Tara actually sounded relieved.

'How did he take it? No, sorry, stupid question.'

Tara chuckled. 'He wanted to go round and thump Greg, but instead, he took me out to dinner and we got drunk.'

Zoe would have preferred the thumping option. She was worried about Tara's drinking. She was worried about Tara full stop. Zoe worried about Shane's drinking too but somehow it seemed a necessary evil at the moment and, strangely, under control. But Tara's growing dependence on alcohol was a direct result of the stress in her marriage. 'Are you okay, Tara?'

'Yeah, fine. It's actually a huge relief that Dad knows.'

'What did Greg's mum say?'

'She's very upset about the whole thing and begged me to talk to him, to come to her house if I'm nervous of being alone with him. She says he's ashamed of himself and will do anything to win me back.'

'How do you feel about that?' Zoe was not going to push her friend one way or the other. Tara needed someone who would just listen without giving advice or standing in judgement.

'I suppose I have to face him sometime. Oh, by the way, he's working away on your house and it seems to be going well.'

'On his own?' Zoe was surprised.

'No, he has a plumber and tiler helping him but most of the work is done.'

Zoe didn't know what to say. She didn't know if the insurance company would pay up and, as Greg hadn't given her a quote for the work, she had no idea what any of this was going to cost. Still, the job had to be done. 'He's very good. Thank him for me.'

'Will do. Give Shane my love.'

'I will.' Zoe said goodbye and, raising her face to the sun, closed her eyes. Would the peace of this beautiful spot help her brother with whatever demons he was battling or would he be better off back in Dublin, facing reality? Her phone buzzed and she picked it up, to see it was a text from Shane.

Where are you?

In the square, she typed back.

On the way.

Alone, I hope, Zoe thought. It would take him at least ten minutes to get down so, before she talked herself out of it, she called Robbie. It rang several times and she was about to give up when the phone was finally answered.

'Hello? Hell*ooo*? Anybody there?'

Zoe hung up. She was ready for anger and recriminations or frostiness but the last thing she had been expecting was Robbie's phone to be answered by a woman.

Chapter Twenty

Terence was almost a head shorter than his son-in-law and much slighter but, when he punched him, Greg Coleman staggered backwards and almost fell into the new bath. Terence's knuckles hurt like hell but there was a grim pleasure in the pain. He hadn't been able to rid himself of the image of the man hitting his daughter. It had been eating him up.

Terence watched Greg massage his cheek. 'I had to do that, you understand.'

'Yes.' Greg shifted a tin of paint and sat down on the loo.

'I'm not convinced you deserve Tara, I never was,' Terence told him. 'But if she does take you back, you need to sort yourself out.'

'I know that but, at the risk of getting punched again, I'm not the only one.'

Terence propped himself in the doorway and crossed his arms. 'Meaning?'

'You must have noticed that Tara has become obsessive about cleanliness? Everything must be exactly so and when it isn't, she explodes.'

Terence clenched his fist. Her kitchen was always gleaming but she was a caterer, it needed to be. But he thought of how she'd carefully lined up her cutlery in the restaurant last night and polished their wine glasses, frowning at the marks he couldn't even see. Still, surely that was an eccentricity and there were worse obsessions. 'You're complaining that your wife keeps your home clean?'

Greg shook his head, annoyed. 'I'm telling you, it's more than that. I didn't realise it until I was at home all day. If I put anything in the wrong place, she'd go mad. The mugs must all face the same way, the glasses organised in order of height. She has different cloths for cleaning different things and when I mix them up she insists on redoing the job herself. I did try to help her, but it was clear that I was causing her more distress than anything else, so I gave up.'

'Then why didn't you get out and work?' Terence retorted. He was angry, mainly because he knew there was some truth in what Greg was saying but he was her husband – it was his place to look after his wife.

'I did try at first but when I came home, unsuccessful, she'd say what did I expect. I hadn't dressed well, or shaved properly or I needed a haircut. Or my approach was all wrong or my presentation skills were basic.' He looked up at Terence, obviously uncomfortable. 'There's only so much of that you can listen to before you stop feeling like a man.'

'Did hitting her make you feel like a man?' Terence said, his anger mounting. Did the man seriously expect sympathy from him?

'No, it made me feel like an animal,' Greg shouted and then sighed. 'I have no defence. I've made her life hell this last year.

I admit it, I resented her success. And the more money she brought in, the more useless and pathetic and angry I became. When I found out she was talking to Shane Hall, exchanging texts with him, I imagined them laughing at me behind my back, maybe more. It brought everything to a head.'

Shane Hall? This was news to Terence: his daughter had left out that particular piece of the story.

'She's been drinking a lot too, but that's probably my fault. Look, I just thought you should know.'

Terence felt completely out of his depth. He had never had to worry about Tara in the past. She had always been self-sufficient, strong-minded and confident and had made her own decisions. He was proud of her and her independence and, he thought with a degree of shame, it suited him. She didn't get upset if he didn't call and made no demands on him. They never fell out, never had cross words. They were close, very close indeed. But then why didn't he know what had been going on in her life and why hadn't she turned to him when Greg went off the rails? And what was going on with Shane Hall? Why hadn't Zoe said anything, or did she not know? He suddenly remembered he was standing in Shane Hall's house with Tara's husband. 'So why are you doing this?' He waved a hand around them. 'Why are you helping this guy?'

Greg shrugged, as if wondering the same thing. 'Tara wanted to help Zoe and it seemed like a way to start mending some fences.'

Terence felt a grudging respect for him. 'I'll leave you to it then. And I'll think about what you've said.'

'Goodbye, Terence, and, for what it's worth, I'm sorry.'

*

Terence walked back towards town, stopping off in Terenure for a much needed drink. As he lifted the glass, he thought of what Greg had said about Tara's drinking and went back over yesterday's events. He'd arrived late afternoon and she was halfway through a bottle of wine. Of course it may have been open already, but she had been dead against going out to dinner until he'd pointed out there was no wine left in the house. She had been brought up in an environment where one had wine with a meal, but she had never been much of a drinker. And once she'd started the business, she was far too conscientious to drink much, at least that's how it seemed. Terence sipped his drink and pondered what to do. He didn't think Tara's mother would be much help. She would be far too direct and judgemental or would simply leave Tara to sort out her own problems.

Once Tara had left school it was as if Vivienne had dusted her hands and got back to her own life, job done. The best decision they'd made was not to marry, acknowledging that despite the passion, they would make each other miserable. And they hadn't proved to be bad parents. Tara was an intelligent and well-balanced young woman, or so he'd thought. Both he and Vivienne had been surprised and a little disappointed by Tara's choice of husband. Greg was much older, although that didn't bother Terence, but he was like a different species and Vivienne had been appalled by his lack of interest in the arts. Like her daughter's chosen career, Greg was an affront to the future Vivienne had envisaged for her child. Terence wondered if his daughter had just craved a simpler and more normal life. Though Tara had taken a different route from her parents, he'd seen creativity in her food and the same painstaking attention to detail and focus that he applied on stage, and he was proud of her. Did caring about what you did and making it as good as you could, mean you were obsessive?

With a sigh, he pulled out his phone and called Zoe. As he expected, it went straight to voicemail. 'Zoe, can you call me when you get a chance – it's about Tara. Thanks, darling.'

He put the phone away. He was feeling a little lost without Zoe. He'd never had a leading lady walk out on him before and he missed her. She was like a sponge, soaking up everything he taught her, and, what's more, she was fun and made him feel young. Ha, he was turning into Jonathan! But he sobered, thinking that Zoe's Isabella might never be seen. She had done an amazing audition and improved every time they rehearsed, living the part and hungry for success. But this business with her brother could put paid to all that.

Terence glanced at his watch and wondered how to pass the evening. It was unusual to find himself at a loss, but then he had cut off contact with most of his usual crowd to spend time with Zoe. He borrowed a newspaper from the barman and studied the entertainment pages to see if there was anything interesting on. He settled on a new play. A couple of the cast were old friends and there was bound to be some fun to be had afterwards. He would slip into a side seat after the lights went down and be able to enjoy the play in peace but, he knew, the cast would be apprised of the fact that he was in the audience.

As he'd expected, a note was slipped to him during the interval, inviting him to the drinks party after the show in a room in a nearby hostelry. The director, an athletic woman he'd met at an arts festival in Kerry – now that had been a memorable weekend – came forward to greet him.

He embraced her, kissing her on both cheeks. 'Brava, Jacqueline, brava. Every production eclipses the last.'

He used his theatre voice to ensure that it was heard by everyone around them.

Her eyes twinkled with gratitude and she steepled her hands and bowed. 'What a wonderful compliment from one of Ireland's greatest actors. How are you, you old rogue?' she added, lowering her voice.

'Much the better for seeing you, darling. Why on earth didn't you call me to play the lead?'

'I did. Your agent said you were busy.'

'Pity, I'd have done a better job.'

'You have no idea of the tantrums I've had to put up with,' she muttered. 'The man's an arse.'

'The arse is on his way over,' Terence murmured, his hand already outstretched. 'Raymond, what a wonderful performance. I was entranced.'

'Too kind.' He lightly embraced Terence. 'Haven't seen you tread the boards recently. Thought you'd been wooed by Broadway.'

'They keep trying but I'm holding out for the private jet. I am very jealous, Raymond, that you've had the pleasure of working with this wondrous woman.' Raymond put an arm around her and Terence smirked at her shudder.

'Isn't she out of this world?'

'A star,' Terence agreed. 'She was just saying she can't wait to work with you again.'

Both pairs of eyes glittered at him.

'Oh, there's Ben Farrell,' Raymond said. 'Must go say hello. Excuse me, you two. Wonderful to see you again, Terence. Ben, Ben darling ...'

'You're wicked, Terence,' Jacqueline said and raised her hand. Immediately, a waitress materialised at her side with two more glasses of wine. 'There's someone I want you to meet. I think he could be the next Terence Ross.'

'Christ, I'm not dead yet,' Terence muttered, shaken by the casualness of the comment. Without even meeting him, he hated the man already.

Jacqueline laughed. 'That was a compliment, darling.'

She beckoned to someone behind him and he turned to see a man with model good looks and a false smile approach, a girl clinging to his arm. Well, they had the same taste in women but Terence took an instant dislike to the man. In his early thirties, he was one of those characters who, he'd bet, had climbed the ladder on the back of his smile and appearance rather than the quality of his acting.

'Terence, let me introduce a wonderful actor recently returned to our shores: Ed McGlynn.'

It took all of Terence's acting skills not to betray his shock. Though he'd heard through Tara about Zoe's husband, they had never actually met; they didn't move in the same circles in those days but that had obviously changed. What had Jacqueline said: he'd moved back?

Ed pumped his hand with enthusiasm. 'A great honour to meet you, sir. I'm a great admirer.'

'How kind. And who is this lovely lady?' Terence turned to the girl whom Ed seemed to have forgotten, obviously a habit of his. Beautiful in a superficial way, she lacked Zoe's poise and class.

'Anita,' she simpered as he kissed her hand.

'You're a lucky man,' he said to Ed.

'Thank you.' Ed barely glanced at her. 'I do hope we get to work together. I've longed to move back to Ireland for some time, but there just wasn't a part strong enough to draw me. Then I was offered a role in the movie being made about the Battle of the Boyne and I jumped at the opportunity.'

'Really? Sounds like a blast!' Terence faked a yawn. The two women laughed but despite the smile he saw fury and humiliation in Ed's eyes. That one's for you, Zoe. Terence watched Ed open his mouth to tell him all about his wonderful role and, turning, swept Jacqueline into a hug. 'Must go and say hello to Ena. I'll never hear the end of it if I don't.' And with a nod to Ed and a wink at Anita, he wandered across the room and gathered Ireland's darling of comedy into his arms. 'Hello, gorgeous.'

She let out a loud throaty laugh and kissed him on the mouth. 'Hi, sexy. What on earth are you doing here? There aren't nearly enough important people here to interest you.'

He laughed. If anyone else had said something like that he'd have taken offence. But not Ena Mulligan. 'You're here, darling – what more do I need?'

'A large whiskey?' she suggested. 'This wine is like piss.'

'Agreed.' He called the waitress and whispered in her ear. Beaming, she hurried off, arriving back moments later with their drinks. Terence pressed twenty euros into her hand. 'Thank you, darling, you're an angel.'

Ena was at least fifteen years younger and mixed in a different professional circle to Terrence; perhaps she would be able to tell him something more about Ed McGlynn. Terence had been watching him out of the corner of his eye, sidling up to all the key people in the room, the girl, Anita, following like a devoted little puppy. He hated the thought that Zoe might have been like that once, subservient to a man who was all front and no substance. He nudged Ena. 'Do you know him?'

She followed his gaze. 'Ah, McDreamy, yes, we've met.'

'And?'

'He's a player.' She shrugged. 'He can act, although he's nothing special and he has that certain something that pulls the women and you know what that means.'

'Bums on seats,' Terence acknowledged and downed half his glass. 'Is it true about the movie?'

She wrinkled her nose. 'The poor relation of *Braveheart*? Apparently, it's going ahead but I've no idea how or why – it's doomed. It will cost a fortune and there don't seem to be any big names involved.'

'Oh good.'

Her eyes sparkled with mischief and laughter. 'Bitchy! What's he done to upset you?'

Terence couldn't smile about it. He'd heard the full story from Tara and seen the doubt and occasional lack of confidence in Zoe that Ed had put there. 'Not me, a friend, a woman that he didn't treat very well.'

'Now there's a surprise.' She scowled in Ed's direction.

'How's the romance with Ken going?' he asked.

'Pah, that's over. He wanted us to marry. Can you imagine anything worse, darling?'

He laughed. 'Nothing.'

She tilted her head and looked at him. 'So you still haven't been snared, eh?'

'No one has been silly enough to try. They know I'm not the settling-down type.'

'Of course you're not – that's why I adore you.'

He caressed her cheek. 'Should we continue this conversation somewhere more comfortable?'

'Let's do that,' she said, then drained her glass and put her arm through his.

Terence lay back in bed with yet another tumbler of whiskey. 'This is lovely.'

Ena stretched and smiled without opening her eyes. 'Isn't it?'

'You've changed the place,' he said, looking around the bedroom, which was decked out in a variety of fabrics and textures running from midnight-blue to the turquoise reminiscent of the Caribbean Sea. There were lit candles on every surface and a heady incense burned, which combined with the alcohol and slow, sensual sex, was making him feel very relaxed indeed. 'I like it.'

'I do too. I'll run us a bath.' She kissed his chest and went into the en suite.

As he lay, listening to her humming as she ran the water, his thoughts turned back to Greg and what he'd said about Tara. He found it hard to think of his little girl as a bully but, if the man was being honest, that's what it amounted to. He pondered discussing it with Ena but he had never been one for sharing his troubles. He'd realised early on in life that it was one of the things that made him attractive to women. He encouraged them to talk about themselves and gave them his undivided attention. But never bothered them with his own worries.

Ena emerged from the steamy bathroom, and held out her hand. 'Bathtime.'

Like a docile child, he followed her, thinking what better way was there to forget your troubles.

Chapter Twenty-One

Celia watched the train pull out of the station and felt both relieved and exhausted. Thomas was being discharged in the morning and Martha had decided to go home the day before so she would have everything ready for him. It had been a stressful time for Celia – between hospital visits, evading Martha's personal questions and living on her nerves, she'd been terrified that Albie would show up. When she got home, she went into the spare room to strip the bed but Martha had done it already and left an envelope on the bedside table. When Celia opened it, she was mortified when four fifty-euro notes floated to the floor. The message was short.

> *Dear Celia,*
> *Don't be cross. It would have cost me a fortune to stay in a hotel or guesthouse and I wouldn't have had your wonderful cooking or the pleasure of your company.*
> *Many thanks for your kindness.*
> *Love*
> *Martha*

Celia felt a lump in her throat. In truth, the woman had been no trouble and they'd had a couple of wonderful late nights reminiscing. It would have been quite enjoyable if Albie's shadow hadn't been hanging over her. She tucked the cash into her pocket and carried the bed linen out to the kitchen. It was true it would have cost a lot more if Martha had had to pay for full board in the most modest of guesthouses. The money would pay the electricity bill and allow her to replenish her fridge. Though she'd got her first cheque for *Isabella*, rehearsals seemed to have come to a standstill. She hadn't had time to think about that but now she wondered should she call Lauren or get her agent on the case. But that might ruffle Robbie's feathers and she couldn't afford to do that. She needed to keep working and the best way to ensure that was to charm the pants off everyone and give no trouble. Her diva days were over. She had to face the fact that, while her name still meant something in the business, it wasn't enough on its own any more. She would have to be dignified at all times and banish any gossip that she was financially embarrassed. To that end, she would need to befriend Zoe Hall, make a confidante of her, help her and support her. She would stick with the story she'd told Martha, but how would she explain her outburst/response when Zoe had called at the door and Celia had mistakenly thought it was Albie back for more? She could say her son was mentally ill; that was better than admitting he threatened and blackmailed her. For a fleeting moment, she wished that Albie had died and not his father, and then buried her face in her hands, ashamed for even thinking such a thing. What kind of a mother was she?

*

Zoe looked across at Shane, slouching in the chair opposite, the sun shining down on him, his teeth gleaming in his tanned face as he laughed with the waiter. At moments like this he could fool her that everything was okay, but she knew in her heart that it wasn't. She topped up his glass, determined to get him talking this time. It was a Penny-free zone, the girl having gone to Granada for the day with some friends. This was the perfect moment to talk, even if there was a rather loud Welsh couple at the next table. Zoe gave the waiter her order and, when he'd left, moved her chair closer and sat forward, arms on the table. 'It's time we had a chat.'

Shane immediately flicked his sunglasses down so she couldn't see his eyes. 'Don't be a pain, Zo. Let's just enjoy our lunch.'

'Tell me we can head home tomorrow and I won't say another word.'

'No!' he snapped.

'Then let me read the play.'

'No. Will you please just leave it?'

'No, no, I won't, Shane. I've been here a week. You have to talk to me so that we can both get on with our lives.' Her voice had risen in her frustration and she suddenly noticed that the couple beside them had gone quiet. She winked at Shane and inclined her head at the couple before continuing.

'You don't want this baby, do you?' she accused, pressing her palm to her flat stomach.

Shane's lips twitched in understanding. 'Of course I do!'

'No,' she sniffed, 'you don't want the baby and you don't want me. It's Hannah you really love.'

The mention of their aunt provoked a snort that Shane

quickly turned into a cough. 'Hannah? Now you're being ridiculous. I know what you're doing – trying to divert me, to take the focus off that baby and who the real father is.'

Zoe gasped and put her hand to her mouth, more to stifle her laugh than for theatrical reasons. 'What a dreadful thing to say – of course it's yours!'

'You kissed Gerry. At Adam's barbecue. I saw you – don't try to deny it.'

'Darling, it was only a kiss—'

'Sea bass?'

Zoe looked up and beamed at the waiter. 'Please.'

'And the langoustines for you, sir.' He set the plate down with a flourish.

Shane pushed up his glasses. *'Bueno. Muchas gracias.* You must try one of these, darling.'

'Thank you, sweetie.' Zoe turned to the couple who were now openly staring at them and raised her glass to them. 'Cheers.'

They hurriedly got up to leave and Shane called after them, 'Hope you enjoyed the show.'

He clinked his glass against Zoe's. 'Ah, just like old times.'

'Yes, but don't think it's going to save you. There's no one to listen in now.' She held up the empty bottle to the waiter and he nodded and went to get a second.

'Are you trying to get me drunk?'

'Yes.' She was happy to see him more relaxed and was glad he hadn't put his sunglasses back on. 'But you're not allowed to pass out until you've spilled your guts.'

Shane set down his knife and fork and looked at her, his expression suddenly serious.

'What's the point of talking, Zo? I was in a crash, it reminded me of Mam and Dad and it knocked the stuffing out of me. I took some time out, end of.'

'So when are you coming home? What are you waiting for?'

He looked down at his plate. 'I'm not sure.'

'You are. You're just afraid to tell me.' He looked up in surprise and she realised that she'd hit the nail on the head.

'There are so many things going on in my head and yes, and I'm afraid to talk about them, afraid of how you'll react, afraid of losing you.'

She reached for his hand. Behind all the bluff, the moods, the sarcasm, he was such a gentle soul. 'I can't believe you said that, Shane. We may argue, we may get upset with each other but nothing and no one could ever come between us. You're my family and I'm yours.'

He looked at her, his expression haunted, and reached for his glass. 'Would you still feel that way if I told you I'm the reason you're an orphan?'

She tightened her grip on his hand. 'What are you talking about? Of course you're not.'

He said nothing but his breath seemed to have quickened. He pulled away from her and dragged his thumb in and out between his teeth, a childhood habit he resorted to when he was anxious. Finally, he raised his tortured eyes to hers. 'I was the cause of the crash, Zo. I was fighting with Daddy, shouting at him, screaming at him, and he turned round to slap me and I shoved him and the car swerved and then I saw the truck coming at us and . . .'

She released his hand and sat back.

'You see? I told you, I knew it. I knew you'd hate me.'

'I don't, Shane.' She looked back at her brother, not sure what she felt. He'd been twelve, a boy. All boys were boisterous.

'You do, I can see it in your face.'

'I don't,' she repeated. 'But to hear something like this twenty-one years after it happened . . .'

That settled him a little. 'I'd forgotten the details or perhaps suppressed the memory. When Rachel crashed, I went into shock afterwards. They gave me a sedative and I lapsed in and out of consciousness. Perhaps it was that or the noises of the hospital, but it all came flooding back' – he gave a harsh laugh – 'in glorious Technicolor too. It scared the life out of me. I felt like a murderer. Poor Mam.'

'Of course you're not a murderer – you were behaving like a normal kid.' Shane said nothing and she reached for his hand again. 'Why didn't you tell me? Why did you run away?'

He looked at her, his eyes luminous with tears. 'It was easier to leave than to see you look at me with hate.'

She shook her head, close to tears herself. 'And do I look like I hate you?'

He shook his head and gave her a ghost of a smile.

'Do you remember what you were arguing about?'

He pulled out his cigarettes. 'Dad was shouting at Mam about something and I was crying and telling him to stop.'

'Then why on earth do you feel bad? You weren't being naughty, you were trying to help Mam.'

'And got her killed instead.'

'It was an accident. You can't keep blaming yourself.' He still looked troubled. 'There's more, isn't there?'

He sighed. 'The play is all about what led up to that night.'

'What led up to it? I don't understand,' Zoe said, confused.

'I abandoned the original play and wrote this one when I came out here. I've one scene left to write.'

'And it's all about Mam and Dad?'

'Yes, but it will never be staged.'

'Then why write it?'

'I didn't want to, it just happened. I seem incapable of writing fiction at the moment.'

And perhaps that's what this was all about, she mused. Maybe when he'd finished it, he would be free of this burden once and for all. On the other hand, maybe it would send him over the edge. 'When can I read it?' she asked.

'Whenever you want.'

She called for the bill. 'Let's go.'

When Shane and Zoe got back to the villa, he fetched his laptop, opened the document and handed the machine to his sister. 'I can't sit here and watch you read – I'll go for a walk.'

Zoe hugged him and looked into his eyes. 'I don't think I could handle you watching me anyway. But I promise, Shane, it doesn't matter what's in this. It won't change anything between us.'

He kissed her cheek, took his cigarettes and keys and left.

Zoe grabbed a bottle of water and took the laptop outside. The sun had gone from the patio and she would be able to see the screen without difficulty. She hesitated, staring at the title: *Para!*. That brought back memories. When they had played rough games as children their mother had worried Zoe would get hurt because she was so much younger and smaller than her brother. She came up with the idea of a code word they could use that would basically mean: This isn't fun any more and I've had enough. But 'Stop' was too easily said and ignored and so she had given them the code word, *Para*, the Spanish translation.

What made him use that as the title for the play, Zoe wondered? She scrolled down to the opening scene, filled with a sense of foreboding. But she should feel happy and relieved. This exercise had to be cathartic for Shane and, once he was able to write the last scene, perhaps he would finally be able to move on with his life. Taking a deep breath, she settled down to read.

And she did. Not stopping to do anything other than wipe away her tears or take a moment to try to digest what she'd read so far.

She sat, stunned, for some time after she'd finished, watching the sun's descent into the sea, altering the light and the mood. Finally, she roused herself out of her stupor. Shane! She had to find him. He'd be going crazy wondering what she thought. It took a few minutes to find her phone and when she did she saw there was a text from Terence, left yesterday. She felt a pang of guilt, but he would have to wait. She called Shane's number and sighed when she heard it ringing in his bedroom. Still, she had an idea where he'd be.

The cove was quiet. Only a couple canoodling under a towel, the occasional dog-walker and some local fishermen remained. Most people were making dinner or filling the tapas bars. The air was so still that the water looked like a mirror and the summer breeze that came in off the sea was no more than a breath on her cheek. There was no sign of Shane, but she knew that, if he'd come here, he'd have climbed up onto the rocks on the far side to enjoy the view in solitude. Having already safely stowed her bike, Zoe took off her shoes and set off across the sand. She had so many questions, she hardly knew where to start. She became aware of her teeth chattering as she walked. She was in shock. It was the strangest feeling, as if the accident that had killed her parents had happened all over again. She was consumed with grief, but she also felt stupid and even cheated. There were specific scenes that brought back memories but they were a different version of her truth. At times she'd found herself saying: That's not what happened. But Shane's perspective was more informed than hers. She hated what he had been exposed to so young, and the loneliness and helplessness he must have felt. It was no wonder he suffered from bouts of depression. How she wished he'd told her years ago. She hoped her knowing would now bring him some peace.

She barely recognised the sick, cruel, twisted father and her mother was not the happy, carefree one she remembered. But then she recalled the times when her mother locked herself away in her room and Shane's version of events began to make more sense. Zoe felt nauseous, thinking of what they had gone through, and more so when she thought about how she had idolised her father. How hard it must have been for Shane to see her run to him when he came home from work and throw herself into his arms.

Had Shane confided in anyone at the time or since, or had this been locked inside him all these years? Zoe understood her brother so much better now. She stopped suddenly . . . Had their aunt and uncle known the truth and done nothing? If they had known before the crash how her father had behaved, she wouldn't be able to forgive them, but even if they had only found out afterwards, she would still be furious that they hadn't got Shane the help he'd so obviously needed. But then, that was the Irish way. Say nothing, pretend it never happened. Shane was young: with time he'd forget, he'd be fine, and no one need ever know this dreadful family secret.

Zoe reached the far side of the cove and picked her way up to the flat stone that Shane liked to stretch out on, but he wasn't there. Which meant he was in the bar, drinking. Zoe was about to turn back but, suddenly weary, she lowered herself onto the rock. Drawing her knees up to her chest, she rested her chin on her arms and stared out to sea. Her teeth were still chattering, though she wasn't cold and her heart was pounding in her chest.

How much of her happy childhood was real and how much just a figment of her imagination? she wondered. Had Shane any good memories? Surely there had been a time when he was happy? She struggled to recall how he had been before, during and after the funeral, but she'd been distracted by the neighbours and her friends' mothers rallying round and spoiling her so she'd hardly seen her brother, let alone talked to him. Had they been deliberately kept apart? She did remember that Uncle Gerry had wanted Shane to say a bidding prayer but he'd refused. Zoe had been sent to bed, but she'd crept to the top of the stairs and listened as the couple continued to try to persuade Shane. Hannah had tried to bribe him with promises of treats, while Gerry, angry, had said it was the last thing he would be able to do for his parents and he should be ashamed of himself for letting them down. But Shane hadn't budged and on the day of the funeral, while Gerry had stood stiff and grim-faced, Hannah had explained to the priest that Shane was too upset to take part in the ceremony.

This prompted another memory that made Zoe gasp. She had made her First Holy Communion shortly before the accident and Hannah had insisted that she wear her pretty white dress, veil and shoes for the funeral. Zoe shuddered at the memory of everyone else in black whilst she was dressed like a bride as she stood at her parents' graveside. An image flashed through her mind of Shane throwing some kind of a tantrum as the coffins were lowered and being led away by one of his teachers. She'd have to ask him what all that had been about.

Zoe was reminded of the occasion after Shane had left for Dublin when she and her aunt had come across old photo albums in the back of a wardrobe. Hannah had become unusually sentimental and maudlin and talked about 'the old days' as Zoe pored over the pictures of her dad with Gerry when they were children, and her parents' wedding photo with Gerry as best man. Zoe had plagued Hannah with questions but, when she brought up the car accident, her aunt had clammed up. She had tried to talk to her uncle too a few times, but he had just left the room. Hannah had reprimanded her, saying that it upset Gerry to be reminded of the tragic loss of his brother and that they had done their best to raise her and

Shane as their father would have wished. Naturally, Zoe would end up feeling guilty and apologise, assuring them that she and Shane appreciated their kindness in giving them a good home. But their silence frustrated her and she found it hard to believe that her uncle was that devastated; the brothers hadn't seemed close and, as adults, had rarely met up.

She sighed as she thought of the revelations in Shane's play. Could she rely on him to answer her questions, to finally tell her everything? It was her right to know: they were her parents too. Her self-righteousness quickly passed. There was nothing normal about Shane's childhood and she hated that he blamed himself for Mam and Dad's deaths. But how could he be anything but scarred by all he'd been through?

Realising it was getting dark, Zoe scrambled down from her perch, jogged back to her bike, and went in search of her brother.

Zoe found Shane sitting in the bar where Penny worked, drinking straight tequila. 'Hey, Zo, come have a drink.' His voice was loud and welcoming and he was smiling but he didn't meet her eyes.

'No thanks. And I think you've had enough. Let's go home.'

He turned and searched her face. 'Well?'

Zoe glanced at Penny hovering nearby and lowered her voice. 'We can't talk here.'

He shrugged and turned away, picking up his drink. 'I think I'm probably past the talking stage anyway.'

'But I have so many questions,' she protested.

'And I'll answer them,' he said, sounding defensive. 'Just not tonight.'

Zoe sighed in frustration. First he wanted to know what she thought, now he didn't. 'Let's go home anyway.'

'Lighten up and have a drink.' He beckoned Penny. 'A Chardonnay for my sis.'

'I said I don't want one. I'm tired.' She hated the fact that she sounded like a sulky kid.

'Go on home, Zoe. I'll make sure that he gets back in one piece,' Penny promised with a smile.

I bet you will, Zoe thought, knowing that meant she'd stay over and the couple probably wouldn't surface before noon. 'Shane?'

'You heard the girl, I'll be fine!' Shane grinned. 'Night, Zo.'

Feeling dismissed, Zoe had little choice but to leave them to it. 'Night,' she muttered, and pushed her way back through the busy bar and out into the night.

Chapter Twenty-Two

For once in his life, Terence was glad not to be working. He doubted he would be able to concentrate, and it would be criminal not to give Isabella his full attention. But he couldn't think of anything but his daughter and what Greg had said about her behaviour. He'd love to have been able to dismiss the guy's words as bitter lies, but some of what he'd said had struck a chord. He longed to discuss it with the one person who knew Tara better than anyone – Zoe – but she was still in Spain. He'd thought of talking to Vivienne – she was his oldest friend and confidante even now – but that would mean betraying his daughter's confidence, and she would be furious with him if he did that. He wasn't sure Vivienne would be much use anyway. She was quite likely to simply plough in and tell Tara to pull herself together and that would be the proverbial red rag to a bull. It had to be handled sensitively. It wasn't as if either of them could drag an adult woman to the doctor, and he was afraid to tell Tara what Greg had said for fear she'd think that they were ganging up on her. As he pondered the predicament, his phone rang and he brightened when he saw it was Zoe calling. What perfect timing.

'Hello, stranger.'

'Sorry, Terence,' she said, sounding genuinely contrite. 'I did intend to call you sooner, but there's a lot going on at the moment.'

'So my daughter said, none of which you want to talk about.' But Terence was too happy and relieved that she had called to be really cross with her.

'Sorry,' she said again, 'but it's not up to me to discuss Shane's private business.'

'Of course it isn't, darling,' he said, thinking how miserable she sounded. 'Nothing to do with me anyway. I just wish there was something I could do or say to make you feel better.'

'Me too.' She sighed. 'I'm afraid I'm still not sure when I'll be back.'

'That's not actually the reason I texted you. It's about Tara.'

'Is she okay?'

'I'm honestly not sure, darling. I had a conversation with Greg that worried me.' He gave her the gist of what his son-in-law had claimed. Zoe was silent when he'd finished. 'Oh, God. You agree, don't you?' he said, his concern mounting.

'I'm not sure, Terence. It's true that she's become fussier about cleanliness and can fly off the handle if everything isn't done exactly the way she likes it. I'd put it down to stress. I mean, she has been under enormous pressure.'

'And the drinking?'

'Mostly, I see her when she's working and of course she doesn't drink then, but ...'

'Go on,' he prompted.

Zoe sighed. 'I did notice more empty bottles in the bin lately and I'm pretty sure that you and I are her only visitors.'

'Oh, Zoe, what do I do?' he asked, although he didn't expect a solution. 'I thought that Greg was the root of all her problems but now I'm beginning to wonder.'

'I wouldn't agree with that. It only started when he went out of business.'

She was silent for a moment and Terence could almost hear her brain ticking over. He hoped it was coming up with more than his addled mind had.

'It must be about security,' she said, 'or rather the lack of it. It frightens her and this is her way of coping.'

'Or not coping.'

'On the face of it, she is,' Zoe pointed out. 'Her business is still going strong, which is one hell of an achievement in the current climate. And the time and effort needed just getting people to pay their bills would have been enough to make me quit months ago.'

Terence flopped back in his chair, feeling both proud and concerned. 'I didn't know about that. I thought all her problems came down to tiredness and having to shoulder the burden alone.'

'Oh!'

'What?' he asked.

'Think about what you just said. She is doing everything alone despite Greg trying to help. I think it's because she prefers it that way. No one else can do it as well as she does – her standards are far too high.'

'But she's happy to have *you* working for her,' Terence pointed out.

'It's not the same. I'm just an extra pair of hands and I'm not deeply invested in the business. I follow her orders to the letter. I know her well and she knows me and it's in my nature to be punctual. Andrea is a great worker, but her social life seems to come first, and when she calls in at the last moment, saying she can't work, it freaks Tara out. As for Greg, well, what can I say? He's a man.' There was a smile in her voice. 'I'll bet the first thing he tried to do was to tell her how she could be more efficient and cost effective.'

'Zoe, I'm disappointed in you. That's so sexist,' Terence admonished her but he was smiling too, 'but probably true.'

'Of course it is. The fact that he used to run his own business would have made it worse. There can only be one boss, Terence.'

'So she only feels happy when she's in control,' Terence mused.

'And secure,' Zoe added.

Yes, that all made sense to him. He knew that Zoe would be able to shine a light on the matter. 'So the ideal scenario would be if Greg found work and they got back together.'

There was a moment's silence and then Zoe answered, her voice like ice. 'Tara is hardly going to feel secure if she's wondering when he's going to land the next slap.'

'Do you honestly think he would do it again?' Terence asked, worried. 'I think it was a one-off – she just pushed him too far.'

'I can't believe you're saying that, especially about your own daughter! You think she deserves what she got, is that it? That she had it coming?'

Terence was astounded that Zoe could even think such a thing and doubly so by the anger in her voice. 'Of course not! I just think he did something completely out of character and that it's unlikely he'll do it again. He's very upset about it. He loves her.'

'That's crap, Terence. A leopard doesn't change its spots, believe me.'

He was at a loss as to why Zoe was suddenly so hostile and was about to ask and then realised the line had gone dead. He took the phone from his ear and stared at it. 'She hung up on me!' What on earth was she in such a strop over? They were on the same side, they both wanted the best for Tara: what had he said? Women – he would never fully understand them.

When John Whelan phoned from Belfast to tell Adam that he would be back in Dublin soon, and to enquire about Shane's progress, Adam reluctantly sent on the script, cautioning that it was not the final version. John's text a couple of days later – *Wonderful script!* – had come as some surprise and, curious, Adam settled down to read it himself and was completely stunned by the time he'd finished. The play was powerful, gripping and, while he hadn't known all the details of Shane's background, he knew enough to recognise that this was autobiographical. There was no ending and though John wouldn't know what was coming, Adam had a fair idea. What on earth had possessed Shane to write this? For over twenty years, he'd maintained his silence and had clearly done everything he could to protect Zoe from the truth and now he was going to stage it. Had he taken leave of his senses? Adam flicked back through the script and shuddered at some of the imagery. It must have been torture reliving the whole business. He was glad that Zoe hadn't seen this . . . or had she?

Adam had called to the house the other day only to find a man gutting her kitchen. When he'd asked where Zoe was, he'd said she was in Spain. Perhaps she had just taken a holiday while the work was going on in the house, but he worried about the pair being alone together. Maybe this was cathartic for Shane but what would it do to his little sister? Shatter the few happy family memories she had, that's what.

Shane couldn't be thinking straight. He obviously hadn't considered his sister's feelings or, indeed, those of his uncle and aunt. Poor Gerry Hall. Surely, he didn't deserve to have his family's secrets turned into a drama. If this play made it to the stage, it would be the talk of their small home town, bringing shame on the family name. And what purpose would Shane's public condemnation serve? His parents were long dead: justice couldn't be done. This was wrong, it was as simple as that.

Adam could understand why John Whelan was delighted with the script, even without knowing the ending. It was electric. But it would not go ahead, not if Adam had anything to do with it. He had to talk Shane out of this or the man would live to regret it.

Adam picked up his phone to call him but paused. If he admitted to having read the play, Shane might just hang up. A call to Zoe might be safer. He could pretend he couldn't get through to Shane and was just checking in, wondering how things were going. If he talked to her, he'd know from her voice and manner if she knew anything. But if Shane was with her, what then? He might not have told her, but if he felt under pressure from Adam, there was no telling how he'd react. Adam sat staring at his phone and finally decided to send a text instead:

Hey, Zoe. Heard you joined your bro in the sun, it's well for some! Can you tell me if he's any plans to come home or if I should go back to stocking shelves in Clerys! ☺

Yes, he was happy with that. It was suitably light-hearted and flippant. He went to get a beer while he waited for a response. But he was now on his second and the phone remained stubbornly silent. He was sorry he'd sent the damn text now. Had she left her phone somewhere and not received it? Was she afraid to answer because Shane was a basket case and she didn't have an answer? Were they together, talking and trying to come up with a suitable reply? Or was she too upset and preoccupied to even notice his text? Adam crumpled up the empty can in his hand and hurled it in the direction of the bin, missing. Fuck.

Zoe was actually lying on a sunbed on the patio, staring at the stars. It was windy and she could not only hear the sea but almost taste the salt on her tongue. Shane and Penny had arrived home in the early hours, drunk and giggly, and the noise didn't stop when the bedroom door closed. Zoe couldn't stand it. It was tough enough listening to their coupling when she was lying in her lonely bed and longing to be in Robbie's arms, but tonight she wanted to storm in, pull Penny out by the hair, toss her out on her perfect arse and confront her brother. How dare he behave like this? How could he present her with that script and then not talk to her about it? Zoe's understanding and empathy had been replaced by a cold rage that would not allow her to sleep. Her heart pounded in her chest and no amount of deep breathing was calming her down. If it were possible, she would leave, right now, this minute, and head back to Dublin. Only she didn't even have enough cash for a cab. Zoe felt a moment's guilt for poor Terence, who had been on the receiving end of her bad temper but the softening in his attitude towards Greg had been like a red rag to a bull. Still, Terence was thick-skinned. He'd get over it.

She felt a yearning to talk to someone. No, not someone, to Robbie. But since hearing that woman's voice answer his mobile, she couldn't bring herself to pick up the phone again. Ed had made a fool of her; she wouldn't allow Robbie to do the same. She was almost grateful now that they'd only had one night together and she could pretend that was the way she'd wanted it. That she'd never have ended up in bed with him if it weren't for the flood. But if, like her, Robbie remembered the tenderness they'd shared and the sweet silence that cushioned them from the world, he wouldn't believe her. In his arms, she'd forgotten about everyone and everything and never felt more at peace. And she had been so completely confident that he felt the same. Though she knew that he might be upset – even angry – at her walking out on him and the play, she was sure that once she was able to explain everything, he would understand and forgive her. Until that woman had answered his phone. She couldn't believe how gutted she'd felt. How had this man got completely under her skin within hours ... ha, minutes!

It was crazy. A couple of weeks ago, she had never even considered Robbie as possible boyfriend material but, within a few days, not only had she slept with him but realised her feelings for him were in a different stratosphere from her feelings for Ed. That first kiss outside the restaurant had taken her to a place that she had never reached with her husband and, it seemed, within hours, they were more intimate than she and Ed had been the entire time they'd been together. It had knocked her for six, elated her, and she'd felt, here was a man that she could really trust. But now, what was she to think now? And if she made it back to Dublin in time to play the role of Isabella, would she be able to work with Robbie? She'd have to. It would be hell but she would do it. It was her big chance and she would not let it pass. She was an actress, for God's sake.

At some stage in the early hours, Zoe went back to her bed and stayed there until she heard the front door slam. She hoped Penny had left on her own or she would be really furious with Shane, and when she emerged, he was sitting outside, dressed, and, it seemed, waiting for her.

'Sorry.'

He looked genuinely contrite and Zoe couldn't but forgive him. It was clear that while she'd been reading the script, he'd been drinking. She'd been upset and had overreacted.

'It's okay.' She poured herself a coffee and sat down opposite him. Now that the moment had come she was almost afraid to ask the questions that had filled her head all night. She started with the most important.

'Is it all true?'

He met her eyes. 'I'm afraid so.'

She put a hand to her mouth and closed her eyes. 'How could I not have known? How did I not see anything, hear anything?'

'You worshipped Dad and he adored you, so he was clever and careful around you.'

The idea that she could have loved her father and been taken in by him disgusted her. What was it in her make-up that she had now been conned by not one man, not two, but three? 'I'm sorry,' she said, feeling guilty that her father had loved her and not him.

He looked startled. 'For what? You were a baby. It was up to Mam to do something but she didn't. I don't know if it was because she loved him, if she didn't want to break up the family or if she just couldn't handle the shame of people knowing what was going on.'

'Why did he do it?'

Shane smiled but his eyes were cold. 'Because he could. And the more he managed to get away with, the more he seemed to enjoy it.'

She flinched, trying to get her head round the fact that this monster was their father.

'You know I used to dream about killing him,' Shane said, almost conversationally. 'I came up with several plans. I might have got away with it too and, even if I hadn't, I would have been a minor. They'd have gone easy on me. I wish I'd done it. Mam would still be alive today if I had.'

Zoe was shocked at the matter-of-fact way he was talking about murder, and feared for her brother more than ever. A shiver ran through her. 'Don't think like that. It's more than twenty years ago – don't let it eat you up.'

They sat in silence. Zoe couldn't remember all her questions; his bare-faced statement had robbed her of rational thought. 'How much had you forgotten?' she asked eventually.

He remained silent and slumped over his coffee mug but after a few moments raised his dark head, his eyes full of pain. 'Just the details of the crash. When I saw Rachel unconscious, it reminded me of the moment when I realised that Mam was dead and it was all my fault.'

'It wasn't—' she started.

'Yes, Zoe, it was.' He looked her straight in the eye.

'Rubbish,' she insisted, tears choking her. 'It was him, all him, and Mam. She should have taken us and left.'

'I begged her to, Zo, honest I did, but she would just get cross and tell me to have more respect for my father.'

Jesus. However bad she herself had been with men at least she hadn't inherited her mother's weakness. Still, their mam didn't go out to work and had no family of her own and it would have been daunting to start a new life with two children and no income. 'Why haven't you finished the play?'

He stared out to sea for a moment before answering her. 'I'm not sure how to.'

'Is it too hard?' she asked.

He shrugged but said nothing.

'Shane, talk to me. Tell me everything. Please?'

He looked up, his eyes begging for her understanding. 'Let me write it down, Zo, please? It's easier.'

Zoe sighed, but nodded slowly. 'Okay, fine. Just one question and then I'll leave you in peace: Did Gerry and Hannah know?'

'No, they knew nothing. I couldn't talk to Gerry after the accident and then he decided I was trouble and just tolerated me more than anything. We've got on better since I left home but what would be the point of telling him? Either he wouldn't believe me and the truce we've finally reached would be destroyed for ever. Or he'd believe me, and the pain and shame would destroy him. And that would come between us too because I'd have told him something he didn't want to know.'

'A no-win situation,' Zoe said, realising that he was right.

'It's not possible to have winners in our story, Zo.' He gave her a grim smile. 'Just survivors.'

Chapter Twenty-Three

Adam arrived at the door, sweating in his business suit, his face a mask of concern. 'I read it, Shane. You can't show it to her, you just can't.'

Shane's eyes widened in panic. He put a finger to his lips and nodded his head towards the patio. 'What are you doing here?' he said loudly. 'Making sure that I'm not idling?'

Adam cursed himself for his own stupidity. What was he thinking? He gave a loud if slightly fake bark of laughter. 'Something like that. Are you?' He dropped his overnight bag, took off his jacket and loosened his tie. If he'd been sweating before, he was positively sweltering now.

'Of course he is. Hi, Adam.'

He forgot his panic for a moment as Zoe appeared at the patio door, dressed only in a bikini, her sunglasses perched on her forehead and her skin slick with oil.

Shane shoved a beer into his hand. 'Close your mouth.'

Adam glared at him before offering Zoe an embarrassed grin. 'Hey, Zoe. How are you?'

'I'm great. You're a little overdressed, aren't you?' she teased.

He laughed and looked at Shane's tanned body clad only in shorts. 'I'm feeling that way, but if you're wearing a suit there's always more chance of getting on a plane at the last minute.'

Zoe's smile was replaced by a frown. 'Is something wrong?'

'John's just getting a bit restless so I thought I'd better get out here and put a stick of dynamite under your brother, as he never bothers his arse to keep in touch.'

'A wasted journey, my friend.' Shane nodded at the laptop. 'I finished it last night.'

Zoe put a hand on her brother's arm and then smiled at Adam. 'We're going out later to celebrate with Shane's teenage girlfriend, Penny.'

'She's twenty-one,' Shane protested.

'Doesn't look or act it.' She turned to Adam and cupped a hand round her mouth. 'Nympho. I'll go shower and let you two chat.'

Shane led him out onto the patio and Adam gave a low whistle at the place. 'Nice, very nice. I can see the attraction, especially with the nympho.' He turned away from the view and glared at Shane. 'What the fuck is going on, Shane? You showed it to Zoe? Have you lost your mind?'

'We can't talk here,' Shane hissed, and, grabbing his cigarettes, went back inside. 'We're going down to the bar, Zo,' he hollered. 'We'll be back to collect you in a couple of hours.' Glaring at Adam, he led him round the side of the house and they headed down the hill.

'What's going on, Shane? I'm not here for a fight, I'm worried about you. I haven't seen you like this since—'

'Yeah, I know.' Shane's shoulders slumped and he slowed his step. 'Hard to know where to start, mate.'

Adam listened as Shane explained in a hesitant, almost frightened, voice about the accident that he'd been in the night before he flew out to Spain and how it had triggered all these memories about his parents' death.

'I never thought about anyone actually reading it. I just had to write it down, you know?'

Adam didn't. He didn't have Shane's talents and couldn't, wouldn't talk about his life. The very idea made him shudder.

Shane turned into a dark, narrow bar and ordered two beers. Adam said nothing until they'd been served. He was glad of the time to get his head together but he still couldn't prevent the first words bursting out.

'But to turn it into a play, Shane, jeez. What about Zoe, what about your uncle and aunt?' Adam could just imagine the shock, gossip and whispers of scandal that would flood their small town.

'I never intended to stage it,' Shane retorted. 'If you remember, you were pestering me and I had to send you something, so I sent that. I specifically told you not to send it on to John unless you absolutely had to.'

Adam sighed in frustration. 'Christ, I thought you were just being precious about it. Why didn't you just give me the old one?'

'Because it was crap. I planned to work on it but every time I tried, my mind went blank.'

'You should have told me what was going on, Shane. Why feed me waffle about being torn over the ending? For fuck's sake, we're friends. Couldn't you have been honest with me? I'd better get on to John and tell him we're scrapping it.' It wasn't good letting a director or the theatre down at such short notice, yet Adam was relieved that his friend had seen sense. If this play went ahead, he imagined the fall-out would be enormous.

'Fiction seemed beyond me,' Shane said, as if to himself. 'Once I started typing, the truth just kept pouring out.'

'Don't worry about it,' Adam relented, thinking of the dreadful things Shane had been through, which he now seemed to be reliving. 'I'll take care of everything.'

'No need.' Shane grinned. 'Weren't you listening to Zo? I finished it last night!'

'But you said you weren't going to use it,' Adam said, feeling a headache coming on.

'No. The original play that I was working on before I came to Spain.'

'But you just said that you couldn't write fiction.'

'I couldn't until I came clean with Zoe. Now that I've told her the truth, I'm back on track.'

Adam looked at his bright smile but wasn't fooled. 'Exactly what *have* you told Zoe?'

'I couldn't actually "tell" her much,' Shane admitted. 'At night, while she was sleeping, I edited my story, made it more palatable.'

'Palatable in what way exactly?'

'I just told her that Dad knocked Mam around a bit.'

Still not the easiest thing to hear but better than the truth, or the bit of it Adam knew. He still felt Shane was holding back. 'How did she take it?'

'She was upset, obviously. She was such a Daddy's girl it's hard for her to learn that he made Mam's life hell. But she's more upset that I witnessed it all. Thinks I should get counselling.' Shane snorted.

'It's not a bad idea. I mean there's only so much you can keep inside.'

'I haven't kept it inside – you and John read it,' Shane protested.

'We haven't read the ending,' Adam pointed out, 'and you haven't been honest with Zoe, so I'm not really sure what's changed.'

'It was good just to talk about Mam, I suppose. Any time Zo has tried to in the past, I've shut her down. I was afraid of what I'd say.'

'And you don't feel that way any more?' This seemed like one hell of a can of worms to Adam. Now that Shane had opened up, surely Zoe would expect more.

'I don't know.' Shane raked his fingers through his hair and looked at Adam with haunted eyes. 'Look, as soon as Rachel went to see her, she knew there was something up and came straight out here to find out what was going on. I had to tell her something, didn't I?'

Adam didn't know. He didn't have the answers. 'I'm not sure but I don't see what good it would do to tell her the full story now. But it means yet more lies and more secrets. Are you sure you can handle that, Shane?'

'I'm fine.' Shane took a swig of beer and grinned. 'Penny gives me all the therapy I need.'

'Is it serious?'

'Lord, no, she's got big plans that certainly don't include a guy like me. She just thinks hanging out with a morose writer in a fabulous pad is pretty cool.'

'And the original play is really finished?'

'Yeah, and it's not half bad. If John likes it, great. If he doesn't' – Shane shrugged – 'tough. There is no way my story is ever going to see the light of day.'

'And you've written that last scene?'

The light went out of Shane's eyes and his smile was grim. 'I did and, no, you can't read it.'

Adam held up his hands. 'That's fine, I was just curious.'

Shane drained his bottle and stood up. 'Come on, Zoe will be wondering where we've got to.'

The four of them sat in the crowded bar and, though Shane was flirting with the sexy bartender, Adam noticed it seemed a bit forced and he was putting away a fair amount of tequila.

'I suppose you're smitten too,' Zoe said, scowling in Penny's direction.

'Not particularly.' Adam smiled at her. 'You don't approve?'

'I don't approve or disapprove – I just wish that she wasn't around so much. I came out here to talk to Shane but it's been almost impossible to get him alone.'

'And now I've arrived unannounced. Sorry.'

'Oh, come on, Adam, you know that I wasn't having a go at you. I'm glad you came, you're his best friend. He probably tells you more than he tells me.'

If only you knew, Adam thought.

'But Penny's a stranger,' Zoe continued, 'and I'm damned if I'm going to discuss our private business in front of her.' She met his eyes. 'I'm right, aren't I? You didn't come because you were worried about the deadline but because of what was in that play.'

Adam shifted on his stool. This was dangerous territory. 'Yeah, when I realised it was based on his own experiences, I thought he might be going through a tough time.'

'Did he tell you about the accident he had before he came out here?' Her lovely eyes widened. 'You didn't know all along, did you?'

'No, honestly.' Adam was glad to be able to look her in the eye when he said it. He decided to ask some questions of his own; that was probably a safer bet. 'It must have been quite a shock for you, reading the play. Are you okay?'

She shook her head. 'I'm still trying to take it all in, really. There are so many things that I want to ask Shane but he doesn't seem able to talk. I'm worried about him. The accident' – she hesitated – 'the recent one, it seems to have brought back so much pain. I asked him to tell me everything about the night Mam and Dad died but he couldn't. He's promised to write it all down, though.'

Adam shrugged. 'Writing is what he does. It makes sense that he would be more comfortable doing that than talking.'

'I suppose, but I wish he'd get on with it instead of messing around with *her*. They were my parents too, I need to know the truth. I won't be able to concentrate on anything until I do and I really should be in Dublin, working.'

'Maybe he's feeling under pressure because you're here,' Adam suggested.

Doubt filled her eyes. It was clear that hadn't occurred to her. 'You think so?'

'It's a possibility. You might get the answers you're looking for faster if you go home and leave him to it,' Adam said, glancing over at his friend. 'He's putting on one hell of an act but he's clearly been traumatised by the crash with that girl.'

'I know. He is either completely hyper or silent. I never know from one day to the next what to expect.'

'There's always the chance that he's imagining all sorts of terrible things that never happened,' Adam continued, anxious to take the worried look from her eyes. 'Remember, the downside to his being a writer is that he has one hell of an imagination.'

'I hadn't thought of that.' She brightened. 'You do hear about people having false memories, don't you? I want him to go and see a counsellor but he just laughs at me.'

'I think that's a good idea but he's been carrying around this burden for a long time – a little longer won't make much difference. Now that I have a play to give John, Shane should relax a little. Maybe if we both go home to Dublin, he'll be able to think straight.'

'You think it was a mistake that I came here?'

'Not at all,' he hurried to reassure her. 'Finally confiding in you has obviously helped him enormously. Thanks to you, I at least *have* a play to take back to John. You're the most important person in his life, Zoe – you always have been.'

'But it's time I backed off,' she said.

Adam smiled at her. 'Just a suggestion.'

Chapter Twenty-Four

'She's back?' Robbie said to himself, staring at the text on his phone by the bed, hardly able to believe his eyes. He hadn't known what to make of Zoe's silence. He knew she had talked to Terence and Tara but she'd made no effort to contact him. Terence had suggested Robbie had done something to upset her, but he couldn't for the life of him think what and his pride wouldn't let him call her again. The very least she could have done was sent a text thanking him for holding her role open for her. He'd expected an earful from Celia for the delay but she was being so understanding and gracious lately it was unnerving.

And now came this text from Terence with the good news that they could carry on with *Isabella*. Lauren would be delighted but he decided to hold off saying anything until he heard from the woman herself. He roused himself to get up and went into the living room, where his children were sprawled.

'Morning, guys, fancy going out and getting some breakfast?'

Samantha looked up from her phone, eyebrows raised. 'You've cheered up. Have you made up with your girlfriend?'

Robbie was regretting having confided in them about Zoe. It had been premature, but he'd felt so excited and couldn't wait for them to meet her. And then she'd disappeared. 'I told you, she's not my girlfriend, just someone I like, a lot. Apparently, she's back in Ireland.'

'When do we get to meet her?' Nick piped up, though his eyes didn't leave the TV screen.

'No idea. Come on, I'm hungry.' Nick could usually be diverted by food.

'Can we go into town?' Sammy asked. 'I need stuff.'

'You always need stuff,' Robbie muttered. 'The apartment is full of stuff. I can't imagine what your bedroom at Mum's house is like.'

'A clothes and make-up shop,' Nick told him.

'Better than your pigsty,' his sister retorted.

'We'll eat first and then go into the city and you can have a wander round while I make a few calls,' their father promised.

'To your girlfriend.' Sammy grinned.

He threw a cushion at her. 'Maybe we'll stay home.'

'Okay, okay, I'll shut up,' she said and, jumping to her feet, went to get ready.

Robbie settled with a newspaper and his phone in a café, having already given his kids a tenner each and sent them off to shop, with the proviso that they stay in the area and keep their phones on. Once he had a coffee in front of him, he called Terence.

'Robbie, how are you?' Terence sounded upbeat, obviously glad to have his Isabella back.

'Confused, to be honest. You said Zoe is home but I haven't heard from her. Does she want to play the part or not?' He closed his eyes, annoyed with himself. That had come out more petulant than businesslike. And obviously, Terence thought so too.

'Patience,' he said, chuckling. 'She only flew in late last night and I think she and Tara were going to move some of her things back into the house this morning.'

'Fair enough,' he muttered. 'What about her brother? Are you any the wiser about what was going on there?'

'Not really.'

'So what's to stop her disappearing on us again the next time he needs her?'

'She assures me that's not going to happen.'

'It would be nice if she assured her director,' Robbie grumbled.

They chatted for a few more moments and then Robbie hung up. It was all very well Terence saying that he should give Zoe time, but he needed to book a room for the rehearsals and Lauren's blood pressure was rising with every phone call, as she tried to pin him down so that she could confirm dates with the theatre and get the posters printed and radio and newspaper advertisements finalised. Just then, a text came through on his phone and his heart lifted when he saw it was from Zoe. But his happiness was short-lived when he read the cool, abrupt message.

Hi Robbie. I'm in Dublin and will be ready to get back to work next week. Let me know where and when and many thanks for your patience. Zoe.

Not long ago that sort of text would have been fine but now it was almost an insult. It was as if he'd imagined those magical couple of days. She'd obviously had second thoughts. Perhaps she was worried about mixing business with pleasure. Or maybe seeing Ed again had got to her after all. God, he hoped that wasn't the case. Their paths would cross on a regular basis if they stayed in Dublin. And he'd never be able to look at Zoe without thinking of her in his bed or wanting to punch Ed. But if she intended to pretend nothing had happened and keep it professional, then he'd play along. He typed a reply.

Thanks for letting me know. I'll be in touch re next rehearsal.

He hesitated for a moment, realising that this would close the door on any hope of a relationship, and then pressed Send. Not giving himself time to dwell on his disappointment, Robbie then got straight down to business. He organised a rehearsal room for the Monday afternoon, sent a text to Terence and another to Zoe and then phoned Celia. It rang several times before she answered and when she did she sounded terrible.

'Is everything okay, Celia?' he asked, remembering what Zoe had told him.

'Yes, fine, it's just that Ophelia, my cat, has gone missing.'

She was upset about a bloody cat? 'I'm sure she'll be back when she gets hungry.'

'I haven't seen her since last night,' Celia fretted. 'I fear the worst.'

'Don't give up hope – I'm sure she'll turn up. I just wanted to let you know that rehearsals will resume next Monday, same time, same place.'

'Zoe's back?'

'Yes, yes, she is.'

'That's good news.'

'It is,' he said, trying to inject some enthusiasm into his voice. 'Well, I'll see you on Monday, Celia. I hope Ophelia turns up soon.'

'Thank you,' she said and hung up.

He shook his head and smiled. Hard-as-nails Celia, broken-hearted over a cat. It took all sorts.

Samantha arrived with a couple of bags. 'Hey, Dad, can I use your phone, I need to call Trish.'

'What's wrong with your own phone?'

'It's out of credit.'

'There's a surprise.' He handed over his own and she tried to call but sighed.

'Damn, where is she? I'll text her.' She went in to write the message and then looked up at him and grinned. 'Zoe, eh? Is that your girlfriend?'

'Nope.'

'Don't believe you.'

He sighed, realising that he'd get no peace until he explained the situation to his daughter. 'She was the one I told you about but it seems she's had a change of heart. Someone must have told her what I'm really like,' he joked.

Sammy didn't smile but put her hand over his. 'Then she'd know that you're lovely. Aw, Dad, I'm sorry. You really liked her, didn't you?'

'We only went out together once.'

'Yeah but when you know, you know,' his daughter assured him with the wisdom of a teenager. 'Don't write her off. If it was such a great date, she must have felt it too. There could be something going on in her life that you don't know about and she just can't think about romance right now.'

'Since when did you become an expert on relationships?' he teased.

'I'm a woman. I'm an expert on everything.'

He tousled her hair and smiled. 'Let's go find your brother and go to a movie.'

Celia had wandered around the neighbourhood for hours, but there was no sign of her darling cat. She asked a couple of shops to put up a notice and gave them her phone number and then, out of sheer desperation, went back to her building and called at each flat to ask if anyone had seen Ophelia. She was surprised at the kindness she was met with when she explained the reason for her visit. The woman on the ground floor immediately drew her inside and sent her three children off to look around the streets and ask some of their friends from other buildings to help.

'You're very kind,' Celia said, deeply moved.

'Sure what are neighbours for, love? A pet is like one of the family, isn't it? I'll make you a cup of tea.'

'Thank you, but I want to get back to the apartment in case anyone calls with news.'

'If we hear anything I'll send up word straight away,' she promised.

'Thank you—' Celia stopped, realising she didn't even know the woman's name. 'Mrs?'

'It's Imelda, love.'

'And I'm Celia.' On impulse, she hugged the woman before running to catch the lift.

Celia had left her immediate neighbours until last. She usually avoided them at all costs, although they seemed nice. But she couldn't bear that they'd probably overheard many of her exchanges with Albie, despite the fact that their television was usually blaring. She hesitated before knocking but the thought of Ophelia out there somewhere drove her on. She had to do everything she could to get her precious cat back. Celia rapped on the door. Betty was the woman's name; she couldn't remember the husband's. She twisted the page with Ophelia's photo and description between her hands and waited.

Thankfully it was Betty who answered.

'Oh! Hello. Are you okay, Mrs O'Sullivan?' Her eyes slid sideways towards Celia's door. Oh, God, damn you, Albie. Celia forced a smile. 'Sorry to bother you, but my cat has gone missing.' She handed over the page. 'She's a Russian Blue and doesn't usually stray far from home so I'm a little worried.'

'What is it, Betty?' The husband came to the door and he looked surprised and then concerned when he saw Celia. 'Mrs O'Sullivan, are you okay?'

'Fine,' she assured him, even though there was a tightness in her chest and her pulse had started to race. She wished she hadn't knocked now.

'Mrs O'Sullivan's cat's gone missing, Pat,' Betty said quickly, and passed him the photo.

'She was a present from my late husband and she's old and more fragile than she once was.' Celia gave a nervous laugh. 'Like her owner.'

He looked from her to the photo. 'A Russian Blue? They're worth a few bob, aren't they? There are some around who wouldn't think twice of nicking a pet to pay for drink or drugs,' he said, sending another dark look in the direction of her apartment.

'You look tired out,' Betty said. 'Why don't you come in and sit down and let Pat go and have a look around. You don't mind, Pat, do you?'

'That's very kind of you but I want to stay by the phone in case anyone calls. I've handed out lots of these in the area, so fingers crossed.'

Betty looked troubled. 'Okay then, but Pat's here if you need him. Isn't that right, Pat?'

'Just shout and I'll be in like a flash,' he said, pushing up his sleeves.

'Thank you, I'll do that,' Celia said, and walked to her door, feeling their eyes on her back. She fumbled around with her keys until she heard their door close and then let herself in.

After the way her neighbours had been behaving, it was no surprise to find her son on the sofa flicking through the channels and drinking gin, the only alcohol currently in the apartment. 'Hello, Albie.'

His head swivelled round and he grinned at her. 'Hey, Ma!'

She studied his eyes and saw the pupils were dilated and his foot was tapping at a manic rate.

'I had some business in the area so I thought I'd call in and say hello.'

She couldn't begin to guess what kind of business. He looked and smelled dreadful. 'You look tired, darling. Why don't you take a bath and I'll make you something to eat?'

'Not hungry. Anything else to drink?'

'No, but I'll go out and get something if you like,' she offered, suddenly nervous of being alone with him.

'No!' he shouted, and was on his feet in an instant, and then he smiled again and lowered his voice. 'No need. I'm not staying. I was just looking for a loan to tide me over. I've a big deal going down and I'm short on cash.'

'You're not the only one. I'd help if I could, Albie, but my advance for the new play still hasn't come through,' she fibbed, looking him directly in the eye.

He grabbed her by the arms. 'Liar!' he shouted, his face so close that she felt his spittle on her cheek.

'No, darling,' she said, remaining calm. 'It's true. You're my son. You know I'd give you anything I had.'

He smiled again, but his eyes were cold and hard. 'Including that moggie?'

The tightness in her chest intensified and she felt weak. 'Oh, Albie, what have you done? Your father gave me Ophelia.'

'You care more for that bloody cat than you do for me.'

'Of course I don't, darling—'

'Stop calling me darling, I'm not one of your fake theatre friends.'

'I'm sorry, dar— Albie, I'm sorry. Look, let me call the

producer and tell her I need the money fast. You can listen and you'll know that I'm telling the truth and I'll be able to give you something towards your . . . business venture.'

His eyes narrowed and he looked around as if waiting for someone to spring out on him. 'You're trying to trick me.'

'Of course I'm not,' she said, her voice shaking as his hands dug into her arms. 'What harm is there in a phone call when you're here to listen to my every word?' He hesitated and she seized the moment. 'But I want Ophelia first. She's far too old to be of any value.'

'Who says I've got the damn cat? What would I want with the bloody thing?'

But she knew from his shiftiness that he was lying. God Almighty, what had he turned into? 'Forget the advance,' she said quickly. 'It would take days for it to come through anyway. I'll go next door and get you something.'

'Why would they give you money?' he asked.

She shook her head. 'Not money. I'm out so much and some of the apartments have been broken into recently so I gave them my jewellery for safe-keeping. Remember the sapphire necklace and earrings and my diamond engagement ring?'

His eyes lit up but then he frowned again. 'Dad gave them to you. You'd never part with them.'

'He gave me Ophelia too and jewellery is cold comfort – you can have the lot.' Celia felt tearful, ashamed of her son as he coldly weighed up his options. He really didn't give a damn about her. This deep pain in her chest must be her heart finally breaking. It was a miracle it had lasted this long.

'Very well,' he said and released his grip on her.

She nearly fell, her legs like jelly beneath her, but straightening her back, she looked him in the eye. 'I want to see Ophelia first.'

'She's in your bedroom, sleeping. You're welcome to her. Damn thing kept hissing and scratching me so I gave her half a Xanax to keep her quiet.'

Celia went over to the door of her bedroom and, right enough, Ophelia was curled up in the centre of her bed, oblivious of the fuss she'd caused. Tears of relief sprang to her eyes and she turned and smiled at her son. 'Thank you.'

'Go and get the jewellery,' he muttered. 'Quick now, before I change my mind.'

'Of course,' she said and hurried out of her apartment and knocked on Pat and Betty's door.

The door opened almost instantly and Pat stood there, his eyes anxious. He'd obviously heard the ruckus. She indicated with her eyes that she still wasn't alone. 'Sorry to disturb you, Pat,' she said loudly.

He nodded in understanding. 'Not at all, Celia, come on in. Will you have a cup of tea?' He closed the door and lowered his voice. 'He's in there?'

'Yes. He's threatening to sell her. I said I'd given you all my jewellery for safe-keeping but that he could have the lot once he left Ophelia with me.'

'I'm sorry to say this, love, but the cat's probably already gone.'

She smiled. 'No. She's on my bed. He must have smuggled her back in under his coat when I was out searching. He gave her something to make her sleep. I just hope that she doesn't have a reaction to it – she has such a sensitive stomach.'

'I can't believe he could do this to his own mother. I'm calling the guards.'

'Oh, no!' Despite everything, calling the police seemed an unforgivable thing to do.

'Is he on something?' Pat demanded.

Celia sighed. 'I'm not sure but I think so.'

'And he's threatening you. Do you honestly think you're the only one he threatens, missus? You have to do the right thing, for everyone's sake, his too.'

Pat was right, Celia knew it, but she was also anxious to get back to Albie: he'd be getting suspicious. 'Okay, call them but I'm going back in. If I'm too long, he'll know I'm up to something, and Ophelia—'

'Wait, I've an idea. Betty! Empty your jewellery box and bring it here and then call the guards. Tell them you think someone's been attacked in the next apartment.' He saw Celia's look of alarm and shrugged. 'If you want them to arrive quickly, you need to exaggerate, love. The Store Street lads will be here in minutes. But I'm not letting you go back in there alone.'

'I have to. If he sees you, there's no telling what he might do,' Celia fretted.

Pat pulled back his shoulders and stuck out his chest. 'I may not be a young fella, missus, but I'm well able for the likes of him.'

'But what will we say?' she asked, her heart fluttering in her chest.

He beamed. 'You're the actress. Proudly introduce me to your son. I'm sure if he's high he'll swallow that. I'll do the rest.'

He was probably right, Celia realised, and it was infinitely preferable to going back in there alone. She never thought the day would come when she would be afraid of her own son. 'Very well, then. Thank you.'

Betty re-emerged with a plain leather box that was not unlike Celia's own jewellery box. 'It's too light. He'll know we're trying to fool him,' Celia fretted.

'Hang on.' Betty disappeared again, returning seconds later with some little boxes and velvet bags and proceeded to fill them with marbles from a jar on the mantelpiece. 'I have these for when the grandkids visit – keeps them entertained.' They arranged the little boxes and bags in the jewellery box and it felt a lot more substantial.

'Ready?' Pat asked.

'Yes.' Celia thanked Betty and followed Pat out to the landing.

He gave her a wink of encouragement as she opened the door.

Albie stood in the centre of the sitting room and his eyes widened in alarm when he saw that his mother wasn't alone.

'Pat, this is my son, Albie. Albie, this is my lovely neighbour, Pat.'

Pat stuck out a big meaty hand and smiled. 'Nice to meet you, son.'

Albie hesitated and then took it, looking slightly confused.

'Your mother was saying that you're going to put her jewellery in the bank for her. Good man. A woman alone is an easy target these days. My Betty only wears her rings going out if I'm with her. It's a sad state of affairs, it truly is. I don't know what the world is coming to.'

'Albie worries too much about me.' Celia played her part and smiled affectionately at her son. 'So if this puts his mind at ease, then I'm happy. I hardly ever wear any of it anyway.'

Albie plastered on a smile and put an arm around her shoulders. 'I'll sleep easier, mother.' I bet you will, Celia thought, looking down so he wouldn't see the bitterness in her eyes.

'She could do with a stouter lock on that door and a safety chain,' Pat said.

'I was thinking that too.' Albie held his hands out for the jewellery box. 'I'll stop by the hardware after I've dropped this off.'

'The three-point lock's the best,' Pat said, leaning against the door and folding his arms. 'Would you consider getting an alarm installed? Betty feels much safer since we got ours. I could give you the name of the lad who did the job – he was very reasonable.'

'Oh, there's no need,' Celia said. 'Sure I only buzz in the people I know.'

Albie was looking anxious to be on his way but if Pat had noticed, he was ignoring it. 'These characters are smart, Celia,' he said. 'They watch the door and slip in before it closes after someone. Then they check the postboxes and target the people living alone.'

Celia put a hand to her mouth. 'I had no idea. What do you think, Albie?'

He was beginning to look agitated now. 'Let me look into it. But I'd better go if I'm to catch the bank before it closes.'

'Of course, thank you, darling.' She handed him the box and he turned to go. 'Aren't you forgetting something?'

Albie looked back. 'What?'

'Honestly!' She pointed at her cheek and rolled her eyes at Pat and, just as Albie kissed her, there was a banging on the door.

Pat opened it and stood back. 'It's for you, son,' he said, shooting Albie a triumphant smile as three police officers walked in.

Chapter Twenty-Five

Zoe stared at Robbie's polite and impersonal text. It looked like that was that. She must have imagined his interest if he was able to move on so quickly. It hurt, but better to find out now than in a few months' time. The first rehearsal would be awkward but she'd just have to grin and bear it, concentrate on the part and not the director. She jumped as the phone rang in her hand. She glanced hopefully at the screen but it was a number she didn't recognise. 'Hello?'

'Zoe?'

'Yes.'

'This is Betty, Celia O'Sullivan's neighbour.'

'Is something wrong? Is Celia okay?'

'There's been an ... incident. She's a bit shook up. I didn't know who else to call and you did say—'

'I'll be with you in twenty minutes.'

Zoe phoned for a cab and, while she waited for it she called Tara.

'Hi,' her friend answered. 'Are you ready to be picked up?'

'No,' Zoe said and explained the situation. 'I'll call you when I know what's going on.'

'But you're still coming over for dinner this evening, right? I want to hear all about Spain.'

'Don't worry, I'll be there.'

'Something's up here, by the look of it.' The driver pulled up behind two Garda cars.

'Oh, God,' Zoe muttered and hopped out. She pushed her way through the small crowd standing outside Celia's building, in time to see a man being pushed into the back of one of the cars, the sun glinting on the cuffs that linked him to the police officer. As she got closer, the man looked straight at her. He gave her a lewd grin and she realised it was Celia's son. Oh, God, what had he done? She went to go inside, but another Garda stopped her.

'Are you a resident, miss?' he asked.

'No, I'm a close friend of Celia O'Sullivan's. Her neighbour, Betty, called me and asked me to come.'

'Go ahead, then.' He stood back.

She glanced over her shoulder as the car screeched away. 'He hasn't hurt her, has he?'

'No, miss.'

'Thank God,' she said, and headed for the stairs. When she emerged onto the landing it was full of people, so she wormed her way through them and was about to go into Celia's apartment when a stocky woman blocked her way. 'Can I help you?'

Before she had a chance to answer, Pat was there. 'It's fine, Imelda. Zoe is a friend of Celia's.'

'Oh, sorry.' The woman gave her a warm smile and stood aside. 'Come on in, love.'

'What's happened?' Zoe asked Pat.

'The bugger was back looking for money again, only this time he took her cat, threatened to sell it. She came to us for help and I kept him talking while Betty called the guards.'

'Well done. Is Celia all right?'

'Upset. Come on in, she'll be happy to see you.'

Zoe sincerely doubted it but followed him inside. A policeman was talking to Betty, while Celia sat on the sofa looking tiny and frail and white as a ghost. 'Celia?' Feeling awkward and unwelcome, Zoe perched beside her. Celia continued to stare straight ahead, her eyes wide with shock and her lips a sickly shade of blue. 'Are you all right?'

'He doesn't mean to be nasty.' Celia didn't even look round. 'It's just whatever stuff he takes makes him that way. I don't mind him having my money. It will all be his when I'm gone anyway. I just wish he wouldn't spend it on drink and drugs. But when he threatened to take Ophelia, I couldn't let him do that.'

'Ophelia?'

'My cat.' Celia snapped out of her reverie. 'Oh my, I forgot all about the poor darling, she must be starved!' She hopped to her feet and went into the bedroom but moments later her cries brought them all running. The cat was cradled in her arms and she stroked it lovingly, tears rolling down her cheeks. 'She's dead. Albie killed my beautiful Ophelia.' And, the cat still in her arms, Celia slid to the floor.

*

This wasn't quite the reunion Terence had expected. They were in a small room off the Accident & Emergency Department, waiting for news of Celia. Zoe sat in a plastic chair beside the door, her head back and eyes closed, while Robbie sat as far away from her as he possibly could, messing with his phone. Terence felt like banging their heads together. 'Hasn't she any other relations?' he asked.

Zoe opened her eyes. 'Her sister-in-law, but she doesn't live in Dublin and her husband's recovering from an operation. As soon as she's arranged for someone to keep an eye on him, she'll come up.'

Robbie raised his head. 'Celia's going to be okay, isn't she?'

'Worried about having to find a replacement?' Zoe said, and then sighed, shaking her head. 'I'm sorry, that was uncalled for.'

'We understand, darling.' Terence patted her arm. 'You've had a dreadful experience.'

Robbie acknowledged the apology with a brief nod.

'I'm not convinced she will be okay,' Zoe said, wiping her eyes with the handkerchief Terence proffered. 'She looked awful when I got there, really sick, and that was before she discovered the cat was dead.'

'I don't get why he killed the cat,' Robbie said.

'He didn't intend to, or at least it doesn't look that way. He gave it a sedative to keep it quiet and apparently the drug was too strong for the cat's system.'

Terence noticed that, despite the apology, Zoe hadn't once looked at Robbie. 'Come on, darling. Let's get out of here for a breath of fresh air and I'll buy you a decent coffee somewhere. You don't mind, Robbie, do you?'

'Of course not. I'll call if there's any news.'

Zoe stood up and allowed Terence to lead her through the busy department and out into the street.

'How come the neighbours called you?' Terence asked, as much to get her talking as anything else.

'Robbie asked me to check in on her the day she went home early, and I met them as I was leaving. They were worried about the son but Celia wouldn't admit that there was anything wrong. I'd met him in the lobby on my way in.' Zoe met Terence's eyes. 'I didn't like the look of him at all. So I gave them my number and told them to call me if anything else happened.'

He put an arm around her shoulders and gave her a squeeze. 'You're a good girl.'

'I wasn't needed,' she assured him. 'Celia may not live in the lap of luxury but she has great neighbours. They all rallied round.'

Terence pushed open the door of a small café, sent her to sit down and returned with two large coffees and chocolate brownies. 'You have to keep your strength up, darling, and sugar is good for shock.'

Zoe nodded and stirred her coffee. 'Do you think she'll be all right, Terence?'

'Of course she will!' He winked at her. 'Celia's a tough old bird and quite fit. She walks everywhere and swims too, I believe.'

'Imagine, if she died that bastard would get everything. It doesn't seem right, does it?'

'From what you've said, I doubt she's much left to give,' Terence replied.

'Pride is a terrible thing. If she'd told someone what was going on before this, the cat would be alive and she wouldn't be in A&E.' Zoe looked at him. 'Hasn't she any close friends at all?'

'I think her husband was her real friend. They were a very united couple. And you know what Celia's like. If Albie was troublesome, she wouldn't have wanted people to know about it. Keeping up appearances would be more important.'

'It's very sad.'

'It is. It's also sad to see you and Robbie not speaking. Tara had great hopes for the two of you. What went wrong?'

She stiffened at the mention of his name. 'I'm not interested in being one of many, Terence. I've been there before, remember, and I have no intention of going there again.'

'You think Robbie is seeing other women?' He laughed. 'What rubbish.'

'I called him one night from Spain and a woman answered his phone,' she told him.

He threw back his head and grinned. 'Oh, my, then he must be having sex with someone else! Did it ever occur to you that it could have been Lauren?'

'Why would she be answering his phone?' Zoe demanded.

'Sorry. Excuse me a sec, will you?' Terence stood up.

'Of course.'

'I'm expecting an important call. Will you answer it if I'm not back?'

'Sure – oh.' She scowled at him. 'Very funny.'

He sat down again. 'Robbie also has a teenage daughter who looks and behaves more like a twenty-year-old than a fifteen-year-old.'

Doubt filled Zoe's eyes. 'But why hasn't he called me?'

'What did you say in your note?'

'That I was sorry but I had to go away, my brother needed me, and he should find someone else ...' She raised her eyes to his. 'I meant to play Isabella.'

'And how is he supposed to know that? Especially as you talked to both me and Tara when you were in Spain – and he knows it – yet you didn't call him.' Terence shook his head, amused at the conclusions both Zoe and Robbie had leapt to.

'You might be right but you might not. The woman who answered *could* have been a girlfriend.'

'Yes, but in all honesty, Robbie has not been behaving like a man who's out having a good time. On the contrary, he's been a moody bugger.'

Zoe looked pleased to hear that. 'What should I do?' she asked.

'Go and talk to him.' He glanced at his watch. 'I have to run. I promised I'd go to the doctor's with Tara and she'll be wondering where I've got to.'

'Of course! I forgot. I hope it goes well, Terence.'

'Thanks darling. Keep in touch and let me know how Celia's doing.' He leaned over to kiss her cheek and left her to mull over what he'd said. Playing matchmaker was an entirely new experience for him but, hopefully, the pair would be able to sort their differences. They would be good together.

Zoe was afraid to get her hopes up, but Terence had made her feel a bit foolish. She had jumped to conclusions on the basis of one call, one voice. But how did she approach the subject without making a bigger eejit of herself? How did she let Robbie know that her feelings hadn't changed? She decided to buy him a coffee and take it back to the hospital as a peace offering and then play it by ear. She reached for her bag and saw Terence's mobile phone on the chair. It must have slipped out of his pocket. She'd drop it off at his house later.

Robbie was sitting where they'd left him, dozing. Zoe winced when the door banged behind her. His eyes flew open and he jerked up in the chair.

'Sorry. I brought you a coffee. Americano, right?' She crossed the room and held it out.

'Perfect, thanks.'

As his fingers brushed against hers, she met his eyes. 'I'm sorry,' she said again.

'What for?'

She sank into the chair next to him. 'For leaving the way I did. I was worried sick about Shane and all I could think about was getting to Spain.'

'I don't understand why you went to Tara for help. Why didn't you call me, Zoe? You could have left your belongings at my place and I'd have taken you to the airport.'

'I thought you'd be furious at me walking out on the play and I had no explanation to give you. I hated letting you down but I'm glad I went. Shane needed me.'

'Don't you think I'd have understood that?' he protested. 'I'd have done the exact same for Nick or Sammy. Work would never come before them. Yes, I was angry at first and so was Terence. Strangely, Celia was the one who stood up for you. She said the role meant far too much to you for you to have left without good reason.'

Zoe smiled. Celia wasn't quite the dragon she pretended to be. It seemed more of an act than anything, probably designed to keep people at a safe distance from her troubled private life. 'Is there any news?'

'They say she's comfortable, but then they always say that, don't they? I imagine they only give out information to next of kin.'

'As if her son would care. He'd be just trying to figure out how much money he'd inherit. I wonder what will happen to him.'

'They should have enough evidence to charge him with something,' Robbie said. 'Extortion, harassment, not to mention animal cruelty.'

'But even if he's jailed it won't be for long, will it?' Zoe shivered. 'It makes my skin crawl to think of someone like that walking the streets.'

Robbie put his hand over hers. 'At least everyone will know exactly what he's like, now it's all out in the open.'

They were silent for a moment and then Zoe plucked up the courage to say what was on her mind.

'I phoned you,' she said.

Robbie frowned. 'When? I didn't get any message.'

'It was while I was away and I didn't leave a message because' – she watched him carefully – 'a woman answered.'

'And you thought ... oh, Zoe!' He chuckled. 'The only woman I've been seeing is my daughter and, trust me, she uses my phone more than I do. She saw your name in my log and asked about you.'

'What did you tell her?'

His eyes softened. 'I told her you were lovely, special, but that you weren't interested in me.'

He thought she was special. 'That's not true, Robbie, not true at all. It was silly and childish of me not to talk to her, not to ask for you. But Ed made a fool of me and I couldn't bear being used like that again.'

He laced his fingers through hers. 'I'm not Ed, Zoe. I care about you. Quite a lot, actually.'

She felt a warm glow spread through her at the tenderness in his eyes. 'I care about you too. Quite a lot, actually.'

He was lowering his mouth to hers when the door opened and a young doctor came in. 'Are you the relatives of Mrs Celia O'Sullivan?' he asked.

'Yes,' Zoe said immediately, fed up of the number of times they'd been asked that question. What difference did it make? They were the closest Celia had to family until her sister-in-law arrived.

'We're moving her up to a ward and you can visit for a few minutes. In the morning, she will have an angiogram and, depending on what we find, possibly angioplasty.'

'What's that?' Zoe asked.

'If any of her arteries are clogged, stents will be put in to open them, allowing the blood to flow more freely.'

'It's a straightforward procedure, Zoe,' Robbie assured her.

'It is. A nurse will come and get you once Mrs O'Sullivan is settled on the ward.' The doctor nodded at them and left.

'That's good news, isn't it?' Zoe said.

'It is. Now, where were we before we were so rudely interrupted?' He pulled her in for a kiss and she wound her arms around his neck. There was always a risk that her heart might still get broken but, she decided, Robbie was worth the risk.

*

'How are you feeling, Celia?' Robbie asked, touching the actress's hand.

'A little sleepy.'

Zoe pulled up a chair. 'You'll feel better after some rest and then we can get back to work again. I'm so sorry for deserting you all but I needed to spend some time with my brother.'

'That's quite all right, darling. Family first, that's what my Albert always said.'

A flicker of concern crossed her brow and Zoe kept talking, not wanting Celia's thoughts to turn to Albie. 'I have your keys. You'll probably be kept in for a couple of days, so tell me what you need and I can go to your apartment and pack a small case for you.'

'Thank you, darling, I'd appreciate it.' Robbie backed away as Celia told her what she wanted and Zoe wrote it down. 'And will you put out some water and food for Ophelia and ask Betty to pop in and check on her?'

Zoe looked at Robbie, not sure what to say, but Robbie smiled at Celia. 'Of course we will.'

'We should go,' Zoe said. 'We were warned not to stay long.'

'I *am* tired.'

'I'll leave your bag at the nurses' station and I'll give them my number. If you think of anything else you want, just ask, Celia.' Zoe kissed her cheek.

'So kind, so very kind,' Celia said, her eyes watering.

'Was I wrong to pretend about the cat?' Robbie asked on their way out to his car.

'No, the nurse said we shouldn't say anything to distress her, that it's important she's well rested for the procedure in the morning. I'm glad she's forgotten. There'll be plenty of time for her to face up to reality,' Zoe said, thinking of Albie.

Robbie turned her to face him. 'Spend the night with me, Zoe?'

She put a hand up to caress his cheek. 'There's nothing I'd like more but Tara's expecting me. We haven't had a proper chance to catch up and, believe me, we have a lot to talk about.'

He raised an eyebrow. 'More secrets?'

She sighed and nodded. 'More secrets, but I'll fill you in soon, I promise. How about tomorrow night?'

He hugged her close. 'I'll be counting the hours.'

Chapter Twenty Six

Tara was feeling angry and upset and tired. She didn't need a doctor, she needed money and decent help and, basically, sleep. Thank God Zoe was back in Dublin. At least she'd have an extra pair of hands from time to time and someone to talk to. When her father had told her he'd gone to see Greg, she'd been annoyed at his interference but not half as incensed as she was when she heard what Greg had said about her. Was he delusional or trying to persuade Terence she was crazy in order to excuse his behaviour? And her dad had swallowed it all and was now convinced that she was sick in the head. He'd even suggested that Greg may only have hit her because of the pressure that she'd put him under. It would be laughable if it hadn't hurt so much. Terence might never win a Best Father award but he'd always supported her and seemed proud of her accomplishments. It was hard not to feel hurt that he'd so readily believed Greg. How she wished this ordeal was over and she was having a good old moan with Zoe over a bottle of wine instead of sitting in her GP's waiting room.

She glanced over at her father, who was engrossed in a novel and oblivious of the surreptitious glances the woman opposite was giving him. She couldn't believe it when he'd insisted on coming along today. It made her uneasy. Dad had become a much more regular visitor. She'd assumed it was because he was concerned about her, what with Greg being unemployed. Now she didn't know what to think.

'Tara? Would you like to come through?'

She looked up to see Jane Burton, her GP, smiling at her and stood up. Her father closed his book. 'Don't even think about it,' she hissed and stalked past him.

'Good to see you, Tara. How can I help?' the doctor asked when they were in the safety of her consulting room.

'How are you at making soufflés?' Tara joked.

'Rubbish.' Jane laughed. 'Is work getting on top of you?'

'It is a bit,' Tara admitted, 'but I'm coping. The only reason I'm here wasting your time is to get my father off my back. He's worried about me.'

'Why's that?' Jane settled back in her chair.

'Greg is still out of work and so I've been taking on more business to compensate. Then Greg and I had a row and he slapped me across the face and I threw him out and now' – Tara sighed – 'now it seems it was my fault.'

Jane sat up, looking shocked. 'Greg hit you?'

'Yes, but it's not about that. It was probably a one-off. What I resent is that I have done everything I can to help him get through a tough time and not only has he thrown it back in my face, he's resented my success in my business and done nothing to help me. He and my father think that I'm upset about the slap but I'm upset because I feel let down and I've had enough. They think that I have some sort of obsessive-compulsive disorder because I make lists, never stop cleaning and get annoyed when things don't work out the way I want. But I believe that in my business it's a positive to be a perfectionist.' She paused for breath, alarmed at the way all of her anger had spewed out. She looked across at Jane but the doctor said nothing, waiting patiently for her to continue. 'Yes, I admit, I like to be in control and I do find housework therapeutic.' She shot Jane an anxious look. 'Is that weird?'

'No.' Jane's smile was kind and understanding. 'And if you run out of things to clean, come over to my house. It sounds to me as if you know exactly what is going on in your life and what you need to do to calm yourself.'

'I wouldn't go that far,' Tara said. 'But I'm under a lot of pressure and pretty strung-out at the moment, but it's just because it's such a difficult time.'

'Difficult because of Greg?'

'Not just him. Customers aren't paying their bills and I don't sleep well but lie awake worrying about the mortgage. And, I know that I'm probably drinking too much. But I just feel constantly tired and stressed.'

'Is your drinking out of control?' Jane asked.

'I don't think so. I couldn't cope with drinking to the point that I blacked out or let a customer down. But I'm drinking to help me relax, to help me sleep, and then, of course, the next day I'm more exhausted because of the alcohol. So, Jane, do I need to check myself into a drying-out clinic?'

Her doctor didn't smile along with Tara. 'I don't think so but I would like you to try and cut down. Alcohol won't make you feel better in the long run. What I think *would* help is a holiday, a break from your usual routine.'

'I don't have time for a holiday and I certainly can't afford one.'

'Do you have time for a breakdown? Can you afford one?' Jane countered, effectively silencing Tara.

Back on the street, Tara thought she would never shake off her dad. He didn't ask any questions but she could hear them in her head and feel his eyes on her. God, she really was paranoid. She invented an errand just to get away, assuring him she was fine and that going to see Jane had been a good idea: she'd given her some tips on how to cope better.

'Has she referred you on to anyone?' he asked.

'No, Dad, because it's not necessary.' She smiled sweetly and kissed him goodbye, hurrying off before he could question her any more. Jane had indeed made her think. Tara was going through the biggest crisis of her life and hadn't had time to actually give it any real thought. There were vague, random ideas but that was it and she saw that Jane was right: she needed to take a break. And, if that didn't help, her doctor had assured her they would find another way to deal with her stress levels. Tara wished she was comforted by Jane's words but she felt it would take a lot more than a pill or meditation to solve her problems. And this evening, despite her promises, she planned to numb the pain with a glass of wine with her friend.

*

Adam was getting out of his car when he noticed Zoe's sunglasses on the floor of the passenger side. It was as good a reason as any to go and see her. He'd only dropped her at Tara's a few hours ago but already he was wondering why he'd been so keen on getting her back to Dublin, when they could have stayed on in Spain for another few days and he'd have been able to enjoy her company. But he knew the answer. Shane had told Zoe only half the truth and Adam felt riddled with guilt for persuading him that he was right to protect his sister. He had meddled where he shouldn't have and he wondered now if he had done more harm than good. For, though Shane had waved them off all smiles, the light had gone out of his eyes.

Tara was the one who opened the door, wearing an apron, a wooden spoon in her hand. 'Oh, hi, *again*, Adam,' she said, her voice dripping with sarcasm. 'Zoe's not here.'

He held out the glasses. 'She left these in my car.'

'Oh, right, thanks.' She gave a sheepish smile and went to close the door.

He turned to go and then, on impulse, turned back. 'Can I have a quick word, Tara?'

'I'm in the middle of something, Adam.'

'I can see that but it's important. It's about Shane.'

Tara, having reluctantly invited Adam in, was now perched on the edge of a kitchen chair, still holding the spoon. 'What's wrong?'

Adam paced in front of her, his heart racing. He would be breaking a confidence if he told her and he wasn't sure that telling her would make any difference. But the truth was choking him and he couldn't rid his mind of the look in Shane's eyes. Still, it was hardly Tara's problem, only Adam had always felt she'd cared. The fact that she'd admitted him the second he mentioned Shane's name suggested that she still did.

'Adam, what is it, for God's sake? Tell me.'

So he did.

The clock in the hall chimed seven. Zoe would be here any minute and Tara hadn't even thought about dinner. Since Adam had left, she'd scrubbed and polished and cleaned, replaying his horror story over and over in her head. It was obvious that he was completely besotted with Zoe and that was why he had made the mistake of thinking that she was the weak one in the Hall family. Tara didn't say so to Adam – the guy was tormenting himself enough already – but she feared for Shane. How she wished he'd confided in her all those years ago. She wasn't sure what Adam expected her to do now; perhaps he didn't know himself. He'd just had to unburden himself to someone who was as close to Shane and Zoe as he was. Should Tara say something? Was it her place? In her heart she was sure that Zoe was stronger than Adam or Shane gave her credit for. Despite losing her parents, despite Ed, or maybe because of him, Zoe had doggedly followed her dreams and never given in to self-pity. Shane was the one who kept running away. And now, Tara could finally understand why.

She heard Zoe let herself in with her spare key and call out a cheery hello.

'I'm in the kitchen.'

'Where else would you be, Cinders?' Zoe walked in, heading straight for the kettle. 'I'm gasping for a cuppa.'

I'm afraid I haven't had time to cook – I've been mad busy,' Tara fibbed.

'Good, because we're having a takeaway, and it's on me as a thank-you for doing such an ace job on the house.'

'Are you happy with it?' Tara asked, distracted. 'Greg wanted me to call and ask you about colour schemes but I didn't think either you or Shane would be in the mood for talking decor.'

'You were right and your taste is much better than ours. I can't believe the difference. That rich yellow makes the kitchen so much warmer and brighter.'

'It is nice, isn't it?' Tara said, pleased with Zoe's reaction.

'Was it difficult for you, working with Greg, I mean?' Zoe asked as she dunked a tea bag in a mug of boiled water.

'I didn't really work with him. I hardly even had to talk to him. Texting is the most wonderful invention.'

Zoe went to the fridge for milk. 'It's a bit sad, though. We don't talk enough to people any more. Then there are all sorts of misinterpretations and misunderstandings and we all get paranoid. Life might be easier because of technology but it has its pitfalls.' She slopped milk into the mug, some splashing on the worktop, and then came to sit at the table.

'I suppose,' Tara said, her eyes riveted on the wet counter and milk carton.

'I have some good news, though.'

'Oh?' Tara dragged her eyes away from the mess and tried to focus on her friend's face.

'I've been asked to play the lead in *Dirty Dancing* in the West End.'

'That's great.' Tara sat on her hands.

'Oh, for God's sake, Tara! I'm kidding!' Zoe laughed. 'Go and clean the bloody worktop before you spontaneously combust. And then you can tell me what the doctor said.'

Tara looked at her. 'Dad told you?'

'He's worried about you. We both are.'

Tara replaced the cap on the milk, put it back in the fridge and cleaned up the mess. 'Well, smart-arse, for your information, my doctor thinks I'm perfectly normal.' She flung the cloth in the sink and came to sit down.

Zoe smiled but her eyes were concerned. 'I've never doubted it.'

'Dad does. He thinks that I'm partly responsible for Greg's depression, and telling me I should forgive him doesn't help.'

'He's a man. He has an innate need to solve your problems and an inability to recognise or deal with grey areas. But he means well and he loves you.'

'I know,' Tara said grudgingly.

Zoe's smile faded. 'Have you decided to make the separation official?'

That sounded so final, Tara's anxiety level cranked up a notch. She stood up and took a bottle of wine from the fridge. 'Want one?'

Zoe shook her head.

'Don't look at me like that,' Tara said, pouring a large glass for herself.

'Should I close my eyes?'

'Sorry, Zo. It's been quite a day.' If only she knew, Tara thought. 'But to answer your question, I haven't decided anything. That's the problem. I can't seem to think straight. The doctor suggested that I take a holiday.'

'Sounds like a great idea.'

'She was lovely. She made me feel a lot better but scared the hell out of me too.'

'How?'

Tara took a gulp of wine. 'I said I didn't have time for a holiday and she asked me did I have time for a breakdown.'

'Wow.' Zoe's eyes widened. 'Heavy!'

'Yeah. It certainly shocked me. And the thing is ...' she looked up at Zoe, feeling close to tears. 'I'm afraid that she's right.'

'Oh, Tara.' Zoe reached for her hand. 'I hate seeing you like this. I wish there was something I could do or say to make it all go away. But, come on, accepting that there's a problem and considering how you're going to handle it, that's a huge step forward. Take a break. Concentrate on what you want for you and for your future. Not what your Dad wants or what Greg wants, just what you want.'

Tara sighed. 'I think it would take a bloody long holiday for me to figure out all that. I'll lose business if I feck off for too long.'

'Then don't admit to fecking off. Divert your phone to mine and, if there are any queries in your absence, I'll say you're booked solid. That will make them want you even more!'

Tara laughed. 'God, you're devious. What a great idea.'

Zoe grinned. 'Where will you go?'

'No idea, somewhere cheap. I haven't the cash for anything fancy.'

'I was about to suggest visiting your mother again, but I suppose that wouldn't help.'

'No, that would most definitely result in a breakdown,' Tara assured her with a rueful smile.

'I have a confession to make,' Zoe said. 'I used to get cross with you for not making more of an effort to keep in touch with her. I thought that, if my mother was still alive, I'd probably talk to her daily and see her every chance I could.'

Tara felt a pang of guilt. 'I suppose I should try harder.'

'I said I *used* to think that way,' Zoe said. 'But I've realised that someone doesn't have to be physically gone to be absent from your life. It's up to Vivienne as much as you to keep in touch and I know that she doesn't make much of an effort to do that.'

'That's rather profound.' Tara studied her friend's face. 'What or who brought you to this conclusion?'

'Celia O'Sullivan,' Zoe said, and proceeded to tell her the actress's sorry tale.

'The poor woman. Her son sounds deranged,' Tara said, thinking that Greg's behaviour seemed positively tame in comparison to Albie O'Sullivan's.

'I think so. Hopefully, he'll be locked up for a while and Celia will be able to feel safe. I just hope she doesn't retreat into herself. She can be a dreadful snob and will hate the fact that people will know her business.'

'I'd say everyone will know soon enough. It's sure to make the papers.'

Zoe sighed. 'Sometimes life sucks.'

Tara took a sip of her wine. 'By the way, Adam was here earlier. He dropped off your sunglasses.'

'Oh, great. I was afraid I'd left them in Spain.'

'Tell me how Shane's doing.'

'I wish I knew. He's better than he was but' – Zoe shook her head – 'something's still not right. You wouldn't believe the things he's kept locked up inside. Apparently, Dad used to hit Mam and the worst part is that Shane knew about it, heard it.' Zoe shivered.

Tara wished she was the actress. Thanks to Adam, she knew all this – knew more than Zoe did – but she did her best to appear shocked. 'That's dreadful. You didn't suspect anything?'

'Not a thing. Well, I was only seven when they died and Dad always behaved when I was around. And because I adored him, Shane couldn't bring himself to shatter my illusions. The night of the crash, Dad and Mam were having a row and Shane tried to help but, as a result, Dad lost control of the car. He blames himself for their deaths. Not that he cares about Dad dying. In his mind, I think life would have been just perfect if Dad had died and left the rest of us in peace.'

'Christ!' This was news to Tara. It appeared that even Adam didn't know the full story. Did Shane even know, she wondered?

'He never told me what happened because he was afraid I'd hate him, wouldn't be able to forgive him. Can you imagine that? So he kept quiet all these years. And then he was in that car crash with Rachel.'

'And it brought it all back?' Tara asked. She hadn't needed Adam to tell her that. It was what both she and Zoe had suspected and the reason that her friend had jumped on a plane.

'Yes. There were some details he'd forgotten and, also, I think, he started to grieve for Mam all over again. He knew that he wouldn't be able to hide it from me so he ran away. He wrote a play about the whole thing.'

'What? You're kidding? That doesn't sound very healthy to me.' Tara congratulated herself for sounding appalled but that had been her reaction when Adam told her Shane's initial plan.

'I don't think he planned to ever show it to anyone. It was just that when he arrived in Spain he felt compelled to write it all down. That alone seemed to help. He panicked when I arrived and told him that Rachel had come to see me. I kept pressing him to talk about what had upset him and, finally, he gave me the play to read.'

'That must have been hard.' Tara searched Zoe's face but, though she looked sad, she wasn't falling apart, not at all; her instincts had been right.

'It was awful. Poor Mam, she had such a dreadful life. I hate what Dad did to her but I just keep thinking about this young helpless boy witnessing it all. Is it any wonder he has moods? I want him to get counselling but he won't hear of it.'

'Perhaps telling you was all the therapy he needed. It must have been a huge relief after all this time, especially given that you didn't reject him as he expected.'

'Yes,' Zoe said, though she looked doubtful.

'You don't think he's told you everything, do you?

Zoe's eyes met hers. 'Is it that obvious?'

'Just to me, I'm sure. You're my best friend, Zo. What's bothering you?'

'I can't put my finger on it. He is better now than when I arrived.'

'But?'

'The last scene in the play is missing, the scene about the crash. At least, I assume that's what it's about. I asked him to tell me about it but he got really agitated. Finally, he said that he just couldn't bring himself to talk about it but that he would write it down and let me read it.'

'But he didn't?'

'Not yet. Adam thought that it would be better if we came home and left him to do it in peace but I'm not convinced. I hated leaving him, not knowing.'

Tara took a deep breath before asking the question that she'd been asking herself since Adam had left. 'Do you think that he might harm himself, Zoe?'

Zoe was silent for a moment and then shook her head. 'No, no, I don't. He might have before we talked but not now. I'm just not sure that he will write it all down and I don't think he will ever fully heal if he doesn't.'

'I'm inclined to agree.' Tara thought about the idea she'd been hatching while they'd been talking; it made sense. She could help, she knew she could. 'This holiday I'm supposed to be taking—'

'You *are* taking.' Zoe eye-balled her.

'I *am* taking,' Tara conceded. 'I could go to visit Shane.' She watched a range of emotions cross Zoe's face. 'You think it's a bad idea.'

Zoe sighed. 'I honestly don't know. He'd love to see you, but I'm not sure being around him would be good for you. His moods are erratic, understandably. Having said that, if you tell him that you don't feel like talking, he will shut up and take no offence. But what worries me most is that because you're both fragile you would become emotionally involved and that could lead to someone getting hurt. I'd hate that for either of you. You've both been through enough already.'

Tara was about to deny the possibility but she knew that

would be a lie. Why, on the basis of Adam's visit, was she ready to hop on a plane to try to help an ex-boyfriend? Did she really want to go out there for his sake or was it because she was in need of his special brand of flattery and seduction to make her feel like an attractive, desirable woman again? Or, worse, did she still love him?

'It's your decision but, if you decide to go ahead with it, please make sure that you're doing it for the right reasons. The doc suggested a holiday because you need a break. I'm not sure going to see a man as troubled as my brother is what she had in mind.'

'But—'

'I'm not saying another word, Tara. It's up to you. Please just think about it long and hard first, okay?'

'Okay.' Tara nodded slowly, understanding and respecting Zoe's concerns. But she was sure that she could help Shane, and that would help Zoe too.

'Now.' Zoe rubbed her hands together. 'Let's order some food. Apart from a chocolate brownie your dad bought me, I haven't eaten all day – oh, damn, he left his phone behind and I meant to return it before I came over.'

'Knowing Dad, he won't even have missed it,' Tara said, and then caught Zoe looking longingly at a cheesecake on top of the fridge. 'I love you dearly but touch that and I will kill you.'

Zoe laughed. 'As if I'd dare! I'll drop the phone over to him in the morning and then I'm free for most of the day if you need any help.'

Tara went to rummage in a drawer for menus. 'Thanks, but I just have to deliver this lot, go to the wholesaler's and I'm done.'

'In that case, I will spend the day putting the house in order.

Although, I have to say, it was a clean job. I must call Greg and thank him.'

Tara ignored that. 'I fancy Thai. You're welcome to stay here if you want, until Shane comes home. I know you don't like staying there alone.'

'Thanks, but I'm tired of living out of a suitcase. And, well, I might not always be alone.'

Tara noted the sparkle in Zoe's eyes. 'Robbie?'

'Yeah.'

Tara smiled as Zoe actually blushed.

'I'm delighted for you.' And Tara truly was, but she couldn't help feeling a pang of envy. 'Not moving back in with him?'

'I certainly am not. That was only because of the flood, remember? This time I plan to take things nice and slow. You know, I've almost forgotten what it's like to date.'

'Yeah, well, don't take it too slowly – you're not getting any younger,' Tara quipped.

'Thanks a lot!'

They agreed on dinner and Tara phoned the order in. 'I'm glad that everything has worked out, Zo. From what Dad says, this play of yours could be a big hit. How come you never told me?'

'Robbie wanted us to keep it quiet for some reason. I never really understood why. Lord knows when it will open now Celia's in hospital.'

'Does she have a big part?'

'Not really but we couldn't replace her – that would be wrong.' Zoe frowned. 'I hope Robbie agrees or this could be the shortest reconciliation in history.'

'You couldn't bear the woman to begin with and now you're bosom buddies,' Tara said, laughing.

'I didn't know her or anything about her life before. With her cat gone, acting is all that she's got left. How sad is that?'

'I may end up the same and I don't even own a cat.' Tara felt the familiar feeling of panic wash over her. 'I have to take that holiday, don't I?'

Zoe's hand closed over hers. 'You have to do whatever is necessary to make you feel better.'

As they ate and drank, Tara noticed Zoe's eyes grow heavy. 'Bedtime but, can I ask you something first?'

Her friend gave a sleepy smile. 'Go on then.'

'If Ed and Robbie were here now, both saying they loved you, who would you want?'

'Robbie,' Zoe said without hesitation. 'When Ed turned up on my doorstep, I realised I felt nothing for him any more. I'm glad he came to see me or I might have always wondered.'

'I'm sorry,' Tara said.

Zoe raised herself up on her elbow to look at her friend. 'For?'

'Not telling you about what Ed was getting up to behind your back. I should have. You would have stayed here, become a huge success and found someone worthy of you.'

Zoe shook her head, smiling. 'No more apologies. I'm happy now – that's what is important. And, although I'll be disappointed if *Isabella* isn't the hit your dad and Robbie think it will be, I won't be shattered. The fact that the two of them have shown such faith in my acting has given such a boost to my confidence. I'm not going to give up. At least, not yet.'

Tara smiled. Zoe's words reinforced her belief that she was strong enough to handle anything that Shane had to tell her.

'Same question to you. If Greg and Shane were here, who would you want?'

Tara had fallen in love with Shane Hall six years ago but he'd upped and left one day, ostensibly to write, though she'd known it was to get away from her. And then Greg had come into her life. His age, steady job and sheer size made her feel safe. But not any more. Though Shane might be moody and undependable, he would never hurt her. It wasn't the greatest choice. 'I don't know,' she admitted, choking back tears. 'Maybe I'm destined to be alone.'

Zoe sat up and pulled her into a warm hug. 'Hey, don't cry! Everything will work out. You're just tired and can't see straight. Once you've had a break, you'll be fine, I know you will.'

Tara said nothing. She couldn't begin to see a way out of her problems. But maybe, just maybe, she could help Zoe and Shane with theirs.

Chapter Twenty-Seven

Slightly the worse for wear, Zoe went home, unpacked and put on a wash. It was almost lunchtime before she finally had a chance to deliver Terence his phone. But as she stood outside the house on Harcourt Street, she wasn't sure which button on the intercom to press as there were no names. She was about to phone Tara for guidance when the front door opened and a guy in overalls stood grinning at her. 'Looking for the boss?'

'I'm not sure I have the right house.'

'Go ahead, first door on the right. He'll be able to help you – lived here for donkey's years.'

'Thanks,' she said, and walked in to what was basically a building site. She tapped on the door.

'Come!'

She frowned and pushed open the door and there, standing at a table, studying plans, was Terence.

'Zoe!' He looked up in surprise and then grinned like a guilty schoolboy.

'I brought your phone. You left it behind in the café.'

'Ah, thank you, darling. I was wondering where it had got to.'

'I thought you said the place was being decorated?' She looked at the plans and saw they were for the entire house. 'What's going on?'

'A complete refurbishment. Let me show you around. Mind where you walk,' he warned her, and led her towards the staircase. 'Let's start at the top and work our way down. I bought the top-floor apartment over thirty years ago. It wasn't a fashionable area to live in then so it was cheap. The apartment was basic but the house was solidly built – they didn't go in much for plasterboard in those days – and red brick is timeless.'

'It's a beautiful piece of architecture,' Zoe agreed.

'It took a few years to renovate the apartment itself. I was the veritable impoverished actor back then.' He grinned. 'But it was worth the wait. There are three floors and the basement and there's only one apartment on each floor.'

'Wow, that's incredible. These days, there'd be four crammed into each and they'd all be ridiculous prices.'

'Well, exactly. The apartment on the second floor was rented by a lovely couple who moved in shortly after I did. They had no family and didn't want to own a property, but spend their cash enjoying life.'

'A good philosophy,' Zoe agreed.

'Indeed. Sadly, Valerie passed away about five years ago and Ronnie couldn't bear living there without her, so he eventually moved abroad. The owner of the building, Maurice Mahon, never got around to reletting it. He lived on the ground floor and, in recent years, was in bad health but wouldn't hear of leaving his home. A nurse dropped in a couple of times a day and I ran errands for him and, if I was cooking, I put a little extra in the pot for him.'

'That was a lovely thing to do.' Zoe smiled. This man was full of surprises and so kind. Terence shook his head dismissively. 'Trust me, it was the least I could do. Remember that I told you someone gave me a start in the theatre?'

She nodded. 'It was him?'

'Yes, Maurice was a director. The first time I met him I was in a crowd scene, pushing a brush across the stage. But he found me at lunchtime, sitting in the wings and memorising all the parts and, the next thing I knew, I had a line in the play. After that, he included me in many of his productions, giving me a little more to do each time. And then he put a roof over my head. Of course I couldn't get a mortgage then, so he rented the apartment to me until I was in a position to buy it. He was a good man.'

'He's dead?' Zoe put a hand on his arm.

Terence nodded. 'Yes, he passed away six months ago. It was quite peaceful in the end.'

'I'm so sorry for your loss.'

'Thank you, darling. Anyway, here's my humble abode.' He opened the door to his apartment and Zoe gasped at the size and splendour of the place.

'Humble? Ha! What a wonderful space, Terence. I can't believe the height of the ceilings.'

'That's the plus of being on the top floor. Mind your clothes – I wasn't kidding about the decorating. All the walls and doors have been done and I'm not sure what's wet paint and what isn't.'

Zoe walked to the window and cried out in delight when she saw the small private patio.

'May I?'

'Of course.' She opened the door and Terence followed her outside. 'It can get a bit noisy at times but when I'm inside I can't hear any of it.'

'I love it, you are lucky. So, now that Maurice is gone, has the new owner decided to renovate the entire building?' she asked, remembering the plans he'd been studying.

'The new owner isn't quite sure what to do. He's still coming to grips with the fact that he *is* the owner.'

She turned and met his eyes. 'You?'

Terence nodded, looking embarrassed. 'It doesn't seem right, does it? But the solicitors say that Maurice had no living relatives and that he made this will a long time ago when he was still working and most certainly of sound mind. They say that, even if some long-lost cousin climbed out of the woodwork, it would be a hard job contesting the will. I still made them put notices in the newspapers but no one has come forward.'

'Wow, that's incredible. What will you do?' she asked, going back inside. 'You don't plan to pull a Howard Hughes and live in this huge place alone, do you?'

He followed her in and closed the door, laughing. 'Lord, no, I'd hate that. Initially, I thought that I'd have it converted, put two apartments on each floor and take the basement for myself. But in light of Tara's situation, I'm having second thoughts.'

'What do you mean?'

'She'll inherit everything I have when I'm gone but it's now she needs help. It occurred to me that the ground floor and first floor would make a first-rate restaurant. This is such a central location and she could live here too.'

Zoe looked at the smug smile on his face. He had it all figured out. She knew that he was waiting for her to tell him what a great idea it was but she couldn't do that.

He frowned. 'What?'

'It's very generous, Terence, really it is, but I'm not sure it's a good idea to jump in and try to sort all of her problems for her.'

'But I'm her father and she's in trouble. What kind of man would I be if I had all this' – he waved his hand around – 'and didn't try to help?'

'Does she know that you own the house?'

'No. I didn't want to say anything until the solicitors were as certain as possible that I really was the only beneficiary.'

'But work has already started,' she said, remembering the workman she'd bumped into on the way in. 'How can you go ahead with anything until you've discussed it with Tara?'

He met her eyes. 'Because whatever happens, I'm definitely moving into the basement. If Tara isn't interested in my proposition then I'll fit the house out in apartments. The income will be my pension and then it will all be Tara's when I'm gone.'

Zoe spun around his bright sunlit living room and gestured at the window. 'But why would you leave this? The basement will be dark and damp and you won't have this wonderful view.'

'Between us, darling, I don't have much choice. I won't be able to manage those stairs much longer and it's too costly to put in a lift. Access will be easier to the basement and it can be fitted with ramps and whatever other paraphernalia needed.'

'You're sick?' She looked at him in disbelief. Terence was the picture of good health.

'Do I look sick?' he demanded, holding out his hands.

'You look great, as always.' And he did, as youthful and attractive as ever.

'I have arthritis and, though it's under control now, it will become more of a problem as I get older. If I've had a bad night followed by a busy day, the two flights of stairs are already a challenge.'

She came over and hugged him and he chuckled. 'I'm fine, darling.'

She drew back to look at him. 'Does Tara know? Does Vivienne?'

'Yes, but I've played down the symptoms, and you're not going to tell them otherwise,' he warned her.

'Of course I won't but they're going to figure it out for themselves when you move downstairs.'

'And I'll tell them what I've told you, that I want to remain independent and I'm taking the necessary steps to ensure that. I want to be in control of my own destiny, thank you very much.'

She grinned. 'You want to be in control, eh? The apple doesn't fall too far from the tree.'

'Take a look at my kitchen and see if you still think that,' he retorted, but his expression sobered at the mention of his daughter's problems. 'How was Tara last night? Did she tell you about the doctor's?'

'Yes, and I don't want to go into details – Lord, it's tough being friends with a father and daughter – but there's nothing to worry about. She's going to take a holiday.'

'A holiday? That's it?' He looked completely unimpressed.

'For the moment. I think it will help, Terence. She could do with a rest and it's easier to think clearly when you remove yourself from a situation.'

'I suppose. By the way, any word on how Celia's doing?'

Zoe quickly explained the situation and checked her watch. 'She should be out of theatre. Robbie and I are heading over to the hospital soon.'

He smiled. 'Together? Does that mean you two have made up?'

'We have and you were right. It was his daughter who answered the phone.'

He raised his eyebrows. 'Of course I was right. You were in doubt?'

She laughed. 'I know, silly of me! So, are you going to tell Tara your plans for this place?'

He hesitated. 'Perhaps this isn't the best time to broach the subject. I'll let her go and enjoy her holiday and see how the land lies when she returns.'

Zoe hugged him again. 'I think that's a good plan.'

Chapter Twenty-Eight

Shane groaned as the ringing started again. Bloody phones, how he hated them. He struggled up in the bed to turn the damn thing off and then realised it wasn't the phone, it was the doorbell and he was on the sofa, fully dressed. Still half asleep, he staggered out to the door.

'Hi, Shane.'

'Tara!' He blinked. Was he imagining things? He'd certainly had enough tequila.

It was her turn to look surprised. 'I told you I'd be here at ten. Did you forget?'

He searched his sodden brain cells and vaguely remembered a phone call and something about a visit. He pulled himself together as he realised she was looking distinctly uncomfortable and embarrassed. 'Forgive me, I'm an idiot! I was working and once it gets dark out here I lose track of time. Why are we having this conversation on the doorstep? Come in. I'm so happy to see you.'

She gave him a shy smile as he picked up her case and stood back so she could go ahead of him. She was casually dressed in jeans and a T-shirt, but she couldn't have looked more perfect to him. He thought of Penny's voluptuous young body, but it was no match for his precious, petite Tara. 'How's Zoe?'

'In good form and in love, I think.'

Shane looked at her in surprise. Zoe hadn't even mentioned there was a new man in her life, although they had been so busy talking about the past, there wasn't much time for the present. 'In love? Who with?'

'Robbie Prendergast.'

'Robbie?' Shane knew of him of course. He had a good reputation in the business and he seemed a decent man. Certainly an improvement on Ed McGlynn.

'It's all very new so that's probably why she didn't mention it.' Tara looked round the large open-plan kitchen and living room. 'Nice place.'

He saw her eyes drawn to the bottle and glass on the counter. 'Want one?'

She hesitated and then shook her head. 'No, thanks.'

'Tea?'

'Please.' She paced the room and then stared out into the darkness. He made a mug of tea and, handing it to her, turned on the patio lights.

'Wow! Zoe wasn't exaggerating. It really is beautiful here.' She stared out at the pool for a few moments and then glanced at him with a worried frown. 'I'm not sure I should have come.'

'Of course you should. Don't worry.' He gave her a sad smile. 'I don't flatter myself that you're here because you were overcome with an urge to see me.'

'I'm here for two reasons. Firstly, I need space to try to

figure out what I want and I remembered your kind invitation.'

'Good. And the second reason?' he asked, hoping that it was more personal and concerned him.

'I'm worried about you.' She went to sit down on the sofa.

'Why?' he asked, surprised, and sat down across from her.

'Don't be mad,' she warned, 'but Adam's told me everything.'

'Oh.' He didn't really mind Tara knowing. He knew he could trust her. He just didn't understand why Adam had confided in her. 'How come you were talking to Adam? You're not exactly close . . . or are you?'

'Of course not.'

Her face was the picture of horror and he was relieved. The thought of them together would have been pure torment.

'He dropped by to see Zoe, but she wasn't there so he took the opportunity of telling me what was going on. He's afraid that he was wrong to encourage you to keep the truth from Zoe and I agree.'

'What's the point of upsetting her, Tara? Writing about what happened has helped me, helped me a lot. Just putting the story down on paper was all I really needed to do. Now I can move on.'

Tara looked him straight in the eye. 'Who do you think you're kidding?'

'I'm fine,' he insisted, but he turned away from her searching gaze.

'No, darling, you're not.'

He felt a lump in his throat at the endearment and the tenderness in her voice. 'Don't be nice to me, Tara.' His voice cracked.

'Why not?' she whispered.

He shook his head, not trusting his voice.

'Shane, you need to tell Zoe everything. She will be fine.'

'You don't understand—'

'No, *you* don't understand, neither does Adam. Zoe is a very strong woman. She can handle this. And then you can deal with it together. But don't kid yourself that you are "better" for telling her a half-truth. I think, if anything, you must feel worse.'

'Rubbish.'

'Is it? Then why won't you look at me? Why are you still here, instead of home in Dublin getting on with your life?'

He turned back to face her. 'God, you could always see right through me. You know, there was a good reason I ran out on you, Tara.'

She flapped her hand at him dismissively. 'Stop trying to change the subject. That's ancient history.'

'But that's just it, Tara, I'm not changing the subject. My father was an animal, that's the only way to describe him. I didn't understand at the time, not until I hit puberty and we had "the talk" in school.' Shane looked into her eyes. 'But the truth is, he raped my mother, and on a regular basis.'

'Oh, Shane.' She reached out and took his hand.

He tightened his fingers around hers. 'Dad seemed to be turned on by her fear or anger and would deliberately pro-voke her. And then' – he swallowed as the images swam in his head – 'then he'd drag her upstairs.'

'It may not have been what you think,' Tara said, obviously trying to make him feel better. 'Some women are turned on by that sort of thing too.'

He shook his head. 'No. My mother was the gentlest woman in the world. I wish you'd met her. She did anything to avoid his touch and I saw the bruises on her body.' He swallowed his tears. 'There were days when she could hardly walk and others when she never got out of bed and I'd have to look after Zoe. Trust me, Tara, she wasn't turned on. She lived in fear.'

'I'm so sorry. Had you forgotten it all? Zoe told me that this recent car crash brought back memories.'

'That brought back what happened the day of the accident, but the rest has always been in here. He tapped the side of his head and met her eyes. 'That's why I left you. We were getting close, so very close, but I was afraid to take it to the next stage, terrified I might be like *him*.'

Tara looked completely stunned. 'Shane, you could never be like that,' she protested. 'You are the sweetest, most wonderful man.'

'Stop, you're making me blush,' he protested, but it was nice to hear her say so.

'And I thought you didn't find me attractive any more.'

'Are you crazy? I spent my life taking cold showers!'

'And I spent my days trying different hairstyles and clothes and perfumes in an effort to attract you. I was convinced there must be something wrong with me.'

Shane touched her cheek. 'You were, and still are, perfect.'

'Now who's talking rubbish? I'm a mess inside and out.' She laughed but it was a sad and lonely sound.

'Greg's not good enough for you.'

'Well, you would say that, wouldn't you?' Tara smiled.

'True. But, seriously, I was glad for you when I thought you'd found someone who would love you and care for you.

But when I heard what he'd done to you, I wanted to kill him. I still do.'

'If it's any comfort, Dad punched him.'

'No!' Shane couldn't imagine the silver-tongued charmer hitting anyone. But then, if something threatened your family, it could drive you to do all sorts of things you never believed you were capable of; he knew that better than anyone.

'He never told me,' Tara said, 'but I went over to your house once to check on progress and Greg had a black eye. In fairness, he admitted it was no more than he deserved and was glad Dad was the one who'd delivered it.'

How big of him, Shane thought, but decided to say no more on the subject. 'I never thanked you properly for organising the repairs. I really appreciate it.'

'What are friends for?'

When Tara smiled it warmed him and he wished he could turn the clock back. If he'd told her his fears all those years ago, they might have been a couple today. 'Friends don't send naughty texts to happily married women. If I hadn't sent it, the rest might never have happened.'

'I didn't have to reply,' she pointed out.

'Why did you, Tara?'

'I was low, sad, worried, fed up and' – she grinned – 'I'd had a few drinks.'

'Huh, so, that's the only reason you talked to me? Thanks very much,' he joked, but he was surprised at how much that hurt.

She shook her head. 'No, I talked to you because I needed cheering up and I could always depend on you to do that – ah, something's just clicked.'

'What's that?' he asked, feeling happier now.

'What you said about Greg. If he's done it once he'll do it again. You were thinking of your dad.'

'Yes. Not only was Dad not repentant, but as time went on he became crueller. The more afraid and upset she was, the more it seemed to excite him.'

Tara stroked his hand with her thumb. 'Do you think your mam was aware that you knew what was going on?'

He was distracted by the warmth of her hand in his. It had more of an effect on him than Penny naked in his arms. He looked into her eyes. 'You're so beautiful.'

She seemed startled and tried to pull away but Shane held on tight and smiled. 'Don't, please, it's nice.' She gave him that shy smile again and relaxed her hand in his. Shy was never a word he'd have associated with Tara in the past: she had always been a confident and assertive girl. Had Greg changed that? A helpless fury built up within him and he felt like getting on a plane home just so he could follow Terence's lead.

'Have you gone to sleep?' Tara was peering at him through the gloom.

'Will I turn on another light?' Apart from the one over the worktop and on the patio they were in darkness.

'No, don't. This suits me much better. It's more flattering,' she grinned.

'I wish you would stop putting yourself down.'

'Sorry,' she said, looking away.

'And stop apologising! Jesus, when we were together we spent half the time arguing and getting an apology out of you was like getting blood from a stone. What's happened to you?'

'I'm afraid, Shane.'

He leaned closer and saw that there were tears in her eyes. He took her mug from her and cradled both her hands in his. 'Of what? Of him?'

The tears spilled down her cheeks. 'No, not of Greg. If anything, of myself and what I've become. Maybe I will have that drink.'

'And I'll get you one but first tell me what you mean by that.'

'Oh, I don't know, Shane. I just seem to be angry all the time.'

'That's understandable. You've been through a lot and Zoe says you work far too hard.'

'Did she tell you that I can't sit still? That I'm always cleaning? That I'm a perfectionist bordering on obsessive?'

'We all use crutches to get us through the tough times. With me it's tequila and cigarettes. Yours sound a lot healthier and more productive.' His heart went out to her when she didn't even smile and the tears continued to course silently down her cheeks.

'Greg said I criticised everything he did and I think he might be right.'

'Maybe that's because he deserved it. Ah, for crying out loud, Tara, he's a grown man. You can't hold yourself responsible for the fact that he didn't get off his arse and find work!'

'You're right, but I could have been more sensitive.'

'Because poor little Greg is easily hurt. Really?' He rolled his eyes dramatically and was rewarded with a giggle.

'You see? You always make me feel better.'

'Then stay with me,' Shane blurted, not giving himself time to think about it. He just knew that, with her by his side, he could handle his demons. He cupped her lovely face. 'I don't care where we live, Tara. I love you, I always have. And I know now that I'm not like my father. I could never hurt you.' And then it registered that, rather than love or happiness in her eyes, there was surprise, even panic.

'Shane, I'm sorry, I can't think beyond dealing with what's going on in my life right now and you have your own problems. This is no time to start anything.' Tara shook her head, clearly even more distressed. 'Zoe was right. We're both too messed up to be trusted. I shouldn't have come.'

He picked up on the need in her voice and ran with it. 'Trusted to do what, Tara?' She gazed into his eyes but said nothing and, emboldened, he brushed his lips against hers. The blood raced in his veins when she didn't move an inch. 'Oh, sweetheart,' he groaned, and kissed her again, and thought he might die of happiness when she responded hungrily, her arms going round his neck, her fingers tangling in his hair, drawing him in. He knelt on the floor before her and pulled her body against his, sliding his hands under her top to caress the velvet skin of her back.

'Stop!'

Suddenly she put her hands on his chest and pushed him away. He fell back on his heels and stared at her, stunned, confused. 'But, Tara—'

'Sorry, I can't, I just, I just . . .'

He saw that she was close to tears again and forced a smile. 'It's fine, forgive me, I was out of order. Let me get you that drink.'

'No, I think I'll just go to bed, if that's all right.'

'Of course. You can have the second-best room in the house,' he said, keeping his voice light.

At the bedroom door she looked up into his eyes. 'It's not you, Shane. I'm just confused. There's so much going on—'

'I understand.' He cut her off, unable to bear the excuses. 'Get some sleep and I'll show you the wonders of Nerja tomorrow.'

She smiled. 'Goodnight.'

'Goodnight, Tara.' He kissed her forehead, went back into the kitchen and poured himself a very large drink. In the six years since he had dated and fallen in love with Tara, he'd shown no signs of having his father's sadistic, perverted traits. Yet Tara pushing him away had shaken him. But it was just as well. She was vulnerable and he'd fucked up her life once; he wasn't going to do it again. Tara had said Zoe had worried about her coming out here and his sister had been spot on.

Shane quietly opened the patio door and went outside for a smoke. He thought about what Tara had said about his sister. He trusted her instincts and, if she said Zoe was in a good place, he believed it. And in a relationship too – well about time! But he still didn't plan to tell Zoe the truth. He was sure that at best it would damage their relationship and at worst he would lose her for good. He had hated seeing Tara cry tonight but he knew that she would be okay if she got rid of Greg. She didn't need him in her life and, truth be told, she didn't need Shane either. He wished it were otherwise. He'd love to be her knight in shining armour, but he'd missed the boat. It wasn't meant to be and, it seemed, he was destined to be alone. His phone beeped and it was a text from Penny.

Finished work. Want some company?

Immediately, he responded, happy that this was one woman he didn't have the power to hurt. He'd enjoyed being with her but now it was time to put an end to their fling. Even though Tara didn't want him, the physical comforts that Penny provided no longer held any attraction.

No, sorry, Penny, I have company, an old friend, and she may be here for some time. x

Within seconds she replied.

Hey, good for you but look me up if you get bored! x

He smiled at the reply but he probably wouldn't be around to take her up on her offer. Diana had warned him that he couldn't stay much longer; various members of her family would be using the villa throughout July and August. What then? He wasn't sure but somehow returning to live in Dublin no longer held any attraction. He'd have to go back to put his affairs in order but he couldn't stay there. Not now.

Chapter Twenty-Nine

Zoe sat in the tiny dressing room, practising her deep breathing, but it wasn't working. She was a nervous wreck. There was a tap on the door and Robbie came in, smiling. 'How are you doing?'

'I think I'm going to be sick.'

He came to stand behind her chair and massaged her neck and shoulders. 'You'll be fine once you're on stage.'

She met his eyes in the mirror and nodded, knowing he was right, but she still felt ill. Hanging around before a performance was always nerve-wracking. Zoe tried to recall the wonderful advice Terence had given her, but brain fog had descended and she couldn't remember a single thing, which was why her throat was dry and her heart was racing. She reached for the water and sipped and then swapped it for one of the orange segments that someone had thoughtfully left, along with lozenges. 'I think my voice might be going,' she said, clearing her throat.

'Of course it isn't.' Terence breezed in without knocking. 'Now, darling, we are going to sing.'

She blinked. 'Sing?'

'Yes, the scales will do and I find a good scream, a shout and some belly-laughs work well too. Come on!' He proceeded to burst into song. 'Doh, ray, me, fah, soh, lah, te, doh!'

Robbie grinned and squeezed her shoulders. 'I'll leave you to it.'

'Sing.' Terence glared at Zoe and she joined in, in a small quivering voice at first but, as he started to dance around the room, she laughed and raised her voice.

'From the diaphragm.' He placed his hand under his ribcage. 'Remember what I told you about projection.'

She nodded and her voice grew clearer and stronger and she relaxed a little.

After a few more exercises, he put his hands on her shoulders and smiled, his eyes full of excitement. 'Forget the audience, darling, forget we are even on stage. We're back in your kitchen that night that we very nearly ended up in bed.'

Her eyes widened and she felt her cheeks flame. 'I don't understand. I thought I'd got it wrong, imagined it.'

'We were both imagining, darling,' he said, his eyes twinkling. 'You were the flirting Isabella and I was the completely besotted Jonathan and that's what we are going to be tonight.'

Zoe thought about his words and looked up at him, an invitation and challenge in her eyes. 'Kiss me,' she commanded.

Terence transformed before her. His eyes filled with disbelief, then excitement and then desire. He tipped her chin with a trembling hand and kissed her. He pulled back and smiled. 'Ready?'

A calm settled over her and she took his hand. 'Ready.' They stopped off to collect Celia who, though quiet, smiled when she saw them, accepted Terence's kiss on both cheeks and hugged Zoe, her eyes warm.

'You will be wonderful.'

'Thank you, Celia.'

Lauren poked her head round the door and gave them a rare smile. 'It's a full house!'

Zoe felt her nerves return, but Celia took her hand and squeezed it. 'They've paid hard cash for their tickets and come here to be entertained. Let's give them a night to remember, darling.'

Terence put an arm round each of them. 'Couldn't have said it better myself.'

Zoe thought of who was out front. Her uncle and aunt, Shane and Adam, Tara and Vivienne and Robbie's children. It was a daunting thought, but tonight she would forget them all. Tonight she was Isabella.

'Oh, my God, she's brilliant,' Tara whispered to her mother at the interval.

'Celia is a veteran,' Vivienne replied. 'She can always be relied upon to deliver. It's why your father has done so many plays with her.'

'You know very well I mean Zoe.'

Vivienne's shrug was dismissive. 'She's playing opposite Terence. He makes all his leading ladies look good.'

'Oh, I don't think that's fair,' Tara said, only to be interrupted by the arrival of Adam, his face alight with excitement.

'Isn't Zoe amazing? The atmosphere is electric when she's on stage – everyone's talking about her.'

'I know! She's wonderful,' Tara agreed, beaming. 'Mother,

this is Adam O'Brien, producer and close friend of Zoe and Shane,' she added, hoping her mother would take the hint to be a little less critical. She needn't have worried. Once Vivienne heard the magic word 'producer', a smile lit up her face.

'Lovely to meet you, Adam.'

'And you, Ms Devlin. Are you enjoying the play?'

'I certainly am. It's an excellent concept and one I'm sure many of the audience can relate to.'

'Yes, gripping.' Adam smiled at Tara. 'Your dad is excellent, as always.'

'He's playing a quiet, reserved introvert so there's no question he's an excellent actor,' Vivienne drawled.

'Just minutes into the first act, I was so lost in the story I'd forgotten it *was* Dad. Oh, look Mam, there's the writer.'

'So it is. Excuse me, Adam.' Vivienne touched his arm. 'Gerald's an old friend and I must say hello.'

'Where's Shane?' Tara asked Adam, looking around. She'd waved when they first came in and he'd waved back but she was disappointed when he didn't come over to talk to her. In fact, he hadn't been in touch since he'd dropped her at Málaga Airport more than a month ago.

'Hiding. Everyone wants to know where he's been, what he's working on, and he doesn't want to steal Zoe's thunder, apart from which, he detests openings, not just his own.' He looked down at her, his eyes searching. 'I heard you went out to Nerja.'

'For all the good it did. He was adamant that he wasn't going to tell Zoe the truth and nothing I said could convince him otherwise.'

'Ditto.' Adam sighed.

'He promised her that he would write to her about the night of the crash but I don't believe he has. Luckily, she's been too busy with rehearsals to dwell on it but I know she hasn't forgotten.' Tara had been uncomfortable talking to Zoe about her holiday, afraid that she would give away her own feelings for Shane. For the most part Tara talked about how well he looked and raved about the lovely places he'd taken her to. The break had done her good but she knew that she'd hurt Shane and was afraid to admit that to his sister.

'Tara?'

'Sorry, what was that, Adam?'

'I was saying that if Shane didn't listen to you he won't listen to anyone.'

She looked at him. 'Why would you say that?'

'Oh, please, you know that he's always worshipped the ground you walk on.'

'We were over years ago,' she protested, but felt the heat flood her cheeks.

Adam shook his head. 'It may have been over for you, but his feelings have never changed.'

It was one thing to hear this from an emotional Shane, but to have it confirmed by Adam was quite another. Before Tara had a chance to reply, they were asked to return to their seats and Tara had no choice but to rejoin her mother.

Celia stood centre stage and gave Terence a look that was both withering and pitying and then, head held high, she tossed her scarf over her shoulder and walked off stage, leaving him, half a man, staring after her. He didn't budge and it was a full minute before the curtain came down. For a moment, you could have heard a pin drop and then the audience were cheering and applauding.

'They liked it.' Zoe looked from Celia to Terence as he joined them in the wings.

'Yes, darling,' Terence said, and pushed her gently onto the stage to take her bow.

The cheering and whistling intensified and then, row by row, people stood. Zoe felt completely overwhelmed and, putting a hand on her heart, bowed. She stepped back and Celia came to take her bow and then joined her, taking her hand and smiling. And then Terence emerged and the crowd went wild. Celia and Zoe joined in. It was impossible not to be moved by his performance. He bowed and then drew the two of them forward and they took another bow together. Then Terence beckoned Robbie and Gerald on stage and the three actors led the audience in applauding the writer and director.

Robbie and Gerald took an awkward bow and then stood to the side and joined in the applause as a stagehand presented each actor with a single red rose. Zoe stared out at the audience, amazed they were still applauding. She looked down and saw her aunt in the second row beaming up at her, Uncle Gerry clapping loudly, his eyes suspiciously bright. She glanced over at Robbie, who was watching her, his eyes so full of pride and love that it brought a lump to her throat. What a night. What a perfect and magical night. When the curtain finally came down, Terence hugged Zoe and Celia. 'You were both magnificent,' he said, tears in his eyes, 'truly magnificent.'

'Likewise, darling,' Celia said. 'Bravo.'

'I feel honoured to be standing here with you both,' Zoe said, tears rolling down her cheeks.

Celia kissed her. 'You're standing where you belong, darling.'

Terence nodded his agreement. 'Brava, Isabella.'

Celia stood, champagne in hand, graciously accepting congratulations but pointing out that it was the wonderful chemistry between the three of them that had made this such a special experience. She was amused by her own generosity. She had never handed out compliments, at least not genuine ones, to young, beautiful actresses before. But Zoe, so considerate and kind, felt more like a daughter now. In hospital, Celia had decided two things: that it was time to retire and that she would leave Dublin, possibly even Ireland. She had changed her mind on the latter when Robbie had brought her home to her apartment and she was swamped with cards, flowers and more home-cooked food than she'd eat in a month. Her neighbours' kindness was humbling, considering that Celia had barely given them the time of day in the past. She'd decided there and then that property size and location were unimportant. These good people had made this her home and she wasn't going anywhere. Now, likewise after she'd stood on the stage tonight and listened to the applause, and looked out on the sea of smiling faces, she knew that she would never retire. It was a privilege to be a part of this and she would cherish every moment for as long as she was able or wanted.

Terence was being his usual jovial charming self and enjoying every second of the attention he was receiving. And while there was a fair crowd around Zoe too, Celia noticed the girl kept close to Robbie's side and he looked as proud as punch. She was pleased for them both: they made a lovely couple. Lauren had pointed out Zoe's ex-husband to her at another opening recently and Celia didn't like the look of the handsome man with the broad but false smile. Zoe was in much better hands now. Robbie was solid and decent, not unlike her Albert, and it was clear from the way his children were chatting with Zoe that there were no problems in that quarter.

How she wished Albie could have been here with her tonight, to feel proud of her and she of him. He was undergoing a variety of tests and attending a psychiatrist now, and there was a suggestion that he might have Asperger's syndrome. That, along with the abuse of drugs and alcohol, might, she'd been told, account for his anti-social behaviour and why he couldn't form close attachments or hold down a job. It was a great comfort to know that there might be a medical explanation for Albie's coldness but she felt guilty that she and Albert hadn't brought him to a doctor years ago. The truth was they hadn't been able to deal with Albie's personality and so had turned a blind eye to it. The psychiatrist waved aside her guilt, saying that many children passed under the radar back in those days. It wasn't a common syndrome and not easily recognised, even by the medical profession. That brought her some comfort and she prayed that, once he was on medication, he would be easier to love. For now, though she was glad that he wasn't in jail, she felt safer that he was in a secure psychiatric unit. She watched Tara throw her arms around her father and prayed that one day she and Albie would have a better relationship. But for now, she was content knowing that her son was finally getting the help that he needed.

Terence smiled as Vivienne, the only woman he had ever really loved, approached. She kissed him on both cheeks and cupped his face in her hands. 'Bravo.'

'Thank you, darling, that means a lot coming from you. Have you seen Tara?'

'Yes, we sat together. She's around somewhere. Why?'

'I don't think she's very happy at the moment,' he said, choosing his words carefully. 'I thought she might have confided in you.'

'Sweetheart, I'm probably the last person Tara would talk to,' Vivienne assured him.

She was probably right. Terence hoped his daughter was at least unburdening herself to Zoe. He hated the idea of Tara dealing with so much alone but wasn't keen on her hooking up with Shane Hall either. She had said little about her time in Nerja, but he'd watched her carefully this evening and noticed her eyes following the guy around the room, although Shane seemed to be keeping his distance. Zoe had told him how their parents had died and that Shane blamed himself for the accident that had killed them. And while he understood that must have been traumatic for a young boy and was full of compassion for him, the last thing that Tara needed was to be around someone that damaged.

'I take it you haven't discussed your plans for the house with her yet.' Vivienne turned her vivid green gaze on him.

'No.' Terence had told Vivienne about his inheritance and his renovation ideas but not the fact that Tara might well be taking up residence in his apartment alone. For some reason, Tara still hadn't told her mother that she and Greg were living apart. Not that it would bother Vivienne. She always thought Tara had been mad to marry Greg.

'Don't be disappointed if she's not interested in your proposition. She's a very independent young woman and moving in to look after Daddy might be more than she wants to take on.'

Terence stared at her, horrified. 'I'm not suggesting it because I want a minder when I enter my dotage!'

'I know, darling.' She smiled, her expression softening. 'You are a superb father. She is lucky to have you. I'm just saying, don't feel hurt if she turns you down.'

'Of course not.'

'Speaking of the house and your dotage, I have another proposition for you.'

Terence looked at her, curious. 'Oh, yes?'

'My voice has been giving me trouble. I can't hit the high notes the way that I used to. So I've decided to retire before I start getting the scathing reviews and unreturned phone calls.'

'I'm sorry, sweetheart,' Terence said, knowing that despite the lightness of her tone this must have been a traumatic decision for her.

She shrugged. 'I'm lucky I lasted this long and, to be honest, I'm tired and ready to go. I thought I might return to Dublin.'

He was completely taken by surprise at that. Vivienne had carved out a life in London and it seemed to suit her. Then the penny dropped. 'Don't even think of giving up your life for me,' he warned her, disgusted at the thought of being the subject of pity. 'It's going to be a long time before I need bed baths.'

She fixed him with an amused look. 'And I've always been the self-sacrificing type, haven't I? I'm telling you the truth, I'm bowing out. I will be making the announcement soon, but I wanted to tell you and Tara first. Though I've loved London as a place to work, it holds little attraction for a lonely old woman.'

He smiled. 'You will never be old, darling. Are you lonely?'

'I am more particular about my companions these days and I like the idea of ending my days with someone who understands me and accepts me for who I am.' She looked up into his eyes. 'And you're the only one who's ever fitted that bill, darling.'

He shook his head, flabbergasted. After all these years, she wanted to come back to him? Vivienne was always full of surprises.

'Well?' She nudged him. 'What do you think?'

He gave a casual shrug that belied the thrill he felt at the thought of having her back in his life. 'Oh, go on then. I suppose it could work.'

Tara hunted high and low but she couldn't find Shane. She was about to ask Zoe where he was but stopped herself. She didn't want to do anything to take from her friend's night. Instead, she made her way round the room towards Robbie. She hadn't had an opportunity to congratulate him yet. She had only met the guy a handful of times, but he had won her approval when she saw how completely in tune he and Zoe were. Tara realised that she and Greg had never been like that. They had always operated as individuals and that's why, when things fell apart, they weren't able to resolve their problems. She had finally given in to Greg's pleas and met him a few times but it had only confirmed what she already knew: they had no future together.

Robbie smiled as she approached. 'Have you had any more luck than me in getting near our star?'

Tara laughed. 'We exchanged a full sentence and half a hug before she was dragged away. I'm so happy for her. I knew she was good but I had no idea how good.'

'Your father has an eye for talent, no mistake about it.'

'Don't tell him that – his head is big enough already,' she said, but she felt equally proud of him. It never ceased to amaze her that every time she watched him perform she'd forget that he was her dad. That was some achievement. And even though Zoe was her best friend and her dad more than thirty years older, she'd found herself rooting for Jonathan and hating Isabella for the callous way she'd cast him aside once he'd served his purpose.

'I don't suppose you've seen Shane,' she asked.

'I think he bailed ages ago.'

'Oh, well, never mind. I just wanted to thank him for having me stay in Nerja.'

'I hear it's quite a place.'

'It is,' she agreed. 'You know what, I think I'm going to head off myself. Will you tell Zoe I'll talk to her tomorrow? That's if, now that she's a big star, she'll still talk to mere mortals like me.'

Robbie grinned. 'I think you're safe.'

She gave him a brief hug. 'Night, Robbie, and congratulations again.'

'Thanks. Night, Tara.'

'Am I ever going to get you to myself?' Robbie growled, his lips brushing Zoe's ear.

'Now, Director, you wouldn't want me to neglect my duties, would you?' she murmured, smiling her thanks as yet another person congratulated her.

'They've taken hundreds of photos and you've given four interviews.'

'But isn't word of mouth the best way to get punters in?' she reminded him.

'Twenty minutes and we are leaving. You haven't eaten since lunchtime.'

'I had a couple of orange segments,' she said, 'and I'm too high to even need food.'

'I'm glad, darling, but the fact remains that you have to do this all over again tomorrow night and the next and the next ...'

'Oh, Lord, yes, you're right.' Zoe had been so busy enjoying her moment in the spotlight that she had forgotten that minor detail. She noticed then that Celia had slipped away and Terence was making his way towards the door. She put down her glass. 'I'll get my bag and be right back.'

'I'll bring the car round. Stay with me tonight?'

She smiled up at him, her pulse quickening at the desire in his eyes. 'Try stopping me.'

She collected her things and then looked around for her brother but wasn't surprised that he'd already gone. She sent a text to let him know that she was spending the night at Robbie's and smiled at his reply:

I thought you might! Congratulations, Zo, so very proud of you. xx

Chapter Thirty

Adam slipped away unnoticed and walked back to the car park, smiling. He was delighted for Zoe and knew, as a producer, that the offers of work would be flooding in from now on and they would be big parts. She was finally on her way. She had presence, and the understated, minimalistic nature of her role had highlighted her acting ability to the full. Fair play to Terence Ross: he'd spotted talent and was able to match it to the perfect role. He'd make a damn good director. Anyone who didn't know Zoe would have been astounded at the contrast at the party afterwards. She was high as a kite, her smile lit up the room, and she was talking nineteen-to-the-dozen as people vied for her attention. Celia O'Sullivan, rather than being put out by this, stood in the background smiling like a proud mother hen. Robbie Prendergast, unlike most of the directors Adam knew, was letting the actors take the accolades, and there was no doubting the pride in his eyes when he looked at Zoe. Adam felt a twinge of envy but no more than that. He'd come to terms with the fact that she didn't see him the way he saw her and was happy that her life was coming together. If only the same could be said about her brother's, although perhaps Adam was worrying too much. Though Shane had remained very much in the background tonight, it was clear he was deliriously happy for his sister.

Adam parked outside his small terraced house and let himself in. 'Only me,' he called out, as he ran upstairs and knocked gently on the bedroom door before going in.

'Hello, Adam.' Jenny was on duty this evening and she smiled up at him. She put down the book she'd been reading aloud. 'Greta, Adam's home.'

Greta looked up and smiled with her eyes and gave a grunt of approval.

'Hello, Mam.' He crossed the room and dropped a kiss on her temple before looking over at the nurse. 'Is everything okay?'

'Just fine.' Jenny turned her head to check the board next to the bed. 'Teresa was on duty today and she said that Greta ate quite well. She wasn't up to physiotherapy but the doctor did say that the new drugs would probably sap her energy until she adjusted to them. I was about to make a pot of tea. Would you like some?'

'I'm fine for now, thanks. You take a break, Jenny. I'll keep Mam company for a while.'

The nurse patted Greta's hand and smiled at Adam. 'Just call if you want anything.'

Adam kicked off his shoes and stretched out on the bed facing his mother to enjoy one of their 'chats'. He'd come to treasure this time together. The stroke that she had suffered four years ago had left her in need of full-time care, but it had brought them closer than they'd ever been. Though she was relatively immobile and her speech slow and somewhat garbled, her brain was sharper than it used to be when she was an addict. She wanted to know everything about him and his life and relayed stories of what he'd been like as a baby, before the drugs had taken hold. She was sometimes tearful, realising how she had let him down, but he wouldn't tolerate that. He had her back now and he wanted to make the most of it.

The nurses were amused by the strange language of hand movements and distorted words that only Adam understood perfectly. It had been his idea to reintroduce her to books. He remembered the wonderful stories she'd made up for him when he was little and now she loved it when he read to her. The doctors weren't optimistic of further recovery, but Adam ignored them and did everything he could to improve her quality of life, giving her goals to work towards. He talked about trips they might go on – she'd always longed to see Paris, she confided, so he promised that would be the first on the list. He brought her food from great restaurants and when she closed her eyes in bliss at the wonderful flavours, he told her he'd take her to them all one day.

She muttered something now and smiled.

'Yes, I am in good form, Mam. I was at this amazing play, it was really wonderful. And you know the best part? The star of the show was Shane's little sister.'

His mother frowned and opened her mouth, struggling to say something. He leaned closer and finally she gasped out, 'Zo.'

He smiled in delight. 'Yes, Zoe, that's right. You remember her?'

She gave a small nod. 'Pretty.'

He laughed. 'She was and she still is and very talented.'

Her eyes widened and she touched her good hand to her heart. 'You?'

'Oh, no, Mam, she has a man, and a good one.'

She rolled her eyes and pointed to his watch. 'It's time.'

'Oh, give over, stop trying to get rid of me. Why do I need a woman? Isn't it enough that I've got you nagging me?'

She touched his cheek. 'You're a good son.'

The clarity of the words and love in her eyes was his undoing and he had to swallow back his tears. 'Get away out of that. Don't go all sentimental on me. Now, how about that tea?'

Shane sat under the gazebo, smoking. It was cool and a misty rain had started to fall, a far cry from the warm sultry nights in Nerja. He wondered had he been more open with his sister if she would have been able to give the performance she had tonight. He doubted it and was glad he'd stood firm against Adam and Tara's pleas. Zoe had been sensational and had class and presence and the chemistry between her and Terence had been incredible.

He gave a malicious chuckle at the thought of Ed reading the reviews. How he'd love to be a fly on the wall, watching the man's bitterness and envy. He'd got Adam to sound out his contacts and word was that the movie Ed was in was already cursed with problems from the budget to the location and rows among the actors. Good, couldn't happen to a nicer guy.

Shane went into the house and returned with a pile of private papers to torch on the barbecue. He had already penned a letter to Adam, along with other business-related matters, with explicit instructions that *Para!* must never be staged. He'd also composed an email to Zoe. Thinking about that now, he fed the paper into the fire and sat back to watch it go up in flames, knowing that he had finally come to the right decision and his house was in order. He smiled at the irony and looked up at their family home. He'd bought it thinking it would help them remember their mother and the happy memories but it had only kept the nightmare alive. Zoe, however, loved it, just not in its current condition. It was only right that Shane should put it in her name. He'd walked around it with Robbie, inspecting the repairs, and the man was full of ideas on how to transform the place. He liked to think of Robbie's kids spending time here and, perhaps, some day, playing with a little step-brother or -sister. It was a relief to finally hand over the reins to someone else, to let go.

He read through the email, double checked the attachment. He figured it was safe to press Send. It was unlikely that Zoe would get home to Robbie's until late and, on such a high, he doubted that the first thing she'd do was check her email.

He drank some tequila and eyed the concoction of tablets on the table in front of him. All he had to do was swallow them and there would be no more soul-searching, no more worrying, no more flashbacks and no more guilt. Perhaps it was wrong to do this tonight, but it would be the last time that he would cause her any pain. Finally, he would find peace.

*

Tara tried to call Shane a number of times but it went straight to voicemail – he must have had his phone switched off. She had a bad feeling about it and, as she stood outside the theatre pondering what to do, a taxi rounded the corner and instinctively she stuck up her hand and directed the driver to Terenure. When they got to Shane's house it occurred to her that if he wasn't in she'd be stranded. 'Can you wait, just in case there's no one home?' she asked as she paid the driver.

'No problem, love.'

She was heartened when she saw a light on in the kitchen and she gave the cabbie the thumbs-up. She rang the doorbell – nothing. Knocked and called his name – nothing. 'Damn.' She turned to wave at the cabbie but he was already halfway down the road. 'Shit, shit, shit.' She went back, rang the bell again and then, remembering how much time Shane spent in the garden, she went to the side gate. It was locked but through the crack she was able to see flames in front of the gazebo. 'Are you having a bonfire?' she called, laughing. Crazy man. And then, when there was no response, she got worried. 'Shane, Shane, are you okay?'

A shadowy figure staggered down the garden towards her.

'Tara?' Shane screwed up his eyes and peered out at her.

'Yes, it's Tara. Now will you let me in?' What the hell was wrong with him?

She heard him lift the rusty latch and tugged open the door. 'What are you doing here?'

'I was worried about you. You vanish from your sister's opening night, I hammer on your door and there's no answer and then, when I come round the side of the house, I see

354

flames. I thought you'd bloody topped yourself, you dense bastard.'

His lips twitched. 'Should I apologise for not being dead?'

She laughed, so relieved that he wasn't, but crying at the same time because of the shock he'd given her. 'You scared me. I thought it was my fault.'

'How could it be your fault?'

'I know things between us didn't end the way you wanted in Nerja. Hey, that thing's going to cause a fire.' She marched past him towards the barbecue, as much to hide her embarrassment as to douse the flames.

'It's fine, leave it, come inside,' he said, following her and grabbing at her sleeve.

She pulled up short when she saw the table beneath the gazebo covered with pills, a bottle of tequila beside them. 'Oh, my God, Shane.' She swung round to face him. 'Have you taken any?'

'Nothing, honestly.'

'Are you sure?' She searched his face, terrified. 'Your speech is slurred.'

'I've had too much to drink, that's all.'

'Jesus, Shane, this isn't the answer. How could you, why would you?' She swiped at the tears rolling down her face.

'But I didn't. I changed my mind.'

'You're just saying that. If I'd arrived ten minutes later ...' She sank into a chair, weak at the thought of finding his body.

'No, Tara, that's not true. You didn't save me.' He crouched in front of her, put his hands on her shoulders and looked up into her eyes. 'Honestly.'

'But why would you even *think* of doing this, Shane? You've talked to Zoe and everything is fine between you and you saw her tonight. She was amazing out there and on top of the world. And she's got Robbie too ... ah.' It clicked. She looked at him, her heart breaking. 'You think you're surplus to requirements. That's what this is about, isn't it? Little sister has a new minder.'

He smiled. 'Well done, Sherlock. Ah, Tara, you know me so well.'

The flames had gone now and the air was filled with acrid fumes. Tara scooped up the tablets in her hands, tossed them viciously into the dying embers then dragged Shane towards the house, where he sat in silence at the kitchen table as she made coffee.

'Just because Zoe's in love doesn't mean losing you would hurt her any less,' Tara said when she finally was able to trust herself to speak calmly.

'Why are you giving me such a hard time? I didn't do it and Zoe would be fine.'

'The way you're okay about losing your mother,' she fired back and immediately regretted it when he flinched as if she'd struck him. She crouched at his feet. 'Shane, talk to me or talk to someone.'

He touched her face. 'I didn't tell any of you the truth in the play, not all of it, I couldn't – oh, shit!'

'What?'

'I emailed Zoe.'

She frowned. 'So?' And then realised. 'A suicide note?'

He nodded, the colour draining from his face. 'I told her everything.'

'She probably hasn't seen it yet. Was she staying at Robbie's tonight?'

'Yeah.'

'And her laptop's here, right? So you can delete it.'

'I don't have her password and, anyway, she has email on her phone too.' He put his head in his hands. 'Fuck.'

'It's okay, relax. She's probably doing something a lot more interesting than reading her emails. Still, I'll call her now and let her know that you're still above ground.'

It took a while before Zoe answered. 'Tara? Are you okay, is there something wrong?'

Tara put her hand over the mouthpiece and smiled at Shane. 'She hasn't read it.'

'Tell her not to.'

'Don't be ridiculous, Shane, as if she'd listen!'

'Tara? Tara, are you there?'

'Yes, I wanted to tell you that Shane's fine. He had some dark thoughts earlier but then he changed his mind. The only problem is he had already emailed you his intentions so I just wanted to let you know that he's okay. I'm here at the house with him.'

'Let me talk to him,' Zoe said.

'He's not in much condition to talk, Zo. He's had a lot to drink. Why don't you read the email and come over in the morning?'

'No!' Shane protested, looking horrified.

Tara met his eyes but continued to talk to Zoe. 'Shane doesn't want you to read it, but I doubt you could stop yourself and I think it's probably best for both of you if you do.'

'No.' Shane moaned, burying his face in his hands.

Zoe took a few moments before answering, her voice trembling. 'I'll come straight over.'

'No,' Tara said firmly. 'It would be a waste of time. He needs sleep.'

'Okay then. I'll be there first thing and, Tara, please, look after him for me?'

'I won't leave his side.'

Chapter Thirty-One

I must have been nine the first time I realised that Dad abused Mam. She had taken his new car to go shopping and reversed into a fence. He probably wouldn't have even noticed if she hadn't owned up. There was only a tiny scratch on the bumper. He didn't say anything, just grabbed her wrist and dragged her upstairs to the bedroom and closed the door. It was odd but I wasn't worried because there was no shouting or anything so I just got on with my homework. But when Mam came back down, her lip was bleeding and she was very quiet. She said she'd fallen getting out of the shower and banged her mouth on the sink. I don't know why, but I didn't believe her. Dad had gone straight into the sitting room and watched the news, as he did every day, and then we had tea as usual so I put it out of my mind.

The next time must have been a couple of months later. Dad had gone out for a few drinks after work and hadn't told Mam and she was furious because she'd made his dinner. She gave out hell to him when he came home and stormed off to bed. Dad poured himself a whiskey, drank it down in one, winked at me and followed Mam upstairs. You were already in bed, Zo, and I sat there, listening to the bedsprings squeaking above my head. I was mortified. I knew feck all about sex, then except what the lads talked about in the playground. But it sounded awful. I could hear him grunting and her muffled moans. As I got older I noticed that while Dad would usually be in great form after these sessions, Mam was miserable. I thought maybe she was embarrassed that I might have heard so I started to go to bed early to spare her blushes. I was twelve when Mr Murray, our religion teacher, gave us the sex talk. It took all of about fifteen minutes – he couldn't get finished fast enough. It was far from educational but he said something that really made me stop and think. He said that intercourse should be a part of a loving and respectful relationship and a man should never force himself on a woman. And I realised then, that's exactly what Dad was doing and I hated him for it.

Mam was always happiest when Dad wasn't around or we were doing something as a family and he had to behave himself. But there was no protection for her at night and there was little I could do to help. I usually knew when she was in trouble, maybe even before she did – it's funny how quickly you grow up when you have to. But I'd see him watching her over the newspaper or rubbing up against her while she stood making dinner. She'd laugh this false, high-pitched, nervous laugh, and push him away, telling him to behave. Sometimes he'd tell a rude joke and she'd be cross but he'd wink at you and get you in on the act. 'Let's find Mammy's tickles,' he'd say. Do you remember, Zo? Except his tickling involved groping her breast or slipping his hand up under her dress. I always had to leave the room. Squeaky-springs were bad enough, but when he involved you in his harassment, it made me sick, especially as I saw how much he got off on that. I started worrying then that, as she got older, perhaps he would start to look at you as a replacement. I knew that if he did, I would kill him. I did my best never to leave you alone *together and, from what you've told me, I don't think you were ever exposed to his disgusting side. God, I hope I'm right. I never had the guts to ask you.*

Anyway, the tickling sessions were always followed by squeaky-springs and I'd sit listening, powerless. I don't know why Mam tolerated it. Maybe she felt she'd no choice.

I was finding it harder and harder to be around Dad and remain civil. But one evening after you were in bed and Mam was visiting a neighbour, all hell broke loose. It started well enough – we'd settled down to watch a movie. It was a whodunnit and I was quite enjoying it until it got very sexually explicit and a woman was raped. I didn't know where to look. If Mam had been there she'd have changed the channel but Dad nudged and teased me, saying wasn't she a fine bit of stuff. 'Don't worry,' he said, 'it won't be long before you get your turn.'

I couldn't help myself. 'Turn to rape?' I said.

'No, of course not, but it's only natural for a man to want a woman and you're a man now, or near enough.'

'But the woman has to want the man too.' I looked him straight in the eye – though, to be honest, my heart was in my mouth. 'If she says no, it means no. That's what my teacher says.'

And do you know what, Zo? He laughed, and said, 'Don't mind that – they say no because they don't want to be seen as easy. But they don't mean it. They want it as much as the lads do.'

That was the night I started dreaming up ways of killing him.

The day of the accident started out as quite a good one. I'd got an A in a maths test and Dad was proud as punch. You were at a party so he took me and Mam out for dinner and a movie. Even Mam was on good form and drank some wine, but I knew by the way that he was looking at her how his mind was working. When we got to the cinema I sat between the two of them. I was delighted with myself, especially when I saw the furious look on Dad's face. Mam squeezed my hand in the darkness, the closest she ever came to acknowledging what was going on. It was a Bond movie and I was really enjoying it, but all the cola I'd had with dinner forced me to go out to the loo and, when I came back, Dad had moved in beside her. I waited for him to move but he blanked me and I was forced to take the outside seat. I couldn't concentrate on the rest of the movie. Every time I looked over, he was groping her and she was squirming in her seat, trying to get as far away from him as possible. But I knew her reluctance and fear were turning him on even more and she'd be in for it later. As we left the cinema, Dad chatted away about the movie, not seeming to notice or care that we barely opened our mouths.

I begged Mam to let me sit in the front, a treat as I had done so well in my test, and she agreed. I still remember the gratitude in her eyes. But Dad was having none of it and told me to get in the back. I knew better than to argue when he had that look in his eye. But I leaned over between the two seats and chatted away about the movie. Mam sat with her back to the door so that she could look at me, but I knew that it was so that he couldn't touch her. It was clear he was disgusted.

He stopped at traffic lights and pulled her closer, saying she wouldn't be playing so hard to get if it was Pierce Brosnan behind the wheel. She pushed him away, telling him to behave himself in front of me. The lights changed and he drove on, sneering at her. He said she was thick if she thought that her saintly son was any different from other men. He said the only reason I suffered her hugs was so that I could rub up against her. She went mad, screaming that he was a disgusting excuse of a man, no better than an animal. Without taking his eyes off the road, Dad punched her straight in the mouth. I couldn't believe it. I lashed out and whacked him across the head, again and again, not thinking of the consequences. He took his hands off the wheel and turned, trying to fend me off and lost control of the car. Then there were screams and shouts and crying and horns and brakes and then . . . then there was silence.

But that's not when I passed out, Zoe. I thought it was but when I saw Rachel I remembered what happened next. Because of where I was sitting I had no seat belt on and I went straight through the windscreen. The undergrowth we'd crashed into saved me. I was spread across the bonnet but conscious and I looked up, straight into Mam's lovely face, covered in blood. She was staring straight at me but not seeing me. She was gone. And then I heard a groan and looked across to see Dad trying to push a lump of wood off his neck. It must have been a bit of the fence we crashed into. He met my eyes and pointed at it, asking with his eyes for help. I could pretend, Zo, that I was dazed, injured or in shock, but the truth was I knew exactly what I was doing. I smiled at him and closed my eyes and waited. By the time help arrived it was too late for him and I was glad. I'm still glad, Zoe. He deserved to die. You asked me why I got upset at the funeral. I couldn't bear the thought of them putting his coffin in with hers. It was like he was laughing at us even in death, like she would never be able to escape him.

So, as I told you, I'm the reason you're an orphan. I'm sorry for taking Mam away from you, Zoe, but not him. I know how much you loved him but, truly, you were better off growing up without him, especially without Mam to protect you. I only wish I'd had the courage to kill him before he destroyed our family.

I can't live with what I did to her and to you but what I did then and now was because I loved you both. Please forgive me and forget me, Zoe. Start a new life with Robbie and be happy.

S.

The phone slipped from Zoe's hand and she fell back on the sofa, reeling in shock. She didn't even realise that she was wailing until she felt Robbie's arms wrap around her. He sat down and, pulling her onto his lap, rocked her like a baby, asking her over and over what was wrong. Eventually, she pointed to the phone and sobbed, her head pressed against his chest as he read Shane's note.

'Christ, Zoe, we had better get over there!'

'Tara phoned me. He didn't go through with it.'

'Thank God.'

She straightened up and looked into his eyes. 'This time.'

Shane had been up since six, drinking coffee and chain-smoking. The evening before, he had let Tara read the note and been moved beyond words when she embraced him and kissed his tears away. She had held him all night as if afraid that if she didn't he would go back outside and finish the job he'd started. But there was no chance of that. He relished that time in her arms and would store it away to remember the next time the darkness threatened. But when he woke, his thoughts were of Zoe. She'd have read the email immediately, he had no doubt of that. He couldn't begin to gauge how she'd react and the closer he came to facing her the more nervous he became.

It had just gone eight when he heard her key in the door. Shane sprang to his feet, and looked at Tara, resisting the urge to light another cigarette.

'It will be fine.' Tara squeezed his arm and went out into the hall ahead of him and embraced Zoe. 'I'll let you two talk,' she said and disappeared upstairs.

Zoe came closer and Shane looked into her eyes, searching for condemnation, but saw only sadness. She opened her arms and he swept her into a tight hug, relief washing over him. 'You don't hate me?' he asked.

'For not helping Dad? No, I'd probably have done the same. But for what you were going to do last night—' She pulled away and looked up at him, her face full of reproach. 'I don't think that I could ever forgive you if you did that. Thank God Tara came by and stopped you; but how do I know that you won't try again?'

'Tara didn't stop me, Zoe. I sat staring at those tablets and realised that, if I took them, it wouldn't change what I'd done and it wouldn't bring Mam back and' – he looked at her – 'it might hurt you.'

'Might?' She looked at him, her eyes incredulous then furious. '*Might*?'

'Well, you have Robbie now and you are going to be a star.' he smiled nervously. 'You don't need me.'

'Shane, I was seven when they died, just seven!' Zoe collapsed into a chair.

His stomach churned. 'I know, I'm sorry.'

'Since they died you've been the closest thing to a parent I've had. You were the one I went to with my problems, not Gerry, not Hannah, you. Even when you hated me when I went to England, I still wanted you to give me away at my wedding. I told you nothing would ever come between us and I meant it. So don't you dare say I don't need you any more, don't you dare!'

'Sorry,' he said again, surprised by her anger.

'Do I seem messed up to you, Shane?'

'No, not at all,' he protested. 'You're amazing. It doesn't seem to matter what life throws at you, you keep smiling and laughing and trying. I admire you, Zo, you've got guts.'

'And why do you think that is?' she asked.

He shrugged. 'It's the way you are.'

'Maybe, but I think a lot of it has to do with the fact that you have been there every step of the way – apart from when I was with Ed – and, no matter what I did, I knew you always would be.' Her expression darkened. 'Until last night.'

'But I didn't go through with it, Zo,' he repeated, at a loss what he could say to calm her.

'Not this time,' she said, and he saw her eyes fill with tears.

So that was it. She was scared he would try it again. Poor Zo, he had to make her understand. 'Why would I do it now? You know the truth now and you forgive me and still love me. I'm happy.'

'What about Tara?'

He frowned. 'What about her?'

'You love her, don't you?'

'Yes,' he admitted. 'And I let her read the note and explained that's why I had to leave her.'

She frowned. 'You've lost me.'

He sighed. He'd forgotten he hadn't told her that part. 'When Tara and I began to get close, I got it into my head that

I might turn out to be like Dad. I was terrified of hurting her so I panicked and ran.'

'Aw, Shane, you wouldn't hurt a hair on her head – or anyone else's.' Zoe reached for his hand, tears welling again. 'It breaks my heart that you lost Tara because of Dad.'

'Maybe it's not too late,' he said, thinking of how close he felt to Tara right now. Zoe looked concerned again and he sighed. 'What? It could happen.'

'And what if she goes back to Greg? Will you run away again or will you kill yourself?'

He flinched at the baldness of her words and her anguished expression.

'If Tara goes back to Greg, I'll just have to accept it, but I'll be at the end of a phone if she needs me. If she doesn't and falls in love with some other guy, I'll wish her well. I've cared about Tara far too long to want anything but her happiness.'

'So, what now?'

'Now,' he said, smiling, 'I'm going to start living, really living. I think I might travel.' He held up his hand when he saw the suspicion in her eyes. 'No, I'm not running away to some far-flung place to drown my sorrows every day. But I like the idea of taking trips to places that would inspire me. But I'll always come home, Zo.' He took her hands and looked her straight in the eye. 'I discovered something last night. Despite everything that's happened, I love life.'

When Robbie arrived, Zoe ran to open the door and threw herself into his arms.

'Are you okay?' he asked, searching her tear-stained face.

'Yes.' She smiled but her voice was shaking. 'I think everything's going to be fine.'

Robbie hoped she wasn't building herself up for a fall. When Zoe left him alone with her brother to go up and talk to Tara, he closed the door. 'Are you really okay, Shane, or is this all an act? Forgive me for being blunt but I care very deeply for Zoe and you scared the shit out of her last night. She loves you and would have been devastated if you'd gone through with it.'

'I know that now, Robbie. I thought I was protecting her all these years but I was just hiding from the truth and hurting both of us in the process. Now' – he shook his head in wonder – 'I feel free. And so incredibly lucky.'

Robbie looked at the undoubted happiness in Shane's eyes and believed him. 'I'm relieved to hear it because your sister would never recover from that.'

Shane closed his eyes and nodded. 'I know that now but, honestly, before I talked to her, I'd made up my mind it wasn't the answer. And now that we've made our peace, I couldn't be happier.' He opened his eyes and gave Robbie a pleading look. 'Now, can we please stop talking about it? It's embarassing. Tell me, how has the play been received?'

'I've no idea,' Robbie admitted, startled. He and Zoe had been so preoccupied with Shane's note they had forgotten all about *Isabella*. It was odd that no one had been in touch. Not a good sign. He pulled out his phone and grinned when he saw that there were lots of messages and texts. 'It looks like there is plenty of news but I had my phone on mute. Want to call your sister?'

Zoe raced down the stairs, Tara hot on her heels, and searched Robbie's face with anxious eyes. 'Well?'

'I don't know,' Robbie told her. 'I've lots of messages on my phone but I haven't checked any yet. Didn't anyone call you?'

Zoe went to her bag for her phone. 'It's dead. With all the fuss' – she glanced at Shane – 'I forgot to charge it.'

Robbie scrolled through the names of people who had contacted him. 'I think I'll call Lauren. She's left three messages so she's probably tearing her hair out. She will have checked all the papers and will give it to me straight.'

'Okay, go for it.' Zoe stood in front of him, rocking on her heels and biting her lip. Shane came to put his arm around her.

'It will be fine, you were great,' he assured her, but Zoe's eyes remained riveted on Robbie.

'Lauren, hey, sorry I missed you. The phone was on mute.' He listened for a moment. 'Oh, okay. Interesting.'

'Interesting?' Zoe muttered. 'What does that mean?'

'Yeah, I'm sure between us we can manage that. Will you contact Terence and Celia? Great. Thanks, Lauren, see you later.'

'Well?' Zoe said, her nerves in shreds.

Robbie couldn't help but drag out the moment. God, he was crazy about this woman and felt so proud of her. 'It's a hit, sweetheart, a big hit, and you, my darling, are a star.'

She stared at him in shock as he went on to tell her all the people who had been in touch looking for interviews and inviting them onto chat shows.

'They mainly want to grill you and Terence to see if there's anything going on.'

'If we're going on any show then Celia is too or they can feck off,' she retorted.

He pulled her into his arms and kissed her. 'Congratulations, sweetheart.'

'Well done, sis. Come here.' Shane swung her round in his arms and shook Robbie's hand.

Tara then hugged her, smiling. 'It's no surprise. It was an amazing play and you were wonderful.'

After a lazy breakfast, Zoe and Robbie left the house to go and meet up with Lauren to hear what the plans were for the rest of the day. Before they got into the car, Robbie pulled her into his arms. 'Do you know something, Zoe Hall? I love you.'

She looked at him, stunned, and he wondered had he got it wrong, was he moving too fast. Damn, he should have kept his mouth shut. 'It's okay, you don't have to say anything—'

She silenced him with her lips, a soft, sweet kiss, and pulled back to smile up into his eyes. 'I am over the moon that the play has been well received, Robbie, but I am even happier that my brother has finally unburdened himself, and thrilled to hear you say those three words. Will you say them again, please?'

He pulled her closer, in awe at the love in her eyes. 'I love you, Zoe Hall.'

She smiled. 'And I love you, Robbie Prendergast.'

Both their phones started to ring but he held her gaze. 'Feck them, they can wait,' he said, before lowering his mouth to hers once more.

Chapter Thirty-Two

Tara sat in the restaurant, wishing her mother had picked a quieter place to have lunch. They had been here an hour and hadn't ordered food yet as her dad was being besieged with congratulations from fellow luvvies for his performance in *Isabella* and the fact that it had been extended for another month. Also, some of Vivienne's old theatre friends were stopping by to say hello and ask how long she was planning to be in Dublin.

'Talk about mutton dressed as lamb,' Vivienne murmured as a woman waved from the far side of the room. 'Looking younger than ever, darling,' she called, blowing a kiss.

Terence grinned at Tara. 'Your beloved mother, not a genuine bone in her body.'

'I learned from the master,' Vivienne said with a wicked grin.

The waiter brought the champagne Terence had ordered. 'You two will have to drink most of this – I've got to go out there and do it all over again tonight.'

Vivienne winked at her daughter. 'How will we manage that, darling?'

Tara gave her a nervous smile. It never ceased to amaze and annoy her how self-conscious she always felt in the company of her mother. Over sixty, Vivienne was easily the most beautiful woman in the room. An expensive, figure-hugging black dress showed off her youthful figure. The trademark red hair was piled on top of her head, making her look even taller, and a pearl necklace accentuated her long neck and slender shoulders.

'There's something I have to tell you,' Tara blurted out before she lost her nerve. 'Greg and I aren't together any more.'

'Oh?' Vivienne said.

Tara nodded. Her mother knew nothing about what had happened; Tara hadn't wanted to tell her, knowing that she'd have to listen to 'I told you so' over and over again. Vivienne had always looked down on Greg. She was grateful her father had respected her wishes and said nothing either.

'I'm sorry, darling. Is that going to be a permanent arrangement or is it a trial separation?' he asked now, his eyes questioning hers.

'Permanent, I think, Dad. Greg's changed a lot since he went out of business and we haven't been getting on. I'm not sure that we can recover what we've lost.'

'I can't say I'm surprised. The foundation was rocky at best,' Vivienne said. 'You're young, darling, there are plenty more fish in the sea.'

That's it? Tara thought. Her five-year marriage dismissed in two sentences? No wonder her mother had never married: Vivienne was cold and selfish. Tara had always felt she should make more of an effort to spend time with her mother, but Zoe was right, Vivienne hadn't tried that hard to remain close either. It assuaged her guilt but made her feel sad too.

'Don't rush into doing anything drastic, darling,' her father counselled, and patted her hand. 'And if there's anything I can do to help, you know I will.'

She gave him a grateful smile. "Thanks, Dad. I do still care for Greg but I think it's time I put myself first for a change.'

'Quite right, darling.' Vivienne nodded in approval. 'I'm proud of you.'

Tara almost choked on her champagne. She couldn't remember her mother saying those words before.

The waiter came to take the order and Tara and Terence selected starters and main courses. Vivienne smiled at the young man. 'Grilled dover sole and green salad, no dressing.'

Tara shook her head as he left. 'You've been eating that for as long as I can remember. There are so many tasty, healthy and low-calorie alternatives to sole and salad.'

'It's stood me in good stead.' Vivienne sighed, and sank back in her chair. 'Until now.'

Tara frowned at the tremor in her mother's voice. 'What's wrong, Mum?'

Vivienne ignored her question and looked directly at Terence. 'I'm sorry, darling. After all these years, I'm still using you. I meant it when I said I wasn't being self-sacrificing and coming home to look after you. I was thinking of myself.'

'You're coming home?' Tara tried to make sense of her mother's words. 'Self-sacrificing? Will you please tell me what's going on?'

The colour drained from her father's face as he stared at her mother. 'What is it, Vivienne?'

'Cancer,' she whispered with a resigned shrug.

'Oh, my poor darling, my love!' He put his hand over hers.

'Now, don't get all maudlin,' Vivienne said with a bright smile. 'I deliberately chose to tell you here so that there would be none of that carry-on.'

'What kind, Mum?' Tara asked.

'It's my liver.' She held up her glass. 'And at least I enjoyed the journey.'

'Don't talk like that,' Terence told her. 'Come home and I'll look after you and get you the best doctors. The treatment available these days is nothing short of miraculous.'

She shook her head. 'They've tried everything, darling. It's over. I just need somewhere pleasant to end my days.'

Tara looked at her father. He seemed to have aged in just a few minutes but he raised a smile.

'And you've found it, darling,' he assured Vivienne. 'I will take care of you.'

Tara gulped back tears, unable to take all this in. Her mother, her vibrant, flamboyant, arrogant, annoying mother, was dying? She sat in silence for a moment and then asked the question that she didn't really want an answer to. 'How long?' she whispered.

Vivienne's eyes met hers and, for once, they were both soft and tender. 'Well, darling, don't bother buying a Christmas present.'

'I can't believe it.' Tara shrunk into a corner of the sofa.

'I'm so sorry.' Zoe had come straight over when her friend called and now sat next to her, rubbing her arm.

'You saw her, she looks amazing.' Tara dashed at the tears

that refused to stop. She was getting really fed up of crying. It was a wonder she wasn't permanently dehydrated. 'I don't know why I'm so upset.'

Zoe's eyes were full of understanding and sympathy. 'She's your mum.'

'She's coming home, going to stay with Dad. I hope he can handle it. Oh, and that's the other thing. It turns out he's inherited the building he lives in and he's offered it to me to start a business and live in, while he moves down to the basement.' Tara shook her head. What a bizarre afternoon.

'I must admit, I knew about that. The day I dropped off his phone I saw the work going on and he told me.'

'I can't accept it, Zo. It's far too generous.'

Zoe shrugged. 'If it makes him happy, why not? Think about it – it would mean you would always be there if he needed you and he's probably going to after ...'

Tara knew what she was about to say and it increased the flow of tears again. 'You know he has arthritis?'

'He told me when I asked why he wanted to move out of his gorgeous apartment.'

'Do you think he's sicker than he's letting on?' Tara shivered. 'I couldn't take losing both of them.'

'I think he's absolutely fine, he just wants to ensure his independence as he gets older. But, to be honest, I'm not sure about the wisdom of him taking on your mother. That's going to be very hard on him.'

Tara shook her head and smiled through her tears. 'No, I don't agree with you there. He loves her, he's always loved her, and he's happy that she has chosen to spend her final days with him.'

Zoe squeezed her hand. 'How lucky to be loved so much.'

'How lucky indeed,' Tara agreed, banishing thoughts of Shane from her mind.

When Zoe had left for the theatre, Tara started to clean the kitchen, not that it needed it. Her movements were, for a change, slow and deliberate as she considered her parents' revelations. She felt more composed now and, as she worked, she thought back over the last few months and the stress and anxiety she had gone through. It all seemed inconsequential when compared to what Shane had been planning and the ordeal her mother was facing. She thought of Vivienne's last words when they had parted earlier.

'You only get one shot at life, darling. Don't waste it,' she'd said, giving her a tight hug. Her mother hadn't dispensed much advice to her over the years but this piece Tara intended to heed. She wiped her hands on her apron and threw it and the cloth into the washing machine and then went to phone Greg. After a long, long conversation, she hung up and called her doctor for some advice. 'Thanks, Mum,' she murmured as she made one final call.

'Another wonderful night and another great performance.' Robbie pulled Zoe's body in against his and dropped a kiss on her bare shoulder. 'Well done, sweetheart.'

She turned in the bed to face him. 'I didn't think I'd be able to pull it off. After Tara told me about Vivienne, I felt numb. But then I got to the theatre and there's Terence, cool, calm and collected. I knew that if he could be that strong, I couldn't let him down.'

'And you didn't.' He kissed her lips. 'The show must go on, and it did.'

Zoe thought of how Terence had given the performance of his life and she wondered at the end, when Jonathan's wife walked out on him, had he been thinking of the day when he would lose Vivienne. As soon as the audience started to applaud, his smile was broad and he had circulated afterwards, as he had every other evening. But when he had come to say goodnight and she had whispered in his ear, 'I'm so sorry,' he'd held her close for a few seconds longer before slipping away.

'The best way that we can help him is to keep life as normal as possible,' Robbie said.

'What if we go on tour?' she asked. 'Terence wouldn't be happy leaving Vivienne.'

'Let's worry about that when we have to. I imagine we're going to be staying in Dublin for the foreseeable future.'

In other words, Vivienne would probably be dead by then. Zoe shivered. Still, the timing might suit Terence. If he was travelling and working, it would keep him occupied and help him through the grieving process. But who would look after Tara? Greg? Shane? Or would Tara be better off without either of them? She sighed and snuggled closer to Robbie. 'I wonder, do they regret not staying together?'

'Terence and Vivienne?' Robbie asked. 'I don't believe either of them are the type to waste time on regrets.'

Zoe smiled. 'True.' But the fact that Terence had immediately agreed to take Vivienne in suggested he still must care deeply for the mother of his child. Which would explain why someone so handsome, personable and in demand had never married. But Vivienne hadn't married either. It didn't make much sense to Zoe. Why would anyone choose to be alone? It seemed selfish that Vivienne wanted to be with him now and let him watch her die. If anything, it was quite theatrical really. Was it Vivienne's final performance? Another shiver ran through her.

Robbie pulled her closer. 'What's going on in that head of yours?'

'Lots of things ... Do you think Vivienne put her career before Terence?'

'Maybe. Would you leave me if some big-shot director wanted to sweep you off to Hollywood and make you famous?'

She pretended to consider it. 'Well, I suppose it would depend how big a shot he was.'

'The biggest.'

He was joking but she saw the serious question in his eyes. She held his gaze and put her finger up to trace the line of his mouth. 'Not a chance, darling. I'm afraid you're stuck with me.'

'Damn,' he said, a wide smile splitting his face.

'We won't ever let work come between us, will we, Robbie?' She searched his face with anxious eyes. It was ridiculously early to be having such serious conversations but there was nothing normal about their relationship or, indeed, what had been going on in her life in the last few weeks. Shane's suicidal thoughts had brought everything into sharp focus for her. She wanted to act, she loved to act, but her family were her priority and Robbie felt like family now – she couldn't imagine a life without him. She had never felt this close to Ed. There was simply no comparison between the two relationships.

'I won't let anything come between us,' Robbie promised with a soft kiss.

And she believed him, filled with warmth from the love in his eyes. 'I'm glad that Sammy and Nick don't have a problem with us getting together.'

'Problem? If we broke up, I think they'd want you to get custody! Apart from the fact that you're funny and super cool, you are now famous too and Sammy's role model.'

'Oh, Lord, that's a lot to live up to!' She laughed. 'They're wonderful kids. You are lucky but they are too. You're a great dad.'

He pushed her hair back from her face. 'And you would make a great Mum. I could see you with a baby in your arms.'

Her heart leapt and she searched his eyes. 'Our baby?'

He pretended to look outraged. 'It damn well better be! You're mine now … aren't you?'

She nodded, feeling close to tears, only this time they were tears of pure joy. 'All yours, darling. Only yours.'

Epilogue

Four years on ...

Zoe sat down on the large comfy sofa by the window to enjoy her mug of warm milk. Though she loved the entire house, this was her favourite room and this her favourite place to sit. They had renovated the house bit by bit over the years but this room was definitely Robbie's pièce de résistance. He had knocked down the wall between the kitchen and Shane's study and created one large open space where they could cook, eat and relax. A glass wall now separated them from the garden, and the room was flooded with the light and warmth the old kitchen had always lacked.

When Shane had told her he proposed to put the house in her name, she wasn't sure if she wanted it or not. Her childhood memories had been tarnished when she found out that her father was not the man she had worshipped. Robbie wanted to buy it but Shane insisted it was her inheritance and compensation for the loss of her mother. She could keep it or sell it, but he would never live there again. Robbie had promised her that he could make her love it again and he had.

Shane had left Ireland, accepting a post as writer in residence at a university in Scotland. He came home regularly, and Adam still produced his plays, although he'd had some success in Edinburgh too. He was a happier man as a result of counselling but, sadly, he was still without a significant other.

Zoe had wondered whether he and Tara might find happiness together, and felt a little resentful for a while that her friend had turned down her brother's proposal. But, when she thought of all that Tara had been through, before and since the night she'd found Shane contemplating suicide, she came to understand why that would be too hard for her friend. Zoe just hoped that someday Shane would find someone else.

She stared out at the gazebo, thinking of the night he had planned to take his own life. She'd wanted to knock it down, to banish the memory, but Shane had begged her not to, pointing out the happy times she'd enjoyed. And she'd remembered then how she'd played there with her dolls as a child and the wonderful night Robbie and Terence had come to tell her that she had the part in *Isabella*, and realised he was right.

As for Tara, she too was alone but, it seemed to Zoe, she didn't want or need a man. After Shane had scared the hell out of her and Vivienne had announced her diagnosis, Tara seemed to dig deep and find a strength that was inspiring. She'd started a course of cognitive behavioural therapy almost immediately, taken up yoga and, when she had the time, went running. Zoe, had at first been worried about all this activity and had taken to joining her for a run, to keep an eye on her friend as much as anything. But it soon became clear that the exercise was relaxing Tara, helping her to deal with her problems, sleep better and it had the added benefit of keeping her away from the bottle. Still, Tara's home was always spotless; but then, Zoe thought with a sad smile, there was no man or child to mess it up. Perhaps Tara would end up like Celia, as she'd predicted.

'Here you are!' Robbie came in, looking handsome in grey jeans, a grey shirt and a black jacket. 'Shouldn't we be making tracks?'

'In a minute. You're looking very James Bond.' She patted the seat beside her, inhaling the spicy scent of his aftershave as he sat down.

'Why thank you, Mish Monneypenny,' he said in a dreadful Scottish accent, and kissed her hand. 'You're looking pretty spectacular yourself. You have that special glow.'

Zoe winced and put a hand on her tummy. 'Don't tempt fate,' she begged.

'Hey, third time lucky and we've never got this far before,' he pointed out, his eyes full of hope.

She couldn't help smiling. 'I was planning to wear my red dress but my bump was clearly visible so I changed.'

'And you look edible,' he said, eyeing up the purple silk skirt and matching top. 'And very accessible too.' He slid his hand up underneath her top and smiled in appreciation. 'It's not just your tummy that's growing.'

She laughed. 'Behave, there's no time.' But he was right – her boobs were bigger and that hadn't happened with either of the other two pregnancies. In fact, she felt totally different this time. How she prayed she would bear their child.

'What were you sitting here thinking about?' he asked, his hand moving down to gently stroke her stomach. 'Junior?'

'No, actually, I was thinking about lots of things, including how uncomfortable I used to feel in this house and how much I love it since you worked your magic.'

Robbie pulled her into his arms. 'I'm so glad to hear you say that. It's not your father's house now, Zoe. It's our family home and hopefully always will be.'

She pressed her lips to his chest. 'I hope so too.'

'Feeling nervous about the play?' he asked.

'Excited as much as nervous. It seems so strange being in something not directed by you.'

'I think you're in good hands,' he chuckled. 'And finally playing the lead in a Shane Hall play too.'

'Yes, I am thrilled about that. I hope he makes it back in time.' Shane had promised he'd do his best to get home for the opening tomorrow night, but there was something on at the university and he wasn't sure that he would be able to get away. At worst, though, he'd be here later in the week.

'Come on, let's go. You know what Tara's like if we're late for one of her feasts.'

'True.' She smiled and stood up. Tara had decided to bring the cast together for a pre-premiere dinner. It was an unusual thing to do, but then this was an unusual play. It did feel odd that Robbie wasn't involved in the production but he had been adamant that he was the wrong person for the job, and she knew he was right.

Walking into the impressive building, Zoe felt a swell of pride and admiration for what Tara and Terence had created between them. The ground floor was a busy bistro, where people came in the hope of catching a glimpse of famous actors as much as for the excellent food. The floor above had been transformed into two small theatres, and Tara lived on the top floor in Terence's old pad, whilst he, as planned, had moved to the basement with Vivienne and had lived there alone since she died. The man was in his element, relishing being surrounded by people. Even on his off days, he could enjoy a glass of wine with friends at the bar, or sit at the back of one of the theatres and watch all the new and exciting talent erupting in his beloved Dublin.

Zoe and Robbie walked past the door that led into the bistro and hurried up to Tara's apartment. The room was already full and Zoe smiled at the buzz of conversation and laughter. Tara came towards them, looking relieved.

'Here you are. I was about to call you.'

Zoe hugged her. 'Sorry. Have we held things up?'

'No, you're just in time to help me in the kitchen.' Tara grinned as Robbie kissed her cheek.

'Ah, back to my real job!' Zoe rolled her eyes. 'I'll just say hello to everyone and I'll be right with you,' she promised. Robbie squeezed her hand and went to join his son, who stood chatting with Adam and his new girlfriend, Jean.

'Your doppelgänger,' Tara had said to Zoe when Adam had first introduced them to her, and there was quite a resemblance, but Zoe tried not to dwell on it.

'Darling, you will be wonderful!' Terence was saying. He looked up and winked when he saw Zoe. 'Tell her, Zoe.' He reached for her hand and kissed it.

She smiled at Terence's customary exuberance. He was looking particularly dashing tonight in a crimson jacket that set off his shock of silver hair. He used a cane now but as much for effect as a walking aid. 'He's right.' She bent to hug Robbie's daughter, Sammy. 'You are going to be sensational. Forget the audience and pretend it's just another rehearsal.'

'I'll try but it's a bit intimidating trying to live up to a director father and superstar stepmam.' Samantha's large blue eyes were anxious but it would be odd if she wasn't nervous the night before her debut.

'Superstar Stepmam has been commanded to the kitchen.' Zoe laughed. 'I stood in your shoes once, Sammy. We all did. Enjoy it, have fun. You know that you're good.'

Terence nodded his agreement. 'That's exactly what I've been telling her.'

'And you have the second-best director in the business,' Zoe added.

'Damn cheek.' Terence brandished his stick and she skipped out of reach, laughing.

When Shane had suggested Sammy for the part in his play, he had wanted Robbie to direct it but immediately understood Robbie's reservations: he didn't think it would be fair to his daughter. Terence had been the obvious alternative. Though he still acted, he was taking more interest in directing and he was damn good at it. Under his gentle and generous guidance, the girl had blossomed and Zoe and Celia had done everything to make her feel comfortable on stage.

It was a charming story of three generations of women and their lovers, and one of Shane's recent forays into comedy.

Zoe went over to say a quick hello to Celia, who was chatting to the comedienne and actress Ena Mulligan. It had been a shock to them all when, shortly after Vivienne's death,

Terence had started to date the gregarious younger woman, but they were good together and Ena exuded a warmth that Vivienne had never possessed.

'Zoe, darling, you're here! Join us.'

'Later, Celia. I promised Tara I'd give her a hand.'

'In that case, go,' Ena ordered. 'I'm ravenous.'

Zoe went into the kitchen and gasped at the array of food. 'Wow, you *have* been busy! You should have told me you were preparing a banquet, I'd have come over earlier to help.'

'You're the star. You can't work as my skivvy the night before opening.'

Tara grinned but Zoe could see she was anxious, not least because of the tell-tale way she was wiping around the edge of every platter at least three times. 'Is something wrong?'

'Nothing. Just about ready to serve. If you could get out the salads and slice the baguettes.' Tara bent her head over the dressing she was making.

'It's a pity Shane isn't here,' Zoe said, wondering if that was why her friend seemed down.

'Yeah.'

'Your dad seems on top form.' The salads laid out, Zoe fetched the bread board and started to slice.

'Yeah.'

'Pity the same can't be said about you,' Zoe muttered. 'I know something's up, Tara. You're a bag of nerves.'

'I'm fine. Now will you please back off?' Tara said through gritted teeth.

Zoe's eyes filled with tears – it took little to make her cry at the moment. 'Sorry for breathing,' she mumbled, and started to carry the food through.

Tara followed with two platters. 'Let's eat, folks,' she yelled above the chatter. They went back and forth with food, while Robbie opened wine and left a large jug of water to the right of Zoe's place at the table. She shot him a grateful smile, but hoped that no one else had noticed.

Tara went to help her father to the chair at the head of the table. It was only when they were finally all seated that Zoe noticed there was an extra place setting. 'Who's missing?' she asked Tara.

'Is that for our absent playwright?' Terence smiled.

Tara stood. 'Yes, but—'

'He's not absent.'

Zoe looked up to see her brother standing in the doorway, smiling. 'Shane! Great to see you, but why the mystery?'

'I wanted to surprise you. I've come home, Zoe, for good.'

She jumped up and threw her arms round him. 'I'm so glad.'

'Welcome home, Shane.' Adam raised his glass to his friend.

'Welcome home,' Terence echoed.

Tara stood up. 'Eh, I have an announcement, too.'

'Well, come on, darling, don't keep us all in suspense,' Terence urged.

Tara looked at her dad and then at Zoe. 'My divorce has come through. I'm a single woman again.'

'Should we congratulate or commiserate, darling?' Celia asked, her eyes sympathetic.

'I'm not sure if either is appropriate.' Tara reddened. 'But I think it's a good thing for both Greg and me that all ties are severed and we can both start afresh.'

'And—' Shane went to Tara and took her hand. 'This crazy woman has agreed to start afresh with me.'

Zoe let out a squeal, Robbie whistled and Terence's face broke into a broad smile. The men had worked on a number of productions together now, and Zoe had been delighted to see them grow closer. Shane hadn't had many male friends other than Adam but that had changed now. She was beginning to believe that he truly had put his past behind him and, judging from the smile on Tara's face, she thought so too.

Zoe went over to her friend. 'At least now I know why you were behaving like a shrew.'

'I'm sorry,' Tara said, hugging her. 'I was sure I was going to give the game away and Shane really wanted to surprise you.'

'I'll forgive you. I presume there have been texts zinging back and forth between Ireland and Scotland,' Zoe teased.

'And phone calls, emails and' – Tara grinned – 'the occasional weekend.'

Zoe couldn't believe that this had been going on under her nose and she hadn't noticed. 'How long?' she asked.

'Since he left,' Tara admitted.

'What?' Zoe stared at her, stunned. 'But then why did he go?'

'We were both too fragile. You said that yourself when I was going out to Nerja. So we decided to take time apart, to be sure of our feelings and that we weren't just clinging together for the wrong reasons. Also, I needed time to sort myself out and I refused to talk to him until he'd signed up for some counselling.'

'Good for you.' Zoe said, feeling tearful again. 'I'm so happy for you both. Does this mean one day that you might be my sister-in-law?'

'I think that's a fair assumption,' Tara replied grinning.

Squealing with delight, Zoe hugged her again.

The evening took on a party atmosphere, although Terence kept reminding his cast that, hangovers or not, he would expect brilliant performances all round.

Celia was the first to call it a night and Terence and Ena said they'd walk her the short distance home. She tried to argue but he assured her that he was supposed to walk daily. Zoe watched him get slowly to his feet, and was glad that Tara had ignored her father's protestations and installed a small lift, arguing that theatres should be accessible to everyone.

'Happy, Isabella?' he whispered when Zoe hugged him goodnight.

She smiled. 'Thrilled, Terence. Are you?'

'Delighted, darling. Your brother is a fine man and I know he'll look after Tara.'

'He will,' she assured him. 'She's the only woman he's ever loved.'

Robbie came and put his arm around her as the party started to break up and Tara and Shane were hugged and kissed and congratulated.

When Nick and Sammy were leaving, Zoe noticed the anxiety in the young girl's eyes. 'You'll be fine,' she assured her.

'I'm terrified I'll seize up or forget my words or lose my voice, Zoe.'

'Don't worry. The singing will take care of that.'

'Singing?' Sammy looked bemused.

'Never mind.' Zoe chuckled, and hugged her. 'Try to get some sleep tonight. You're ready, Sammy, and Terence is an expert at soothing actors' nerves.'

Zoe stood with Tara in the doorway, calling goodbye as her husband and brother went downstairs to see the guests out.

'I can't quite believe this. Your dad didn't put you up to it to distract me and Sammy from first-night jitters, did he?' Zoe said, as Tara led her back inside.

'No, it's all true.' She went to pour the dregs of a champagne bottle into their two glasses.

'Not for me.' Zoe quickly put her hand over hers. 'You heard what the director said.'

Robbie came back in with Shane. 'Ready to go, Mrs Prendergast?'

'Ready.' She gave her brother another hug. 'I'm so happy for you and I'm thrilled you've come home.'

'I knew better than to try and take Tara away from you or Terence,' he joked.

Zoe marvelled at the change in him. His eyes shone clear and bright, and she realised that he'd grown into the man Tara needed.

'I'm happy for you too, Sis, and I can't tell you how proud I am that the famous Zoe Hall is playing the lead in one of my plays.'

'I'm the one who's proud,' she told him, swallowing hard. Lord, these bloody hormones would be the death of her.

'Come on, Terence will murder me if you have bags under your eyes tomorrow,' her husband said, putting a protective arm around her waist.

Zoe hugged Tara one last time. 'See you tomorrow.'

'I'll be the one in the fourth row clapping and hollering and basically making a show of you and your brother' Tara promised.

Zoe crossed her fingers. 'I hope so!'

Robbie came out of the bathroom, slid into bed beside his wife and switched off the light. Zoe snuggled into his chest and sighed in contentment. Would she ever get tired of the feel of this man's skin against hers? She didn't think so.

'Quite a night,' he murmured in her ear.

'Quite a night,' she agreed.

'You had no idea what was going on?' Robbie asked.

'None.' While Zoe was close to her brother and friend, she could understand and respected why they had handled things the way they had. 'It's quite romantic really, isn't it? A proper, old-fashioned courtship.'

'Is that a complaint? Suppose I can't blame you. Dinner, a flood and then huddling up in your bed, exhausted!'

'Ah, but we made up for it the next night, didn't we? I'll never forget that night. It was wonderful.' She kissed his chin.

'So wonderful that you run out on me the next morning,' he retorted. 'And then we make up in a hospital waiting room.'

She laughed into his shoulder. 'It may not sound very romantic but, you know what?'

'What?'

'I knew as soon as you kissed me that night outside the restaurant that you were the one.'

'Mmm, that was quite a kiss.' He tilted her mouth up to his.

'So was that,' she sighed when they eventually came up for air.

'So, no complaints, Mrs Prendergast?'

'No complaints, Mr Prendergast.'

'I have to tell you, I found it very hard to keep my mouth shut tonight,' Robbie said. 'I can't wait to tell everyone about Junior, especially the kids.'

'It's too soon,' she protested, although she'd felt tempted too. 'Do you really think Sammy and Nick will be happy?' It had always worried her that if she and Robbie had a baby, his children might feel they were being replaced.

'They'll be chuffed. Wow, I just thought of something.'

'What?' She looked up into his face.

He stroked her stomach, his eyes full of wonder and pride. 'There will be three members of my family on stage tomorrow night.'

'So there will.' She smiled and put her hands over his. 'I suppose that's what you would call a true family production.'